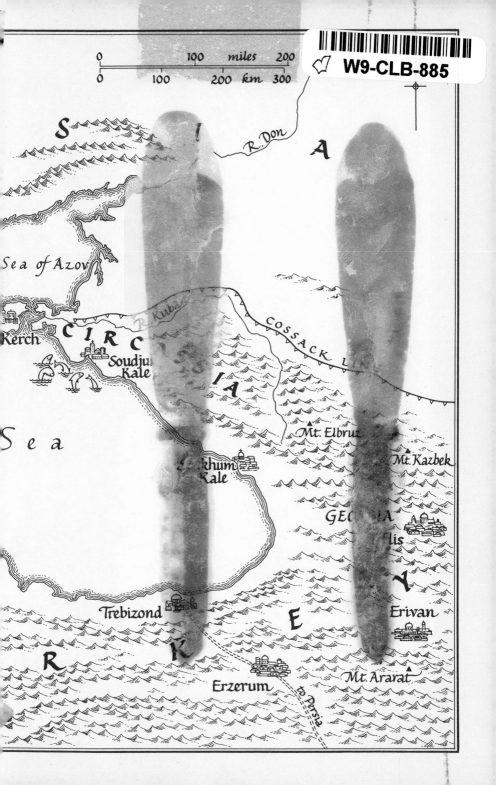

0   100   miles   200

0   100   200   km   300

S   I   A

R. Don

Sea of Azov

Kerch   C I R C   S S I A

R. Kuban

COSSACK L.

Soudju Kale

Sea

Mt. Elbruz

Mt. Kazbek

khum Kale

GEORGIA

lis

Y

Trebizond   E   Erivan

R   K

Erzerum

to Persia

Mt. Ararat

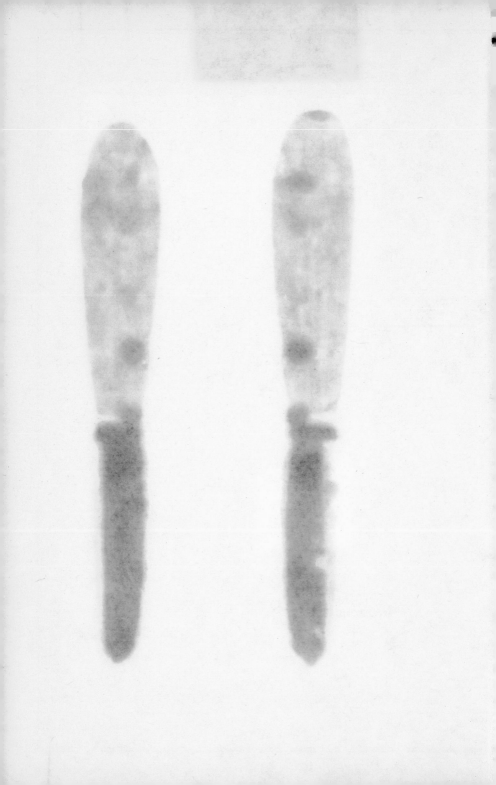

MISSION
TO CIRCASSIA

A JOAN KAHN BOOK

F
O

MISSION
TO CIRCASSIA

Kathleen Odell

When a man hath no freedom to fight for at home,
Let him combat for that of his neighbours;
Let him think of the glories of Greece and of Rome,
And get knock'd on the head for his labours.
                                    LORD BYRON

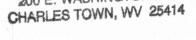

HARPER & ROW, PUBLISHERS
New York, Hagerstown, San Francisco, London

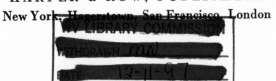

Map drawn by Reginald Piggott

FIRST U.S. EDITION

LIBRARY OF CONGRESS CATALOG CARD NUMBER: 77-3802

ISBN: 0-06-013287-6

77 78 79 80 81 10 9 8 7 6 5 4 3 2 1

PART ONE

Chapter 1

IT WAS COLD and blustery on the height overlooking the Golden Horn. A bitter wind out of the steppes blew down the Bosphorus, hurrying the waves before it, and dust skirmished across the waste patches of the city, and drove between the shabby, wooden houses. A few weeks earlier the mosques had been ringed with snow. The snow had now vanished, but the grip of winter was still unbroken. The minarets of Stamboul transfixed a dark and lowering sky, and the celebrated panorama which Robert Wilton had paused to contemplate, on his way back from a circuit of the ruined walls, was all in black and grey. The plane trees were tattered, no green showed yet, except for the dark, eternal cypresses. In the streets of Galata the passers-by were cloaked to the eyes, and no hint of sun lit the tumbled water racing down from the Black Sea, the inhospitable Euxine which was the goal of this traveller's desire.

Yet the prospect was still a splendid one, however ramshackle the ruins of Byzantium, despoiled through the centuries, however desolate the empty acres which the ancient walls now enclosed. While he admired it, Robert Wilton felt unconsciously for his pocket-book, for robbers were apt to frequent deserted places, and the afternoon was drawing on. His fingers encountered the wallet which contained, as well as his letters of credit, two more letters much worn by folding and re-folding, and a small sheaf of newspaper reports relating to the capture of a British ship, the *Vixen*, by a Russian gunboat off the coast of Circassia the previous November. This arbitrary seizure, which had inflamed British opinion, already on the side of the Circassians in their heroic resistance to the Russian invaders of their country, had given rise to awkward questions as to the legality of the Russian blockade in the Black Sea, and had taxed to the full the Foreign Secretary's determination not to disturb the *status quo*. Lord Palmerston had been induced to negotiate some compensation to the *Vixen*'s owners for the loss of their ship and her cargo of (technically contraband) salt: but England was not going to war with Russia over Circassia. As winter went by, the dust which had blown furiously in the corridors of Whitehall at the time of the affair began to settle and thicken, at first a smoke screen, later a pall which would smother the outlines of an inconvenient international incident, and the hopes of the pro-Circassian faction. From time to time flurries of indignation continued to rise in the columns of the Press at the government's supine attitude, but they died away without provoking any official reaction.

By the end of winter Robert Wilton, who was filling his days with strenuous perambulations of Constantinople, had almost given up reading the English newspapers in any event. They were so far out of date by the time they arrived that most of their news meant little to him. At first he had seized on each successive copy as an echo of the life he had repudiated, and devoured the pages, but the gulf of time and distance was now too wide. He had definitely quitted that world – but where lay the future? Certainly it was not here, in this sprawling, semi-European town, where coal lighters unloaded in the shadow of the Seraglio, and the West, in the form of iron ships and the new uniforms of the Sultan's troops, was gradually reconquering its former domain. He had come to the East with the object of joining the Circassian cause in the national struggle against the Russian armies, and he was anxious to get to the seat of war as soon as possible.

This was not proving as easy as he had anticipated. He could not find anything like the recruiting agency for foreign volunteers which the Circassian appeals, widely circulated in Europe, had led him to expect. And although he had quite reasonably expected the sympathies of the Turks to lie with the Circassians, their co-religionists, in their resistance to the Russian infidels, he found everyone in Constantinople strangely disinclined to discuss the campaign at all. This was strange, as many of the Sultan's principal ministers were themselves Circassians by origin, sold by their families as young boys into the Turkish service, while nearly every pasha's harem contained Circassian girls who had arrived there in the same way. After some weeks of futile attendance in the reception rooms of the pashas, Robert was no further forward, when he fell in with a young Greek of the Ionian islands, Giorgio by name and a dragoman by calling, who professed to have a good deal of information on the subject. Giorgio told him that he had been making an entirely wrong approach, and could have spent many months of inquiries in Stamboul without making contact with a native Circassian.

'They are all afraid of Russian spies here!' Giorgio exclaimed. 'They see Russians everywhere. The Turks –' he gestured eloquently, as if over the body of a defeated foe –'the Turks are very frightened to annoy the Russians. That is why they will not tell you anything about Circassia. Besides, they think you may be a Russian spy yourself. They are fools, these Turks! I know an English gentleman. I have myself travelled with an English lord. The English fought for the freedom of my country. That is why I love them.'

Although Giorgio promised he would in his own way be able to make immediate contact with the Circassian envoys known to be somewhere in Constantinople, his methods were no more productive of speedy results than Robert's fruitless coffee drinking with the pashas. There was a whole chain of inter-mediaries to be worked through link by link. First of all came Greeks : a barber in Pera, and his cousin who had a ship's chandlers business in Galata. The cousin in turn was able to provide an introduction to a Turkish ship's captain who maintained an illicit trade with the Circassian coast, and ran in the supplies of salt and gunpowder so urgently needed by the tribes.

A meeting was finally arranged with the captain, in a coffee-house at Kassim Pasha on the Golden Horn, and on the appointed day Robert made his way thither, the indispensable Giorgio accompanying him. The bazaar, when they reached it, via Galata and the Thursday Market, was like a dozen others in the city. Shabby wooden houses, gently crumbling away, a trellis across the street with a vine trained along it, a sheep, which bleated incessantly, tethered in a doorway. A group of silent Turks sat over their doll's-house sized cups and their narguilès in the coffee-house. At first sight it seemed to Robert a most public place for a confidential discussion, and one where his Frankish clothes were uncomfortably conspicuous, but it

4

turned out that there was an upper room to which Giorgio led the way, while the turbaned patrons of the room below, seemingly sunk in contemplation, took no notice of them whatsoever.

The captain was awaiting them in the room upstairs. One wall of this consisted of a wooden lattice work, beyond which was the open air. Round the other three walls ran a low wooden shelf covered with mats, on which the captain and Robert seated themselves, after Giorgio had performed the introductions. Each endeavoured to study the other unobtrusively. Robert found himself bad at this, lacking experience, and was caught out several times by the captain, whose wooden, stubby features relaxed each time into the semblance of a smile. Then when Robert looked away in embarrassment, the captain had his chance to stare his fill. After about five minutes of this Robert felt the time had come to open the conversation. But there was an interruption. An old Turk shuffled into the room with the paraphernalia of coffee, which he proceeded to dispense in minute quantities. Dealing with this took another ten minutes, silent except for the sound of the captain absorbing his allowance. Then the captain cleared his throat, and Robert hoped that this was a signal that conversation could commence. But it only indicated the captain's intention to send for a narguilè, with which he proceeded to fill the room with its sickly smell of shavings and burnt paint. Robert declined to participate. He was tired of etiquette, and wanted to get ahead.

'Ask him,' he told Giorgio, 'what port he comes from.'

He thought this would be a suitable opening gambit, and that after this it would be permissible to approach, by gentle stages, the matter in hand.

Giorgio put what may have been the question, but he did not translate the answer, if there was one. For the next five minutes Robert, to his vexation, was a passive third in a conversation of which he could barely understand a word, although Giorgio, after each sentence he contributed, turned to Robert smiling brightly, as though seeking confirmation and then, as though he had received it, resuming his flow of words. He talked three times as much as the captain who, as befitted a seaman, was a man of few words. At last the captain got in a sentence which sounded to the point.

Giorgio said to Robert, 'He has asked you how much you are willing to pay for a passage to Circassia.'

'First of all, I want to know when he is going to sail.'

'No, no, you do not understand. He will not take you to Circassia, only to Trebizond. After Trebizond it will be a matter for his friend, who also has a ship. But this captain will make the arrangements for his friend, as well as for himself.'

'Tell him I will discuss the matter of money as soon as I am satisfied that he is in earnest. I want first to know who this friend is, and what contacts he has in Circassia. Will he be carrying a cargo, or –'

But Giorgio was off again and there was no stopping the flow of words. Finally the captain got up, fixing his eyes on Robert and uttering phrases of leave-taking. The session was over. Robert bowed, while Giorgio gabbled off some formula on his behalf. His joints were aching from the uncomfortable way he had been sitting, and his left foot had gone to sleep. He was not sorry to break off. The captain left first, then the other two made their way down the decrepit wooden staircase. Giorgio went to settle with the master of the coffee-house who, Robert fancied, was rather glad to see the back of them.

Outside, a purple dusk enveloped the Golden Horn. The sun had just sunk into Europe, leaving the tips of the minarets still gilded. On the other side of the water the black cypresses of Eyup marched up the hillside, mounting guard over tottering headstones and untidy graves. Some figures too distant to be made out clearly, but which might have been shrouded women, were sitting in groups among the trees. There was hardly a sound as men and beasts padded down the lanes to the water-front, where the off-shore was iridescent with the outfall of the open city drains, and little waves lolled against the landing steps. The whole of this little quarter smelt of age and decay – not a new house, not an unpatched garment – while not a few hundred yards away was Galata with its Frankish merchants, its jostling crowds and the babel of tongues.

They parted outside the coffee-house, the old Turk padding away in the direction of the waterfront, while Robert turned in the direction of Pera. He dismissed Giorgio, saying he would find his own way home. In fact, Robert had now reached the stage where his knowledge of the city made it a pleasure to go about on his own. He was able to walk the streets like a conqueror who had reduced Constantinople into his possession, quelling any unfriendly notice which the occupants might give him, and rising superior to those other travellers he saw being herded by their dragoman into the shops of the latter's choice. He made his way through Galata, climbing the steep streets which led from the crumbling Turkish bazaars on the Golden Horn to the region of cosmopolitan hotels, foreign shops selling pigs' bristle tooth brushes and French cosmetics, and women with unveiled faces. These foreign influences did not, however, conduce to greater cleanliness in the streets, in fact the squalor of Europeanized Pera exceeded, if it was possible, that of the wooden shacks by the waterfront. There the dirt was mainly the dust of casual neglect, the unheeded rejecta of nomads who expect to move on to a new camping ground next day. The tiles fall from the kiosk, but it is not worth while to replace them: tomorrow the Sultan will call for his horse! In Pera, men were daily adding to the refuse which it was the business of nobody, except the resident tribe of scavenging dogs, to remove.

Just now, with the approach of evening, in every quarter of the city and in the cemeteries, those same street dogs were sending up their chorus of wailing barks, the big yellow dogs which had arrived in the wake of Mahomet the Conqueror's armies, and were now the night watchmen as well as the scavengers of Constantinople. As Robert approached his lodging he saw a couple of them asleep in the gutter, curled into balls against the chill of the coming night. At his approach they each cocked an ear, and opened their eyes. The bigger of the two, a male with battle-scarred ears, got up and approached, hoping for a pat, or perhaps a morsel of something. He was amiable enough, despite his savage appearance, but full of fleas.

'Usht!' said Robert, with true Turkish intonation.

The dog retreated to its former pitch and lay down again, with its eyes still fixed on him. It watched him mount the steps of the house with neither animosity nor expectation. Feeling in his overcoat pocket, Robert found the remains of some bread which he had pocketed after his midday meal. It was now as hard as leather, but he managed to tear it in two and throw half to each of the two dogs. He heard the snap of their jaws as they met on the food. The yellow dog could easily have snatched

7

her portion from his smaller mate, but he was content with his share. There was a community spirit among the members of these bands of animals, each of which policed its own district and would have torn to pieces any outsider which ventured in.

The lodging-house smelt as usual of cooking and his landlady's scent, with other less agreeable overtones. He gained his room as quickly as he could to consider the alternatives before him, which were to dine in the nearby hotel, which was his usual routine; to eat in a café, which was amusing when he wanted to feel himself a tourist, after all; or to order a meal from the landlady's kitchen to be served in his room. He finally settled on the last course. There was plenty to think of. Although the interview with the captain had not been fruitful in immediate results, yet he felt a start had been made in the business and that he was nearly done with Constantinople. The vision of Circassia became stronger and clearer. He could even picture the coast he had read so much about that he knew already the outlines of the mountains.

The dinner came in due course, brought in by an old Armenian woman with only one eye, but a handkerchief bound over her head partly concealed the defect, as well as giving her a rather rapscallion appearance. Robert dreaded this old crone slightly less than he dreaded Madame Boutiadis, her employer who, once she got into his room, was singularly difficult to get out again. Exuding scent, patting her too-black hair with a casual hand, she told him at length about the expenses of her daughter's education, and eyed him during the pregnant pauses of the conversation with a knowledgeable eye, but without ever making it clear whether it was the charms of Madame herself or of her daughter, Miss Calliope, a statuesque girl with a plaited coiffure like a horse at a fair, which were being put in issue. The upshot of these unsatisfactory interviews was that Madame would eventually retire from the room with a pitying sigh, closing the door behind her with the silence of the serpent. The crone was easier to comprehend. She was an old woman, she had only one eye, but she had survived, and presumably for an Armenian, that was enough. Robert recalled the Armenian gravestones in the cemetery at Pera, with the effigies scratched on them of men hanging meekly in nooses, or sitting with their decapitated heads placed neatly beside them, and the sculptured

8

inscription setting out the virtues of these victims of Turkish rapacity and oppression, and the manner of their deaths.

Already the different races inhabiting Constantinople were becoming clearer to him, and their characteristics. The Armenians were second only to the Jews in their dogged capacity for endurance. The Greeks ran them close in commercial acumen, and formed the most lively stratum of the visible life of the city. It was clear that the sub-European sophistication of Pera was the product of Greek skill and ability, while all the gaiety to be found in the little Bosphorus villages drew its life from the Greek women chatting in the chilly winter sunshine. For any laundering of clothes, for a trunk needing repair, for the changing of money, one went to the Greeks.

Each faction vied with the other in reprobating the manners and morals of the rest. 'Oh, oh, Galata!' Giorgio would exclaim. 'That is not a good place to go, after dark. The coffee-houses! All those pretty boys with their curls. Jewish boys . . .' and Giorgio would smirk, and his two hands sketch a curl on each temple.

The Armenian crone, after Robert had established communication with her, whispered to him with her one eye on the door through which Madame Boutiadis might at any moment appear.

'These Greeks, they stop at nothing! First the man offers his wife, then his daughter, then the girl offers her little brother. What a people!'

Only the Turks themselves, the true believers, did not bother to particularize in their contempt between one brand of infidel and another. When obliged to deal with foreigners they hid their unwavering dislike of giaours, of Western habits and influences generally, behind a front of urbane official courtesy.

In fact, the least conspicuous of all races to the view in this city were the Turkish masters of it. Robert's favourite pursuit was to wander the shadowy ghost-streets of Stamboul, the stronghold of orthodox Islam, where it was possible to sit on the kerb of a broken fountain, contemplating the scattered stones of a former civilization, with no living creature in sight save for the sparrows rustling about among the plane leaves. Very occasionally an old man, or a shrouded ghost-woman would sidle by. Sometimes as he sat he sensed that eyes were

9

watching him behind the wooden lattices which masked the upper windows of the houses. On one occasion a wicket in a street door opened a crack, and Robert saw the sullen face of a black porter, eyes blood-shot under his turban, peering out.

Such glimpses half-fascinated and half-repelled him. The life they disclosed was so unbelievably strange it was as though the world had spun round, and was disclosing its unknown side.

Constantinople was, however, but the ante-room to distant mysteries. Chronicled, reconnoitred, described over and over again in countless books of reminiscences and ladies' travel impressions, replete with hints on how to find the cleanest lodgings, purchase the most reliable antiquities and pick a really trustworthy caiquejee, Robert, even with his new-found confidence in his pidgin Turkish, was getting tired of standing indefinitely on the threshold, while the inhospitable Black Sea still lay between him and his goal. He turned again to the Circassian phrase-books he had been studying intermittently. Unfortunately, none of these gave any deep analysis of the language, but contained merely a list of words, with their Turkish equivalents, which the respective authors had found to be useful in their passage through Circassia. Something of the nature of the passage could be gathered from the particular author's choice of words and phrases. Robert opened one of these works, by an English traveller.

'Open the window', he read.
'It is too dear, have you change?'
'Carry my luggage.'
'I wish to have my linen washed.'
'Can you make me some chicken broth?'
'Conduct me to the mullah.'
'Help! Help!'

None of these phrases seemed to be the passport to a life of military adventure. He tried a Frenchman, whose offerings, although more limited in context, were certainly more promising

'I will kill you.'
'I love you (very much).'
'I do not love you.'

There followed the Circassian words for legs, and a woman's breasts. Robert did his best to commit some of the more likely phrases to memory, but it was not made very clear how to pronounce them. It looked as though everything connected with Circassia was going to be difficult.

Giorgio told him a few days later, with a fine air of mystery, that matters were progressing, and although Robert did not know how far to believe this, he knew enough by now not to expect miracles in a day. Meanwhile, he applied himself to learning more Turkish, reasoning that this language would be understood by at any rate the more cultured elements at his destination, while any words of Circassian he mastered would be a sort of extra bonus. This did not, however, occupy all his days, and sight-seeing was beginning to pall. He had already gained admittance to the principal mosques under the authority of the usual *firman* granted by officials of the Porte, and had sampled the doubtful pleasure of strolling round among the hostile worshippers. He had also tried, under the challenge and in the company of an adventurous acquaintance, the more hazardous experience of putting on Turkish dress and entering without the *firman*.

This venture had been completely successful: they had mingled with the crowd and got in and out without being detected. During the time they spent in the mosque (S. Sophia itself was their choice), a party of well-dressed foreigners entered, with their attendants. Their disregard for the hundreds of Moslems who thronged the holy place was complete. Sweeping their trains over the carpets, the unveiled and hatted Frankish women strolled to and fro among the men, pointing up at the roof and indicating objects of interest with their lorgnettes, while their escorts, evidently jaded with an excess of such spectacles, laughed and joked together. But they were Russians – the hated word ran through the huge building – and no official of the mosque dared protest. For a moment Robert, understanding the words which his neighbour murmured to him under his breath, thrilled to feel himself a part of that alien life which he had daily observed, without approaching any nearer to the central mysteries. But he was not tempted to repeat the

11

experience. He could not summon up any feeling of reverence for S. Sophia as she was now, or share Giorgio's vocal indignation at its rape by the conquering Turks. It seemed to him to be now nothing but a hulk, a derelict of both religions, unrecognizable as a Christian edifice, yet strangely resistant to Islam, which had attempted to cant its altar sideways, and to force the structure into its own service.

He could not summon up, even in a Christian eye, any picture of the great basilica as it had once been, and might again be. The shining floor, once picked out in precious marbles, now covered by layers of overlapping carpets, was beyond his power to imagine. The great golden angels of the dome were cut off, not only by plaster and whitewash, but by the glaring ceiling of lamps suspended low over the floor, like a cartwheel, or a huge lid pressing the congregation down into the ground. It struck him as typical of the Moslem faith that its worshippers, instead of lifting up their eyes through the huge spaces of the church to Heaven, should be constrained to grovel on the floor and perform their ritual head-knockings. The incongruous bad taste exhibited in this, as in the other big mosques of Constantinople, offended him, the English grandfather clocks ticktocking away in odd corners (to what end he could not imagine, as the Turks did not reckon by European time), the meandering Arabic inscriptions which placarded the pillars, the unmended pavement, the unheeded dust.

The congenial companion of the S. Sophia escapade moved on southwards en route for Egypt, and none of the other travellers who from time to time passed through the boarding-house replaced him in interest. Robert inwardly pined for contact with another European, if not a fellow countryman. He bethought himself of the casual words which an acquaintance had let fall before his departure for the East, about a certain Mr Eugenius.

'I don't know what nationality the fellow is,' his friend had said, 'but he certainly speaks English almost like a native, and he seems to have pots of money. Rather an outsider, perhaps – I heard some talk about his wanting to settle down in the East and give up Europe altogether. But he certainly knows his way about in Constantinople, and could give you some useful tips. I never succeeded in discovering what his business is, but the bank could put you in touch with him, I am sure, since he is well known. A letter from me would be no use, I don't expect he would remember me, but he seems to keep open house. If you do see him, give him my regards.' Now seemed the time to seek out this mysterious and hospitable Mr Eugenius, who might possibly be able to help him on his way.

The official in the bank was all comprehension.

'Lord Shuttleworth directed you to Monsieur Eugenius? Your friend was here how long ago? Two years? I understand perfectly. I think you could best approach Monsieur Eugenius by going over to Kadikoy on the Bosphorus – it is a village on the Asiatic side, very pretty in the summer – and inquiring for the yali – the villa – of Egenye Bey. Yes, you will find the bey at home at his villa at Kadikoy. He will tell you what you wish to know about Monsieur Eugenius.'

It was blowing half a gale when Robert embarked on the Bosphorus, and it took all the skill of the boatmen to set a course for Kadikoy in the teeth of the current setting dead against them down the straits. Chill drops of rain fell as Robert balanced himself at the centre of the caique, and he wondered whether it would get worse, and if so, if the boatmen would want to turn back. He himself was filled with the intrepidity of a trusting passenger in the hands of an expert crew, and found the passage exhilarating. As soon as they ran under the lee of the Asiatic shore, however, the wind subsided, and the rowers could take it more easily. Nearly all the villas at the water's edge were shuttered and deserted for the winter months. The owners had moved back into their houses in the city, as the yalis were practically impossible to heat. The villages also looked desolate, but the villagers were there, huddled inside their houses, each in his own quarter, Turkish, Greek, Armenian or Jewish, keeping out the cold as best they could. Only on a distant hill could moving dots be faintly discerned; a shepherd must be bringing his flock down hastily, as if he felt in the air the presage of late snow to come.

Robert was watching the hill and not the shore, when the caique turned alongside the landing stage of the yali, and to his embarrassment he was thrown off balance, endangering the equilibrium of the craft. However, he managed to scramble on

13

shore. The boatmen, told to wait, swung their craft into a back-water from which they continued to watch him. Robert wished they had not. He would have liked time to reconnoitre the yali before making a frontal assault.

From what he could see of it, it looked smarter than most. The wood was painted, and the landing stage had gilded posts to tie up to. The yali stretched along the waterfront, the windows overhanging the Bosphorus. Where the women's quarters were, at one end, the windows were closely covered with wooden grilles, and there was also a line of posts some distance out in the water to prevent any unauthorized approach from that quarter, even though it would have been difficult to squeeze so much as a hand through the lattice work. On the landward side there appeared to be a garden of some size, and a creek ran up from the landing stage and was barred with a chain. But ahead was a door, massive like all Turkish doors, and furnished with a spyhole. Conscious of the boatmen's gaze at his back, Robert raised his hand to the knocker.

The door fell back, it seemed, of its own accord as soon as he touched it. It was only then that he realized that a visitor approaching by caique was in full view of the yali long before he arrived. Before him stood a handsome young servant who bowed politely as he accepted Robert's card and desired him, in very passable French, to enter. Inside, Robert found himself not in the ante-room of a Turkish house where no sign of life is visible, but in a warm and light apartment furnished in a mixture of European and Turkish styles. A carpet patterned with roses covered the floor, swags of roses in painted stucco festooned the walls and ceiling. The servant disappeared through an arch which led to more rooms beyond. A little white lion-dog, like those Robert had seen in Malta waiting for their masters at service-time outside the doors of the cathedral, ran out and stopped short at the sight of a stranger. A smiling, plump young man, dressed in what at first sight appeared to be a fancy-dress of apple green and pink, advanced through the arch and greeted Robert in excellent English.

'Do I have the honour of addressing Monsieur Eugenius?' hazarded Robert. However strangely he chose to costume him-self, his host was certainly European, but of what nationality Robert could not conjecture.

'My dear sir, your servant Egenye Bey has the pleasure of welcoming you. But when the good friend of us both, Lord Shuttleworth, was in Constantinople two years ago, your servant was plain Mr Eugenius. I am delighted that Lord Shuttleworth has still remembered me, and more delighted that you should have braved this weather to pay me the honour of a visit. Tell me, how is our friend?'

Egenye Bey stepped back smiling, with his head on one side. He was clean shaven, except for a slight moustache, his skin was pink and fresh, and his face shone with health and benevolence. A modified Turkish turban of rose-patterned silk was pushed back to disclose thin blond hair. He could be Austrian or Hungarian, thought Robert.

'But let us go where we can talk more comfortably.' pursued his host, leading Robert through the archway. 'The rooms which face the Bosphorus are very well in the summer, but in the winter I retreat into my little sanctum.' Lifting a heavy curtain, he ushered Robert into a small room furnished in oriental style with a divan running round three sides, panelled walls painted with more roses, with little bits of looking-glass stuck here and there, and another painted stucco ceiling. On the fourth side a wood fire snapped and crackled under a marble chimney piece.

'You see, I know how to make myself "cosy" in your English fashion.'

Obviously Mr Eugenius, as Robert still thought of him, had left the divan to greet his visitor. The cushions were crumpled and his narguilè was there on a Moorish table. The good-looking servant was lounging over it, the white dog at his heels. The room contained two other occupants. Languidly disposed the length of the divan was a dandified young man, black-haired and black-moustached, in European dress. Mr Eugenius moved without hesitation into French as he introduced Robert to Monsieur de Beaumont. To Robert's ear, his French was as good as his English. The fourth person present was a little old Turk in a big turban who sat with his eyes cast down and his feet tucked up under him on one corner of the divan. He never spoke, never raised his eyes, and was never introduced.

Robert took a seat on the divan, slightly puzzled by the whole establishment. Mr Eugenius (or Egenye Bey) clapped his hands, and a file of servants entered the room, bearing the whole apparatus of ceremonial coffee-taking, the embroidered, gold-fringed towels, the tiny cups in jewelled stands and the coffee pot over its censer of glowing coals. Coffee was served with the serious attention given to this ritual in the pashas' establishments which Robert had already visited: somehow it had in these surroundings a flavour of the theatrical about it. The coffee, too, had a peculiar taste as if some alien substance, costly no doubt, but unwelcome to the European palate, had been infused with it. The Frenchman waved his cup aside. The old Turk in his corner for the first time took an interest in the proceedings, and imbibed his ration of coffee with serious appreciation, but in complete silence.

The ceremony was completed, the servants took back the gilded cup-stands, offered the gold-fringed towels and withdrew. Monsieur de Beaumont rose from the divan and began to take his leave, with not so much formality. Robert was in some doubt as to what to do. This would be a convenient moment to break off a call which he was beginning to wish he had never made – he had already a surfeit of coffee drinking to no purpose – but on the other hand it was really too soon after his arrival to talk of going. It became clear, however, from references to Monsieur de Beaumont's horse, that he had arrived at his host's residence from the land side, as it were, and if Robert were to announce his simultaneous departure, it would put Mr Eugenius's politeness to a severe test, to honour both guests appropriately. As it was, the two men left the room together, leaving Robert with his *vis-à-vis*, the silent old Turk. The old gentleman did, it is true, steal one sideways glance, but immediately looked down his nose again and resumed staring at nothing. Not even the appearance of the little white dog which ran in, sniffed at Robert's trousers, and ran away again, roused him – or did he draw his feet a little further under him as the unclean animal frisked up to his end of the divan?

The silent presence irked Robert, who would have liked to be free in his host's temporary absence to look at the room and its contents more closely. He could see no European object, and he wondered if Mr Eugenius possessed a still more private retreat, with a roll-top desk, perhaps, where he could relax in a chair from the strain of life *à la turque*. But just then his host re-appeared and spoke a quick word to the old man, who put

16

himself down off the divan and retired, silent to the last. Whether he was there as a mentor, servant or companion, Robert never knew.

Mr Eugenius was most affable.

'Tell me now, how is our good friend Lord Shuttleworth?'

They talked about London and Paris. Mr Eugenius was better informed than Robert about recent events and Robert asked him if he had recently visited Europe. (He hoped to elicit his host's place of origin.) But Mr Eugenius shook his head.

'I have thrown in my lot, as you see, with the East.' He glanced down at his flowing robes. 'I must forever forgo the pleasures of giaour society. Once I knew it, now I shall know it no more. But I have my compensations. The flowers here are very beautiful in the spring. I hope you will be staying long enough to enjoy them. You should be here to see spring come on the Bosphorus. It happens in a flash, overnight. Then you will see how beautiful Constantinople can be. There is a *douceur de vie* which one can never experience elsewhere. But I know how restless you Englishmen are. I expect you will be on the high road – or the high sea – before long.'

'I plan to go to Circassia as soon as possible.' said Robert.

'Ah yes, Circassia, that is a country where I have never been, but I have heard that it is very interesting. Very fine scenery, too, if you care for that. And the customs of the people are truly original. But it will not be easy travelling – there is a little war going on there now, do you know?'

Robert admitted that it was to join in this little war that he had come all this way. Mr Eugenius was most sympathetic.

'So you are a friend of Circassia, too. Another splendid Englishman! I hear that there are several more of your countrymen there already. They are certainly brave, these Circassians. But you will find them funny people to deal with,' he added, obscurely.

'In England we greatly admire the fight they are putting up against the Russian invasion,' said Robert.

'Oh, fighting, fighting, that is the breath of life to a Circassian, you know. That is the business they understand best.'

Robert said something about finding less sympathy for the Circassian cause in Constantinople than he had expected, particularly when so many Turks were of Circassian descent.

Mr Eugenius was pursuing his own line of thought, however.

'Circassia is *par excellence* the country of beautiful girls – that is something more important than scenery – and they have very interesting customs, these girls. You know they are not veiled, and they are allowed a good deal of freedom with the young men. They can give the young warriors every encouragement but one – no kissing is allowed.'

'A good many of these beautiful girls find their way to Constantinople still, I believe,' said Robert.

'Yes, their families sell them, it is their staple export, a sister or a daughter is just so much merchandise to the family. But the girls are anxious enough to come. Circassia is a poor country and backward, life there must be very uncomfortable, while here they find themselves in a state which is luxury to them. In fact, there is a little Circassian girl in the women's quarters of this house who has just arrived, a new importation. Would you like to see her? I cannot take you to the harem, custom would not approve, but she is just a child, I will have her brought here.'

There followed a long dialogue in Turkish with the servant who was summoned to give effect to Mr Eugenius's intention. At last the servant departed, and after some delay a curious pair entered the room. In the forefront was an enormous negress, the fattest woman Robert had ever seen. In spite of the fact that her attractions were minimal, she held a cloth firmly over most of her face so as to conceal all but one eye. With her free hand she dragged behind her the Circassian girl, who was resisting with vigour. Once she was fairly in the room, however, the Circassian quieted down, and when the negress let go of her, she stood panting in the middle of the room with her eyes cast down. On her head she wore a handkerchief, but her face was not covered, and she raised her eyes to shoot a furious glance at the two men.

At first sight her costume of billowing trousers and overskirt seemed to Robert to be a grotesque parody of a European girl child's dress, the outline was similar, long plaits hung down the girl's back, but the Circassian's trousers were made of gaudily striped silk, and the tunic was a sort of gauze, dotted over with spangles. Her waist was clipped in with a girdle plated with silver, and the neckline, open almost down to the waist, in no way resembled the demure round décolletage of the schoolroom Miss. Robert found it difficult to judge her age, but the figure exposed by the low-necked garment was barely developed.

The Circassian panted and glared alternately, while the negress kept a restraining hand on her shoulder from behind, and with her single eye she seemed to dare the men to approach too close.

'She doesn't seem very tame yet,' said Robert at length. 'How long is it since she was caught?'

Mr Eugenius laughed.

'Actually she does not belong to me, but to one of the *ladies*,' (he gave a peculiar significance to the word, as a Turk might) 'so I am not very sure. But one thing is certain, she will not have lived in a house like this before. She probably thinks she is in a palace!' He said something to the negress, who replied in a guttural rumble. 'She is quite happy, though, and is eating well. She should turn out quite a good investment. She can hope to be placed in some pasha's harem if her looks keep their promise.

'It is a pure Circassian type, you see,' he went on, looking at the girl critically from several angles. 'No snub nose – that is important. They say that already the influence of the Russian prisoners the tribesmen have taken is making itself felt with the Circassian ladies.' He laughed, and made to brush the little girl's nose with one finger, but quick as a tiger she struck his hand away, while the old negress remonstrated. Robert tried out one of his halting phrases of Circassian, which to his chagrin had no effect. The girl relapsed into sullen immobility, and Mr Eugenius told the negress to take her back to the harem.

'Perhaps you will have better success when you meet her grown-up sisters! How I envy you your courage and enterprise. I wish I could do something to speed you on your mission. Unfortunately I have no contacts who could help, except – yes, there is one man, an old acquaintance of mine who might be a useful acquaintance for you, also. He is an Armenian merchant who carries on business in Trebizond, and he is, or at least he was until recently, in touch with elements in Circassia. He is a man of business, of course, and his interests are in that line, but you might find it useful to meet him. His name is Papandian, and he is well known in Trebizond. If you sail from that port, and I think you will have to, make a point of seeing him and let him know that you come from me. I am sure he will do all he can for you.'

There was little left to say, and it was clearly time for the visit to end. A servant entered the room bearing a tray covered with another gold-fringed napkin. This when raised disclosed a glass in a filigree holder studded with jewels (or with what looked like jewels), containing a turbid greenish liquid. The servant offered the tray to Robert.

'Violet sherbet,' said Mr Eugenius gaily. 'One of our specialities. I had the recipe from the Palace.'

Robert took the glass and sipped. The first mouthful seemed to him inordinately sweet. The liquid was flavoured sugar-water, with a peculiarly sickly taste, and it touched a raw nerve in a back tooth which immediately gave a warning twinge. Robert suppressed a grimace of pain, for Mr Eugenius was watching him closely. No doubt the offer of sherbet was a rite of hospitality which could not be refused, and some guile was necessary. One of the oldest dodges would have to suffice. Drawing his host's attention to something on the other side of the room, Robert contrived to knock his knee against the inlaid table on which he had put down the glass. The table tilted : Robert made a grab and saved the glass from falling, but the contents trickled down the inlay and dripped stickily on to the carpet.

Amid the profuse apologies and expostulations which followed, the little white dog jumped down off the divan and began to nose at the sticky patch. Then with a reproachful look at his master, he licked over his lips twice with a pink tongue, shook his head, sneezed, and returned to a corner of the divan.

Ceremonious to the end, Mr Eugenius escorted his guest as far as the entrance hall, where he restrained the white dog which seemed disposed to follow Robert as he went down the landing stage to the waiting caique. Robert took his seat and the boatmen were ready to push off, when the white dog followed in full pursuit. Behind him, waving his arms, ran a servant, shouting and cajoling. The dog reached the steps first and squattered down them. The caique was still alongside, the gap was not unsurmountable, and the dog scrambled on board and began to frisk about, barking with delight. The servant coaxed and threatened without effect, nothing would induce the truant to return. Robert tried to pick the little dog up so as to return him bodily to shore, but he wriggled so violently that he was out of Robert's hands in a trice and nearly in the water between the caique and the shore. By this time Mr Eugenius himself had arrived on the scene, in his pink and green robes.

'You keep the dog,' he called. 'I make you a present of him, Mr Wilton. He will go to the wars with you in Circassia, and keep you company.'

Any doubts which Robert might have entertained as to the suitability of appearing on a campaign accompanied by a white lap-dog were unavailing, for there was no chance to refuse the gift. In obedience to Mr Eugenius's gesture, the boatmen were pushing off. They turned the boat's head towards the European shore, while at Robert's feet the white dog, evidently no seaman, was already being sick.

The brief storm of the afternoon had blown itself out, however, to be succeeded by a windless calm, although the current still raced down from the Black Sea, and it was a heavy pull across the strait. Ahead of them the city of Constantine crouched on its seven hills and spread itself along the European shore, the domes and minarets of the mosques rising above each quarter like the tents of an invading army. By one of those strange contrasts of climate to which Constantinople was so prone, the breath of evening was almost balmy compared with the gales and icy sleet of the afternoon. The flowers, as Mr Eugenius had predicted, were stirring into bud. Soon the willows would be turning golden, and the lumbering arabas drawn by milk-white oxen would be carrying their rainbow-coloured loads of harem beauties to walk on the grass at the Sweet Waters, on their one outing into a world at other times forbidden to them.

Before willow-time came, however, Robert was tossing on the Black Sea en route for Trebizond – on the way to Circassia at last.

Chapter 2

ROBERT'S DEPARTURE happened in a rush. Giorgio was full of conspiratorial excitement, leading him to strange rendezvous, in a cellar at Galata, under an upturned boat beached somewhere near Seraglio Point, in the back room of a house on the way out to the Adrianople Gate. The Turkish captain reappeared, and as well as he, each individual member of the crew had to be brought into the discussions which once threatened to become interminable. But things were moving, and there had to be an end. Robert bought stores and travelling requisites, bearing in mind that he was bound for a country where nothing at all, by all accounts, was to be had, and filled his baggage with the lengths of cloth he had been assured passed as currency in Circassia. He paid a last visit to the bazaars to procure more of the massive gilt chains and the other trinkets which had been recommended to him as suitable gifts for the Circassian matrons who would be his future hostesses. His luggage was conveyed down to the harbour by porters in the chill of a surreptitious early morning departure. Giorgio followed close behind, leading Fop. For this was the name the white dog had chosen to answer to, after Robert had tried many others more suitable without result. At the last moment Robert had tried to bestow the dog as a parting gift on Mistress Calliope, but it had been declined. Perhaps he had made it a little too clear that his interest was not so much in the girl as in getting rid of an embarrassment. Anyway, Fop, shivering with excitement, was off to the war. As Robert followed in the wake of the porters down the steep streets, the water seemed to rise to meet him.

For once there was no delay, hands seized the corded boxes and the travelling trunks, and Robert, stepping on planks still wet from the night air, recoiled from the frowst of the cabin and looked round for a place on deck where he could lodge himself out of the way of the activities of departure. Then they were cast off and were gathering way, slipping from side to side of the narrows, keeping under the lee of first the European, then the Asiatic shore. Few were astir to see them pass in the villages of the Bosphorus, and along most of the water's edge the mist still trailed, hiding the habitations of rich and poor alike. The yali of the mysterious Mr Eugenius, otherwise Egenye Bey, was hidden from sight and Robert could only guess when they were abreast of it.

Robert had not repeated his visit, as he had at parting been politely pressed to do, but he was now better informed about Mr Eugenius. He owed this to a chance meeting in the covered bazaar with Monsieur de Beaumont, then languidly appraising a stock of antique weapons on display, who was amazed at Robert's ignorance of their host's history.

'But he has become a Moslem – undergone the step, or operation, should one say? of initiation. What intrepidity! Now he has his reward : no wine, of course, officially, but when one has the compensation of a harem, one can do without it. He is very much in the confidence of the Porte, millions must pass through his hands. The villa was a gift from the Sultan only three months ago. The last owner was a Greek banker, he was decapitated in December. Egenye Bey has had the decorations changed, I think, and imported quite a constellation of ladies which I was never privileged to see, although I hinted quite strongly that this was really the object of my visit. It seems that he has become quite Turkish in this respect since his conversion. When he was an unregenerate giaour, I am told his entertainments were famous, rose-water flowing in fountains, lovely fat unveiled women on every side, ready to play a little tune, or do a little dance, or otherwise make themselves agreeable to the guests. Now he has got all these women ministering to himself alone.

'I wonder if that is as enviable a state as it sounds? There they are, the ladies of his selection, locked up safely behind bolts and bars, nothing for him to do but send for the one he fancies. But would one fancy any of them in such circumstances? Would one feel any desire for a woman delivered like a trussed chicken, so to speak? No trials to undergo, no competition, no jealousy – at least, for the man – and above all, no conversation. What can he find to talk about? For each minute of pleasure, there must be at least one hour of boredom. And he is a European, a man of intelligence. One wonders how he can live like that!'

'Is not what you are describing the lot of every man who takes an Eastern mistress?' asked Robert.

'Ah, you are thinking of our colonial ventures, your mind is turning to India, to punkahs and little, bright-eyed brown girls! Yes, but in India, and in Algeria and elsewhere, our compatriots were the victors. The West had conquered the East and of course despised it, as all men despise the countries where they have defeated the men, and slept with the women. But our friend Monsieur Eugenius has not conquered, quite the reverse. He has succumbed – gone native. Still, it has paid him, so long as he keeps his head. It was an interesting experience to meet him, and I only regret not having seen the ladies. But perhaps you were more fortunate in that respect?'

Robert explained about the Circassian girl.

'These Circassians one hears so much about,' said de Beaumont, indifferently. 'They sound a savage lot. Unwashed also, I suspect. Imagine in this century coming upon a man in chain mail wielding a sword like this –' he pointed to a blade which looked fit only for a giant, but de Beaumont picked it up and expertly tested the balance. 'There's an inscription on it too, which needs a good cleaning.' He rubbed the blade with his thumb and bent over it. *'Parmi Dey y par my Rey,'* he read. 'That helps to place it. Toledo, I should think.'

'Do you collect?' asked Robert.

'Oh, when I have the chance I do so, but usually his arms are the last things a Circassian will part with.

'They are good fighters, these Circassians, but the Russians will have the country in the end. How can they fail to? The Russians have guns, which are better than Toledo blades.'

He watched for Robert's reactions a trifle maliciously, but Robert said nothing. It occurred to him that he knew little about Monsieur de Beaumont, and that it would be wiser to keep his intentions to himself.

But now he was off. Constantinople, just waking to the day, was well behind them. The sun was up now, and drying the wet planks, glancing through the mists which were rising from off the water and from the trees at the water's edge, the giant plane trees with roots like ancestors reaching deep down into the soil. Soon he would be able to stretch out on deck in the shadow of the sail while the old captain cradled the tiller under his arm, and the crew settled down to their tasks. He listened to the strange sea-language they used, a mixture of Turkish and Genoese sailors' jargon.

The maistra, he found, meant the mainsail. Ala! was the cry of the look-out man, always with his eyes ahead, for the entrance to the 'false Bosphorus' claimed many ships in a season. Poco alabanda! he intoned. Put up the helm! Orsa alabanda! Hard alee! At times of great excitement a concerted cry was raised of Issa! Issa! Issa! which produced prodigies of effort from the crew.

The water rushing past the bows gave the illusion that they were speeding forward. To be breasting the steady cataract of the Bosphorus, the lighter, less saline water always pouring down from the Black Sea into the Sea of Marmara, was like climbing a ladder, the prize at the top a Golden Fleece. But the golden lads and girls were gone from the classic shores past which they were to sail, the city walls had been broken and the temples had gone up in flames, and, camped where he had conquered, the Ottoman herdsman sat in the sun and watched his flock. Only the sea-words of a nation of seafarers had taken hold. The old Turkish captain talked of the 'anavasya', the annual migration of the fish from the Black Sea to the Mediterranean when the more northern waters became too cold for them, and the 'ratavasya' when they returned in the spring. He also told of the terrors of the 'ayandon', the dreaded storm which usually swept the Black Sea about the middle of January, without knowing that St Anthony's day fell about that time.

It took a whole day before they sighted the lighthouse at the entrance to the Black Sea. Here the captain put the ship on an easterly course, flanking the twin mountains on the Anatolian shore. Robert had heard all about the violent currents, produced by the rivers which poured themselves into this inland sea, and the sudden storms which sprang up without warning and before which a small vessel had no choice but to run for port, which in the case of an illicit voyage like theirs, would have been inconvenient. But they were fortunate in their weather. The Euxine was kindly, almost gay, and its waters were as blue as any other sea under the sun. They kept fairly near in to the coast, while bay and promontory succeeded each other, and the hills ran thickly wooded down to the water's edge. Somewhere, somehow, Robert had formed a picture of the ancient Greek settlements standing much as they must once have been, with colonnaded temples and marble palaces, a marble statue, perhaps, on the quay, with its arm raised as a beacon to foreign merchantmen.

He might have known that the temples and the villas would not have survived the Turk. The cities themselves had vanished entirely, the ports where traders from the Mediterranean had moored were ports no longer. The coast contained empty bay after empty bay, with a few low Turkish houses, perhaps, huddled together where a river ran down into the sea, but no mole, no beacons, not a wink of light at night. Behind the villages, vast shaggy forests clothed the hills.

Robert questioned Giorgio. He was curious to find out if the boy knew the legends of his own people, and if it meant anything to him that this was the Pontic shore to which the Argonauts had found their way, but Giorgio replied to all questions with his usual brand of practised omniscience, the fruit of serving many masters with this uncomfortable predilection for travel. Amastria, Sinope, Amisus – yes, these were old cities and gone to ruin now, he agreed. Robert tried him with the Ten Thousand – the same result. It was not worth while pursuing. Giorgio stared disdainfully, so long as Robert was in safe sight, at the Turkish sailors, who were better seamen than they had at first appeared to be, and played with Fop. Fortunately the Turks did not seem to find this provocative, in fact Robert fancied they looked on the little dog as some strange variety of foreign cat. Robert himself fell into the tranced state which a sea voyage imparts : the hours and the days went by, and they crept slowly along (for the wind was fitful) towards Trebizond. Sometimes they tied up in one of the deserted bays, while the small boat they carried put off and presently returned with fresh food and water, and sometimes with surreptitious visitors. Then the turbaned heads nodded together in mysterious conclave, until the visitors returned as they had come, averting their eyes from the Frankish party.

Robert found this rather irritating. It was as though these silent old men had drawn aside the hems of their garments, a gesture which he had yet to see put into practice, although Egenye Bey's domestic prelate had come very near to it.

An ironic turn of fate nearly deprived Robert of his first view of Trebizond. An onslaught of toothache had kept him awake the greater part of the night, and in desperation, as dawn came on, he had taken an opium pill. Thus he was lying still asleep in the cramped little cabin when he became aware of the check and change in the rhythm of the ship's progress, and of Giorgio's voice raised in excitement. The captain was calling orders to the crew, and by the sound of his suppressed yaps, Fop was striving to get free and join them. Robert struggled into wakefulness, became conscious of a muted but bearable ache in his tooth, and raised himself on one elbow. Red roofs and white houses, and a green headland, passed across the little square of vision vouchsafed to him. He hastily emerged on deck, to see before him a town, gay in the morning sunshine, running inland up a deep cleft crowned by old, ruinous fortifications. There were many minarets: it seemed a big place. There was a small harbour where a fair number of local craft were lying, also one or two foreign merchantmen. There was also what looked like a private yacht.

Then Robert saw, with some surprise, that they were heading away from the town. They were holding straight on their course, past the harbour and the shipping, towards another point of land, leaving behind them the mole, surmounted by a fort, holding rusty cannon. These clearly had not seen service for many a year, but sitting sunning himself, with his back against the wall, a Turkish irregular soldier gazed unseeing out to sea. He seized his long gun too late at the exclamation of another lounger. The boat, with Robert's tall figure conspicuous on deck, was out of range.

'Trabzon?' said Robert to the captain.

'Trabzon!' said the captain.

'Trebizond, we have arrived, Excellency,' said Giorgio.

'Then why are we carrying on?' asked Robert.

Giorgio answered. 'There is a better place to anchor round this corner. It is more private. The Russians will not see.'

27

And so it was they came to anchor by another ancient mole whose stones had tumbled long since beneath the shallow water. No other craft was near.

Giorgio promptly embarked upon a long argument with the captain, concerning the means of their getting ashore, Giorgio maintaining that the contract included putting Robert and his party ashore at Trebizond, and that steps must immediately be taken to get a shore boat to come out to them. The captain, while not disputing the basic validity of this, was not disposed to take active steps. He was of the opinion that a boat would come out to them by and by. Meanwhile Giorgio was having the luggage assembled. Robert noticed for the first time that there was a fresh breeze, and went below to finish his dressing. Nobody had any time for Fop, and the little dog, tied to a bolt on the deck, barked and danced on his hind legs in his excitement. After some delay a flat-bottomed craft, high at prow and stern and manned by two very old men, was seen approaching. It came alongside, and after intermittent parleying with the captain, one of the ancients scrambled on board and proceeded to hand down Robert's travelling bags and boxes to the other. The process took some time, and when at last it was finished, Robert asked Giorgio to find the captain, who had unaccountably disappeared from sight. But Giorgio only urged Robert to get ashore without more ado.

'We should not stay here,' he kept on saying, turning his head this way and that, the very picture of a stage conspirator. Robert could see no menace from the nearly empty bay, and the shore seemed equally deserted, but he decided to comply, and to omit a leave-taking with the captain. So he scrambled over the side and into the lighter, Fop was passed down to him, and Giorgio came last. Slowly they were ferried to the beach where the luggage was unloaded, still in slow motion, on the shingle. Structures which had looked like a row of derelict sheds now revealed themselves to be the habitations of fishermen, where a few tortoise-like beings were sunning themselves in a placid dream, broken by Giorgio's vigorous hail for porters. When the boatmen added their voices, there was a response from two or three of the loungers. They came over to the boxes, and Giorgio apportioned the loads. The boxes were carried up over the shingle to the green sward above, where the men

promptly put them down again. Giorgio stared round in disgust.
'This place is no good. There is nowhere to stop here.'
'Is there anywhere in the town?' asked Robert.
'In the town, yes. It is a big town. There will be a hotel.'
'Then let us go to the hotel,' said Robert with decision.

There ensued a delay while Giorgio went to the village further up the valley, which he said was a Greek village, to find horses. Eventually he came back with two, the porters were roused again, and the cavalcade moved off.

As they left the shore, Robert realized that this part of the country was much more fertile than any of the regions along which they had coasted. Thriving orchards and neat plantations lay on either hand. Pretty houses – for they were in the suburbs of Trebizond – were shadowed by magnificent trees. About half an hour's ride brought the party under the shadow of the crumbling walls, then they were in the main street through which flowed the commerce of east and west. Caravans from Mosul, Baghdad and India trod on each other's heels. The strings of camels and donkeys were too long to be counted. They were like an irresistible tide. Giorgio was riding ahead and endeavouring to clear a way befitting a traveller of distinction, but in vain, for the caravans kept the centre of the road. Forced to retire precipitately into alleys when a more than usually numerous band of laden donkeys invaded the street, constantly ducking under poles and trellises when his mount was forced into the gutter, menaced by toppling piles of merchandise, Robert was glad when the main street debouched at last into an almost equally crowded main square. The lines of camels and convoys of little jingling, tripping donkeys, bound in opposite directions, still forced their way past each other as half the caravans tried to make their way to the sea, while the other half were coming away from it, but there was more space to manoeuvre. The open space seemed to be used as a marshalling place for goods. Men bent double brought up incredibly heavy loads of boxes from Manchester and Hamburg, which were being roped on to grumbling animals. Some large and cumbrous pieces of iron, unidentifiable machinery of some sort, were lying there waiting to be transported into the heart of Asia Minor, over the mountain passes which were just then blanketed with heavy cloud. Buyers and sellers carried on their inter-

changes in the open air, by the side of the merchandise, vendors of roasted indian corn threaded their way among them, crying their wares, water sellers clashed their brass cups, while the heavy-eyed beggars of Trebizond indolently moved their limbs out of the way of the horses' hooves.

Only the caravan men, the drivers of the animals, had a look of men apart about them. Gnarled, weatherbeaten, wild of aspect, they strode in the dust beside their loaded beasts. Ceaseless travellers, living and dying on the road, their eyes under the clouts tied round their heads were looking forward to the hills, while the shopkeepers of the bazaars stood at their doorways and watched them go by.

Then the travellers and their train of porters were through the square and turning up a short street of steps. A house slightly more imposing than the rest – it had two storeys – was in front of them. They had arrived at the hotel. Robert obtained a room with a fairly reliable bed, and the luggage was carried in under the superintendence of Giorgio and stacked in a corner. Robert opened his travelling bag and sent out for water to wash. The first stage of the journey was over.

The large pile of boxes stacked in the room suggested a rich and therefore important private traveller, an English milord, in fact, and Robert hoped they would not attract undue attention. Indeed, he wanted to have as little contact as possible with the innkeeper and the officials of Trebizond. He had no intention of perambulating the town and bringing himself to the notice of the pasha, or of calling on the British consul. He wanted to be off again as soon as possible, and he hoped the captain would carry out his undertaking to secure him a passage on a ship bound for Circassia without undue delay.

In the meantime he unpacked only one travelling bag, and remained where he was, apart from one brief exploration. The main activity of the town appeared to be the transit traffic. The bazaars, where the manufacture of wooden cradles was the staple industry, offered little of interest, although an old man sidled up and pinched Robert's arm, making gestures indicative of wishing Robert to follow him. It turned out, however, that he had nothing more interesting to offer than wine. It would

no doubt have been rewarding to have explored the general locality of Trebizond, where many traces of the antique could be discerned, in the usual state of fearful dilapidation, but Robert judged it prudent to remain in the hotel, where he kept to his room, only emerging at the hours of the table d'hôte to see his fellow guests. Fortunately a common language was hard to find, which made it easier to avoid awkward questions. But after twenty-four hours of incarceration, waiting for the sea-captain to appear, or at least send news, Robert grew impatient and cast caution aside. Finding that Giorgio was not at hand, he asked the landlord of the hotel if he could tell him where Mr Papandian might be found.

The request seemed to arouse no curiosity.

'He is most probably in his shop, at this hour,' was the reply. 'Shall I tell him to come here, or will your Excellency go to him?'

Robert hastily considered. The room was reasonably private, while Mr Papandian's shop was probably in the bazaar, which was anything but private.

'I shall be obliged if you would ask Mr Papandian to make it convenient to call and see me.'

'He shall be told immediately of your Excellency's wishes.'

The landlord must have moved with an un-Oriental speed, for in less than an hour Mr Papandian was in the room, inquiring with extreme outward civility in what way he could be of service. Robert looked at him with interest, but it was not easy to take in Mr Papandian at a glance. Something remote and mournful lurked at the back of his eyes, and his obliging manners gave the impression of masking other qualities as well as an extreme skill in negotiation. Robert took the plunge.

'I have been given your name, signor' (for Mr Papandian spoke passable Italian) 'by Egenye Bey, in Constantinople, when I was recommended to apply to you for any assistance I stood in need of.'

'It would be an extreme pleasure for me to be of service to a friend of Egenye Bey. I trust the Bey enjoys good health?'

'It seemed excellent when I saw him' ('Good, good,' breathed Mr Papandian.) 'The Bey thought you might be able to assist me if I found myself in difficulty in a particular matter.'

Mr Papandian repeated his protestations, and Robert had an

31

idea that he already knew what the matter was. His alert eye had already taken in the presence of the boxes.

'I wish to take passage to Circassia,' continued Robert, 'and I had made my plans to do this. Unfortunately there seems to have been some hitch, and I do not know whether my ship will sail as I had expected. As I would like to make the journey as soon as possible, I wonder whether you can arrange it for me.'

'With whom had you arranged this passage, Mr Wilton?' Mr Papandian sounded all efficiency.

'That I cannot tell you, I will have to ask my servant who took charge of the details. If you will wait a minute, I will call him.'

Fortunately Giorgio was somewhere at hand, and answered the summons without delay. Mr Papandian questioned him directly in rapid Turkish. At the answer he received he made an expressive little gesture and turned to Robert, obviously waiting for him to dismiss Giorgio, which Robert did. Giorgio rather sulkily left the room again.

'Your servant says he does not know the name of the man who owns this ship, on which you were to sail, but he has told me enough. I know who the man is. He was hanged yesterday.'

He waited for Robert's exclamation, then he went on. 'He was caught returning from a trip to Circassia. The ship and her cargo were confiscated, and the captain was hanged. This was done at the orders of the Russian consul here. Oh, the pasha of Trebizond gave the instructions, but it is known who was behind them. You see, it can be rather dangerous for a Turk to break the embargo on trading with Circassia. You are quite safe, of course, you are an Englishman and a brave man, but all the same this is not a good place to discuss this matter. It would be better if you would honour me by coming to my house. It can be this evening, as soon as you please. And I hope I will be able to arrange matters for you as you wish.'

Mr Papandian's house was in the Armenian suburb, some half an hour out of town. It stood next to the curious squat church, square and fortress-like, which was the centre of the village, and the house also, with its blank outer walls, seemed built for defence. Inside was a warm welcome, however. Refreshment was offered on arrival by a smiling elderly woman in black, who was presumably Mr Papandian's wife, and not a servant, for diamonds flashed in her ears under the black veil which covered her head, and the appearance of two Europeans did not disconcert her. There were also two girls who did not appear beyond the threshold of the room, and were shooed away by Mr Papandian when they attempted to get a closer glimpse of the visitors. Robert was amused by the altercation which seemed to be going on between the ladies about the nature of the refreshment. Finally Mr Papandian intervened, with authority.

'The women have prepared a sherbet to celebrate your arrival. It is their best, but not such as Egenye Bey would offer. But perhaps you would prefer tea, Mr Wilton?'

'If it is not too much trouble,' said Robert.

'Trouble? There is no trouble. It is only women who make trouble –' and Mr Papandian said something in a rapid undertone to the senior lady, who trotted out and returned with the tea. Robert drank it, under the baleful stares of Mr Papandian's ancestors, whose portraits adorned the walls. Only one of them had his eyes closed, but then he was dead and in his coffin. These portraits were evidently much prized, for vases with dusty flowers were ranged below them, but Robert hesitated to allude to them when the fate of the subjects was so uncertain.

The room in which they sat was crowded with a jumble of objects, samples, and piles of goods, among which lay the shipping directories of several nations, and cuttings from the English, French, German and Italian press. It looked as though Mr Papandian could read English, although he did not offer to speak it. Tin plaques, emblazoned with legends such as 'Rowland's ODONTO', 'Walker's Needles, supplied to Royalty', 'Chubb's New Patent Detector Locks', and 'Parr's Life Pills' hung on the walls, as much for ornament as for advertisement. There was also what looked like official documents in Russian, on which Robert recognized the script and the double eagle at the head of the paper. At least he thought he recognized the script, but when he looked that way again, the papers were no longer there.

'It is unfortunate that your servant can only speak Turkish – as well as Greek, Italian and some English, of course,' Mr Papandian had said. 'Where you are going you really need a man who can speak the Circassian dialects, and Russian and Georgian could always be useful. I could have arranged this, but not without a certain amount of notice. Some of the men who offer their services are outlaws, *abreks* as they are called in Circassia, and they are not very trustworthy characters. Also, they cannot go amongst another tribe with which they have a blood feud, and this can be inconvenient. But the chiefs of the Circassian tribes nearly all speak Turkish, so you should be all right as you speak such good Turkish yourself. The most important thing is to arrange for your *konak* – your host – who should be a man of high rank. Otherwise the first Circassian chief into whose hands you fell would have the right to sell you as a slave – and you might find yourself right back in Constantinople.' He laughed gaily. 'They would not do that to you, of course, you are an Englishman, but they are very suspicious, these people, and nervous of strangers, now more than ever. But once a chief becomes your *konak*, he is bound to protect you, at the cost of his own life, if necessary.'

Robert began to feel rather nervous himself. 'How is this host to be found?' he inquired.

'Oh, it is simply a question of money,' answered Mr Papandian. 'They are desperately short of funds. It costs money to fight a war. The country is self-supporting in normal times, but the war supplies they need have to be bought from outside. A suitable contribution to the expenses of the campaign will assure you a welcome, and all can be arranged. They would prefer to have part of it in kind, gunpowder for choice as this is very hard for them to obtain on account of the embargo. This is a risky affair, though, and I do not know if the man I have in mind for the voyage will be prepared to undertake the carriage of the gunpowder, but I will endeavour to persuade him as it would undoubtedly be best for you. You are a brave man, and I can see the risks of the embargo do not trouble you.'

'I am in some difficulty,' said Robert at last, 'in that I do not know how far matters have progressed with my first contact. It might be embarrassing to find that I have two hosts.'

'Matters can have progressed nowhere,' said Mr Papandian, 'as the man is dead. He was waiting off the coast, hoping to come in after dark, but they were watching for him. I have not found out where the Russian consul got his information, but there it is. The man cannot have taken any steps in your affair, and you should be able to recover any money you have paid. Your servant should be able to do that, as he introduced the man.'

Robert raised this matter with Giorgio as they jogged home on donkey-back in the dust, with a rising moon creating a deeper darkness under the big roadside trees, and dogs barking a challenge behind the walls of the nearby farms. Giorgio was sulky, and clearly put out at the turn matters had taken. However, early next morning a turbaned visitor was ushered into Robert's room who, without a word, counted out in Giorgio's presence the money due.

While waiting, once more, for departure, Robert took the opportunity, on Mr Papandian's advice, of augmenting his stock of presents by purchasing a number of small compasses (indispensable to the conforming Moslem, as Mr Papandian pointed out, for ascertaining the direction of Mecca), and some pocket looking-glasses, something which Robert would never have thought of himself as acceptable gifts for mountain warriors. One more thing also remained to be done. The nagging tooth had subsided again into temporary quiescence, but this state of things could not be relied upon to continue. It seemed more sensible to have the tooth pulled now, in the comparative civilization of Trebizond, rather than later in conditions entirely unpredictable. Robert instructed Giorgio to send for the town practitioner, who turned out to be the barber, reasoning once again that this would be more private than having the operation performed in full view of the bazaar.

It was in fact a relatively private occasion, The barber arrived, with his assistant bearing his chair and paraphernalia, and the full complement of guests, servants and hangers-on of the hotel congregated to witness the operation and to cheer and encourage the patient. The barber fortunately was skilful, and the tooth came out easily (it must have been in a pretty bad way anyhow), and once the extraction was over, Robert felt more comfortable than he had for some days. The onlookers dispersed, loudly praising his courage and endurance, as did the barber, who once back in his shop in the bazaar, which was one of the meeting-places of the town, lost no time in spreading the news of his foreign client, and his importance and wealth.

Mr Papandian, who was in his own shop, heard the news, as indeed he heard everything which was going on round him, but not by one flicker did his dark, wide-set eyes show that he had heard. He continued to deal with the several problems which were engaging his attention : the non-arrival of a consignment of English horsehair to stuff a set of cushions for the pasha's harem (for several of the ladies were modern, and aspired to live *alla franca*), and the unpleasant, not to mention threatening attitude of the pasha's agent who had come down to the shop; the fistful of uncut gems, of very doubtful provenance, which had been offered to him by a ragged Kurdish muleteer; the new regulations which the Russians had promulgated concerning Black Sea shipping. As he listened with humility to the threats and insults of the Turk, Mr Papandian turned over calmly in his mind the present he would have to give the agent at the conclusion of the interview, and re-calculated the profit on the horsehair. The other transaction was quite satisfactory : the Kurd would be drunk by now, and lying helpless somewhere in the bazaar. Tomorrow he would have to set off with his animals on his return road and he would have no opportunity to make trouble. Later, when Mr Papandian reached home, there was a more congenial matter awaiting his attention. His eldest daughter had been asked for in marriage, and the two families were waiting agog to hear what would be the dowry, for Mr Papandian was a devoted father.

He was also attentive to his client's interests. Late that evening Robert received a message to have all ready for an early departure the following morning. Thanks to Mr Papandian's admirable organization, everything went smoothly. Mounts were waiting outside the hotel before the first light, and porters were ready to take up the baggage almost before the last straps were fastened. On the beach of the secluded bay where Robert had landed, Mr Papandian was waiting to see his client off.

The boat in which the trip up the coast was to be made looked at first sight alarmingly small, but Mr Papandian had assured Robert that Ismail, her captain, was an experienced sailor who made regular trading trips to Circassia. Ismail was a wiry and muscular young man, the first 'real' Circassian Robert had seen. His face was partly obscured by the fur cap which he wore and he was dressed in ragged grey woollen garments, cut high to the neck and belted in tightly at the waist, the national dress which looked most un-nautical. He wore light morocco slippers on his feet. Four other men made up the crew.

The luggage was hastily put aboard. It took up all the space in the tiny cabin, and Giorgio surveyed with distaste the utter discomfort of the undecked vessel in which they were to spend a day and a night, at least. He did not look enthusiastic for the voyage. Robert, now that his fate was in the hands of Ismail and Circassia nearly in sight, felt a prickling of the nerves which was due to the solemnity of the occasion rather than the possible dangers ahead, but he did not feel loquacious. Only Fop, adventurous as ever, panted and danced in excitement, and made strenuous efforts to scramble on board. When Ismail perceived the dog, his look at first boded ill, and Robert half expected a demand that the unclean animal should be removed, but then the severe face relaxed and Ismail actually stooped to pat the infidel's pet, while Fop frisked unsuspectingly at his feet. The Circassians could not then be very diligent Moslems, and Robert had second thoughts about the acceptability of the compasses. Still, as he reflected, a compass could always be useful on a campaign.

The moment of departure had arrived. Ismail hurried the business of leave-taking along, anxious to make the most advantage of the early morning mist, and also hoping to pick up a breeze off the coast. Mr Papandian shook hands with Robert, his eyes sad and unfathomable as usual.

'May God protect you!' he said rather unexpectedly, at the last.

Mr Papandian remained on the shore until the small boat was out of sight, and then he mounted his donkey. The business of the day was waiting, in his shop.

Armed riders were frequently to be seen in the streets, parties of Bashi-Bazouks, and men of the pasha's bodyguard. When a small group of them, gaudily caparisoned, but well mounted, and lavishly armed, clattered through the bazaar and made for the hotel, Mr Papandian did not raise his eyes from what he was doing. The pasha's secretary, the bearer of compliments and invitations, drew a blank, however, at the hotel. The English milord had flown.

37

The travellers were lucky. The mist protected them nearly the whole of the way, although from time to time it cleared in patches, and the sun came through. There was a moment of drama, when in the late afternoon a vessel suddenly loomed up ahead which seemed of vast size in the delusive light. There was extreme agitation on board the Circassian's boat, but the patrol ship, or whatever it was, sheered off and the two vessels passed unseen within a shot's length of each other, Ismail creeping gingerly on his course, with the sail close-hauled, and Robert with his hands clamped firmly round Fop's jaws. There suddenly came into his mind the situation of Lord Byron's *Mistico*, lying becalmed off Missolonghi with the Turkish frigate in the offing. But fortunately for Greece, his Lordship's dogs had not given tongue, and Fop's efforts to do so were frustrated on this occasion. But it was a near escape and shortly afterwards, when darkness fell altogether, the captain hove-to. During the night which followed captain and crew huddled together and snored in the bottom of the boat, but Robert slept little.

The next day he felt was going to be a hot one as soon as the sun rose. They were quickly under way. The mist began to stream off, but not quickly enough for Robert. He fancied he could smell the land – it was maddening to be off the coast of Circassia and not be able to see it. Then a crack appeared, and a patch of intense green showed through. They had come right in close to the shore without his having realized it. The patch became a large opening, the clouds rolled away, and before him was the sea coast of Circassia, green hill after green hill rising one upon the other till their crests vanished into the low-hanging clouds behind which the high mountains must lie. Forest trees ran down to the water's edge.

Choosing a small beach, Ismail ran the boat in. The men jumped out and manhandled her up the shore and unloaded Robert's belongings. He himself stepped dry-shod on to the sand. It was only a couple of steps to cross the little beach and reach the grassy slope beyond. The sun shone down with early morning vigour, familiar flowers, daisies, cowslips and scabious, strange only in their enormous size, thrashed and fluttered in the light sea breeze, and a cloud of buzzing flies descended on Robert's face and hands. It was like a stage drama. One minute the scene was empty: the next minute there were the flies, glittering precursors of events. Then the Circassians had sprung up in the foreground, fierce swarthy figures dressed in the same fashion as Ismail. The smell of meadowsweet and crushed turf came to Robert's nostrils faintly tinged with the aroma of the big sheepskin caps which every man wore pushed back from his brow. The Circassians were all round him, smiling broadly, embracing Ismail and the rest of the crew, and greeting, with ceremonious politeness, the stranger from England.

Chapter 3

IT WAS FORTUNATE for a visitor from Europe, that custom required any Circassian of position to lodge his guests in a cabin to themselves, removed from the main house. It assured the stranger a nominal measure of privacy – if only it were possible to exclude the crowds who came to see him. Robert was at first acutely embarrassed by, then he became reconciled to and began to take for granted, the enormous interest which his person, his property and his behaviour inspired in the local inhabitants. They watched him get up, and saw him go to bed. They watched him dress and undress, eat, read and wash. They made it difficult for him to pursue his English-style ablutions without the risk of shocking the veiled matrons and handsome unveiled girls who peered into his wattle hut at all hours, and it was impossible to dispose tactfully of the strange and un-appetizing meals which were carried out to him from the main house, or alternatively to supplement them with his own provisions. Robert blessed the forethought which had led him to lay in a supply of foreign comestibles. He calculated that he had sufficient stocks to see him through until he had learned to subsist on Circassian food, or had taught his hosts to supplement the universal meat and grain which appeared at every meal with the delicious-looking vegetables which abounded on all sides but, so far as he could judge, were made no use of at all for food.

The fact that he was under continual observation himself made it difficult for him to observe, as closely as he would have liked, the family circle of his hosts. But the family which he saw consisted of the old prince, Arslan (the Lion) Bey, who was to be his *konak*, a fine-looking old man who seemed honest and straightforward. The princess, his wife, was a matronly figure, richly but curiously untidily dressed. Robert had not seen her unveiled, but she seemed quite friendly disposed towards him. The young princess, their daughter, Paka by name, went quite

40

unveiled, and Robert was able to study her discreetly. She was not exactly a beauty (Robert felt a secret pang of disappointment at this), but she was a handsome enough girl, albeit a trifle rigid and unbending in her carriage. Robert wondered if this was due to the famous deer-skin corset, sewn on in childhood and never removed until marriage, which he had heard so much about in Constantinople and read of in the travellers' tales. She was certainly very slim, at least in the top half of her figure.

Both the mother and daughter had disconcerted Robert by rising to their feet when he was first taken to their quarters to meet them, and by remaining standing for the whole of the visit. Later he discovered that this was not a compliment to him, as he had imagined it to be: the ladies stood up at the sight of any man, be he one of their own serfs. The two princesses also did a good deal of domestic work, including farmyard tasks, but except in these two particulars, the women were treated with a considerable degree of respect for a Moslem country. From time to time Robert observed the old princess putting her husband to rights. Paka, too, seemed to enjoy a considerable amount of freedom which quite often involved her in chasing the straying chicken, lamb, or whatever it was, in front of Robert's quarters. He carefully refrained, however, from making any use of the opportunity, if such it was, so afforded. He had no doubt it would be the height of imprudence to make advances to his host's daughter, while how Paka would receive an approach he was not entirely sure. Her expression was so stern, so impenetrably Asiatic as she ran flourishing her switch and calling objurgations at the runaway livestock. Her hair, which at first appeared to be flying in wild Medusa-locks, was in fact tightly braided into many little tails, each one weighted with a silver coin, just as her bust was first laced in, then clipped with silver plates. Perhaps because of this tight lacing, she very easily got out of breath, and then she leaned on any support available, gasping and giggling with the serf women who were glad of any excuse to put down their water buckets, or their loads of wood.

The male side of the family was represented, besides the old Lion, by his son Hassan and a couple of younger boys, relatives of some sort, who were attached to the household in the capacity of squires, attending on the old prince, his arms and his horses. They appeared to be on more intimate terms with Arslan Bey than was his own son, who had been sent away, following the Circassian custom, to learn the arts of war, horse management, and falconry, in another princely family, from which he had only lately returned. Part of the coldness which the old man exhibited towards him might be due to the Oriental convention which forbade a father to display affection for his son in public, just as Hassan's respect seemed exaggerated – standing in his father's presence with downcast eyes, not eating at the same table, and so on – but there seemed to be little affection between father and son. Out of the old chief's sight Hassan was a lively enough young man. He was dark, like his sister, with the same wasp waist displayed by the tight fitting Circassian tunic and the same air of nervous hauteur, but much less reserved and unapproachable than she, and his curiosity often made him seek out the Englishman.

He threw himself down now in the long grass which stretched from Robert's quarters to the stream (ice cold, like most Circassian rivers) where Robert was wont to wash, hiding himself as much as possible behind the alders and the hazel bushes. Robert went over and squatted beside him: they both spoke an indifferent Turkish which made it quite possible to converse. Hassan brought out a cracked pocket looking-glass and showed it to Robert.

'Have you got another one, Jibrahil Bey?'

Robert's first name was one the Circassians could make nothing of, but when he told them that his second name was Gabriel, rather doubting whether such a Christian-sounding appellation would be acceptable, his hosts had adopted it – or the local variant – immediately.

His cargo of compasses and looking-glasses had been an instant success, but not quite in the way he had anticipated. The men had dismissed the compasses with one glance, after Robert had explained their use. 'We know where the north is without that little iron to tell us!' they had exclaimed disdainfully. The women, however, had seized on them as a most diverting toy which might or might not contain a genie of a benevolent variety, and therefore a *porte-bonheur*. Paka and her mother each wore theirs on a chain round their necks, and consulted it from time to time. The looking-glasses, on the other hand, had disappeared into the pockets of the men as soon as these warriors caught sight of them. There were, unfortunately, frequent breakages (the fragments, down to the smallest, being seized on by the servants and retainers), and Robert foresaw that if he met all the demands for replacements, he would be soon out of stock. He could not, however, refuse the chief's son, so he went and unlocked the box and got out another looking-glass. Hassan took it without thanks, and began to study his face in it.

'When are you next going to make an expedition against the Russians?' asked Robert.

Hassan gestured towards the main house.

'They are still talking about it now. My father has not decided. In any case, we shall have to wait until the moon is right.'

'I should like to come with you.'

'I will tell my father what you say.' Hassan sat cross-legged and twisted his moustache carefully over one finger, squinting into the glass. Then he saw that at the far end of the clearing one of the young men was pantomiming his action, with an imaginary looking-glass in his hand, and a clownish grin on his face. Hassan sprang to his feet and closed with the offender – for one moment Robert expected daggers to be drawn. Then the young men grappled together until one tripped the other, and they were rolling over and over on the ground, laughing and crushing the stalks of the fleshy, bell-shaped flowers which grew there in profusion. They got up and wandered off together, hand in hand, by the stream side. Robert, watching them while they were in sight, saw Hassan pass what was presumably the cracked mirror to his companion. Then they passed out of view, tall figures bristling with weapons, pushing their way through the thickets of dog-roses which grew riotously up and down the river banks. They would be off on a day-long hunt of wild animals, if not of Russians, skulking through the enormous forests which covered most of their land, like soft-footed beasts themselves. Robert, left behind, went back into his own hut.

A sharp vision rose up in his mind of those golden October days when either very early in the morning, or in the evening, when Henry could be spared from the farm, they had gone out together with a gun and Henry's old dog, Sam. He could smell the autumn mists rising off the stubble, remember the nervous excitement, hear the sudden clatter as the golden bird rose in flight.

There were other expeditions, further afield, and although he was the younger, it was always Henry with his knowledge of country lore, with his strength and his ready hands, who guided their adventures : if he deferred to Robert as the nominal leader, both knew well which was the better man. But all that was long ago, and far away. Around him the forest flamed and glittered as the sun grew hotter. At a little distance a group of serfs who were hacking in a desultory way at a patch of cultivation watched him out of the corners of their eyes.

Robert suddenly wished with all his heart that Henry was there, and that he had the support and comfort of his presence. To have somebody to talk to – and Henry was always a good listener, his sensibilities were developed far beyond his station in life. Henry would have sympathized with him even if he did not understand the emotions which had launched his friend on this present venture. But there was nobody at hand but Giorgio – and Giorgio was not a good listener.

Peering out through the interstices of his rustic pavilion, Robert could see his servant some distance away, very much occupied. Almost immediately on their arrival the young Greek had secured himself a welcome in the feminine community of the kitchen quarters, presided over by the old princess in person, by making himself a willing and obliging assistant. There he was now, hanging round the back door as usual, holding forth in what language Robert could not imagine to a bevy of stalwart waiting women, who were one and all convulsed with giggles. Cheerful, snub-nosed, undersized, it would take a half a dozen Giorgios to make one Henry.

Giorgio shortly after appeared as the bearer of a summons from Arslan Bey to a *tamata*, or consultation of chiefs, to be followed by a festive dinner, in preparation for which, Giorgio assured him, the princesses had laboured to produce a special cake, under Giorgio's direction.

'Plenty of honey, plenty of nuts,' said Giorgio. 'Just now I teach these ladies Greek cooking. Soon I teach them to make English rice-pudding, as I used to serve to the English Lord. Rice-pudding, rosbif, tea-and-toas'. These people are savages. They need to be taught everything.'

But Robert was not interested for the moment in food, he was intrigued by the chiefs' consultation. Tedious and uncomfortable as he knew these functions to be, having been exhibited (as he felt) at a number of them, there was always a hope, however small a crumb, of action resulting, and action he was determined to see. He suspected from time to time that his hosts were for some reason reluctant to admit him to full participation in the campaign, but he would impress upon them that he had come to a war to see fighting.

Robert's wish seemed quite shortly to be on the verge of fulfilment, for although no news came in of Russian moves, Arslan decided to keep the pot boiling by making a raid across the Kuban river, which was the southern limit of Russian territory, into the vast Kuban plain beyond. Here were the Cossack settlements, peopled by a race of warriors almost the equal of the Circassians, who were bred to hold the perilous acquisitions which the Tsars had added to their empire against all counter-attacks from the Circassian side. The settlements were also the base from which the Russian armies thrusting into Circassia operated. Raiding the Kuban was always an effective counter-move which raised the Circassians' spirits, and could also afford them an opportunity for driving off some cattle.

The raiding party was mustered under the leadership of Arslan himself, and included both Hassan and Robert. Then at the moment of departure the rain began to fall, first in spasmodic showers, then in a steady downpour which blanketed the hills. With resignation, the men unsaddled. As Hassan explained, even if they got through the mountain passes, they would be unable to ford the Kuban river which ran on the other side of them. The expedition was postponed, and Robert returned to the hut to watch the rain fall out of the clouds in straight lances which hammered down the grass and the Circassians' standing crops. There was the sound of running water everywhere : the stream was coming down in spate, and after a few days of this, Robert came down with a fever.

It was not at first very serious, but it was a miserable business. To begin with, his habitation was far from being watertight. Men were sent over from the main house to mend the roof, but the result of their efforts was to exclude most of the light and air, while the drips above the divan on which Robert lay continued. He kept on his feet as long as possible, hoping to avoid the ordeal of a public illness among these well-intentioned but uncouth strangers, but finally he collapsed, shivering and sweating, burning hot and icy cold by turns, into his blankets until the worst of the attack should be over.

The first day was comparatively peaceful. Giorgio brought hot drinks and such food as Robert was able to eat, and doctored him from the medicine chest. Then the Circassians discovered their guest lying there, his eyes closed and his face clammy with sweat. They gathered, twenty-five, fifty strong. All who could find standing space forced themselves into the hut, where they sang and clowned. Those outside banged on drums, on pans and on buckets. The idea was, as Hassan later explained, to make sure that the patient did not go to sleep, as this was certain to entail fatal consequences. At the end of a morning of this, Robert's temperature had rocketed, and he was very ill indeed. Then the old Princess appeared with a potion which she insisted he should swallow. It tasted of nothing worse than leaves and hay, but it left a bitter after-taste which would have made Robert apprehensive had he been in a state to think more clearly. But by now he was fairly light-headed, and not even the presence of the handsome Paka and of several other girls who leaned over the divan stroking and patting him could divert his mind.

It was Hassan, more perceptive than the others, who came to his rescue. Hassan succeeded in getting the hut cleared of spectators, and in silencing the musicians outside, when it became apparent that local remedies were failing to have effect. Giorgio, summoned again to take charge, administered one of Robert's remaining opium pills, and Robert fell into a half-stupor which was not unpleasant, when his soul seemed to be suspended in mid-air, detached from the discomfort engendered by the fever within and the rasp of the rough blanket, which Giorgio would not allow him to throw off, under his chin. The shafts of bright sunlight filtering in from outside (for the rain had stopped and the sun had burst out again with furious force) did not worry him: he lay gazing at the humming insects which darted in and out of the bars of light. Hassan came in from time to time, and then another man appeared in the hut, a tall clean-shaven man wearing the Circassian dress, although it seemed to Robert that he was not a Circassian : but he was too weak and disinterested to question a stranger's presence there. Later on this new guest – if he was a guest – returned. Robert watched him out of half-shut eyes moving about the hut, touching things, lifting clothes and books, then going into the corner where the boxes were, which was out of Robert's sight. But just then Giorgio entered, and the stranger said something to him and left the hut hastily, stooping under the low lintel.

A day or two later, when he was nearly recovered, Robert recalled the incident, and asked Hassan who the man was.

'His name is Shekhir Effendi.'

'But is he a Circassian?'

'No, he is a foreigner. He was formerly with the Russians, but now he has come to help us, a man of noble heart, like yourself. He knows everything about cannon. We are hoping to capture enough guns to have a battery of our own. Then we shall blow the Russians into the sea. Shekhir Effendi will show us how.'

Robert was still unsatisfied. The behaviour of 'Shekhir Effendi' struck him as strange, and in retrospect, disagreeable. He did not want to have any further contact with him.

'Is Shekhir Effendi staying here with your father?' he asked.

'No, he left at dawn today for the coast. We have news that the Russians are moving.'

This was satisfactory in one respect, at least.

'I should like to go to the coast myself, and see where the Russians have built their forts.'

'You shall go.' replied Hassan, 'you shall go, as soon as you are able to ride. That will be tomorrow, or if not tomorrow, the day after. We will go together to the country of my people's ancestors, of the little men no higher than your knee, who live in caves among the rocks, and ride out on hares. Did I tell you that they wear chain mail, like a chief's coat of mail, and when they fight, they fight with bows and arrows? They fight with bows and arrows, and they are miniature men, yet sometimes a sword is found under the rocks which is too heavy for our strongest warrior to wield, with writing on the blade which none of our most learned mullahs can read.'

47

Sitting cross-legged on the carpet, he went on intoning his stories till Robert was almost lulled to sleep. Finally Hassan took Robert's watch, shook it and put it to his ear. Then tiring of being indoors, he sprang up and went out into the sunlight.

Next day he returned when Robert, now fully dressed, was pottering about setting things in their proper places, but this time he brought his sister with him. Paka's colour was high (they seemed to have had an argument), and her mouth was as tightly shut as ever.

'Go in, girl,' said Hassan, giving her a push. 'Talk to him. Englishmen are human. He is like other men.'

With this encouragement Hassan left her to her own devices, and Paka, as soon as she was in the house, regained her ease. An initial difficulty arose in that she refused to sit down until Robert had taken his place on the divan. Once he was in his rightful seat, however, she indicated that she was prepared to enter on the business of entertaining him. This promised to be difficult without a word of a common language, other than Robert's few tags of Circassian, but he had the bright idea of calling for Fop. The little dog had by now acquired quite a repertoire of engaging tricks (some of them undoubtedly learned at the cook-house door). The dog made her laugh, the ice was broken, and by the time they had tired of throwing a ball for him while Fop sat panting but bright-eyed, watching for them to continue the sport, all constraint had vanished. In some ways it was like amusing a little girl. Robert showed her how to blow a feather along and Paka, overcome with laughing, collapsed on the divan. He put his hands on her waist to lift her up.

She did not seem to resent this : in fact she did not seem to notice it. Perhaps through the rigid corsetry, which reminded Robert of the pinched waists of the girls he had danced with at home, she could not even feel his touch. As he raised her to an upright position, she swung round and rested her head against his chest. The pungent smell of her hair, sleeked with some unfamiliar oil, filled his nostrils, attracted him while it made him want to sneeze. Her head was heavy on his shoulder. This was not at all like the girls he had danced with, who had held their heads at a decorous distance from him, and smiled at him shyly when their chaperone's eyes were elsewhere.

When she had recovered from her laughing fit, Paka sat up

48

demurely on the divan. Robert made to take her hand – he now felt well enough to make the most of the occasion – but instead she took his, and began to enumerate for his benefit the Circassian words for the fingers, the thumb, the hand, the wrist, and so on, up to the arm, while Robert repeated the words after her. There seemed no reason why they should stop at the arm, and Robert tried to show that he was willing to continue with the lesson a little further : but Paka clearly thought that she had done her duty by him for the day. She restored his hand to him with decision and got up. Robert could find no words with which to restrain her : he tried to look bereft, but this had no effect. Paka only laughed, and making a gesture which clearly indicated that enough was enough, she left him.

Robert was at a loss. He was not sure if Paka attracted him – but she provoked him. He watched her disappearing figure, in some ways so disproportionate in appearance, and wondered what difference, if any, her clothes made. Dressed in the Circassian costume she seemed to him to look bottom-heavy, with her voluminous trousers and voluminous overskirt, all bundled round the lower half of her body. From the waist up, the woman became a child, so tight was the clasp of her bodice and overdress. To be sure, the neck line was very low, but as with the London young ladies' ball-dress, the expanse of bare skin did not in itself constitute an allurement to the senses. The suggestion of budding curves below had been ironed away by the grip of whalebone – or deerskin.

Did she like him at all, Robert wondered. Did she always look so fierce, so unyielding as she looked to him? (Except, of course, when she was amused by something : then she went off into peal after peal of laughter, but even so, she always laughed *at* Robert, he thought, never with him.) He would have liked to inspire some emotion in this self-possessed young creature, but it was difficult, when he had no idea how far his advances would be permitted – or expected – to go. Was Mr Eugenius right in saying that only kissing was debarred? Had Paka been sent to him by her father and brother as a solace to his solitary hours of convalescence? He had read that in some Eastern countries, offering a daughter or a wife was a rite of hospitality. In that case, he must have shown himself grievously backward, not to say discourteous, in not making use of the opportunity so offered. Yet however passive and quiescent Paka had shown herself, some instinct told him that if, when he had put his hands round her waist, he had instead of lifting her up, drawn her down on the divan beside him, Paka would not have tolerated his importunities for long before she took the sharp little dagger which hung at her waist, like a lady's *nécessaire*, in a pretty case of shagreen studded with coral and turquoises, and thrust it into his flesh.

No, he had been wise and prudent not to push things any further. All the same, his mind continued to dwell on Paka. Those bisque brunette cheeks : what would be the effect of a good bath with soap and hot water ? Would it produce the white skin which made the Circassian girls famous ? Was her skin white at all ? Perhaps the brown was only sunburn, and a few months behind the grilles of a Turkish harem would produce the necessary pallor. If her hair were to be shampooed, and the strange-smelling unguents washed away, would there be a cloud of chestnut ringlets to braid with pearls instead of the snaky black locks of Medusa which he had felt against his chest ?

How long would it take before the untamed girl, the herder of lambs and goats, the dexterous embroideress (for Paka, he learned, had made with her own hands the silver lace which ornamented the Circassian tunic he had been given), the warrior's helpmeet, turned into the harem beauty, lolling away her life behind the window grilles ? That is, if her fate led her to Constantinople. If, on the other hand, her father and brother decided to dispose of her to the son of another family of equal rank, he could see all too clearly what her life would become – the example of her mother was there in front of his eyes. Weighed down by her *embonpoint*, as well as by the cares of her family and household, the old princess, swathed in veils, waddled on her pattens between her divan, her kitchen and her farmyard, putting her hand to tasks which if left to her serf women would probably have never got done at all, and standing back with downcast eyes whenever a male came in sight. No doubt she scolded her husband and her son roundly when she had them to herself: and Paka too, thought Robert, could probably be a shrew when she wanted to. A strange and provoking girl, but not, as he had been led to expect of Circassian girls, the embodiment of feminine charm.

50

A day or so after Paka's visit, Giorgio hastened into the hut and informed Robert that the foreign mullah desired to speak with him.

'Who is this foreign mullah?' asked Robert, baffled.

Giorgio spread his hands.

'Nobody knows. These men say that he is very holy, very wise, a learned man, but nobody can understand what he says, and they do not know where he comes from, whether from the east or from the west.'

'Where is he, then?'

'He is approaching now,' said Giorgio, pointing to a figure in flowing robes which was advancing slowly across the grass. Looking at the approaching visitor, Robert remembered something which he had thought at the time must have taken place in a dream. Either in a dream, or in his delirious fancy – for it had occurred when the fever was at its height. He recollected this same robed figure by his bedside, reading aloud, or rather chanting, in an unknown but strangely soothing tongue some incantation out of a book. After chanting for some time, the stranger had fallen into a rapt meditation, and as the book he held was now closed, Robert was able to read the words on the cover, upside down, while his sick mind struggled with the problem of turning them right side up. *Y Beibl* was what he finally achieved. It meant nothing to him, and he abandoned the attempt to make any sense out of the episode. In his memory, though, he retained the impression of a vaguely beneficent personality, quite unlike the sinister Shekhir Effendi.

The mullah entered, and saluted. Robert could not understand anything he said, but after glancing briefly at Giorgio, who was equally at sea, he replied with his best selection of Turkish and Circassian phrases, and invited his visitor to take a seat. He told Giorgio to bring tea, hoping to ease the situation, and Giorgio disappeared to execute the order. The mullah put his feet off the divan to the ground, and straightened his back.

'A cup of tea, now, would be a very welcome thing,' he said, in English, but with a lilting accent strange to Robert's ear. 'That was a kindly thought in you, Mr Wilton, or Jibrahil Bey, as I should be calling you while we are in these parts, especially as I have not tasted tea these six months. The people here gather herbs and make a kind of infusion of them, which they

51

call tea, but it is poor stuff, as I expect you have by now found out for yourself.'

The tea was brought, and Giorgio withdrew again. While he was in the room, the visitor laid down in front of him the black book which he was carrying, joined his hands on top of it, and exhaled a pious sigh, directing his gaze meanwhile at the air in front of him. By squinting slightly downwards, he was able to make out what was in the tea equipage. Robert read, once again upside down, on the cover of the black book *Y Beibl.*

'I think I must have seen you during the time I was ill. You were reading to me from that book.'

'I read the Scriptures to you in your extremity,' was the reply, 'as the best office I could render you. Yes, sugar if you please, Mr Wilton – what a pity there is no milk! Would that I could reach the hearts of these poor heathen here as easily.'

'Are you then a missionary in these parts?' asked Robert. 'For I take it, sir, that you are a minister of religion.'

'I was, sir, until a year ago, a man ministering to his flock in a green and pleasant place. Now I am but a voice crying in the howling wilderness, with none to hear but ravens and jackals, or men who have no more understanding than these. You may well ask me, Mr Wilton, how this came about. My name, for I should introduce myself, is Lewis Jones, the Reverend Lewis Jones, till lately pastor of Zion Chapel in Pant-y-dillon.

'Yes, thank you, another cup of tea would be very welcome.

'It was wickedness, Mr Wilton, which drove me from my charge, wickedness, and the conspiracy of evil doers banded against me. They traduced me, Mr Wilton, these wicked men set themselves up in league to destroy me. They disobeyed the rules of our church: in that they were the wrong-doers, not I. They made themselves deacons. It was not properly done in accordance with our regulations for the church government. The thing was out of order, and I told them so. They said 'What of it, we are the deacons and we shall alter the rules.' I told them, you cannot do this thing, your election is in all respects irregular, I cannot have any dealings with you. You are not deacons properly appointed by our church rules, therefore I cannot regard you as the proper spokesmen of the congregation.'

Mr Jones was getting increasingly agitated, his teacup was

shaking in his hand. He put it down, and from the depths of his robes he drew out a folded paper, much worn and soiled at the edges, and proceeded to read from it, stabbing his forefinger from time to time to give added emphasis. Robert listened bemused to the catalogue of precepts, adjurations, prohibitions and sanctions which followed. It was a very long one.

'I ask you, Mr Wilton, what could be more plain than the way it is all set down,' said Mr Jones, restoring the paper to its hiding place, 'and yet it is nothing more or less than these written rules that these wicked men sought to question. How could I give ear to them, when they were plainly in error? And it was these same men who expelled me, their duly appointed minister, from their midst.

'I was glad to go, seeing that I could not lead them away from their error. But one thing I did not leave to them. I took the trust deed with me. That at least has not fallen into the hands of unbelievers.'

Mr Jones's eyes flashed, and he looked the picture of an Old Testament prophet.

'So you took to the missionary field instead, and came here. How splendid!' said Robert, when he could get a word in.

'Ah no, it was for the newspaper that I came here, as the war correspondent it was,' said Mr Jones.

Visions of *The Times* flashed through Robert's mind. Had he perhaps been reading Mr Jones's despatches?

'My cousin it is who owns the newspaper,' continued Mr Jones. 'That is my cousin Emrys Jones, who is living now in Swansea. The *South Cambrian Independent*, he calls it. Only a small circulation as yet, you will understand, but great things may yet come of it.

'There were many problems, however, over the war news. It became very hard to send it out. That was the one difficulty, and there was the other difficulty over the money. There was no way of sending it here. So when the opportunity came of doing the Lord's work among these poor people here, I willingly embraced it. They have given me food and lodging, not very good it is true, but I accept the hardships as my own small offering to the faith I serve.'

'Are you hoping then to reconvert the tribesmen to Christianity?' asked Robert.

'I doubt that reconvert is the word,' replied Mr Jones. 'It would surprise me greatly if these people here were ever Christians as you and I would understand the word.'

'I understand that they have now turned Moslem, at least nominally,' said Robert, 'but I have not so far seen any signs of Moslem observances, and I surmise that their profession of Moslem beliefs is not very profound.'

'At heart they are pagans, Mr Wilton.'

Mr Jones gazed gloomily through the open door. In the bright sunshine outside one of the men-at-arms was loitering with two unveiled girls, whom Robert recognized as being Paka's constant companions. What he was saying to them Robert could not tell, but the girls were holding their hands in front of their mouths to hide their giggles. One of them ran back into the kitchen quarters, uttering little screams. The other, the prettier of the two, sauntered off, twitching her plaits over her shoulder, in the direction of the stream. The young man followed and in a pace or two caught her up, The swinging hazel branches dropped behind them.

'Such wantonness!' said Mr Jones. 'That at least is a sight which you would never see in a God-fearing Moslem country. Wantonness and pride, those are the twin faults which must be rooted out, if the weeds are not to choke the good seed. They are the mildew that cankers the crop, before the sheaves are gathered in.'

'Surely these people have quite high moral qualities for pagans?' queried Robert, going back a little.

'The thieving that goes on,' said Mr Jones, 'does not lead a man to think very highly of their morality.'

'Well, you have more experience than I,' said Robert, 'but nothing so far makes me think that they are lacking in honesty.'

'You are in a privileged position.' said Mr Jones. 'You are the honoured guest of their chief. They may covet your goods – covetousness is a sad failing here – and they may even ask you for them, as I have no doubt they do, but they would not steal them. But it would be different, I assure you, if you were a stranger coming among them without protection.'

'I was warned that I would be sold as a slave if I did,' said Robert, but Mr Jones was not listening.

'Now I myself have no possessions worth the taking, and I

have to grant that they respect my position as a minister of religion. But that brings me to the crux of the matter, Mr Wilton. As I have said, these people here, poor sinners of course, but not entirely without hope of redemption if they could but overcome the sinful pride which puffs them up and hides their failures from themselves, have some respect for my mission, and indeed they have lodged me and fed me as befits their ideas of what becomes a spiritual leader. Yet there are times when we needs must bow down to Mammon if our better ends are to be accomplished. I think it would be better for the success of my work if I were to be seen to be concerned in their patriotic as well as their spiritual regeneration. How would it be, Mr Wilton, if I were to become your secretary? In these parts of the world, it is not usual, you know, for wealthy and distinguished persons like yourself to be travelling without a certain number of attendants, so the arrangement might be mutually advantageous.'

Robert was considerably taken aback.

'I am afraid I am neither wealthy nor particularly distinguished, Mr Jones. I am just a well-wisher like yourself, and I am afraid I cannot see that I would have any use for a secretary – except, perhaps, to teach me Circassian, and I do not know how familiar you are with that language.'

'Circassian language!' said Mr Jones. 'You will be aware that a different dialect is spoken in nearly every valley in this country, all of them sounding, according to competent authority, like the rattle of stones in a bucket! How to spread the enlightenment of the Scriptures in such circumstances is indeed a sore problem. But as I see the suggestion I propounded just now is not to your taste, Mr Wilton, we will say no more about it. Indeed, I meant it for your help as much as mine. Just now my duties call me, so I trust you will excuse me if I take my leave of you, for the time being.'

As soon as Mr Jones had departed Giorgio hurried in to remove the tea cups. His attitude towards Mr Jones was not very reverent, and he was dying to impart information about him. Robert at first gathered from him that Mr Jones lived in a tree. This sounded incredible, but it was apparently entirely true.

Shortly before Mr Jones had appeared in Circassia in his capacity as war correspondent for the *South Cambrian Inde-*

pendent, there had died a 'saint' (according to Giorgio) who as far as local memory went back had lived in a sort of crow's nest lashed to the summit of one of the loftiest trees in one of the groves revered by the Circassians. He never washed, never changed his apparel, never cut his hair, and never descended to the earth, but prayed incessantly to the God of the Christians. Although he never spoke to them, and indeed spurned all their overtures, the local people treated him with veneration, and daily climbed the rope ladder conducting to a platform on a level a little below the saint's look-out, to leave there the few cakes of coarse bread and the pitcher of water necessary for the holy man's sustenance. More than that he would not take, although not a few of the women, hoping to gain blessings, had sought to offer him delicate dishes of honey and nuts, and bread made from pure white flour. So he had lived for very many years, only growing more and more weather-stained, while his skin became like leather, and his long and matted hair turned white as snow. Then one day he had died. The villagers found him still on his feet in death, but slumped over the side of his crow's nest like a paper figure broken in the middle. With some hesitation, they had carried him down and given him burial after their own fashion.

Not so long after, Mr Jones had arrived, and had disclosed quite soon that he was not only a foreign well-wisher, but a priest. So when Mr Jones had announced that he found it necessary, as his paper was not supporting him, to depart, the local people had bethought themselves of the tree now untenanted, or perhaps Mr Jones had himself come to hear about it. At any rate, he had established himself there, and had even prevailed on the Circassians to build an additional hut at the foot of the tree, since the crow's nest was too small to permit of anything but a standing position, and Mr Jones, unlike the saint now deceased, was unable to sleep in such conditions. He had also managed to convey that he was not as exigent in matters of diet as his predecessor, and would welcome variations.

All this and more Giorgio poured out, but Robert had only half his attention to spare for Mr Jones, surprising as his appearance had been. He was turning over in his mind that the Russians were moving on the coast, and wondering what it portended.

Chapter 4

AFTER MR JONES's visit, Robert felt a renewed craving for action. The leisurely deliberations of the chiefs, which kept them immobilized for hour after hour while the Russians encircled their country, were becoming unbearably irksome. He was convinced that the opportunity was there and should be taken. It was madness to ignore the chance of moving against the Black Sea forts while the forests provided their heavy summer cover, and an attack would be wholly unexpected. He knew that the Russians themselves never undertook military operations during the summer because the risk of an ambush was too great. But neither Arslan or the neighbouring chiefs could be induced to move. 'In the summer we get in our crops,' was what they had said. It was only after long persuasion by Robert that they agreed to send a small party to the coast to find out what was going on there. He determined to go with it himself.

Just when the party was on the verge of departure, one of Mr Papandian's agents, an Armenian merchant who made his way inland, presented himself with bowings and compliments before the old chief. As well as bringing trade goods, he carried a packet of letters for Robert, readdressed from Constantinople to the care of Mr Papandian.

All the links which had been so remote as to be meaningless in Constantinople reasserted themselves in full force. Now that he was indeed in the wilderness, Robert craved a contact with his own people. He opened the packet with delighted anticipation.

Alas, it contained only one letter. The rest of the contents was newspapers, now several months out of date. He wondered why they had been sent. There were passages marked in emphatic pencil. He glanced through them, saw nothing of great interest, and turned to the letter, which was in his father's handwriting. Instinctively, he hesitated before opening it. Holding it in his hand, he experienced once again a faint return of that inward commotion, the grip of an iron hand on the vitals, which had accompanied the receipt of communications from the Rector, all through his Oxford days. At last, despising his own weakness, he opened the letter.

News of his mother : mention of his brother, serving in India. Parish intelligence. Village news (the Rector, of course, never descended to gossip). A name caught his eye in the closely-written pages – Henry. He read what followed with painful concentration.

'You will remember your old companion, Henry Ginger,' the Rector wrote. 'I am sorry, although not entirely surprised, to have to write that he has turned out badly. There have long been suspicions about his poaching, and Handyside, Lord Shuttleworth's gamekeeper, had told us that he nearly laid hands on Ginger last season, but the gang (for this has certainly been an organized affair) was too much for him. The next time they repeated their criminal enterprise, however, the forces of law were ready for them, and after a struggle three of the wretches were apprehended, Ginger among them. The rest, I am sorry to say, escaped. The three will come up for trial at the next Assizes, when we hope such sentences will be passed as will deter others from these offences, now too sadly prevalent. Your mother wanted to take the woman Susan Ginger as a scullerymaid, as of course she has had to leave their cottage, but I could not allow this on account of the bad example it would give to the village.

'All these things are very worrying.' the Rector had added. There was more in the letter besides local matters – criticism of the Government's weak handling of the *Vixen* affair was mentioned – but Robert could not go on reading. The news of Henry's arrest was a disaster before which he felt completely impotent.

It came as no surprise to him to learn that Henry had been poaching. If he had been at hand, he might have been able to dissuade his friend, for he was pretty sure that it was the adventure, as well as the gain, (and with three mouths to feed, a farm-worker's wage did not go far) which drew Henry out on dark nights into the keepered woods of the Rector and the Squire. Now he was caught, and with the feeling against poachers as strong as it was, he was almost certain to be convicted. A bird weighed more in the balance than a man, his wife and their child. The penalties were severe – it could mean transportation.

Why did it have to be? If only it had been possible to have Henry educated, so that he could rise step by step in the world with the Rector's son! Why had he not overcome his father's implacable resistance to all his ideas for Henry's improvement? As it was, he felt it was he who had deserted his friend. First to go away to school (although their friendship had continued unabated during the holidays), and then for the years at Oxford, during which time they had seen less and less of each other. That was his fault, and so were the years which came after. Other friends, other distractions, had intervened between him and Henry. But he still had Henry's last letter to him in his pocket-book, laboriously written on lined copybook paper. He carried it always with him as a sort of talisman.

'Dear Robert,' Henry had written.

'It was very good to hear from you and to know that you are in good health. Things are much the same down here as they have always been. We are very busy as we are short-handed. Head-cowman is off sick, so I am having to do his work. If he does not come back I am going to ask for his place, but I expect they will say I am too young. I do not get much time for reading these days as you may imagine, but I remember all those games out of books we used to play in the old days and the names of those old Greek heroes.

'I was sorry to hear in the village about your engagement. To my mind the young lady made a mistake. Perhaps she will discover too late what she has lost, as other silly maids have done. In case you should hear about it later Robert I am to marry Susan Whitgift soon. We are promised old Miller's cottage as he is too old to do his work. But it will never make any difference to our freindship.' That letter had been written over a year ago. He had not seen Henry since, but he could imagine what had happened. The marriage with Susan Whitgift, an uneducated village girl. Miller's cottage – he knew it very well, the one which seemed to be sinking into the ground, it was so low and huddled. A child on the way, Susan not able to work. The bitter struggle to keep a family on a second cowman's wage, living never out of the grip of poverty. The only escape to something worthwhile, something which used all Henry's qualities, his nerve, his imagination, his power of decision, his wonderful woodcraft, was this nightly sortie with the poacher band. And it had come to nothing in the end, while he, Robert, had abandoned his own unsolved problems to wander in the East, and to throw himself finally on this Circassian shore. It occurred then to Robert to wonder whether he had not himself made as futile and hopeless a gesture as that for which Henry was now lying in jail.

As it was, he pulled himself together and wrote a letter, to go off with Mr Papandian's agent to Trebizond, and thence posthaste to Constantinople. It was to the only London solicitor he knew, instructing him to do his best for Henry. He also wrote to his banker to supply the necessary funds for the defence. He could only hope that the letters would get there in time. At least his mother could be relied upon to see that Susan and the child did not starve, whatever were the Rector's scruples about lending her aid.

Before he sealed the letter to the bankers, he added a postscript directing them to make funds available to Henry should he apply for them in person. The hope of release was always there, however slight, and freedom would be useless to Henry if he were turned loose penniless and workless. Robert joined to this a further direction that if Henry desired to join him in the East, his travelling expenses should be met. This done, he turned to his own preparations for the journey to the Black Sea.

The Euxine, seen from the top of the wooded hill where the reconnaissance party had established themselves in cover, was blue and inviting. Dim, boulder-like shapes which were dolphins rose from time to time out of the water, turned over and disappeared again with a splash and a trail of bubbles. In the morning a milky haze, in the evening a magnificent sunset, lingered over the water. The Circassians were indifferent, however, to the beauties of nature. They cursed every time

they looked down at the bay. Anchored some way off the shore was a Russian transport, unloading stores for the neighbouring fort into two lighters.

The Circassians had already ambushed one train of carts, with considerable success, but now the Russians were on their guard, and the landings were heavily protected. The fort, too, was alerted. Although Hassan and the other young 'braves' could ride up at full gallop to the earth and wood walls in clear view of the sentries, and rein back their horses within rifle shot, flourishing and caracoling, then spur off at top speed before the shot could touch them, there was no hope of rushing the fort, particularly as there was no major Russian church festival in prospect.

'Easter is the best time,' Hassan had explained. 'Then they are drunk for several days and nights together.'

The two boats which moved backwards and forwards, always covered by the guns of the transport, were the targets they yearned for. The Circassians prowled to and fro on the heights like cats, licking their lips. It was not an easy country, however, to get about in. For this expedition Robert had put on the Circassian clothes which had been presented to him shortly after his arrival, the long belted tunic with its high collar and rows of silver cartridge pouches, the breeches, very baggy to the knee and tight below, which he had thrust into his English boots, all topped by a round sheepskin cap which had struck him, when he had first seen it, as patently unsuited to a day of blazing heat. Now he found it an invaluable protection. The heat was extreme on that hillside, clothed with dusty thickets of laurel and rhododendron. Dense clouds of pollen and leaf particles blew up the nose of any man forcing a way through the undergrowth, while clouds of shrilly whining flies rose from their lurking places on the leaves and immature berries. The sea and the ships on it were indescribably alluring.

'How to get hold of them?' said Hassan.

'On a dark night, perhaps, it could be done,' said Robert.

'If a man could swim so far,' said Hassan.

'The distance is not so very great, I think,' said Robert. It was difficult to judge accurately with the eye, but he thought the transport must be lying about half a mile out.

How far was half a mile to swim? He was certainly a strong

swimmer, but he had not before tested his ability to cover a long distance. The Hellespont was about a mile across at the spot where Leander was supposed to have swum it, but Lord Byron, who had repeated the feat in more modern times, had swum no less than four miles between points. By comparison with that achievement, half a mile seemed a puny distance.

'Can you swim so far?' asked Hassan.

'I can try,' answered Robert.

It was a dark night, and the water, although warm enough, was inky black when he entered it. He had shivered as he stripped by the shore, but more with excitement than with cold. The darkness and the solemnity of the occasion kept the Circassians quiet. They desisted from their usual chatter, in fact they were almost glum as they sat around on the stones, watching his preparations. The sea was not their accustomed field of operation. At his waist Robert carried a small, sharp knife. It was not a particularly suitable implement for boring holes in the bottom of boats, but nothing better could be found.

He had marked down during the day a place where the sand seemed to run out a fair distance. He had no desire to stumble over an expanse of shingle, or to wade through mud, and he knew that the shore shelved very gently all along this coast. He began walking steadily out to sea, but it took a long time before the water reached above his knees. Something finny flickered past his ankles. The lapping touch of the water crept higher. Robert kept his eyes on the lights of the transport. He realized that it would be very difficult to keep a sense of direction once he began to swim.

All at once he heard a splashing behind him. It could not possibly be heard by the Russians at this distance, but Robert turned round in irritation. Were the Circassians on the shore trying to attract his attention? But it was somebody running through the shallows towards him – Hassan.

'I am coming with you, Jibrahil Bey.'

They were face to face but could hardly see each other. Robert tried to dissuade the boy. The enterprise was chancy enough with one man: what was the use of risking another? But he could make no headway against Hassan's determination. It was ridiculous to stand there arguing, waist deep in the sea. If Hassan wanted to try it, let him. Robert let himself down into

the water and began to swim, as quietly as he could. Hassan, with a strong although not very scientific stroke, and making considerably more noise, kept level with him.

Once he was swimming, Robert found it less difficult than he had feared to keep going straight, as by raising himself in the water from time to time he could keep the lights in sight. But the water seemed heavier and less buoyant than he had expected. He *could* have gone on, but he was glad when the outlines of the lighters moored to the transport suddenly loomed up in front of him, even though the danger of being spotted and shot at became more real.

He let himself float and rest for a few moments. There was utter silence on board the transport and the lighters, when any sound would have carried in the quiet of the night, and a complete hush on the water. It was then Robert realized that Hassan had vanished.

In the faint starlight, he could make out nothing but empty sea around him. The boy must have let himself sink without a sound and go to the bottom. Then some distance away, a long shape surfaced, and began to sink again. Robert made a few desperate strokes towards it. The body had gone under by the time he reached it, but he got beneath it, and seizing Hassan by the arm, turned him on to his back. Thank God, Hassan did not struggle with his rescuer, but supporting his waterlogged weight as far as the nearest lighter's side called for a final effort Robert had not thought himself capable of making. When he reached it, the lighter rose up like a wall, but there was a chain hanging down, and when he guided Hassan's hands to it, they took hold. Then Robert began the struggle to get himself over the lighter's side.

There was a dreadful moment when he thought he could not do it. The strength had gone out of his arms, and the Black Sea would not give up his body from its hold. Then trembling in every limb, with knees and elbows skinned, he tumbled inboard and somehow dragged Hassan after him. Leaving the boy to come to himself on a pile of sacks, he began a hasty but cautious exploration, expecting any moment a challenge to come from the transport, even if, unbelievably, no guard had been left aboard the lighters. The two of them were side by side, and only the inner one was tied up to the steamer. Robert saw almost at once that they were empty of stores. This was disappointing, but on the other hand, if the transport had not finished unloading, the loss of the lighters would be crippling.

Robert moved round without a sound on his bare feet, too occupied to notice the cold night air on his flesh. He tried to summon up all he knew about boats. The problem was to dispose of both lighters, with the minimum of noise. From hearsay, he thought a boat must have a plug in it somewhere, which if removed would admit the water, and the boat would sink. Or somewhere there should be seacocks, whatever they were, the opening of which would bring about the same result. But search failed to disclose any device of this nature, while with a knife, the only tool he had, it was clearly impossible to pierce the planking. Robert was sitting on his heels, considering the problem, when there was the sound of violent retching behind him. Hassan was coughing up sea water, and making an appalling noise. It was not a time to linger.

An inspiration came to Robert. He dropped a bit of wood overboard and craned after it to see what happened. At first imperceptibly, then slowly but surely, it drifted away to the southward. The next step was to study the mooring ropes and how to cast them off. The outside lighter presented no problem. With some assistance from Hassan, who was on his feet again, he succeeded in releasing it. They pushed it off as far as they could, and saw it gradually drift away, a grey patch on the darkness of the water. Then they tackled the task of getting the second lighter loose from the transport, which meant cutting through ropes calculated to blunt the edge of any knife. They both sawed away doggedly. The work seemed to take a desperate time and Robert, seeing or imagining he saw a faint light appearing in the sky, began to feel that dawn would see them still at it. The air was suddenly chill, too, and he shivered with cold, nerves and exasperation. Hassan's body, glistening as he bent over his rope, exuded a faintly feral smell. Every moment they expected to hear a hail from the transport, and there was one rope left with the strands half-severed, and the chain to which it was attached clanking against the ship's side.

The last strand gave. They both shoved off from the steamer as hard as they could. A little breeze which had sprung up came to the aid of the current, and the distance between the lighter and the transport began to lengthen. Then, for the first time, there flashed into Robert's mind the question of how they were going to get back to shore. He was quite sure that neither of them could swim that distance a second time. There were sweeps in the bottom of the lighter, but they needed two men at least to handle each one of them. He was wondering how he was going to communicate the problem to Hassan, when he saw that the boy, who had been doing some exploration on his own account, was laughing. In the stern of the lighter he had found a small, upturned dinghy with the oars under it.

Curiously enough, Hassan could not row, and Robert later remembered that he had never seen a Circassian do anything but paddle. It fell to Robert, therefore, to get them back to shore, while Hassan gave the direction, and it was in this way that they made a landfall just past the mouth of the bay from which they had set out. There they fell, exhausted but triumphant, into the arms of the shore party, who had hurried to the spot to welcome them, and Hassan recounted the story of his rescue in terms which grew in fervour with every telling.

'My breath had left me, my eyes were darkening, and my last moment had come, when Jibrahil saved me. I felt myself seized, as though a magic bird had swooped down out of the heavens and grasped me in its claws, and I was drawn up out of the water by a mighty force. So I came back to life . . .' and so on.

Robert felt less elation. His raw elbows and knees were smarting furiously, and the salt water had inflamed his other bites and scratches. But as he dressed again in the Circassian clothes he had worn (for the first time) to come on the expedition, clothes which had already left their imprint on him, he felt that he had now earned some right to wear them. It was a bloodless feat of arms he had performed, but it had changed him, just as the heavy fur cap he put on had made a weal across his forehead which would take weeks to fade. He had forced a threshold he had never before succeeded in crossing. There would be a feast, no doubt, when they got back to the village, and he would take part in it as of right. At the same time, a door had closed behind him. Never again would he be the man he was.

The party lay up after this exploit for one or two more days, during which Robert saw no further chance of action. Men were sent singly as scouts, but none of them could detect anything unusual at the fort, except that the settlement round it, where time-expired soldiers and Cossacks had built cottages for their wives and families, had grown visibly. The settlers were cultivating the rich virgin soil, and accumulating livestock. Unfortunately this last consisted mostly of herds of pigs, which were not worth driving off to the Circassians. They spat as they mentioned the unmentionable. In this at least, they exhibited Moslem prejudices. But the enlargement of the settlement round the fort did not arouse their interest.

Then one of the scouts returned with intelligence which was at first the subject of an intense discussion, frustrating to Robert, who could only understand one word in fifty and could not follow the drift at all, nor could he get any sense from Hassan's garbled explanations in Turkish. He regretted having left Giorgio behind, but he had scruples about exposing him to the risk of action, especially against his co-religionists (or near-religionists), the Russians. After much parleying, the Circassians began to saddle up. Whatever it was they had been told of, they were going to see it.

Their course took them north, parallel to the coast and some distance to the east of the fortress, through the region of thick woods which covered the foothills, where Robert lost his sense of direction entirely. It was Hassan who first drew rein – his sharp ear had caught the sound of axes being wielded in the forest where such a thing had never before been heard. The sound came from somewhere ahead of and below them. They dismounted and led their horses forward between the trees. There was a trembling and shaking amongst the topmost branches where the canopy shifted, then with a rending crash one of the lofty beech trees toppled and fell. The fall was followed by a cheer, and a medley of men's deep voices in the distance.

The Circassians left their horses and moved forward with precaution through the undergrowth. With a touch on the shoulder, Hassan showed Robert a mounted Cossack sitting motionless on his horse at a point where a goat path snaked over the edge of the defile. Horse and rider blended so exactly with the background that Robert would have walked straight up to them. One of the young men tapped his dagger with a smile,

66

but Hassan frowned and grunted a negative monosyllable. Making a cast round to avoid the sentry, half crouching, half crawling, in complete silence, the Circassians (and Robert with them) reached the edge of the ravine, and looked over.

In the formerly untrodden forest, empty and untouched year in and year out, a crowd of men was working. The tree whose death throes they had witnessed had not fallen alone. A swathe had been cut through the wood, and the trunks lay in stacks for burning later. A swarm of men in white linen blouses and blue trousers was moving in the glen. Robert thought at first that they were woodcutters until he saw the rifles and realized that in spite of the non-uniform dress, these were soldiers. The swarm was engaged in an organized activity. Clearly they had finished their work for the day, and were about to retire. There were carts as well, some harnessed with horses, others with oxen. Some of the drivers wore the Circassian dress.

Two trumpet notes floated out from somewhere down the valley, evidently the signal for recall. The soldiers put their axes on to the carts, which started to move. Hassan was biting his fingers and scowling as he watched the Russians prepare their withdrawal, but he did not give the order to get back to their horses which Robert expected. It seemed also to Robert that the Circassians' fingers would be itching for their triggers, but no man made a move. It seemed madness to Robert to miss the opportunity of harassing the retreat, when they had apparently penetrated the cordon of sentries without being perceived. He tried to convey this to Hassan in dumb-show, but could arouse no response. He tried words:

'It is a road.'

Hassan did not answer. Instead a dumb and sullen look came over his features. Paying no heed to Robert's remonstrances, he gave the signal to return to the horses. Once more the painful progress through the briars and thickets was accomplished. As they were about to ride off, Hassan regained his ferociously cheerful mien. Bending down from the saddle, after an obvious effort to put his words in order, he answered Robert.

'That road leads into the valley of the Shapsugs. Why should we fight for them?'

He made a contemptuous gesture which drove the words home. Then barely giving time for Robert to mount, he was off like an arrow. As the party streamed after him Robert reflected once again that the cause of United Circassia which had been such a trumpet call in Belgrave Square, sounded less thrilling a chord on its native heath.

The triumph of the party's return – for the news of the taking of the lighters had run ahead of them, and produced a great effect in the Circassian camp – was mitigated for Robert by his distress and anger at his total failure to make any impression on Hassan over the question of the Road. For he was insistent on the importance of this development, and there seemed to be a deliberate refusal on the part of the Circassians to accept his point of view. Hassan, turning sulky, would not or could not understand such a complicated issue. His ideas preferred to remain on familiar ground, and lingered on blood feuds, hereditary hatreds, and the pleasures of inter-tribal raiding. The Shapsugs had made war against his father. Why should his father go to war with the Russians for their benefit? Let the Shapsugs deal with the road which was advancing into their valleys.

'Any day, the road could change its direction,' said Robert.
'If it points towards us, then we shall attack it,' said Hassan.
They were sitting outside the chief's house, in the dusk. In the beaten open space before them a circle of young men with their arms linked was dancing, stepping slowly yet jauntily in their furred hats and thin mocassins, revolving outside a circle of girls who moved with set faces and tiny, almost imperceptible steps.

'It will be too late then,' said Robert. 'Once the Russians have taken that valley, they will build a fort and mount guns. Once they have a fort and a settlement in the Shapsug country, you will be outflanked. The Russians can come against you from two sides, from the coast and over the hills.'

Hassan was unimpressed. 'The Russian soldiers could never get across the passes, Jibrahil Bey. If they tried to do so, we would turn them back. They are men of the plains.'

Robert gave it up. The dancers had broken their ranks and now stood in groups, men and girls apart, laughing and talking. Round the clearing the white veils glimmered in the dusk, as the matrons surveyed their daughters. Bats began to flicker through the air, and drowsy insects, rolled into balls, dropped out of the high branches of the cherry trees overhead and plopped among the fallen leaves and twigs on the grass. One fell on to Robert's neck. All at once the sun dropped behind the hills, furry with trees to their very tops. The darkness seemed to grow up out of the ground, and the company dispersed. Robert went back to his quarters, where he found himself alone.

He would have talked to Giorgio, but his servant had disappeared, he knew not where. In spite of the language difficulty, Girogio had managed to establish himself in this community, so utterly foreign to his Greek nature, where there were no shops, no markets, and no money. He contrived nevertheless to come by supplies with which to supplement the Circassian meals sent down for the guest's consumption. He appeared also to have formed a promising acquaintance with several of the local young ladies, and Robert suspected that even the old Princess herself was not unmoved by Giorgio's flattering address, and bold black eyes. For some inexplicable reason, it was considered perfectly correct for Giorgio to be in and out of that female sanctum, the kitchen, when such an intrusion would have been absolutely unthinkable in the case of Robert himself.

Who else was there to talk to? Mr Jones nad clearly returned to attend to his devotions, and besides, Robert was getting a little tired of hearing the tale of Mr Jones's expulsion from the Zion Chapel, which was his main topic of conversation. Robert would have tried to establish some communication with Shekhir Effendi. It seemed absurd indeed that they should be there presumably in a common interest, and yet should seem to refrain from concerting their ideas and their resources. But he sensed an unwillingness, not only on the part of the Circassians, but on the part of Shekhir Effendi himself, that they should have much to do with each other, and as well as that, the personality of the man himself was peculiarly unattractive.

Robert speculated on his nationality. There was something northern, if not Nordic, about the man's narrow head and pronounced forehead, those curious light, piercing eyes, but he was clearly not an Englishman, or a Frenchman, or a Dutchman, or a German.

Deprived of other company, Robert turned to books, to the

travelling library he had brought with him, selected with anxious care. He had tried to strike a balance, and his choice had finally fallen on:

Horace (a handsome copy presented to him on his 12th birthday by the Rector, and suitably inscribed)
Dante
An Account of the Late Campaigns in the Peninsula, by a Veteran (useful hints on bivouacs, and how to find food in a seemingly desolate country)
A Turkish Dictionary and Grammar
A Complete Guide to Travel, in very small print, and crammed with information on such subjects as cholera belts, the theory of loads and distances as applied to asses, small mules, large mules, horses and camels, and how to find wild honey ('catch a bee and dredge him with flour').

By way of light relief, he had brought *Childe Harold's Pilgrimage*, and he reached up for it now, then changed his mind and took down the Horace. Something fell out from between the pages, a folded paper containing a list of Turkish words and their Circassian equivalents which he had been making out. He was about to replace it when a thought struck him. He had not left that paper there, he was sure of that, but in the back of the dictionary. Who then could have moved it? It was most unlikely that Giorgio had carried his domestic activities as far as dusting the books. It could only be that one of Robert's uninvited guests had been fiddling with the books while the hut was empty, yet of all his belongings, books were the least likely to interest the Circassians.

Perplexed, but seeing no solution to the problem, Robert went outside. It was now quite dark, save that an enormous moon had swung up in the sky above the eastern ranges, just in the place where the morning sun would top them later. Out on the hillside the serfs had been cutting the hay, which lay ready to be turned. The smell of hay mingled with the flower scents, while a nightingale in the elder brake began the song which it would carry on and on, effortlessly, careless of the dogs which were barking in chorus, and the intermittent croaking of the frogs. Perhaps on this night, at midnight, the bracken would flower, and as the Circassians said, he who saw this happen would have omniscience thereafter.

The scent of flowers, the nightingale hidden in the bushes, recalled to Robert those other moments of flowers and nightingales when life had seemed to him too precious to be wasted in mere existence. There must be some way of living it to the full, of not only absorbing the magic quality, but of passing it on, which so far had eluded him. He thought of the people he had cared for most, Lawrence, the friend of Oxford days who had now left him far behind – and Harriet. Where was she now, he wondered. At Cheltenham for her mother's nerves, at Baden for her father's liver, or simply at home in Hampton Wick? Did she ever think of him, and regret her decision to face life without his help? But it was no good thinking of Harriet. In the end, she had found she did not need him, while Henry, who *had* needed him – had he failed Henry? Unconsciously he put his hand to his breast where Henry's letter reposed in his pocket-book. He had come to these shaggy mountains and forests to justify his existence, and here he was, once more alone, smelling the flowers and listening to the unbearably sweet notes of the nightingale.

Then something leapt up at his feet and rushed scaringly away into the darkness, leaping and twisting. It was one of the semi-wild cats which lurked about the place. Out of the darkness came Hassan, laughing and swishing at the heads of the tiger-lilies, stepping like a cat himself, with Giorgio close behind him.

'Tell me some more about life in London. Tell me what it is like to go to the theatre – perhaps we shall have a theatre in Circassia one day! Tell me what you must do to hire a carriage in the street. How much money does it cost? How much money would it cost to have a coat made like yours?'

Outside the hut the nightingale sang on and on, and the dogs howled, while Robert recalled for the benefit of Hassan, and Giorgio translated and hung on the tale, the habits of Pall Mall and St James's.

71

Chapter 5

THE DAYS PASSED and lengthened into weeks. Summer advanced and the crops began to ripen in the field patches. Despite the evidence of their eyes which he and Hassan had brought back from the coast, Robert found it impossible to persuade the chiefs that the enemy was likely to make a move before harvest-time was over. Meanwhile, lengthy hours of confabulation and speech-making went on round Arslan's hearth, or in the open air, while the chiefs' horses and attendants waited in the clearing, and their men were fed in near-by houses. Robert sat stoically through it all.

Then came news. The Russians had made a sudden advance, not along the road they had constructed into the Shapsug country, but into a valley not fifty miles to the north, inhabited by the small tribe of the Bezleni. The move was so sudden that there was no effective opposition, the Russians had burned the houses, and laid waste the crops. The inhabitants, all but the fighting men, who had taken to the forest, had fled from their ruined villages and were making their way south, struggling over the passes, driving their remaining livestock before them. They began to arrive in the village in twos and threes, famished and exhausted. A small group of women, ladies of noble family, arrived with one weary horse which they had ridden, turn and turn about, and they were accommodated in hastily improvised quarters adjacent to Arlsan's own house. The other refugees were all on foot, the old women hobbling with the support of branches torn off the trees. The animals were in hardly better shape than the people. Many of the cattle had died on the pass, said their owners. The survivors were hastily driven into wattle enclosures before they could eat bare the pasturage of their hosts.

This influx gave an impetus to the preparations for war.

Orders were given by the old Lion to reap all the fields remaining, and the whole community, fighting men as well, turned out.

It was an odd way of harvesting, thought Robert. First of all the 'harvest supper' was consumed, at least, enormous quantities of boza were drunk. Then all the able-bodied men rushed into the field and began to slash furiously with their daggers at the standing crop, snatching handfuls from each other in their excitement, and laughing like madmen. Many free fights developed. Half the field was trampled down, the rest of the crop was gathered more or less haphazard. Round the edges and in the corners of the field the ears that no one had bothered to touch still stood erect, but the reaping had been done, more or less, and the men were free to go to war. The women would creep on to the field to glean later in the day and would finish the job, and they would also strip the small patches of maize which grew by every house.

There were more long talks that evening, and the fields smelt piercingly sweet as the first chill dew moistened the stubble. Once again there was feasting, and once more Robert watched the circle of warriors and the circle of girls sidle slowly round, one file of dancers moving clockwise, the other revolving in the opposite direction. From time to time a couple would slip out of the dance and wander off into the brakes of fern and alder, where the nightingales were beginning to call: the mothers seemed less vigilant that evening. Robert looked to see if Paka were there, and if so, what was her mood. He made her out, among the girls, but she was dancing with her face as stern and rigid as ever. On an impulse he broke into the men's circle and linked hands with two of the dancers. His feet in English boots began to sidle round in the slow yet insidious rhythm. As the circles revolved, he came opposite Paka, who brought her gaze back from the distance and focussed it on his face – for one moment their eyes met – then the dance carried them apart again, but not before Robert thought he saw a smile.

Two days later he and Hassan, and a small party, were again riding westwards towards the coast. Arslan and the other chiefs had decided, after more persuasion from Robert, that it was after all necessary to ascertain what moves the Russians were making. The old Lion himself was leading another party to reconnoitre the northern passes.

Covering the same ground a second time, part of the way seemed familiar to Robert. He began to realize that this wilderness was not quite as trackless as he thought : there were ways through it, but the heavy summer growth meant that the path might be imperceptible for long stretches, especially as each rider preferred to make his own way round the fallen trees and other obstructions. Feeling confident that he knew the general direction, he became less apprehensive of being separated from the extended file of horsemen.

It was when they were rather more than halfway to their objective that he lost the others. He was riding in the rear of the file, and he dismounted for no more than a couple of minutes, but when he got into the saddle again, the other riders were all out of sight. He was not alarmed though, he thought he could see the branches shaking, and the route they had taken was quite clear, so it seemed, on the ground. He followed it at his best pace, but quite soon, and before he came up with the party, the path divided. He sat in the saddle for a minute, in a quandary. The movement of branches had stopped, he could hear nothing but the ordinary forest noises, and there was nothing at all to indicate which direction the others had taken. He chose the most likely looking path, which seemed to peter out again half a mile further on. Once again he was in a quandary.

There was the sound of a horseman coming up behind him, and Robert turned, his pistol in his hand, to see one of the party, a short and not very prepossessing man whose name he did not know, riding in his tracks. The new horseman pulled up, and it at once became evident that he could not understand a word that Robert addressed him. However, it seemed that he knew the way. He pushed his horse into the undergrowth, and started off in a right-hand direction, signing to Robert, who was glad enough to follow him.

Although there was no obvious path, the going was not too bad, and the new direction seemed to be the correct one. Then the rider ahead, who kept on turning round to make sure Robert was still in sight, began edging more and more to the right. It seemed to Robert they must be heading altogether too far north, and he called out to the man ahead, who neither stopped or answered him. The going was becoming very difficult. The ground was rotten and full of holes. Robert slowed to a trot and then to a walk. He was too much occupied with guiding his horse to pay much attention to the direction. The guide pressed on into a ravine full of gloomy fir trees, many of which had fallen, uprooted by a winter gale. The place was choked with dead vegetation. The skeletons of the fir trees, festooned with grey and yellow lichens, lay about in all directions, too big for his horse to step over, too closely packed for a horse to jump.

Robert could not remember having passed through a place like this on his way to the coast, and his sense of having gone wrong increased. What a fool he had been to assume that the Circassian knew the way! It would have been better to rely on his own instinct. Then he became aware that the man had disappeared. There was no sign of him, or his horse. They had simply vanished out of the landscape, leaving him to extricate himself from this place!

It took Robert an hour to accomplish this, and by the end of the hour both horse and rider were flagging, and the afternoon sun was dropping in the sky. When he finally broke out of the ravine, he found he was still in deep forest, and there was no sign of a path of any description. He looked round in utter bewilderment, quite uncertain of what to do. There was an absolute stillness all round him. The ground was thick with pine needles, and now there were pines on all sides. He could not recollect having ridden through any pine wood on the way to the coast. The earth was bare except for these pine needles and a little creeping plant bearing a berry which he did not know. Robert looked at it, and realized that he had no food at all with him. The Circassians seemed to derive nourishment from chewing the leaves of an umbelliferous plant which grew in the woods: often they went the whole day without any other sustenance. But even if he could be quite certain of identifying it, no plant of such a species grew anywhere near. For a moment Robert came near to panic.

Reason rapidly reasserted itself. There must, he reflected, be a sensible course to follow. He decided to ride on due west, until he came to some vantage point from which he could get a general view, and perhaps pick up the traces of his party, who must by now be looking out for him. If he had not been re-united with the others by nightfall, he would sleep on the ground and continue next day. He could guide himself by the sun (for all the pocket compasses had long since been distributed).

Robert moved off due west, as he reckoned, picking the easiest possible ground so as to spare his tired horse, while at the same time trying not to deviate too much from his chosen course. He came across old tracks, but they mostly led in wrong directions, so he ignored them. He was so much concentrated on the direction that it happened that he broke through the screen of trees and into a clearing before he realized that there was anyone there. Thus it was only when he was within a few paces of them that he saw the two men – the Russians.

They must be Russians, he realized, after the first moment of surprise. The man with a slight moustache, who seemed to be the younger of the two, was sitting on a fallen tree trunk with a pencil and a notebook in his hands. He wore a pair of blue trousers, a white shirt, and a shapeless white linen cap, rather resembling a butcher boy's. He was smiling, and looked up at Robert with pleased expectancy. The older man wore something more like a military overcoat, and a similar cap. He was standing with an expression of astonishment on his face, and the pistol in his hand, which he had just drawn, was pointing straight at Robert, who pulled up. The horse put its head down and snorted, while Robert's heart gave a tremendous thump.

The man with the pistol held it quite steadily pointed. A half smile appeared on his face, and he gave the stock greeting:

'*Khabermi?*' (What news?)

Robert knew the standard reply, meaning Good News, but it seemed to him hardly appropriate, and anyhow it was pointless to continue with a conversation in Turkish. Wild ideas rushed through his head. He too had a pistol in the back of his belt, but before he could get it out the other man would have plenty of time to fire. Spur his horse and ride over him? But they were two to one, and could he also deal with the younger man? What if the horse were shot – then he would certainly be in a fix! There was nothing to be heard in the twilit wood except his tired horse tearing at the grass.

'*Bonjour, monsieur,*' replied Robert politely, and continued to sit on his horse as nonchalantly as possible.

The younger man said something to the other in what Robert took to be Russian. He thought he hear the word 'angleesky'.

Then the younger man addressed Robert in very fair French.

'I see that you are a foreigner, sir, in spite of your clothes. Can it be that you are the English gentleman of whom we have heard, who is living with "our friends" over there?' He waved his hand in the direction of the mountains.

'I am an Englishman,' said Robert, 'and I am at the present time living in the direction you indicate.'

'Oh, how splendid!' was the answer. 'I must say that I knew it. I knew monsieur for an Englishman the first moment I set eyes on him. I could have told you, Andrei Sergueievitch' (this to the other man). 'Look at that brow. Such calm! It could be none other. And living with those magnificent fellows!

'Permit me to introduce myself – ' the young man's talk rushed on torrentially. 'My name is Soutkine, Nikolai Petrovitch, ensign, at your service. This is Captain Lopakoff.'

The man addressed as Andrei Sergueievitch bowed. He had contrived to put the pistol away inconspicuously, but his manner was still wary. Robert bowed and gave his name, which the other two repeated with some difficulty, while apologizing for having no card with him.

'It is indeed an unexpected pleasure to meet monsieur in this, shall we say unlikely, spot,' observed Captain Lopakoff.

Robert felt that it was necessary to offer some explanation, but at the same time he was determined to say no more than was necessary.

'To be frank with you,' (for there was no point in concealing the obvious), 'it is an equally unexpected pleasure for me. I have, I am afraid, missed my way. The light is very deceptive at this hour. But I have no doubt that I shall pick it up in the morning.'

'In the morning?' It was the captain who spoke. 'But that would mean a night in the open, I am afraid in considerable discomfort. We can offer you better than that. No luxury, but at least we have a roof, and possibly a bed. No, it will not be any trouble, I assure you. We are a little community, you know, so we are always delighted to see a stranger.

'What are you doing there, Nicolai Petrovitch?' This was to the young ensign, who had left his notebook and pencil on the log, and was bending down, parting the bushes with his hands.

'There are wild raspberries here, just the same as ours. Not

77

quite as sweet, perhaps. You remember when we picked them in the woods that summer, at my grandfather's house in the country?' He licked a red stain off his hand, and straightened his knees.

'Who would have thought to find them here?'

His eyes fell on the notebook, and he went over and pocketed it.

'We had best be getting back, or there will be more bears in the bushes than raspberries,' replied the captain.

'This way, monsieur. It will be necessary to lead your horse for a short way. The path is very steep.'

Robert dismounted, and followed the captain out of the clearing and down a short but fairly precipitous track (he had ridden down many worse places, he reflected), to where a man in the Cossack uniform sat on his horse and held two others. At the sight of Robert he seized his weapons.

'He thinks we have caught a Tartar,' observed the ensign, with a smile, and said something to the Cossack in Russian. The Cossack stared at Robert, but did not take his hand from his sabre. The two officers mounted their horses. Robert got into the saddle again, and all four of them cantered off and in a few minutes they were out of the forest, where the rays of the fast-sinking sun were now touching only the topmast branches, and pouring their glow on to the distant mountains behind.

It was astonishing to find how near the fort they were. Robert was chagrined to find how far out he had been in his calculation of his position. He was miles further north than he intended to be. For the last hour he must have been blundering about nearly on top of the Russians – the Circassian had indeed guided him badly. He reflected that it was fortunate in one way that he had fallen in with a couple of officers. Dressed as he was in half Circassian clothes, the Cossacks of the garrison would have picked him off, he was sure, without hesitation.

Now they were trotting among cabins, and vegetable gardens. There were benches outside the cottage doors, and men and women were sitting together on them. The sunflowers in the cottage gardens stood as tall as a horse and rider. Used as he was to the cool, fir-scented gloom in which he had ridden for most of the day, the air at this low level seemed to Robert to be saturated with the varied odours of freshly-turned rank soil, middens, and the smoke from the cottage chimneys. A bush which grew alongside the path bore clusters of white blossoms of a smothering sweetness, like beanflower.

Round the fort itself, which was an earth and wood erection, was first a ditch, then an expanse of bare and hard-beaten earth, like a drill ground. Robert could see the sentries posted on the walls. Instead of making straight for the fort, however, the party pulled up outside one of the larger houses. Running round outside it was a wooden verandah, where an elderly man in baggy breeches and a tunic belted over them was sitting. A girl in a long cotton dress with a handkerchief over her head appeared as the officers and Robert dismounted, and went back into the house at a word from the man.

'This is where we are offering you our luxurious hospitality,' said the captain gaily. 'Quarters are in short supply in the fort itself at the moment, but we have contrived to make ourselves reasonably comfortable here, as you will see.

'Chai, chai, Fedushka!' he called, leading the way inside. Glancing back, Robert saw out of the tail of his eye the man on the verandah and the mounted Cossack talking together, with a look in his direction.

'I have given instructions for your horse to be taken care of,' said the captain, 'so you need not worry.'

Inside the house was a big room with two windows. It was strange to Robert to walk on a boarded floor again, and he was embarrassed by the clatter which his boots made. The room seemed to be appropriated to the two officers. There were two camp beds, and other gear, a table with a wooden bench on either side of it, and something which Robert, although he had never seen one before, instantly guessed to be a samovar. A thick-set, snub-nosed man, who Robert judged to be a soldier-servant, although his dress was no more orthodox than that of the two officers, was setting out the glasses and making tea. Robert was pressed to sit down, and he took in his hand, with some discomfort to himself, a glass of the boiling liquid.

The first glass of tea drunk, the conversation languished, and there was a slightly embarrassing silence. The servant moved about lighting lamps. Both windows stood wide open. Outside it was nearly dark, and moths and other night insects came blundering in. The young ensign seemed distressed to see them

79

gravitating inevitably towards the lighted lamps and extinction, and tried to brush them away. When this proved to be a hopeless task, he relapsed into a moody silence. The captain murmured some inaudible excuse and left the room. Robert heard his voice outside, round at the back of the house.

Left alone, the young man with a moustache seemed to recollect his duties as a host.

'Is this your first visit to the Caucasus, monsieur?' he inquired politely. Hardly waiting for Robert's monosyllabic reply, he went on in a torrent of words.

'For me also, it is the same. What a magnificent country! I have never in my life seen anything like it. Before I arrived, I had been trying to imagine it. I had been telling myself during all that long tiresome journey – a whole month of travelling from St Petersburg, across plains, plains, plains – that when I arrived there would be mountains, and forests, and Tartars galloping on horseback. The first sight of the mountains in the distance excited me so much that I could hardly endure the rest of the journey. I wanted to gallop towards them as fast as a horse could go – but I was in a telega, how would you call it, a sort of cart? Not fast at all. So I had to wait. But now I am here, the mountains are all round, I breathed the air, I see the eagles. And the first Tartar I meet turns out to be an Englishman!'

He burst out laughing, and then slowly recited something in an unknown tongue, which Robert incredulously realized to be English.

'The curfew tolls the knell of parting day,
    The lowing herd winds slowly o'er the lea' –

He pronounced 'lowing' to rhyme with 'bowing', and did the same thing with the first syllable of 'slowly'. He laughed again, and reverted to French.

'I know some more, but you will remember that it is a very long poem, by Mr Gray. Do I pronounce it correctly?'

'We say lowing,' replied Robert, 'and slowly. Otherwise your pronunciation is excellent, I compliment you. Do you speak much English, may I ask?'

'Oh no, I cannot speak it at all,' returned the young ensign. 'All that I know I have learned by heart, like this poem of Mr Gray, and that I learned first of all in Russian. We have an excellent translation, made by one of our Russian poets, Zhukhovsky. Even the metre is the same.'

He repeated, musingly, two lines which were indeed in the same metre as the *Elegy*, but in strange, musical syllables. The vowels slid so caressingly over his lips that they seemed to be quite fluid, and to take any shape that his tongue chose to utter.

'It is a poem not quite as easy to translate as you might think,' went on the young man, 'because your English poets use these poetic expressions which are not, I suppose, what one would say in everyday life. What is this "lowing herd" that Mr Gray sings about? It seems to me they are cows. Now why does he not say "cows" I wonder?' The ensign used the English word, which he pronounced 'coes'.

'I don't think it would sound right to talk about cows in verse,' said Robert, sticking to French and dodging the issue of pronunciation.

'But why not? Surely your Shakespeare, if he wished to mention a cow, would call it a cow?'

'I think Shakespeare always spoke of cows in the plural, so he was able to call them kine,' said Robert. He went on rather diffidently. 'To my mind the most beautiful line in the poem occurs in the next stanza.

"Now fades the glimmering landscape on the sight"–
And that contains no poetic diction at all.'

'Perhaps you are right. "Glimmer" – I do not know exactly what that word means. What a pity we have no dictionaries here – for that is all my library.' He pointed to a short row of books on a roughly made wooden shelf. 'I had to pack in a hurry when I was posted to the army of the Caucasus with orders to leave within twenty-four hours.

'It was such luck for me to be posted to the same company as Andrei Sergueievitch. One of my oldest friends, and how I have missed him in these last two years, since he volunteered for the Caucasus. What a crazy fellow, but as keen as mustard.'

'What made him volunteer?' Robert was emboldened to ask.

'Oh, the usual things. Money – or rather, no money. There was plenty to start with, from his father, but Andrei Serguei-evitch was fond of the bright lights, in his young days. He travelled abroad as well, in Italy, in France, until one day there was no more money. Then there was also a girl. There is always a girl!

'Now he has forgotten the girl, I think, for he is passionate for the Caucasus, and for those splendid fellows, your tribesmen. He is even learning to speak their language.'

At this point the captain re-entered the room with his usual half-smile, and called to the servant to bring him more tea.

'What have you been talking about?' he asked.

'About you. Also about English literature.'

'Literature! There is a subject you had better keep off. Remember it was your "literature" which brought you here at twenty-four hours' notice.'

'That was not English poetry. My interest in English verse has never displeased any of the powers that be. And if it was my literature, as you call it, which brought me here, well, it was a lucky day for me.'

The captain smiled indulgently, and asked Robert if he could speak the Tartar language.

'Very insufficiently, I fear,' said Robert.

'I do not find it at all easy, but they say that when you have mastered it, you can cross Central Asia from the Black Sea to the Pacific and be understood.'

It occurred to Robert to wonder if the captain had any ambitions towards doing this, but it seemed to him to be more tactful to leave this question unasked. The young ensign adroitly led the conversation back to general topics. Robert would have liked to inquire further as to the 'literature' which led to his being posted so abruptly to the seat of the campaign in the Caucasus, but this, he realized, was impossible. He glanced idly along the row of books, and thus was able to sustain a discussion of Lord Byron's works, and to impress his hosts by declaiming some of the livelier cantos of *Don Juan*.

The glasses of tea had been refilled several times. It was getting on for ten o'clock, and Robert, who had started his day at dawn, was wondering if Russians sustained life solely on tea when the soldier-servant began to lay out plates and cutlery. Dinner was on the way, and the smell of cooking began to make itself noticeable, while the conversation re-animated itself.

It was strange to take a meal at a table again, and to handle a knife and fork. Nothing matched: his hosts were evidently pooling their joint resources. Robert got a crested silver fork, a wooden-handled knife, and a tin camp spoon with which to eat the excellent soup which the servant ladled into metal containers. These implements were extracted, he noticed, from a cardboard box bearing an undecipherable Russian name followed by '& KO' in ordinary letters, and then the inscription

'Tiflis – Maidan Jelezni Riad –
GANTERIE FRANCAISE
NOUVEAUTES ANGLAISES ET FRANCAISES'

Salt was handed in a tin surmounted with the picture of a black child in a loincloth and chef's cap standing in front of a cocoa plantation and pointing to the legend ЩОКОЛАДЪ emblazoned on the tin. The servant put candles on the table, in a pair of silver candlesticks with black designs hammered into them.

The meal was enormous. Jokes were passed about the constricting effects of Robert's Circassian tunic, and the slimming results of a diet of honey and wild locusts. The two Russians ate like children, talking and laughing, laying down knife and fork altogether at times when the conversation carried them away, and then gobbling to catch up. The servant, variously addressed as 'Fedushka', and 'Batushka', carried on a familiar conversation with his masters as he moved about refilling their plates. Refilling the glasses, too : they were drinking a very tolerable red wine which came, the hosts said, from Georgia. They bought it by the buffalo-skin full, as it came cheaper that way, but it was necessary to bottle it as soon as possible and then to let it stand, if it was not to be tainted by the skin. This no doubt accounted for the diversity of labels on the bottles. Robert hoped he would keep his head. He had become so unused to wine in the last months, and enormous quantities of it were being poured out. There were quite a few good-natured jokes about the Circassians and their boza. The ensign said it sounded just like the stuff he and his school-fellows had succeeded in brewing, in secret, when they were about twelve years old.

As the meal wore on, more guests began to drop in, to have a look at the Englishman. Robert was surprised to see how old some of these comparatively junior officers were, but all comers seemed to be greeted by the hosts with the same affection and delight. They all found seats somewhere, and the room filled with conversation and with smoke.

The last of the dishes was cleared away, and a green cloth was laid down on the table in their place. Evidently cards formed a staple ingredient of the evening's amusements at the fort. Everyone clamoured for *shtoss*.

Robert did not join in the play. He found it sufficiently amusing to watch those who did, and anyway most of the players had reverted to Russian from the sometimes laboured French which they had been keeping up for his benefit. He tried to follow the rules of the game, and the names of the suits, but it all went too fast for him, and he was only able to catch a few familiar words from time to time, such as 'bank', and 'punt'. There were other distractions, however, besides cards. The handsome Cossack girl whom Robert had noticed in the verandah on his arrival passed outside the window in the light of the lamps, with a bucket in her hand and the same white kerchief tied over her head. The officers nearest the window leaned out and called to her, but she affected not to notice, and passed on with her head held high, and a look of disdain on her face. The officers spread their hands with comical expressions of distress. Their chaff was mainly directed to one of their number, Robert could see, a fattish young man who gazed out at the world rather disconsolately from behind large round spectacles. He looked an unlikely suitor to be courting that magnificent girl, as he stood rubbing his handkerchief over his heated face and glancing in an embarrassed way out of the window.

Robert was intrigued also by the figure of an elderly officer who sat on a chair in the midst of the hubbub apparently un-moved, holding in his hand a glass of tea instead of the wine which everyone else was drinking. Although it was a warm night of summer, and the atmosphere of the room was stuffy to a degree, this officer sat wrapped in his bourka – a long felt cloak – and had his feet thrust into felt boots. He sat there with his head sunk on his chest, showing grizzled hair, but then feeling, perhaps, Robert's eyes upon him, he lifted his head and asked something in Russian, which one of the bystanders translated.

'Do you think this is good tea?' with a gesture of lifting his glass.

Robert of course praised its excellence, although he had in fact found it difficult, having regard to the unfamiliar way in which it had been served, to judge the taste of the beverage he had drunk. The elderly officer then observed in tolerable French :

'That is a good thing. I know Englishmen like tea. We have difficulty in keeping up a supply of good tea here, and our soldiers are making experiments with growing it. This is not difficult, it is the preparation of the leaf which presents the problems. So far we have not solved them. This is *very* good tea. It must be imported – what we call caravan tea.' He relapsed into his former silence, and the fattish young officer, seeing Robert disengaged, turned to him.

'That girl – I assure you, you must not judge by what these gentlemen say – really, she means nothing to me. Why, I have never even spoken to her.'

'She seemed a very handsome girl, what I saw of her,' said Robert.

'Oh yes, very handsome, no doubt of that, but not my style. Yet they are always making these jokes . . .' He gazed at his hands in an embarrassed manner. Robert could not think of anything more to say, but he was rescued by the young ensign, who handed over the bank to another player and came to his side.

'It is very hot in here. Shall we sit on the verandah ?'

They went outside and placed themselves on the bench where the man in the baggy breeches and blouse whom Robert had seen on arrival was still sitting. He took no notice of them.

It was quite dark, and the moon was not yet up. There were other cottages quite near, in fact a sort of street had been laid out, where there were more lights, and conversations could be heard coming through the dark. It was all so settled and peaceful, the menacing forest had been pushed well back from the edge of the cultivated land. A couple of Cossacks trotted quietly by, their horses' hooves muffled by the sand of the road, and passed through the circle of light. Robert noticed that like the Circassians, they rode almost standing in their stirrups, and their saddles were similar to the Circassians', small, and (to Robert) very uncomfortable. He had insisted on using his own, thankful that he had brought it with him, although it looked rather incongruous on the small unclipped native horses.

The young ensign drew out his cigarette case and opened it, and made as if to offer it to Robert, and then with a look at their silent companion, put it away again. The gesture did not go unnoticed. The old Cossack said something in Russian which made the ensign laugh. He got out the case again and offered it to Robert. Robert accepted a cigarette, rather puzzled by this piece of by-play. Could Cossacks be Moslems, he wondered.

The ensign lighted their cigarettes.

'It would be no use to offer one to our companion. It is against his principles to smoke, or to drink. But he says that as we have already polluted his house with smoke, we can do no further harm here in the garden.'

The old man sat unperturbed while the other two continued to smoke their cigarettes in silence. A white shape appeared round the corner of the house, the handsome girl with the bucket, now empty, in her hand. This time, however, she did not ignore the young men. She approached with a smile, and said something in an unexpectedly harsh, deep voice to the ensign.

Before he could reply, the old man intervened with a sharp command. The girl smiled, and dawdling from one foot to the other, she passed them by on the verandah and went into the back part of the house.

'That's a fine girl,' said the ensign.

Just then a pistol shot banged out in the room behind them, followed by a hubbub of excited voices. The ensign sprang to his feet and ran back into the house, closely followed by Robert.

Inside, the smoke was curling up to the ceiling. Cards were lying scattered on the floor, and two of the officers were grappling with the fattish young man in glasses, each holding an arm. Standing up facing the door was the old officer Robert had noticed before, still with his bourka on his shoulders, but the shirt he had on under it was open halfway down his chest, and he was in his bare feet. His face was fixed and stern, and one hand was raised in an attitude of denunciation. Opposite him the fat man gasped and floundered like a stranded fish, and made desperate efforts to break away. It was a dramatic tableau. Could it be depicting Cheating at Cards, wondered Robert, or even The Evils of Drink? But there was no way of finding out this, or who had let off the pistol, or where were the old officer's boots. Round the opposing parties a ring of bystanders stood expectantly. As Robert watched, the elderly officer slowly drew a pistol from his own belt, and advancing a few paces, ceremoniously offered it to the fat man who was, however, prevented from accepting it by reason of the fact that his arms were tightly gripped by the men on either side of him.

Cries of alternative encouragement and restraint went up from the spectators. Some were unable to control their mirth. At this point Captain Lopakoff, who seemed much less drunk than the rest, entered the scene. With calm good humour he succeeded in soothing the fat man, whose captors let him go. He stumbled to a chair and sat down heavily. The elderly officer was persuaded to put away his pistol and resume his own seat. Someone found his boots and helped him to put them on. The cards were picked up from the floor but nobody seemed to want to go on with the game. Instead, the glasses were filled up.

From then on, Robert became increasingly unclear as to the events of the evening. He talked a good deal, mainly in French and sometimes in English, but it seemed to him that his understanding of Russian was improving miraculously. There were recitations in Russian, French and English, and all were equally applauded. Later, Robert again found himself side by side with the young ensign, who was pouring out the praises of his friend, Captain Lopakoff.

'He is so keen on soldiering, and yet so sympathetic. He can seize the spirit of the country. He has a Circassian who is a great friend of his, a chief's son. The young prince comes secretly through the lines, to talk with him.'

'What do they talk about?'

'The chief wants to know everything about Russia, the way we live, what our houses are like, what we eat, how much things cost in the shops, how our laws are administered, everything. He asks questions for hours. Andrew Sergueievitch explains to him. He thinks the young man will come and join us fairly soon. He would do well if he did, as if he stays where he is, he has nothing to look forward to, whereas in our army he would be certain of getting a commission.'

Robert was startled. 'You would offer him a commission in

your army? But how could you ever be certain he would not betray you? Surely, once a Tartar, always a Tartar, as we say?'

'I do not think that is always true. Russia offers the Circassians something that many of them want – security, and stability and a settled way of life. Imagine a life without books, without literature, without law (for savage customs don't make law), with nothing to look forward to but living for ever in that state on a barren mountain side. As for treachery – well, most of them hate the man from the next village a hundred times more than they hate us. That is what they are doomed to, unless we take over the country: a life of endless vendetta.'

Robert could have marshalled many arguments to refute the ensign's view – the divine right of peoples to live their own lives, backward and brutish though they might be, in their own way: the divine smell of freedom, sweeter in the nostrils than the fleshpots of a foreign despotism, the wrongness of aggressive policies – but his head was about to refuse its office. He was dizzy with want of sleep, and with the unaccustomed wine. He heard the voices going on and on: it sounded as if they were coming from somewhere far away. He tried to respond, but could not collect his thoughts. He opened his mouth once or twice, but no sound came. He had, after all, been abroad since dawn, and had ridden most of the day. They were sitting at the table. His glass was filled up once more. Robert reached out for it, but missed. It was easier to put his head down on his folded arms and listen that way. Gradually he heard less and less. Robert slept.

He was shaken awake by the captain only a few minutes later, it seemed to him, but already it was light. Robert got to his feet and looked round him. Soutkine lay along the bench on the other side of the table, his knees drawn up so as to accommodate himself to its length. His face was turned towards the window, and he was snoring slightly. The captain twitched his legs down as he passed. The ensign began to come to, making small grumbling noises. In the corner the elderly officer still sat in the same chair with his bourka draped round his shoulders, sound asleep. Captain Lopakoff had apparently slept on one of the camp beds, while the other had not been used at all.

Robert felt a great and immediate need for a wash, and a cup of tea. The second need was in the course of being met: the servant was crouching and blowing up the charcoal under an iron teapot. There seemed to be no possible means of obtaining the first requisite.

Outside the house the dew on the bushes sparkled in the early morning sunlight, for the sun was already up. Coming back into the house Robert washed his hands in the dew, and rubbed them over his face. The dew was cold and refreshing. It was a beautiful pale, still morning. Cocks crowed, and smoke ascended here and there in the settlement, but as yet there was nobody to be seen about. The window shutters had been opened, however, in the private part of the house which Robert had not penetrated, and inside he could make out a large room, almost empty of furniture. On the further wall were nailed some holy pictures, of saints Robert supposed, with very dark faces to which were nailed metal crowns. The old man was standing facing them, with his lips moving. As Robert looked in, he crossed himself and bowed.

The same red-hot glasses of scalding tea were distributed. Nobody said much. The captain looked much as he did the night before, outwardly imperturbable, and his clothes were as tidy as ever. The young ensign was in poorer shape, and he kept rubbing his eyes and yawning and then excusing himself. The captain glanced from time to time at his watch, and seemed anxious to be off.

The officers' horses were brought round, and Robert's with its English saddle. The old Cossack mounted the fourth horse and he followed behind them as they retraced the road of last night, past the cottages and the sunflowers. A small detachment of soldiers was returning to the fort, strolling at their ease. They took no notice of the riders, but the men who were getting ready to go to the fields, the cultivators with carbines on their backs, watched them with narrowed eyes and shouted to the old Cossack, who answered them in a gruff undertone as the horses jigged through the dust.

Now they were out of the cottages and the cultivation, and in front of them was a belt of razed and burnt land, where the trees and bushes had been cleared down to the bare earth. On the other side of this the forest began.

The party halted at the edge of the bare land. The old

Cossack brought his horse up into line with the others. They remained motionless, in line abreast, a few paces apart.

Robert noticed that although the Cossack was hung with weapons in the Circassian fashion so as to resemble ornamental trappings rather than engines of war, the two officers were to all appearances unarmed. The horses shifted restlessly, but otherwise no move was made. They seemed to be waiting, but for what Robert did not know.

The Cossack said something very quietly, without turning his head. He was watching intently the edge of the forest.

The captain said quietly to Robert :

'Your friends are not very far away. Just over there, behind those big trees.'

'How does he know ?' asked Robert. It was obvious that the information had come from the old man.

'The hare would not have run out otherwise, at this time of day.'

Speech seemed to have released the tension. The captain reined back slightly, and turned to Robert with a smile. The Cossack ceased to study the wood and turned his attention to his horse.

Robert realized that the moment of action had come for him. He held out his hand to the captain.

'I am extremely grateful for your kind hospitality,' he began, but found then that it was not easy to go on. Memorable experience ? Unexpected experience ? Both might have unfortunate overtones.

'I shall carry away with me an unforgettable recollection of your Georgian vintages,' he finally fixed on. It was a successful gambit. The ensign, who was drooping again, straightened up, the captain laughed outright and clapped his junior on the shoulders. Even the Cossack smiled, grimly.

'It has been a pleasure,' said Captain Lopakoff.

'It has been a great pleasure,' said the ensign. They shook hands with each other, and then it seemed to Robert that they quite clearly were waiting for him to go. He urged his horse forward on to the stretch of no-man's-land, keeping at first to a walk. He wondered whether to turn round and wave farewell, and then decided not to. Would they still be as they were, watching him, or would the Cossack be unslinging his carbine and getting ready for his shot ?

When he was about halfway across the open space, his horse broke of its own volition into a trot. Scanning the forest ahead, Robert could see no clump of particularly tall trees for which to aim, so he simply made for the place where the scrub grew thinnest. As he got nearer, he saw that it was in fact a brake of wild raspberry canes, the fruit falling off the stems with over-ripeness as his horse trampled through the bushes. A twisting path opened up, of the sort which usually went nowhere, but this one led through the screen of woods into an open meadow where enormous weeds and thistles grew high. Here he found Hassan who almost fell on his neck in his pleasure and relief at seeing him. Hassan had turned back on finding the night before that Robert had become separated from the party, he had retraced his path and then followed Robert's tracks as far as the edge of no-man's-land. Desperately anxious to know what had become of his friend, he had left his horse in the woods, and after dusk had fallen he had attempted to make his way into the settlement on foot, but had found this to be not as easy as it would seem, for there was not only a ring of sentries but a mobile picket as well. Actually he had got through the line of sentries (Robert could imagine him, completely in his element, enjoying every minute of the exploit), and was congratulating himself on his success, when he was discovered by a small dog.

'No bigger,' said Hassan, 'than your little white dog, but possessed of a devilish spirit.' A large dog he could have closed with and despatched with a knife thrust, but this little beast danced round him, keeping always at a distance, and followed him along, yapping persistently all the while. Hassan threw stones, but the only result was to excite it more. Men began to come out of their cottages to see what was the cause of the noise, and Hassan was forced to retreat. The moon was up by now, and he had some difficulty in getting across the open stretch without being detected. In fact he was in the end spotted by a sentry who sent a bullet whistling after him.

After this he lay up in the woods till daybreak, in a lair among the giant docks and grasses, although, as he explained to Robert, he hardly slept at all for thinking of the disgrace he had incurred in letting his father's guest, the man who had saved his own life, fall into the hands of the Russians.

'Did they treat you well?' he kept asking anxiously.

'They gave me food and shelter,' Robert replied. It was a diplomatic answer, for he really did not know how to describe his reception in terms which Hassan would understand. 'I should be anxious about you,' he went on, 'for the risk you took in coming after me.'

'It was nothing. I have often been into the camp. I know all about it. I know at what hour the sentries are changed, I can tell them one from the other. There is a very big one with big moustaches who is a particularly good shot – nearly as good as I am. Then there is a small man with authority, although he is not an officer. He swears and drinks very much, but still he is respected, I do not know why.'

'How do you know that he is not an officer, and how do you know that he swears?' asked Robert, laughing.

'As to swearing, I know their words –' Hassan emitted a string of strange-sounding expletives. 'I have learnt them so as to know what to call the Ivans. The man is not an officer because he does not live as the officers do. He has no room of his own, or servant to wait on him.'

'You have discovered a good deal,' said Robert.

'I know what they are like,' agreed Hassan.

'How have you come to find out so much?' asked Robert, intrigued.

'Oh, by going there to watch,' returned Hassan.

This seemed to be taking an excessive risk, but it was useless to point this out, and Robert contented himself with asking what Hassan intended to do next. Should they ride south and find the party on the coast? Hassan said it was too late, and anyhow not now necessary. The others would by now have reached the Road, and would report all there was to be learnt about it. The two of them had better return directly to the village.

Confident that Hassan would know the right direction, Robert followed behind him on the narrow path. When they reached the head of the glen, he turned in his saddle and looked back. They had been climbing steadily, and he could see through the tops of the trees to the stretch of bare earth beyond. But there were no figures to be seen of Cossack horsemen or any others. The settlement and the fort which lay beyond were lost in the shimmering haze which cloaked the Black Sea coast.

PART TWO

Chapter 6

ON THE LAST stage of the journey, in the early afternoon of the following day, Robert remembered to ask Hassan about the identity of the solitary horseman who had led him so badly astray (although as he had, inexplicably, been allowed to leave the Russian camp, the disaster was not as great as might have been expected). Hassan considered the matter.

'A short man? There are not many such. It could be the cousin of Aladji, the one who walks with a limp. Was it he?'

Robert replied that as he had never seen the man off his horse, he could not tell if he limped or not.

'Or if not Aladji's cousin, then it could be Kaplan, who has a scar on his chin. Had this man such a scar?'

Robert considered. He had only had a fleeting glimpse of the man's face. Had he, or had he not, noticed a scar?

'Kaplan rides a bay horse,' volunteered Hassan, helpfully.

'No,' said Robert decidedly. 'It was a black horse. I am sure of that.'

Hassan thought again, then shrugged his shoulders.

'It is hard to say who it was. Perhaps it was not one of our men, after all.'

'Who else could it have been? That part of the country is empty.'

They were just topping the rising ground beyond which lay Arslan's village, although the trees were too thick for it to be seen. Suddenly, before Hassan could answer, there was the sound of shots – of heavy firing – coming from the direction of the village. They both without a word to each other put their horses into a gallop, and made their way independently through the woods. Nearer the village the trees began to thin out on account of the villagers felling them for firewood, and for the repair of their houses. Over the pounding of the horses' hooves, it was hard to hear if the firing was continuing, but as they came into the narrow twisting paths between the huts and the maize patches they had to slow down, and they heard the shots recommence. Two or three more: then silence again. They seemed to come from about half a mile away, somewhere on the opposite hillside.

Hassan called out as they approached the first house, but there was no reply, nor were there any shrouded women working in the little cultivated plots. The village was apparently deserted. In the space of beaten earth outside his father's house, where there would normally be a dozen or more horses held by the chief's attendants, and always a good number of the village men sitting in the sun, polishing their accoutrements, or simply gossiping, there was nobody except one old man, a one-legged cripple maintained by Arslan on account of past services, who piped out something in answer to Hassan's questions.

Although no women were anywhere visible, Robert could hear a monotonous high screeching, as though a corpse was being wailed, coming from the back of the chief's house.

'He is in the Red Tower,' said Hassan, turning his head.

This was the name given to an ancient stone building, now ruined, which stood high up on the wooded hill opposite. Robert had been up there to explore it, and thought that it might originally have been a Christian edifice, from the evidence of the crosses carved on some of the stones, but it was unlike any church architecture he had ever seen. For one thing, it appeared to have been fortified.

'Who is there?' Robert also looked in the direction of the tower.

'Ibrahim. The *abrek*.'

Abrek meant outlaw. Robert had heard of these desperate men, belonging to no tribe, whose lives were lived in conditions of even more savage vendetta than those of the tribesmen, for every man's hand was against them. Having no friends, they plundered from all sides alike, and many of them succeeded in amassing considerable quantities of arms and horses, while they lived on the best the land had to offer. They were dangerous men to approach.

Robert followed Hassan out of the village confines and up the way which led to the Red Tower. Halfway up, in a cup of the hills, they found all the women of the village huddled together who seemed to be watching for some event expected to take place higher up the hill. Hassan did not speak to them, but rode in silence round the rim of the hollow, turning his face away.

A little higher up, where the woods began, the firing broke out again, seemingly under their feet. Robert could make out the ruined Red Tower standing on its knoll. A puff of smoke came from the battlements now and again, but most of the shots were coming from the surrounding woods, where the men of the village were lying in a circle round the outlaw's refuge.

'He is trying to hold us off till night,' said Hassan, turning his smiling fox's mask towards Robert. 'If he has enough bullets, perhaps he will succeed. If not –'

There was the sound of a shot, a puff of smoke from the tower, and a yelp of pain from somewhere in the undergrowth. A high thin voice from the tower screamed something which made Hassan slide down from his horse and unsling the long gun from his back.

One of Arslan's young men came running through the bushes, bending double. He blundered nearly into them, and Hassan caught at him and demanded the whole story.

From the flood of words which followed Robert gathered very little, but at that point Giorgio appeared, looking very martial with a dagger at his hip and a large pistol sticking in the back of his sash. It looked like one of the local manufactures, showy but unreliable in performance. Probably Ibrahim had little to fear from it.

Hassan, leaving his horse to stand, had disappeared with his friend into the bushes, and Robert judged from their direction that they were working round to approach the tower from the other side.

Giorgio was delighted to see Robert again and was filled with importance at being the bearer of news. He recounted rather incoherently that Ibrahim was indeed in the Red Tower, beseiged by all the men of the place. He was not alone, however, he had with him in the tower the senior princess of the family of noblewomen to whom Arslan had given refuge.

The older ladies had been working that afternoon in one of the barley fields which lay on the higher slope, while the younger princesses remained at home and occupied themselves in the house. A number of women from the village were also at work in the field. The Bezleni princess was alone in one corner, when with a shaking of the earth Ibrahim had galloped up on his black horse and reined up in front of her. Flourishing his dagger, he had dragged the princess off into the thicket, where none of her terror-stricken companions dared attempt a rescue. Instead, they congregated to listen in horror to her cries and appeals, and to her subsequent lamentations, which made it quite clear that the outlaw had ravished her. Then they ran back in a body to the village to call for help.

By the time the men came up, Ibrahim, his horse and the princess had disappeared, and the tracks led off into the deep woods. Realizing that if he was cumbered with the woman the outlaw could not make much speed and they ought to be able to overtake him, the men followed. Before they had gone more than a mile they came upon the black horse, lame. Ibrahim and the princess were both in the Red Tower, but whether the woman was still alive they did not know. They had not heard her voice, and it seemed quite possible that the outlaw had knifed her to keep her quiet, or to prevent her from hampering the defence of his position, which was a strong one. The tower commanded a wide field of fire, and already one man who ventured imprudently into the open had been fatally wounded. Shots began to spatter again, this time on the other side of the hill. It sounded as though at least two marksmen had succeeded in establishing themselves there. The net was closing, and Robert's sympathies began to go out to the *abrek*, one man against many. Not that he saw any signs of hatred, or even of great animosity, on the faces of the tribesmen. They set about the business with the cheerful though serious attention a man might give to a hunting expedition, and they had clearly settled down to a pleasurable afternoon, or rather, to what remained of the afternoon, for the shadows were lengthening perceptibly.

Robert remembered Hassan's words 'if he has enough bullets'. Bullets, and even more so, powder, were deadly scarce owing to the Russian blockade. The tribesmen, he reflected with some irritation, were wasting enough of both commodities to decimate a company of Russians, and all to no purpose, as Ibrahim was firing through loopholes, while remaining well protected himself.

He had not replied, however, to the last fusillade. Was his

ammunition already running low? One of the besiegers must have thought so, and determined to put the matter to the test, for a tribesman left the cover of the trees and ran forward over the bare expanse of turf in front of the tower, to gain the safety of some rocks at its base. To Robert's horror, Giorgio proceeded to follow him, but when he was halfway across, a bullet hit the ground beside him. Giorgio turned in his tracks and bolted back. In the same instant, however, a second man rushed across and joined the first.

There was a cessation of shots from the tower, and in the bushes and thickets surrounding the grassy knoll there was a rustling and a movement of branches as the hunters crept forward. The sun's disc lay on the western horizon, poised for the plunge. There was not much time left before it would become completely dark. Robert was waiting for the forward rush, for despite his distaste he could not tear himself away before the kill, when he heard the screaming voice of the *abrek* again, this time from somewhere lower down, and he saw something whisk across the hole at the base of the tower, which was the only entrance.

The tribesmen immediately began firing at this hole, and all movement ceased. Again, there were no shots in reply, and the tribesmen emerged from their hiding places and converged on the tower, from behind the walls of which Ibrahim continued to howl his insults. His ammunition must have gone, but his position seemed as impregnable as before. The opening behind which he lurked was less than four feet high – whether because the tower had been built for the pigmy men described by Hassan, or in order to prevent cattle and other beasts from entering a sacred building, Robert could not tell – and only one man at a time, crouching low, could get through the hole. No doubt in the end Ibrahim's arm would tire and his blade would get blunt, but in the meantime it was a poor prospect for those in the van of the attackers, and the tribesmen drew off to one side to confabulate. If the outlaw was to be taken at all, the place must be rushed, and rushed quickly, for there were not enough men to prevent Ibrahim letting himself down over the walls and making his escape when darkness came. Giorgio, who had been with the attackers, lost his martial ardour, and came back to join Robert.

The Circassians remained where they were gathered in a group at each side of the opening, and they began to answer Ibrahim's taunts with counter-insults, obviously hoping to lure him out into the open. This went on for some time, with Giorgio chuckling at the exchange of epithets, until there was a scuffling and commotion within the tower. Shouts mingled with curses and the sounds of a struggle. The man who was nearest rushed to the hole and made his way through unmolested, followed by another and another.

'They have caught him!' shouted Giorgio, as the Circassians emerged from the hole, pushing and dragging their captive, a struggling, spitting man, the outlaw Ibrahim. His sheepskin hat had fallen off, disclosing sparse grey hair, and his face was smeared with blood and grime. Beyond tying his hands behind him the tribesmen offered him no further violence, but Ibrahim, finding himself in the midst of his enemies, continued to make rushes first at one and then at another, while the men shouldered him off and laughed. With no weapon left him but his teeth, Ibrahim was ready to bite and tear like a wild beast. The tribesmen had had enough, however. They mounted their horses. One kept hold of the rope attached to Ibrahim's wrists, another rope was put round his neck, and so they prepared to take him back to the village, fully content with the afternoon's work and repeating to each other how Hassan and Ali had scaled the tower and so taken Ibrahim from the rear.

'But where is the princess?' asked Robert. 'What has he done with her?'

Someone jerked the rope round Ibrahim's neck, but the outlaw remained silent. Some of the men began getting off their horses again, but most of them were for doing nothing more. They were anxious to get down to the village and exhibit their captive. No one wanted to hang around searching the ruined tower in the darkness for an old woman who was probably dead anyway.

'But the poor woman may not be dead,' said Robert.

'If she were not dead, we would have heard her,' said Giorgio.

'Well, I will go and see,' Robert said.

'Take care of the snakes,' said Ibrahim, raising his head like a sly old wolf. 'You will find plenty there.'

'The biggest snake of all has been caught,' said Giorgio.

The last of an angry sunset still reddened the sky, but when Robert scrambled through the hole into the tower he could barely see anything. The only light came in at the top, where the roof had once been. Hassan, and after him Giorgio, also made their way through the gap and peered round the ruined shell.

'There is no woman here,' said Giorgio. 'He must have thrown her away into the forest, and she will be dead by now.'

There was a sudden mooing noise almost under their feet, and something moved. Robert recoiled but it turned out to be a pair of hands, which were scrabbling vainly at the edge of a pit which yawned in the floor, the remains of a vault, the wooden ceiling of which had long since disintegrated. Robert knelt at the edge and peered down. Something was moving in the gloom below, something which emitted the mooing noises and reached up with hands which could touch the lip of the chasm, but no further. It was the Bezleni princess, blinded and gagged with the cloth which had been tied over her head, blundering round and round in her prison.

It was hard work getting her up to ground level, and would have been impossible but for the fact that there was a sort of ramp of fallen stones and rubble in one corner of the pit, up which they lugged her. The princess was past giving them any help, she lay back like a barrel of fat, but at least she was quiet. As soon as they got her out, however, and released the cloth over her face, she found her voice again, and began shrieking and beating her breasts which were liberally exposed by the disordered condition of her clothing. Her veil was entirely missing (this was in fact the piece of white stuff which had been used to gag her). Fortunately it was by now almost dark, and the princess seemed oblivious of the state of her attire. As soon as they raised her from the ground on to which she had subsided, she rushed for the entrance hole and advanced on the group of men who were still waiting under the trees. Giorgio, quicker-witted than the rest, ran and got a bourka which he threw over her shoulders, leaving her head still uncovered. Someone had brought a torch, and in its light Robert got for the first time a view of the princess unveiled. Her hair had fallen out of its plaits, and hung about her face. Her eyes were black gashes above the pendulous cheeks. Her frantic gesticulations had caused the bourka to open, and showed the upper half of her body, the body of a fat old woman, almost bare, with the breasts hanging down to her waist.

The princess was eventually persuaded to leave the spot, and the party proceeded back to the village, where the victim was confided to the care of the women, and the men settled down round the fires to talk about the event until late into the night. Everybody had forgotten about the coastal reconnaissance party. Tired and hungry, Robert returned to his quarters to find the hut not only empty, but damp, cold and unswept. There was no food prepared, for Giorgio and the women had been too much occupied to cook any. Even a slab of Circassian bread, as heavy as lead when it was cold and about as digestible, would have been welcome, but there was none of that. Every crumb had been accounted for by pious Moslem mice, or else by the birds which flew freely in and out of the unglazed window apertures. Chilly, empty, and frustrated by the absence of any news of the missing party, Robert lay down to woo sleep. Just before it came to him, it occurred to him to wonder where was Fop.

Fop was in the princesses' quarters, so Giorgio informed him next morning. The little dog gave the ladies amusement, and lightened their hearts. It was to be hoped that they would soon begin to cook again. In the meantime, he had procured some not very appetizing cold viands on which Robert breakfasted.

The morning went on much the same as usual. The village women and the serf girls led the ox carts out to the fields, water and firewood were fetched, and a man appeared, blinking and drowsy after last night's verbal carousal, in the patch of sunlight before each house. But Hassan did not appear, and Robert looked in vain to see Paka with her switch in her hand, driving out the livestock which were her special care. He decided to go for a walk, and he struck up through the empty stubble fields, scaring off crowds of tiny birds which darted away with cries like the sharpening of myriads of blades. Apart from the nightingales in the thicket, there were surprisingly few real song-birds about.

Higher up on the hillsides, flocks of sheep and goats were

101

browsing in the charge of urchins who Robert knew well enough by sight, and their dogs were disposed to tolerate his approach, in daylight. The boys had inherited the oldest coats of the community, patched and repatched till little of the original substance remained. But they wore their rags with the same swagger as their elders exhibited, and they saluted Robert as he passed. For some time after he had left the grazing slopes, Robert heard the boys discussing between themselves the event of his passing, their strong fresh voices carrying without effort from one side of the valley to the other.

The further valley in which he found himself was quite un-inhabited, and there were no signs of cultivation, but a strongly marked path led him on towards a grove of large old trees, mainly beech trees but with some oak and chestnuts intermixed. As the path entered the grove, Robert noticed numerous tags of coloured material and strands of sheep's wool attached to the lower branches of the trees. Curious to see what was coming, he pressed onwards. The path was so much worn by use that tree roots traversed it from side to side above the level of the ground, and one of them, catching his foot, nearly brought him down. He let out a short exclamation.

'To think I should hear a Christian man invoking the devil in this spot,' said a familiar voice. 'You are picking up bad habits from the people here, Mr Wilton. They are forever calling on Shaitan, Shaitan, Shaitan, all day long. Indeed, it is evident they are better acquainted with that name than with the name of God, poor benighted creatures.

'Sit yourself down, Mr Wilton, and let me do you the honours of my quarters, such as they are. The manse, as you might call it, is a thought small, and a trifle draughty, but the minister of the Word here, as in other countries, should be above the needs of the flesh, at least that is what the congregation think, and so it should be. So you'll find no rich Persian carpets here, or gilded teaspoons, but a bed of the fir branches and a drink of water fresh from the spring, which are sufficient for my own simple needs.'

The Reverend Lewis Jones, wearing a clean white robe, had materialized beside him, and was showing him a neat cabin, thatched with branches, rather like an enlarged version of the wattle beehives whose vicinity Robert always avoided when leaving or entering the village, as the animosity of the insects seemed every bit as great as that of the dogs.

It was an agreeable scene. The clearing lay at the heart of the grove, and in the middle of it stood a tree which had attained a truly remarkable size. A dangling rope ladder provided a means of access to the gallery which had been constructed at the top of the tree. At the foot a flat slab of stone had been set up on others to form an offerings table. There were ancient carvings on the slab, worn and undistinguishable, which might or might not have been Christian symbols. On the ground nearby lay unstoppered jars, and plates neatly stacked, empties waiting to be taken away. The holy man's hut was set back a little in the shelter of the surrounding trees, out of the way of the winter winds. The door was open, and Robert got a glimpse of the tidy interior. Most of the floor space was taken up by the couch which was softened, not as in the guest house, by a carpet, but by the dressed skin of a bear which was thrown over it. Its paws, complete with claws, dangled down on either side. It looked a companionable beast. A few household utensils were arranged on shelves, and outside a wash line stretched between two trees bore some of Mr Jones's inner clothing. It occurred to Robert to wonder where *Y Beibl* was kept – possibly up in the prayer gallery. He was also amused to see, tucked into the rafters of the hut, the form of a sleeping owl.

'It is a fine day. Shall we sit outside the house?'

Mr Jones rolled up two lengths of tree-trunk to serve as stools, and arranged them side by side.

Robert commented on the well-kept state of the path leading to the grove, although the valley seemed to be entirely remote from all human habitation.

'This place has, I think, religious associations which go back to remote antiquity, although they are not all of the most elevated kind. The inhabitants are still accustomed to come up here for some of their festivals; for instance, there is a three-day feast in the spring when they honour the god of Thunder. That is a mere pagan survival, of course, but in some of the other celebrations it is possible to detect a Christian influence. This is one of the reasons which decided me to embrace the opportunity of remaining in this country and working for its spiritual salvation. These poor people are accustomed to coming here to worship their false gods. I hope that in time they may turn to the truth. As soon as I have a sufficient command of their tongue, I can begin my mission in earnest – probably with a children's class. In the meantime, I can only hope to influence them by my example, to love their neighbour, to keep their hands from stealing, and their hearts from other forms of sin.'

'It has occurred to me to wonder,' said Robert, 'whether your mission is not made more difficult by the fact that Christianity is the religion of the invader. The Russians have given it out, have they not, that a reconversion to Christianity might well occur, if they conquered the country.'

'To what sort of Christianity! The people would be better off in their ignorance, poor souls, than bowing down before idols. On its practices alone, the Russian church stands condemned. If the people of these parts are to be brought back into the fold, it must be by another hand. The Orthodox rite is bound to be repugnant to them, with its priesthood and its near-heathen ritual, but I am convinced that the Protestant church has a future in this country. I have been talking to that Greek boy of yours, Mr Wilton, in these last few days. He is a frivolous young fellow, as no doubt is only natural at his age, but he tells me that he was greatly impressed by the chaplain to the English gentleman who last employed him. This chaplain was, strange to say, a dissenting minister like myself.'

Robert immediately began to feel how deficient was his state, travelling with no chaplain in attendance, and in case Mr Jones should again offer his services in this capacity he turned the conversation by asking Mr Jones if he had any idea when the chief was expected to return.

'They say it will be soon,' replied Mr Jones, 'but time means very little to these people, as I expect you will have discovered. It is useless expecting him one day or any other day. But they have sent messengers to tell him that they have captured this man Ibrahim, and you may be pretty sure that Arslan will come back as soon as he hears that news.'

Robert tried another question. 'Do you know who is this foreigner, Shekhir Effendi, who seems to be on intimate terms with the chiefs? What is his nationality, do you think?'

'He is a Pole. That is nearly all I have been able to find out about him. His real name is Zletzki. He is a Pole, and a deserter from the Russian army. How long he has been with the Circassians I do not know. He seems to spend his time travelling between the tribes. But one thing I can tell you – he is no friend of yours, Mr Wilton.'

'I cannot think of any reason why he should be my enemy,' said Robert.

'In the first place he suspects you and your coming here,' said Mr Jones. 'In the second place he is jealous of you, in case you should supplant him as Arslan's adviser.'

'I cannot prevent him being jealous of me, although he has no reason at all for it, but why on earth should he suspect me?'

'Suspicion is in the air here, Mr Wilton, as you know. The Circassians are a suspicious race. After all, they are only half civilized, and savages always fear that which is unfamiliar. They are always mistrustful of strangers, and particularly so just now.'

'Shekhir Effendi is not himself a Circassian.'

'A man in his position, a Russian subject who has deserted from the Russian army, has his own reasons, I should say, for disliking newcomers. I am only telling you what I have heard, Mr Wilton, but these people spend most of their time in idle talk, and three-quarters of it is probably lies. For instance, about your letters –'

'What letters?' asked Robert, sharply.

'While you were away these last days, I am told another Armenian man came here with trade goods, and also brought letters for you. They are being kept in the chief's house until Arslan Bey returns with the Polish man, who will be able to read them.'

Robert found himself too angry to speak. He got up from the stool in a state of agitation which escaped Mr Jones, sublimely complacent as the bearer of bad news.

'How long ago was it that this Armenian came, do you know?' Robert asked.

'Well, it might have been about four days ago now. I expect that you will get your letters in time, Mr Wilton, after Arslan Bey returns. It is irritating, I know, but these people here are very backward.'

Cutting the conversation short, Robert set off in haste, with the intention of finding Hassan and demanding that the letters should be given up immediately. When he reached the village, however, he found it buzzing with excitement. The inhabitants had been rudely awakened by the return of the reconnaissance party, one of whom had a bullet in his shoulder, the hole rudely plugged. Robert's medicine chest had already been requisitioned, and Giorgio was acting as surgeon. To facilitate this, the wounded man had been brought into Robert's quarters, and a number of his companions had pushed their way inside with him, while the rest hung round the door. Robert could make nothing of their story, and he was glad to see Hassan approaching. When the hubbub had subsided he ascertained that this group, and the injured man whose name was Mehmet, comprised the whole of the coast party. They had reached their first objective, the Russian fort which commanded the bay and anchorage of Djookbe. Taking the route ordinarily used by the tribesmen over the shingle, which avoided the difficult terrain of the coastal hills, the party had come under unexpectedly heavy fire from the fort. One of the sentries, a better marksman or luckier than the rest, had winged Mehmet. The boy had ridden on without acknowledging that he had been touched, but later he had nearly dropped from loss of blood. His companions had hastily plugged the wound after their own fashion and had got him back. Now the girls would cure him, said Hassan.

'That was a foolish thing to do!' exclaimed Robert. 'Why did they show themselves to the Russians, and ride under the enemy's guns? There must be another way round the fort. They could have got round without being seen.'

Hassan's face darkened.

'This is our country! We go the way that we have always gone. Are we children, are we women, to hide from the Russians, and skulk in the bushes like boars, or bears? We will never lower our heads. Better for us to die fighting, one by one, than submit to having our land taken from us.'

'I know that, Hassan,' said Robert. 'But you are few, and the Russians come in numbers which cannot be counted. Each of your fighting men is like a piece of gold. So that is why I say, do not throw away lives unnecessarily.'

'Mehmet is not dead,' said Hassan. 'The Russians have tried to kill him and they have failed. Tomorrow he will kill ten Russians. That is how we will deal with them. Now we know that they have put another garrison in that fort, we will drive them out.'

'And what is the news of the road which these men went to see?'

'The road? There was not much to see. The Russians are cutting down many more trees. They have also burnt two villages of the Shapsug people. But there were no people living there. Those villages have been empty a long time now.'

Hassan dismissed the subject as being of no further importance. He was going into the hut when Robert tried a last question.

'Are the Russians building more roads in that valley?'

'Nobody has talked about it, but perhaps the men did not go so far. They had to come back, because of Mehmet.'

With this, Hassan went into the cabin and exchanged greetings with the wounded man. The men outside pressed in so as to hear better, and at the same time take advantage of this convenient opportunity of gratifying their curiosity about such of Robert's belongings as were in view. With delighted fascination they buttoned and unbuttoned his coats, examined his boots and boot trees, and speculated on the use of his brushes and combs.

Then there came a diversion. The figure of a girl appeared, advancing rapidly towards the hut with arms swinging like a grenadier. At first Robert thought it was Paka, then he saw it was another girl, bolder and more stalwart, who came straight up to the men, demanding to know where was Mehmet.

Robert imagined that she had come to minister to the wounded man, but he was rapidly disillusioned. Standing over Mehmet as he lay on the divan, the girl harangued him in loud and angry tones while Mehmet, the fighter, made weakly deprecatory gestures and smiled in a feeble way.

The men were all laughing, Giorgio translated quickly.

'The girl is his sister. She is scolding him for being such a fool as to let a Russian fire at him and hit him. She says he is a useless good-for-nothing lying there while at home she has to do all the work. She says the bears were in the maize crop last night. It is his business to sit on the platform and fire the gun to keep them off. It is not woman's work. She says that while he lies there feeling sorry for himself the rest of the crop will be taken, and there will be nothing to eat this winter.'

Mehmet began to answer her, but the words were not out of his mouth before she shouted him down, repeating everything she had said more loudly than the first time. Mehmet looked inexpressibly sulky, then slowly he sat up and put his feet down to the ground. He began to fasten his tunic, while the girl goaded him with shouts and gestures. For a moment he seemed to be about to protest: then he shook his head and walked unsteadily out of the door. The men outside said nothing, but they opened their ranks to let him pass through, then slowly, one by one, they began to drift away, till Hassan and Robert were left alone.

'The party did not find out so very much,' said Robert.

'No,' agreed Hassan. 'You and I should have gone with them, Jibrahil.'

We would have been with them, but for a false guide, thought Robert. Aloud he said:

'Hassan, I hear that there are letters in your father's house which have arrived for me. Will you please send them to me.'

Hassan looked startled, then a little embarrassed.

'I did not know of this. It is my father's business, but if there are letters for you, certainly I will ask for them.'

'Without delay?'

Hassan frowned. Such persistence verged on ill manners, but Robert persisted, none the less. Hassan's embarrassment became painfully obvious. There must be something at the back of this, thought Robert. That Polish turncoat, Zletzki, possibly. Hassan finally gave way.

'If there are letters, I will see to it that you have them.'

But when he brought the packet to Robert later in the evening, it turned out to contain only one letter, from the Rector. No newspapers, no other letters.

'It is a letter from my father,' Robert felt bound to explain.

'Ah, from your father.' Hassan looked satisfied. That, to him, explained the urgency. Robert opened the letter, but it was getting dark, and he had to take it outside the hut to make out the Rector's tortuous handwriting. The first name that met his eye was Henry's.

'Henry Ginger and his accomplices came up for trial at the Assizes the week before last,' wrote the Rector. 'All seven of them were found guilty of poaching and received appropriate sentences. Ginger and one Edward Perry, whom I do not think you would remember, who were undoubtedly the ringleaders, were condemned to transportation to Van Diemen's Land. Your mother is extremely worried at the plight of these men's families, and indeed one of the most dreadful features of this case, to me, is the complete disregard these men have shown for the needs of those who are dependent on them. We try to do what we can at the Rectory, but there are so many cases in which one fears that money gifts can do little to touch the root causes of the current misery and distress. What is wanted is a complete change of heart, and the will to do an honest day's work . . .'

Robert put down the letter in consternation, then took it up again to look at the date. It seemed to have reached him remarkably quickly, all things considered. The letter contained no word to suggest that any defence had been put up for Henry. His own letter, then, had miscarried, or perhaps it was still on its way to London, while justice for once had been expeditious.

Hassan was watching him, smiling. 'The news of your father is good,' he asked.

'Yes, my father is well,' said Robert. He was thinking furiously. What was to be done now? He would write another letter to the lawyers and get it sent off as soon as he could. Even though the opportunity for a proper defence at the trial had gone by default, there might be a possibility of an appeal from the verdict, on some technical point. He had heard of such things. He would also write to his mother about making some provision for Susan.

Hassan lingered, watching him.

'Tell me more about London, Jibrahil.'

'Not tonight, for I must write a letter while there is still light to do it. Has the Armenian man left the village yet?'

'Probably he has gone, yes. If you have things to do, I will take my leave of you, Jibrahil. Till tomorrow!'

'Till tomorrow,' Robert answered.

A wind got up later that evening, and the light burned so poorly that it became impossible to read or write. Robert occupied himself for some time in rearranging his belongings which had been left in some disorder by his recent visitors, and with some annoyance he discovered that the volume of Horace was missing. It was too dark by that time to make a further search for it, and there was nothing for it but to go to bed. Robert lay awake, listening to what sounded like an absolute chorus of noises : the jackals yapped and squealed with children's voices in the woods, foxes barked – or were they deer ? – and above it all, the village dogs howled incessantly. As well as all these creatures which could be heard, there were others which moved in silence about their business in the night. The wild cat lay along the branch, as silent as a ball of lichen, but with eyes which missed nothing. The bear, silver-coated in the moonlight, moved noiselessly into the maize field, there to sink his bulky body into the crop and embrace between his shaggy paws the sheaves at his leisure. The wild boars, secure in their immunity from human pursuit, were rooting along the game paths. The eagle owl floated ghost-like between the trees, to freeze the blood of the crouching hare with its hunting-call. An owl's screech above the roof made Robert start in his blankets.

Cautiously he got up and unbarred one of the window shutters. The expanse of silvered grass led right away to the edge of the forest, and the dark shadows where it was always possible to imagine movement. He was almost certain he saw a bear by the side of the woods : but on looking again, he saw it was a tree. The shadows cast by the moonlight had deceived his eyes. The moon, which was now quite high, had a curious reddish tinge, he noticed. Hassan had told him that this redness of the moon, when rising or sinking, meant that a snake had bitten it, and that was a presage of bad weather to come.

Robert went back to his hard bed. The frogs which had been croaking in chorus in the earlier part of the evening now, for some unaccountable reason, chose to stop, but the jackals continued to squeal, the dogs barked, and some small unseen but energetic rodent began to make gnawing sounds in the corner of the hut. It was impossible! Robert resisted the impulse to fling one boot at the rat, the other at Giorgio, who was snoring vigorously in his corner. Instead, he pulled the blanket over his head, and in five minutes, he too was asleep.

Chapter 7

ARSLAN BEY GALLOPED in, with his standard flying and his tribesmen surrounding him, a few days later. He was not alone. Accompanying him were several other chiefs of equal importance, each with his own escort. All the horsemen dismounted in the open space outside the chief's house, where they were welcomed by Hassan, bowing respectfully before his father and his guests. They then went inside the house, leaving the attendants to look after the horses, while a wild flurry of cooking engulfed the women's quarters. Giorgio was very soon sent for to assist the princesses, and Robert was summoned shortly afterwards to join the assembled chiefs.

The matter which he found them debating was the news that some of the Shapsug tribe, who had been driven from their coastal valleys by the burning of their villages, had entered into a treaty with the enemy. They had agreed to forgo further hostilities and return peaceably to their old homes. In return, they had accepted Russian protection, and a large sum in gold. The men had started to come down out of the hills where they and their families had been hiding, and were rebuilding their houses, and getting in what remained of their crops.

Opposite Robert sat the striking figure of Kherim Agha, a famous warrior of whom Robert had heard much, but whom he was now seeing for the first time. Quite young, with an air of smiling ferocity, Kherim sat squarely on the carpet with his hands on his knees, and gazed about him with the look of an animal of prey, still benevolently intentioned, but with all that inclined to look on every creature round him as a possible morsel. From time to time he stroked his beard which was dyed red with henna, and his eyes followed the progress of the unveiled girls, Paka among them, who were now filling the cups of the guests with a rather sickly-tasting liquid in the composition of which honey predominated. His dignity would not allow him to turn his head. His lambswool cap was set at a rakish angle, and his waist was encircled by a richly coloured shawl: the elaborately damascened hilts of dagger and sabre protruded from it.

Was it his imagination, or was Paka unusually coy in trying to avoid giving direct attention to Kherim, while watching like an assiduous hostess over Robert's own wants? Tense with concentration, her snaky plaits falling over her face, she refilled his cup with the curdled, semi-opaque brew, while Robert tried to fish out a drowned fly inconspicuously with his little finger and felt uncomfortably conscious of Kherim's light gaze flickering over himself and the girl. When Robert turned to face him, however, the Circassian had hooded his eyes like a cat, and was looking along the carpet into the distance.

Something of this must have caught the old Lion's attention too, for with an abrupt gesture he ordered the women away. Paka left with almost contemptuous slowness, dawdling from one foot to the other as long as Robert could see her. In the background, the shrouded figure of the old princess, her mother, beckoned her agitatedly. Kherim also watched Paka go, out of the corners of his eyes, and there was no mistaking the dislike with which he looked at Robert. But Hassan was standing beside the stranger, and it was to Robert that the old Lion addressed himself, after the Shapsugs' defection had been discussed.

'What does our noble guest say?' he asked. 'This is an act of treachery to all our nation. Shall these traitors not be punished?'

The sentiment expressed in this rhetorical question was clearly acceptable to all present. Robert was thinking furiously in the respite afforded by interpretation.

'You know what is in my thoughts,' he said at last. 'A shot fired at a fellow Circassian means one bullet less for the Russians.'

'We have plenty of bullets,' said Kherim.

'That is exactly what you have not got,' retorted Robert.

'Bullets are not important,' shouted Kherim. 'We have our daggers. We shall carve them into pieces, the cheating cowardly dogs. The jackals and the pigs can take care of what is left.'

The old Lion got to his feet and took a few limping steps, then he recollected himself and sat down again heavily on the carpet. He looked puzzled and baffled. No one else seemed to want to speak – an unusual circumstance in itself. Robert attempted to sum up his point of view in simple language which they would understand.

'What do the Shapsug people want? To go back to their own homes and live there at peace. If their land is now under the Russian guns, they have no choice but to come to terms. It is not they who are the enemy but the Russians.'

There was a glum silence, broken by Kherim, who shouted:

'What choice had they? You ask what choice? The answer is not far to seek. The choice between living like cowards, or dying like free men. What they have done – creeping back like rats into their holes – is a disgrace to all of us. We cannot let it pass.'

'What help,' asked Robert, 'what help did you give to the Shapsug people when they were driven out? They fought alone, then. I have heard that half the men of the tribe were killed before the Russians could count that valley as theirs. Did any of the other men of Circassia come to their aid then? When the rest of the Shapsugs fled into the hills, leaving their crops ungathered and their cattle to be driven off by the Russians, did you and your followers offer them lands and a place to live?'

'The Shapsug people have never lived over here,' muttered Hassan. 'They have their own valleys, just as we have ours.'

Robert sat silent, but Kherim sprang to his feet.

'This stranger does not know our ways. He would have us all think like cowards, and act like women, except that our women would be ashamed to let a traitor live at peace on their own door step. These words may suit men of the west who sit in houses and build towns where they may live under the protection of their King, who has many regiments of soldiers to do his bidding. We are poor people, we have nothing but our lands, and we will fight for them. We have no regiments, and we cannot afford traitors.'

Another oldish chief who was present gave a long-winded recital, coming down first on one side, then on the other, while Kherim looked sulky and Robert had difficulty in suppressing his impatience. At the end all waited to learn what Arslan Bey had to say. His reputation and his authority were undisputed.

'The matter is too weighty a one for the few of us here,' he said, after a pause. 'It is proper that it should be decided by the chiefs of all our people.' There were nods and murmurs of approbation from most of those present: only Kherim stared straight ahead of him, silent and mutinous. 'Our guest is right in much of what he says. We must all move as one. If it is the decision of the assembly to destroy these Shapsug traitors, then I will obey it. I will place myself at the head of our men. But just now we are too few. Also we have other matters on hand. This is the season when the men must watch the maize crops, or the bears and the wild boars will strip our fields. And there is also the affair of the outlaw Ibrahim, who has fallen into our hands. It has to be decided what to do with him.'

Kherim who had been looking more and more glum, started up with interest.

'You have caught Ibrahim the outlaw, then?'

It was Hassan who answered, permitted by his father to tell the story. He recounted the details of the capture to an appreciative audience. It seemed particularly to tickle Kherim that Ibrahim's downfall had come about as the result of his assault on the Bezleni princess.

'An old woman!' he kept on saying. 'What did the old fox see in her? He must have been mad.'

'The old fox saw an old vixen,' said somebody.

'He must have been mad!' repeated Kherim incredulously. 'Not a virgin, not even a young woman.'

'Still, rape is rape,' said the Lion.

'Rape is rape, even on an old woman,' agreed Kherim.

'He must be judged for his crimes, and suffer his deserts,' said Arslan. 'It is not only the matter of the woman, who is my family guest, there is the affair of Aladji, who was shot dead by Ibrahim. The family are entitled to the blood money, or to a life. He also broke the arm of another man.'

'He must have gold hidden somewhere,' said Hassan, 'but gold in a hole is no use. He will have to lead us to it.'

'That hole will need to be deep,' said Kherim. 'The old thief has been filling it for many years. Last year he stole one of my best horses.'

'A black horse?' asked Hassan.

'Yes, it was a black horse.'

'A black horse with one white ear, and a white forefoot? It is here, that horse.'

'That is my horse!' Kherim burst out laughing. 'Well, I see

that this is my cause as well as yours, Arslan Bey. I will be one of the judges to hear this man's case.'

Robert was about to point out that no man could be judge in his own cause, but then he refrained, as he doubted that his maxim would have any validity in the surroundings in which he now found himself.

'There is yourself, there is myself,' went on Kherim. 'We need a third, and there he sits. The noble foreign bey, your guest. He can hear and judge the case for us, in his wisdom. We will be the better for his counsel.'

Robert was about to protest that he knew nothing of the laws of Circassia, and was not competent to adjudicate in a case of rape, murder (or manslaughter), and horse-stealing, having no idea of the relative seriousness of these offences or what were the local penalties in force were the case to be proven, but again, he did not demur when Arslan Bey added his voice to Kherim's and called on him to judge. It was, after all, a chance of seeing that some ideas of civilized justice were observed which could not fail to be a good example to the tribesmen.

'Oh, very well,' said Robert.

The trial of Ibrahim the outlaw before a tribunal consisting of Arslan Bey, Kherim Agha (who was also the complainant in the matter of the stolen horse) and Robert, opened on the following day. It was held largely at the insistence of the accused, who was tired, so he said, of spending so much time under a roof, and demanded a judgment, or his release. He also complained that the food given to him was unpalatable, and that the incessant chattering going on outside the hut where he was kept confined reminded him of jays in a tree.

A thatched shelter had been built in one day at the end of the open space in the centre of the village. Robert wondered why, as the verandah of the chief's house would have afforded adequate shelter for the three chief personages. The shelter had three sides only, one long side being left open. Under it the Lion, Kherim and Robert took their seats, flanked by their attendants. The fields were all deserted, as every living soul in the village had come to see and hear the proceedings. The men sat or stood on one side, the women, huddled into a compact group, sat opposite to them, their veils pulled well over their heads. Robert found the sight of these rows of masked faces distinctly unnerving, and wondered what effect it would have on the prisoner.

When Ibrahim was produced, however, at the old chief's word, he was quite in command of the situation. He appeared to Robert, who studied him with interest, to be not so much old as ageless, now that the grey hairs which Robert had remarked previously were covered again by a fur cap. Shackled and surrounded by his enemies, he still walked with a confident swagger, enjoying to the full the attention he was commanding. But every inch of him proclaimed the outcast man: the negligent dress, the sly and drooping eye. Although the days of confinement had no doubt added to the general untidiness, he wore what looked like a collection of rags belted round him, which were ragged indeed, even by Circassian standards – but possibly Ibrahim had no wish to proclaim the success of his calling. There was an air of quiet ferocity about him, which Robert had remarked before, like a clever old dog which always gets its bite in first. That roving eye, ever seeking for a loop-hole for escape from the situation which had gone against him, meant that he never looked quite straight at anybody, and there was no resemblance to the open, sunny looks with which the tribesmen told the most outrageous falsehoods. Just now Ibrahim was full of bravado as he shuffled along between the two men who were escorting him. They stationed him in the middle of the space which had been left open, facing his judges.

Ibrahim himself opened the proceedings.

'What sort of treatment is this for an honest man, Arslan Bey?' He raised his arms and shook the chains which dangled down to the ground. Hassan and Giorgio were working furiously to keep up with the translating. 'Where in the world do you think I am going to fly to? Here I am surrounded by your warriors, an old man, and not a single man's hand is for me except my own. Do you think a djinn is going to lean down from the sky and make me vanish away from you like a puff of smoke, prrrrrrrr. I can hardly walk, as it is, and you have taken my horse from me.'

'Your horse!' shouted Kherim. 'You old liar! That is my horse which you stole from me.'

Ibrahim regarded him with an indifferent eye.

'Was it your horse, Kherim Agha? I had forgotten that. In any case, the beast was always broken-winded, and has now gone lame. If I wanted to steal a horse, I would steal a better one than that.'

'Broken-winded!' Kherim was in a fury. 'Thief! Liar! Brigand! Before you lamed it, that horse went like the wind. I loved it like my son, I treated it like my brother. The horse never was broken-winded.'

'Is this a black horse with one white forefoot that you are talking about?' asked Ibrahim.

'Yes, my black horse has one white forefoot and one white ear.'

'Well, the only black horse I know with one white forefoot and one white ear is broken-winded, and as Kherim Agha says his horse is not broken-winded, then the horse I am speaking of and the horse Kherim has lost cannot be the same horse.'

Ibrahim looked round the circle in triumph. There was some laughter from the men's side. The women continued to sit in silence. The judges with some difficulty suppressed their exasperation.

'We will see this horse by and by,' said Arslan. 'It can be brought here, and Kherim Agha will tell us if it is his own. But we have more serious matters to consider than a horse. There is the complaint of the most honourable princess who has been violated by this man.'

'Yes, yes, that is indeed more weighty,' chimed in Ibrahim. 'Horses are stolen every day, and I have stolen plenty in my time, but who would dare to violate a most honourable lady? Who is this princess who accuses me? Surely she makes a mistake. I am an old man, and in any case I have always been one who trembles before women.'

'Villain, do not attempt to deny your guilt,' shouted Arslan. 'She accuses you before God.'

'Who is this woman?' shouted Ibrahim.

'The most honourable princess, wife to the chief of the Bezleni.'

'That one! Why, she is an old woman, nearly as old as I am. If I wanted to steal a woman, would I choose one like that? Besides, there is no need for any stealing with that most honourable princess, I can assure you of that, oh men of this place, if you need any assurance. For many years the noble prince her husband has been cuckolded. Even now, although she is nothing but a ruin, she is lifting her veil for men . . .'

A shocked murmur ran through the crowd of women. They drew closer together.

'Why, she respects nothing, that one, not even the sanctity of a holy man. How often do you think she has been going up the path to your sacred grove in the last weeks, hoping to fix her eyes on the foreign mullah? She thinks that no one sees her, but i have seen her. I have been watching.'

'Cease your wicked tongue,' said Arslan. 'You only make matters worse for yourself.'

'How can matters be worse for me than to be falsely accused, before all this company?' said Ibrahim. 'Still, continue, continue. How am I supposed to have violated this noble matron?'

To Robert's surprise, one of the veiled women in the front row got to her feet, and called:

'When she was in the barley field with all of us, three days ago.'

'She was with all of you!' cried Ibrahim, in surprise. 'Why then should I have taken *her* with such beauty to choose from?' He turned to the men, with a smile and a swagger, conscious of a point well made.

Another woman jumped to her feet.

'She was alone, in a corner of the field. None of us was near her.'

'Ah, the princess was all alone, in the corner of the field. And what was the princess doing there alone? Perhaps she went to see if there were men gathering nuts in the woods next to the field.'

'She was reaping . . . she dropped her reaping hook . . . you came out of the wood on your black horse . . . you dragged her away . . . she screamed . . . you raped her . . . we heard her screams!' One veiled woman after another got to her feet and shouted. Some actually shook their fists. But Ibrahim's confidence was not shaken.

'You saw nothing. You heard her scream, so you thought I had raped her. That one! I had to fight her off!' He turned back to the men.

'Listen. I will tell you how it happened. I was in the wood –

why I was there is my business. She came creeping into the wood after me, speaking to me gently. "Ibrahim! Ibrahim!" – like that. Then she dropped her veil before me – aie, what an old grandmother! Not a tooth left. Oh, the wicked old woman! She took my hand and held it against her bosom, so.' (He made a face.) 'All the time she was speaking to me as sweetly as a serpent, saying "Ibrahim, no one will know. I have a dagger with a silver hilt, I will give it to you, I will give you a gold ring, Ibrahim!" '

The air was ringing with the indignant outcries of the women.

'Not true, you forced her!' – 'She screamed, why should she scream if she were willing?' – 'Her veil and dress were both torn!' – 'Ask the son of Arslan Bey whether her dress was not torn!'

'Her clothes were certainly torn when we found her,' said Hassan. He turned to Robert for corroboration.

Robert was seized with acute embarrassment. He had not bargained with giving evidence in the proceedings as well as acting as judge, and this was a situation which seemed to him to be totally irregular. Fortunately he was not required to speak, for Ibrahim again seized the initiative.

'Her clothes were torn! Oh men of this place, are you all like little children? We have here a woman, a woman whose character is known. She tears her dress right down, and shrieks Rape. How many women have not done just that thing! The man is seized, and charged with a most vile crime, and all the woman loses is a dress. If such a trick is to be believed, then justice hides her face, and no man is safe from a revengeful woman.'

He had the men clearly on his side, and they settled themselves to listen with appreciation, but dissatisfaction made itself apparent among the ranks of veiled women. The faceless heads turned from side to side and nodded and becked like an assembly of ghouls. Ibrahim then brought off his coup.

'If the so virtuous princess denies what I have said, then let the princess appear and accuse me herself.'

This was greeted with silence. The men muttered together, while a quivering sigh rose from the women's side. Arslan looked perplexed.

He turned first to Kherim, who had retreated into his

inscrutable mood and was stroking his beard with a look of infinite boredom, and then to Robert.

'It has never been our custom –' he began. Kherim snatched his words from him.

'What does it matter, Arslan Bey? If the woman desires justice, let her come forward. The man is lying, but equally it should be no trouble to a woman to tell lies. We shall see which of them tells the better tale. Or else we shall surely be here all day, listening to this man.'

Arslan turned to Robert.

'What do you say, my guest? You saw the woman after her rescue. Where is the truth of the matter? Is it proper to ask the princess to testify to her dishonour?'

'If she accuses the man and he denies it, then it is surely proper that she should confront him. How else will the truth be known?'

Arslan looked worried, then his dignity reasserted itself.

'The request is a just one, and it is granted,' he said to Ibrahim, who plumed himself: then to everybody and to nobody in particular:

'Let the noble princess herself come forth and repeat her accusation against this man.'

There ensued a lengthy wait. It did not seem to trouble the old Lion and Kherim, who tucked up their feet under them and froze into figures of stately immobility. Robert wriggled himself towards one of the posts supporting the shelter so that he could at least get his back against it and obtain some slight alleviation of his discomfort.

After what seemed like a quarter of an hour at least, but which was probably half of that, a procession was seen issuing forth from the chief's house and approaching the seat of judgment. It consisted of the Bezleni princess, heavily veiled, of course, but Robert recognized her waddling gait, escorted, or to some extent supported, by a pair of girls, one on either side, who were holding her arms. The one on the right-hand side, Robert saw, was Paka. Having their faces uncovered, the unveiled girls scowled vigorously at the outlaw, Paka in particular resembling to Robert's eyes a young Athena, with her flashing silver breastplate, and little helmet-cap. Ibrahim was not abashed.

'Ah, if it had been one of those two there! Your girls are comely, Arslan Bey. Such pearls! But look to them well. How could any man resist them, even with the noble princess offering herself!'

This last speech succeeded in enraging both the Lion and Kherim, and it had a galvanic effect on the princess. Tearing her veil aside so as to confront her adversary more clearly, she began to scream at the top of her voice, hurling accusations and insults pell mell. Hassan faltered, then finally gave up translating the storm of invective, but the impact was fairly clear. Ibrahim began shouting back, shaking his fettered arms. The princess, less restricted in her movements, raised her arms to heaven to witness her words, and then made as if to tear her own face and clothing. From this she was firmly restrained by the two girls, who pinioned her arms, while they in their turn began to shout at the prisoner.

The uproar was appalling. Arslan turned rather helplessly towards Robert.

'Adjourn the hearing. Tell them we will adjourn until order is restored,' whispered Robert, drawing on vague memories of court-room procedures at home. Arslan looked round uneasily. The group of women was surging and murmuring ominously, and it was by no means clear by what escape route the tribunal could make a dignified exit from the scene. The accuser and the accused, each flanked by their attendants, continued to hurl words to and fro with unabated vigour. The princess was the first to collapse, slowly subsiding to the ground and nearly dragging down with her the two girls who were still endeavouring to hold her up. They gave up, and let her down to the ground where she settled, moaning and wailing. At intervals she raised her face and her arms to heaven, as though imploring assistance.

It looked as if the serried ranks of women were going to take up the cry, but before Arslan could put Robert's suggestion into effect, one of the men pushed his way to the front.

'Enough of this,' shouted the unknown man. 'Arslan Bey, are we to hear these women's tales all day? We will never know the truth of it between these two, if we stay here until doomsday.'

This was clearly true, but to Robert it seemed that there was a certain danger in allowing the control of proceedings to fall into the popular hand. Arslan however saw his chance.

'Let the princess now withdraw,' he said with some dignity. 'We will consider this matter and give our decision in due course.'

With some difficulty, the Bezleni princess was raised from the ground by her two supporters, who got her up and into motion. The trio retraced their steps through the group of women who opened a way for them to pass. Growing dissatisfaction remained, however, and cries for justice made themselves heard from the women's side, but with the departure of the princess the cries became less frenetic.

A man who had shouldered his way to the front raised his voice again.

'When do we come to the affair of my kinsman Aladji? He died two nights ago, shot through the body by this Ibrahim. What about the blood-money, Arslan Bey? Has Ibrahim got the money? Aladji's son is only ten years old, and not strong enough to bear arms yet. Who is to look after the women of the house? The family calls for justice.'

'How was this Aladji shot?' This from Kherim.

'Why, everybody knows that! Ask the young chief sitting there beside you. Ask the Frankish lord. It was when we were all surrounding the Red Tower. Aladji was beside me, in the bushes. He said to me, I am going over to the tree there, I shall be able to see better. I told him to take care what he was about, but Aladji was always impetuous, he stood up and paf! There he was, lying beside me with his life running out. I tried to raise him, but I could see he would never hunt again. He was a brave man, a fine hunter, a fine shot.'

Ibrahim was furious.

'A fine shot, you call him? I can tell you, none of your boys knows how to shoot as well as I could when I was *so* high. How many of you were there against me, one old man on my own? Fifty? A hundred? It would have made no difference if there had been a thousand of you. Not one of you could hit me.'

'You were behind walls – and you kept jumping about,' grumbled the other.

'Jumping about – yes, I know your idea of shooting. You think that your beast, or maybe your Russian, is going to stand still for you to fire at him, that he is going to walk very, very slowly, then he is going to stop and give you all the time in the world to get ready for your shot. Any fool can hit the mark that way, but I got your Aladji on the move and toppled him over with one shot. That's the way to do it.'

'You admit the deed, then,' asked Arslan.

Ibrahim was astounded.

'You all saw me do it. And who else, do you think, could have succeeded with a shot like that, at such a distance?'

'You murdered Aladji.' The tribesman stuck to his guns.

'You say I murdered Aladji?' Ibrahim's voice was light and contemptuous. He seemed to be as bored by the repetitive style of these exchanges as was Robert.

'When the bear is surrounded by yapping dogs, it breaks their backs with blows. When the boar has been chased far enough, it stands at bay and uses its tusks on the pack. Would you call that murder?'

Ibrahim sourly contemplated the army of glowering faces which confronted him. Many of the women had already melted away. The rest were preparing to follow, all but one or two whom Robert guessed to be relatives of Aladji. They sat on the ground, wrapped in their cloaks. The men crowded up round the outlaw, shouting and waving their fists.

'Aladji is dead: you are his murderer,' they repeated.

The judges looked at each other, and Robert was about to ask What of the princess? when Kherim jumped up and said in a loud voice for all to hear,

'The man has confessed. He is guilty – condemned out of his own mouth. What are we waiting for?' he added, only slightly less loudly: then he raised his voice again so as to carry to all those standing round.

'Ibrahim has confessed that he killed Aladji. What is the law here in your valley, Arslan Bey? Is it not right that he should pay blood money for this life?'

'That is our law,' said Arslan.

His voice, and any further objection Robert might have made, was drowned by the shouts and cries of acclamation which followed Kherim's words. A howl for blood money rose from all throats.

'But has he got it?' The shout came from the unknown man who had pushed himself forward before. It worked the assembly into an even greater frenzy. One of the group of veiled women which had remained on the scene rushed up to Ibrahim.

'Where is the gold, you son of Satan! Where is the gold you owe us for Aladji?'

'Yes, where is the gold? He must have gold somewhere,' chorused the men. 'Where is it, Ibrahim? Show us where you have hidden your treasure.'

'The fine may be paid either in gold, or in cattle,' said Arslan.

'I am a landless man. Where do you think I keep my cattle, Arslan Bey? Up there?' Ibrahim pointed up into the sky where small fleecy clouds were floating.

'You keep your cattle in other men's byres, you old thief,' shouted the men. 'What other men own is yours, by your reckoning.'

'Your cattle are indeed easy to steal,' retorted Ibrahim, 'when you keep them in the byre next to the kitchen where the bread is baking. Let me tell you, I know a trick none of you would ever have thought of. You take one of the hot loaves, quick, when the housewife's back is turned, yes, you steal it without her noticing –' he grinned diabolically – 'and you clap the hot loaf on to one of the cow's horns. When the bread has cooled a little, you can turn the horn, like that, in your hand. Who can swear to his own beast then?'

Some of the men laughed, but most of them raised anew a howl of execration.

'That is the way my own cow was lost, my best cow! And my cousin's, too! Robber! You deserve death! Where are they now, all the herds you have stolen?'

'I have no herds,' shouted Ibrahim.

'Then give us gold,' shouted the men.

Ibrahim cackled.

'You seek gold, my friends? Then look about you, for it may be anywhere. It may be buried under your feet.' Everyone looked down. 'Dig then, scrabble in the dirt. You never know where you may not find gold. I may have hidden it in one of the trees. Cut down the forests, then, and take care to search every branch. It may be hidden in any one of them. Or perhaps I lowered my treasure down a well, or scattered it in many places. It is a foolish man who hides all his gold in one place.

He had better make gold shoes for his horse – but not for that horse of Kherim Bey's, that broken-winded beast.'

'Where is it? Show us, you devil! Curses on you, Satan's son!' The men were all round him. With difficulty his two guards kept them off, and also the furious women who would have attacked him.

'I will not show you,' shrieked Ibrahim. You can find it for yourselves, diggers of dirt.'

Arslan intervened, His heavy old voice restored order.

'Think well what you say, Ibrahim. If you cannot pay the blood-price which is rightly due, then it is your life. That is the law. Pay the fine, or pay with your life. The choice is yours.'

'I will never give up my gold to you!'

It was Ibrahim's last scream of defiance. Baffled and angry, the men round him drew back, and turned towards the judges.

'It is death, then,' said Kherim.

'Yes, it is death,' said Arslan.

He said something in an undertone to Hassan, who went away, leaving Giorgio to cope with any interpreting which might become necessary. Robert saw that the boy's face was alight with interest and anticipation. He himself felt slightly sick. The further delay which ensued was not made any more pleasant by his ignorance of what was to come.

Hassan reappeared, on horseback, with attendants leading the horses of the chiefs, and also mounts for Robert and Giorgio. An ox-cart lumbered up, on to which they piled Ibrahim, cumbered with his chains. The men had been disappearing to fetch their own horses. Now they were all reassembled.

Robert mounted. There was nothing else he could do, but his mouth was dry and his heart thumped painfully. 'Where are we going to?' he asked Giorgio, who shrugged.

'To the river somewhere,' was the answer.

They did not move off at once, however. Something clearly remained to do. They waited, sitting on their horses, the prisoner in his cart. Then out of the chief's house came a serf with a burning brand in his hand. He brought it over to the shelter which had served the judges, and thrust it into the roof. The dry twigs and branches caught fire. The torch was re-applied to the walls at several points. They too smouldered, and then burst into flames. In a few minutes, with a mighty crackling the flames were devouring the whole construction.

Ibrahim as well as the rest of the men watched the fire in silence. Not until it had died down, having consumed everything consumable, did they move off. Then they rode down the valley and took a path which, as Giorgio had predicted, brought them to the side of the stream, at a place where rocks, on which branches and whole tree trunks had been caught at the time of flood water, made a natural barrier across the river. On the upper side of the barrier was a deep pool which Robert had come across and noted on one of his solitary walks. He had thought it would be an excellent place to swim, but the chance of doing so had never presented itself. This was where they now stopped, and the men who were escorting Ibrahim began to knock off the chains which fettered him.

While they were riding, the whole sky had darkened, and a hot wind had begun to blow in gusts at their backs. Suddenly, without warning, thunder crashed out over their heads, followed by a pelting shower of drops which Robert at first thought to be rain, but which he saw as they lay on his clothes and on his horse's mane to be hailstones, as big as peas. When he shook them off, they rolled on the grass. In a trice men and horses were powdered with white pellets, then the shower ceased as suddenly as it had begun.

They had got the chains off now, and were securing Ibrahim's arms behind him with rope and attaching something – was it a stone ? Robert did not care to look too closely. The horsemen had pulled up at the edge of the river. Some of them who must have gone another way and crossed by a ford now appeared on the opposite side of the pool, where they lined up along the bank. Robert was on Arslan's right hand, with Hassan beside him. Giorgio was a little behind, craning to see. The horses steamed : the hailstones were melting and trickling in droplets down their heated skins. The sudden storm was over, but claps of thunder could still be heard at intervals, although they were now very far away. The valley here was at its narrowest. When Robert looked up, all that he could see through the tangled treetops was the black mass of the mountain lowering overhead. The lesser hills which intervened between the valley and the heights were cut off from view.

Nobody spoke. In the silence the river could be heard rushing over the stones with a melodious gurgle. Big drops of wet fell from the branches and spattered on the grass. Bridles jingled as the horses grew impatient with standing still and tossed their heads, juggling with their bits, but the final act was yet to come. Still in silence, Ibrahim fought and resisted as the men urged him nearer and nearer to the brink of the water. Robert could hear them panting as they strained and struggled. A line from an old Border ballad he had once read was running through his head. He tried to concentrate on it.

'The bangisters will ding them down –'
What did it mean? Who were the bangisters? They sounded desperate characters. Robbers and outlaws themselves, most likely. The Border in the middle ages must have been like Circassia was now.

'And will them sair compel!'
He could remember no more of it. Beside him, Hassan uttered a word of command, and the silent struggle was intensified.

The storm had passed right away into the distance, and overhead a serene and beautiful evening sky was arching itself, cold and clear like a gemstone. Robert's eyes lost themselves in the tranquillity of the heavens, and he was only recalled to the earth by the splash which announced that the judgment to which he had been party had been duly executed. Hassan, who had been leaning slightly forward, sat back in his saddle. Arslan seemed immovable and unmoved. There was a low ejaculation, a grunt almost, from the man immediately behind Robert, and somebody, who might have been Giorgio, laughed nervously, a laugh which was instantly cut off. When Robert reluctantly brought his eyes down again, there was nothing to be seen but a ripple spreading in circles on the surface of the pool, now quite a small ripple, and that was all. One might have thought that it was the evening rise.

Chapter 8

THE END OF Ibrahim was by no means the end of the matter. Bitter recrimination still issued from the home of Aladji's family, who complained that Kherim had ridden away the morning after the trial, leading the black horse of which he had once more resumed the ownership without waiting for the formality of a decree to that effect, thus removing from their grasp the sole asset of the dead man. Their spokesmen were besieging Arslan with their demands. In the quarters assigned to the visiting noblewomen, the Bezleni princess, feeling that her character had not been sufficiently vindicated by the proceedings just concluded, passed most of her time in renewed lamentations. In their turn Arslan's ladies, so Giorgio reported, were becoming a little bored with the troubles of their guest, and were beginning to think that she protested too much.

Coming out of the house a day or so after the trial, Robert found Paka standing in the clearing. She was leaning against a tree and doing nothing in particular, but as soon as she saw that he was approaching, she turned away. Her lashes were very long and very dark. When she lowered her eyelids, all sorts of inscrutable emotions might be hidden behind them: on the other hand it might be that she had no thoughts at all, and that her mind was like the late season's butterfly which was drifting erratically among the bushes, trying to recapture the last savours of summer.

'Where is my dog?' he asked her (he knew the Circassian word for dog). 'Where is Fop?'

Her answer was incomprehensible, but Giorgio hurried up and stepped into the breach.

'The princess says the little dog is in the house. Does you Excellency wish it to be fetched?'

When restored to his master, Fop's first action was to scramble up on the divan where he installed himself to scratch and sleep, thus making it perfectly clear what indulgences he had been allowed in his previous quarters. It boded ill for the future unless he could be retrained into the model of an English dog, but before Robert had time to make progress with the rehabilitation of Fop from his acquired habits of native sloth and uncleanliness, a succession of visitors made their appearance.

The first to arrive was the Reverend Lewis Jones. Giorgio saw him coming in time to announce his arrival, but Mr Jones made an entrance considerably more hasty than was his wont. In fact he almost scuttled in, throwing apprehensive looks over his shoulder. Alas, though, the purpose of his visit turned out to be to discuss the *affaire* Ibrahim. It transpired that Mr Jones conceived that he had been in some way failing in his spiritual duty in absenting himself, albeit involuntarily, from the scene of the outlaw's end.

'But Ibrahim was a Moslem, at least officially,' protested Robert, 'so I do not see that your ministrations, even had he accepted them, would have benefited him.'

'At least I would have had the opportunity to proclaim to him, in his extremity, when his ears might have been open to receive the message, the news of the Gospel.'

'Surely you would then have taken from the man the only consolation he had, namely that as a Moslem he alone could be sure of Paradise, and that the rest of the world consisted of infidel dogs condemned to damnation?'

'I could not reconcile it with my conscience,' declared Mr Jones, his eyes flashing, 'to allow even a follower of the perverted creed of Mahomet to die in that error.'

Robert sighed. He found theological argument with Mr Jones uncongenial, and regretted having let himself be led into it. Then he saw that Mr Jones was in genuine distress.

'I cannot think, Mr Jones, after seeing this man Ibrahim at close quarters for some hours, that he would have derived much benefit from the ministrations of any man of religion. If there was a natural sceptic, it was he. He had a very glib tongue, but whether that will avail him when he comes to be judged according to the tenets of his own faith, which I believe owns to such a judgment, is a matter which perhaps fortunately, we need not concern ourselves with.'

'From what I have heard,' said Mr Jones, 'he was indeed a

man of wicked tongue. Such lies and falsehoods can rarely have been heard, even in this country, such calumniation of innocent persons.'

Robert was somewhat surprised to hear Mr Jones espousing the princess's case so warmly. Ibrahim's guilt or innocence on the rape count was still a matter of some doubt to him. It became clear, however, that Mr Jones was not so much concerned with the wrongs of the princess as filled with indignation on his own account.

'Ibrahim testified in the face of the multitude that he had himself hidden in the hill, and watched the woman coming away from my house, and that on more than one occasion.'

'Well, hardly that,' said Robert. 'He said, as far as I can recall, that he had watched from the hill and had seen the princess going up in the direction of your house, but he did not say that she entered it, on pretext of visiting the sacred grove. I do not know why anybody should have thought she went there for other than religious reasons.'

'It is the same in all countries,' declared Mr Jones. 'The old man will out! It was the same thing in Pant-y-dillon, Mr Wilton, the same thing, mark you. They accused me, my own church members, on the word of one traducer who set himself to ruin me, and not only myself did he seek to ruin but also an innocent woman who had sought me out for spiritual guidance when she was sore beset with her troubles.'

The circumstances of Mr Jones's departure from Pant-y-dillon were now becoming clearer to Robert, and it struck him as unfortunate that the same combination of circumstances seemed to be about to recur in Circassia, but he was to hear no more, for at that moment Giorgio announced that Hassan Bey was on the way to visit Robert. Mr Jones immediately took himself off.

Hassan came in, welcomed vociferously by Fop. He brushed the little dog aside, having evidently become accustomed to such demonstrations, and threw himself down on the divan at Robert's side.

'How is my friend?' he asked.

'I am well enough,' answered Robert. 'How is Hassan Bey?'

Hassan smiled but gave no answer. He drew his feet under him and sat cross-legged, concentrating all his attention on one of Robert's pistols which lay within his reach. He snapped it, cocked it, squinted down it, and took a casual aim at Fop who was still sniffing round his feet.

'What is the news?' asked Robert.

'There is no particular news,' answered Hassan. He put the pistol down. 'What did that old man want?' he asked.

'The priest came to talk about matters of religion,' said Robert, diplomatically.

'Matters of religion? Oh, oh! He looks very sad, that old man. Evidently his religion makes much trouble for him. Or is it his religion?' He burst out laughing.

'It is true that he is troubled by things which were said by the man, Ibrahim.'

'Ibrahim! Think no more of him. Do not trouble your heart about him, Jibrahil, the man is dead. Unfortunately, we still have the old woman, and she is a trouble-maker. All the time she makes complaints about the way she is treated here, yet she is a great expense to us. She would like to get another husband, but who is going to marry the old – ?' The expression he used was too idiomatic for Robert to understand.

Giorgio brought in more wood and piled it on the fire. The wood was wet, and a cloud of smoke filled the room. Hassan, hardened by years of custom, took no notice, but Robert began to cough, and his eyes to run. It must be possible to find out, he thought, how to build a chimney which would draw, even in a wooden hut. Not for the first time since his travels began, he regretted that he was not better equipped to remedy the invincible ignorance of the natives of the east towards the fabrication and properties of starch, of buttons, and even more important, of soap, his own dwindling supplies of which were rapidly becoming a matter of concern.

'What is your father going to do now?' he asked Hassan.

'My father will soon be returning to the assembly.'

'What assembly is this?'

'It is the meeting of chiefs which will decide what is to be done with the Shapsug people. Will you go with him, Jibrahil Bey?'

Robert remained silent. He felt the campaign was making little headway, due to causes of which he was as yet only vaguely aware. One thing, however, was quite clear: there could be nothing more fatal to the Circassian cause than the spectacle of the tribes pursuing their vendettas in the face of the Russian armies on their soil. The question was, could he persuade his host of that?

'Tomorrow I will speak with your father, Hassan,' he said.

'I will tell him,' said Hassan politely.

He was about to go when Robert noticed, lying in the divan in the place where the boy had been sitting, the missing volume of Horace. Obviously it was Hassan who had left it there. Hassan followed the direction of his eyes.

'I have brought you back your printed book,' he said gaily.

'Thank you,' said Robert, 'but keep it longer if you wish to.'

'No, I do not need it any more.' Then possibly feeling that some explanation was due, Hassan said, 'I wished to see what your English writing was like, so I took the book to read.'

'It is not in the English language,' said Robert. 'It is in Latin, a dead tongue which was spoken long ago.'

'Yes, I know that now, that is why I have brought back the book.' Hassan smiled again without embarrassment, and faded away, leaving Robert too much amused to be seriously annoyed by the fact that the boy must have taken his book to the Pole – how else could he have learned that it was not written in English?

Early next morning, long before Robert reached the point of sending Giorgio to the chief's house to announce his impending visit, both Arslan and Hassan were at his door with the news which had just come in. The Shapsug tribe had seized the Russian officers who had been circulating among them arranging the details of their 'resettlement' as a pacified people under Russian protection. The arms, which under the terms of the treaty were to be given up, when the tribe accepted protection and a large sum in roubles, had been hidden instead, and the fighting men whose numbers had been understated by various carriers of false information (which information, needless to say, the Russians had paid well for), had lain in ambush and fallen upon the carts containing the money, and on the military escort. The Shapsugs had killed many of the escort, but they had captured the officers unhurt. The officers were being sent as prisoners to the most remote villages of the region for safe-keeping, and the boy who had rushed into Arslan's house with the news had actually seen them passing through a place some miles to the north. There were three officers, reported the boy, and one of them seemed very much exhausted. The party had stopped to find food for him. The Russians were mounted behind Circassian horsemen, and each had one arm tightly secured behind his back. They were bound for another and yet more inaccessible village in the interior.

Within an hour the good news was round the valley, and the men, roused from sleep earlier than usual, gathered before the chief's house where they discussed the event again and again, telling the tale to each other with more and more embroidery and roaring with laughter at the Russian discomfiture. All talk of Shapsug treachery was naturally at an end. Men had also crowded on to the galleries outside Arslan's house where they let off their guns from time to time at nothing in particular. The women, perfunctorily veiled, gossiped at the back of their houses. Nobody was in the fields, for the serfs and the women servants, sensing that a gala occasion was afoot, went about their tasks even more erratically than usual. Some of the men were shoving around from one to another, without any particular malice, a man dressed like a serf, but distinguished by his height, his bulk, his blue eyes and his snub nose. Although he was a much bigger man than the Circassians who were baiting him, the serf made no attempt to protect himself, but reeled about with a helpless grin on his face, in a sort of protective buffoonery.

'Look at the Ivan!' said Hassan.

'Who is he?' asked Robert. They were crossing the open space to the chief's house, where an impromptu banquet was in course of preparation.

'He is a Russian soldier who ran away from the army,' was the answer. 'He was captured by our people who found him hiding in the bushes, and they sold him to my father for field work.'

Although Robert supposed there must be quite a number of such captives, he wished that Hassan had not chosen that moment to draw his attention to the unfortunate deserter. However, when they reached Arslan's house, he found an even more unpleasant surprise awaiting him. 'Shekhir Effendi' had returned and was at the old chief's side. Speaking little, never smiling, his presence none the less dominated the noisy expressions of joy which were going on all round, and Robert noticed that Arslan turned to the Pole rather anxiously from time to time, as if seeking his approval to the proceedings.

Later however Shekhir sought Robert out, rather to the latter's surprise, and seemed to be disposed for conversation. Robert asked him what effect he thought the capture of the Russian officers would have on the campaign. He himself was inclined to think that it would be met by immediate retaliation. The Pole discounted Robert's conjecture that there would now be an initiative on the part of the Russians.

'You do not understand,' he said. 'To the Russians, individuals mean nothing. The whole of the operations in the Caucasus are directed by the Emperor himself, and the Emperor is in St Petersburg. What does he care about the fate of his officers? His army are to him like ants, and how does one tell one ant from another? That a certain Major and a certain Captain have been so careless as to fail in their duty and let themselves be taken prisoners would mean a black mark against them in their records, if it was not on account of their records that they were sent to serve in the Caucasus in the first place. Who knows? They may be free-thinkers, intellectuals, liberals, even! Or perhaps they are the sons of liberals and intellectuals. The Emperor never forgets, even to the third and fourth generation. However distinguished they may be, such officers will never get promotion, so if they are captured, they are not much loss to him.'

'That may be so,' said Robert, 'but what about the breach of the treaty which the Shapsugs made with the local commander? They had signed it, they had agreed to lay down their arms, and it was after that they ambushed the convoy. Surely there will be retaliation?'

'I do not think the Russians will undertake a big operation just now. It is the wrong season, the gales on the coast will prevent them getting supplies, and above all, there is no indication of a major move from any of the forts.'

'How do you know that?' asked Robert.

The Pole smiled a slightly superior smile.

'From our observations, of course. Opposite every fort we

have a sentry, posted on the highest hill nearby, or else in the trees, to keep watch on the garrison.' (I could tell you of at least one fort where there is no such sentry, thought Robert.) 'The sentries are used to seeing the ordinary activities, the driving in and out of cattle, for instance, but they would be sure to notice any movement of troops.'

'What would the sentries then do?' asked Robert.

The Pole made an impatient movement. 'Why, they would alert the tribes. These fellows know their own country, I assure you. The Russians would find that they had walked out into a hornet's nest.'

Picturesque but hardly explicit, thought Robert, the whole point of his question being that unless the local tribe thought themselves to be directly threatened, they probably would not take any action. He swallowed his irritation, however, and observed that the total absence of maps made it difficult for him to appreciate the present state of the campaign from the point of view of the other side.

'Oh, there are maps,' said Shekhir unexpectedly. 'There is a Russian one, not very good, the five-verst map, but I have it. I will show it to you tomorrow, if you like.'

Shekhir was as good as his word. There was nobody else in the guest's house when he brought the map to Robert and they settled themselves on the divan. Robert told Giorgio to bring tea, and after that had been dispensed, he was free to study the map. The place names were of course in Russian, and Shekhir had to read them for him. They were most of them, apart from the names of the forts, which had been given patriotic Russian appellations, Russianized versions of the local name, which Robert had some difficulty in reconciling with the version which he had already heard. A good deal of the map, so far as it covered the territory they were now in, was plainly conjectural, but what it made clear to him for the first time was the degree to which the Circassian tribes were encircled by the Russians. The Russians were along the Kuban, to the north. They were on the rich, sub-tropical coast to the south, and in spite of what Shekhir said about fevers and deserters, they were firmly entrenched there and were recruiting from the local tribes, and they already held the ancient kingdom of Georgia to the south of the Caucasian chain. The Georgian military highway which ran through the Dariel defile, the main pass in the Caucasus, linked the Georgian capital, Tiflis, with the garrison towns on the north of the mountains. These towns were now so well established that some of them were becoming quite fashionable as watering-places, for there were many mineral springs, and numbers of society ladies and gentlemen frequented them in the season, drawing an additional thrill from their proximity to the seat of warfare. There was always the chance of seeing a real Circassian!

The military highway also separated the two centres of resistance, so dissimilar anyhow that they were most unlikely to combine, the dour, fanatical Mussulman peasantry on the Caspian side, fervid followers of Islam and dominated by their mullahs, and the aristocratic societies that made up the tribes living on the Black Sea coast and inland, from the Kuban to the main mountain chain. Robert, who had loosely referred to all the native inhabitants of the Caucasus as Circassians in his ignorant London days, had by now realized his error. The western tribes that made up the Circassian people numbered in some cases as few as five thousand souls, but they were rigidly ranged in the five castes, princes, nobles, freemen, vassals and slaves, each with reciprocal rights and duties. It was only when Robert had grasped the structure of the tribal society, and the precarious relations which existed between the tribes themselves, that he came to realize why federation, under the London-embroidered banners, was still far away. Yet the thing was not quite impossible, he thought. A union of tribes, casting aside their traditional differences to fight together for their homeland against a common aggressor, was a noble idea which must surely appeal even to the Circassian temperament, so fatally engrossed with internecine feuds and vendettas. Indeed, there was reason to think that the *idea* did appeal to many: witness the hours spent by Arslan Bey (and also, with reluctance, by himself) in those interminable conferences of ceremony. Alas, the hope of seeing any practical results from these confrontations was beginning to recede.

Robert attempted to voice something of this to Shekhir Effendi, but that strange man listened to him in silence and without response. Robert grew tired of trying to draw the other out, and put a direct question.

136

'Is it known what are the numbers of the Russian garrison at Soukhum-Kale?' This was an old town on the coast. The Russians had gained a foothold there about ten years before, and had established a fort, since when the local tribe, the Azras, had come into a reluctant alliance with them.

'At Soukhum-Kale? I should say there are about –'

The Pole pulled himself up as if he had been about to let out some secret of great importance to him. Instead of completing his sentence, he laughed and looked aside. 'But of course it is very difficult to say. To begin with, not all the garrison are Russians. They have a number of Azra men serving with them, that is the Russian system, you know, to integrate their local recruits into their ranks rather than to form special regiments which I understand is your English practice. The idea is both to Russianize these recruits as far as possible, and at the same time to keep them under surveillance. I do not think, though, that the Azras could be relied upon to fight with the Russians on all occasions.'

'Would they then rise against the rest of the garrison?'

The Pole shrugged his shoulders.

'Perhaps, but I do not think it would be very probable. They would more likely just slip away and go back to their villages.' He hesitated, and seemed to choose his words, or rather to overcome some deep hesitation at speaking at all, but then he went on with more feeling than Robert had yet seen him display.

'Think of the unhappy thousands, Mr Wilton' (why did he use the English name, Robert wondered, instead of the honorary Circassian title which Robert had been given, and in any case, how did the Pole come to know the English name at all?), 'who have been pressed into the Russian service, who are struggling helplessly in the net, forced to fight, many of them, against their own countrymen! There are many of my own people here, in the army of the Caucasus, who have been in just that position –' he broke off, apparently overcome with emotion.

'How many Poles are there in the Caucasus, would you say?' asked Robert. He was anxious not to let this promising opening peter out, as did so many of Shekhir's conversational gambits.

'Yes, I am a Pole,' said the other. Although reluctant to

137

impart information, the Pole seemed equally unwilling to admit any statement of fact of which he was not himself the source. 'To answer your question, Mr Wilton, there are six thousand Poles in Tiflis alone at the present time.'

'Good heavens, that is a very large number, is it not?' said Robert, but his voice was drowned by Shekhir Bey's rising tide of passion.

'That figure represents thousands of mourning Polish homes, thousands of Polish families, which have lost one, two, or all of their sons.

'After the Rising, Poles were deported wholesale and sent eastwards into Russia. I was a boy of nineteen then, Mr Wilton, but I fought. Here is the scar –' he put his finger on his left temple, and Robert looking at it saw that the bare skin which made the hair grow so far back was in fact wrinkled and discoloured, the mark of an old wound. '*That* was a Russian lancer. I have other scars too, which I could show.' He indicated various parts of his body, but to Robert's relief did not attempt to expose them further. 'The doctor who eventually treated them, a Russian but a good man, said he would not have believed it possible that any man could have received such a wound as I had in my stomach, and yet live.' For the first time he laughed with some humour. 'Probably it was the cold that saved me. I was left for dead, lying on the freezing ground. That froze my blood and kept it in my body. The doctor said that even our winter was on the Polish side. That was about all we had on our side – that, and our bodies.'

Robert, summoning up his recollections of recent Continental history, thought that the Polish insurrection of which he spoke had taken place some eight to ten years ago. In that case, Shekhir Effendi, if he had been aged nineteen at the time of that event, was a much younger man than Robert had previously imagined him to be. Perhaps it was the wound which had shorn away much of his hair that aged him and gave him such a curiously bleak appearance. His eyes too were the most extraordinary colour. Robert previously thought they were light green and expressionless, but they seemed to flash fire as the Pole dilated on his national grievances.

'And what did you do after you recovered?' asked Robert, with curiosity.

The Pole shrugged his shoulders, a favourite gesture with him.

'I was incorporated into the Russian army. What alternative was there? My country was in chains, my family proscribed. I could not return home.'

So you served voluntarily in the Russian army, thought Robert. Aloud he said,

'These six thousand of your countrymen in Tiflis, are they there as deportees, or are they also serving in the Russian army?'

'It does not matter. They are all ready and waiting for the call of liberty.'

This was hardly informative. Robert tried again, although he was conscious that the conversation on his side was becoming an interrogatory.

'Are there many of your countrymen with the Circassians, do you know?'

Shekhir sprang to his feet.

'Wherever the struggle is carried on in the name of Liberty, wherever there are free men fighting the Russian oppressors, there you will find a Pole,' he declared, gazing round as though he expected to see a banner waving before his eyes. There was nothing, however, in the open space before the house except a figure half visible, hanging about in the undergrowth, but whether attempting to get away or to approach them was not clear. Used to the openly-demonstrated curiosity of the natives, who made nothing of standing directly before the entrance to his quarters and studying all within, Robert's attention was caught by the semi-crouching man, particularly as he then raised himself to his full height. It was the Russian prisoner who turned his face towards them with an expression of such acute misery that even at this distance Robert was struck by it.

The Pole had also remarked the man, apparently. He gave a stifled exclamation, then muttering some excuse about having to go to the chief, he left the clearing by the side opposite to where the Russian was standing. The Russian made a move as if to follow him, then drew back among the branches. Later Robert noticed the Russian hanging round at the back of the guest's quarters, still with the same hangdog look and the same air of wanting to approach, but not quite daring to. Finally, Robert sent Giorgio to ask him what he wanted, but Giorgio came back and said the man had gone away.

Next morning the rising sun dissipated the chill and dripping mists and promised to shine brilliantly all day. In spite of the cold nights, the flowers were blooming all round in a late efflorescence, white and purple flowers mostly, in the forest, in the long tangled grass of old clearings, in the cracks of the rocks. The high mountains came back into view. Away to the south was a revelation : the main chain of the Caucasus, spread across the horizon. Up and up rose the distant mountains, steeper and steeper grew their sides, the striated cliffs of rock which seemed to be falling sideways, shrugging off the surviving trees which clung haphazardly to the ledges as if terrified at the gulfs beneath. Cliffs of black rock fell vertically from a towering height, and above them, snowy pinnacles shot into the sky at angles so sharp that they might have been cut out of paper. These were the regions of snow and ice where even the hardy Circassians feared to go.

By midday the visions had faded, however. Clouds came up, and a hot wind began to blow unexpectedly from the east. Mr Jones, who had picked up various pieces of local lore, said that this wind was unhealthy and generally brought fever. Whether this was the case, or whether the fever was the result of the drinking-bout the day before, Hassan succumbed to it, and a message came down to the guest's house asking for medicine. Robert sent quinine, and instructions as to taking it (he knew better than to counsel quiet repose in a quiet room, as he knew this was quite unattainable). When he went up to see his patient the next day, he found Hassan considerably better, although he was lying in the midst of a hurly-burly which made Robert's head reel. Hassan raised his head on Robert's approach.

'Your bitter medicine is strong, Jibrahil Bey! It is stronger than our willow bark. I fought with it all night and this morning, as you said, I am cured. But I am tired.'

'I said I would cure you,' said Robert. He sat down beside the boy. The other men who were sitting and lounging round got up and moved unobtrusively outside, where they settled themselves once more in a circle and resumed their chatter. The air in the house was thick with the aftermath of their occupation, the dominant odour being, as ever, that of the sheepskin caps which were rarely removed, although some of their owners were now searching them in the sunlight for insects.

Hassan raised himself and fumbled beneath the divan. He unearthed something wrapped in an old piece of rag tied at the corners. Undoing this parcel, he disclosed an object like a collar, or perhaps a bracelet, which he handed to Robert.

Robert took it and examined it with interest. He could not tell whether the ornament was intended to go round the neck or the wrist, it seemed an awkward size for either. But it was unquestionably made of gold, and most elaborately and perfectly worked. The scrolled terminals of the circle ended in sphinxes, female sphinxes, for the breasts were clearly delineated, with their heads crowned with laurels. In their paws the sphinxes held rings which were intertwined to clasp the two ends of the circle together. It was a perfect work of art, clearly not Circassian, but the product of some older and superior civilization.

'It is very beautiful,' Robert said, handing it back to Hassan. 'Where did it come from?'

'It was found in an old grave near Soudjuk-Kale. There is an ancient city there, all in ruins and buried underground. It used to be full of gold and silver. Whole coffins have been dug up there, full of money.'

'Are there any of these coffins left now?' asked Robert, smiling.

'No, they have all been taken since long ago. Besides, the Russians are there now. The place is near their fort.' Hassan held out the gold circle to Robert. 'Take it, Jibrahil Bey, it is yours.'

Robert drew back, making gestures of polite refusal.

'No, no, you are too generous, I cannot take it. It is too great a gift.'

Much as he would have liked to possess it, he had nothing approaching the value of the gold circlet to give in exchange, he thought rapidly, unless he parted with one of his English pistols, which he knew Hassan coveted, but he was not going to do that. Hassan however continued to press the ornament on him, and was really distressed when Robert persisted in his refusal to accept it. It was at this point that Paka joined them, the first time Robert had seen her for some days. She said something rapidly to her brother which Robert could not understand, and pointed to the gold circle, now in Hassan's hands.

'He will not take it,' said Hassan.

Paka took the ornament from him and looked at it critically. Outside a man began to sing softly in a high falsetto which crept over and round the tones. The song was a popular one, and Robert could catch and understand most of the words. 'The black-eyed girl . . .' crooned the singer, with many a shake and quaver, 'high on the hills . . .' Then came a mournful-sounding refrain,

'Oh, your two black eyes
Flash fire into my soul!'

'It is a bad thing,' said Paka at last. 'Heathen!' She ran her finger over the sphinx breasts. 'It is not a good thing to have.'

Hassan snatched it back from her quite roughly. Paka made no protest, but smiled contemptuously. Hassan pulled up the sleeve of his drab woollen tunic, disclosing a gay silk shirt below. He slid the circle up his arm and passed it above his elbow, then pulled his sleeve down again with a defiant expression. Paka continued to look aloof and contemptuous. With a groan Hassan lay back again on the divan.

'Hold my hand, Jibrahil Bey, as you did last night. Cure me – I am sick again.'

Robert took the wrist extended to him and felt the pulse. It was perfectly normal, he thought.

'You are cured already,' he said.

'How do you know that?' Paka pushed herself between them, her eyes now bright with interest. 'Hold my hand also, Jibrahil Bey, and tell me if I am well or not well.' She put her hand into Robert's. It was warm and firm, a plump little hand. He could feel the tips of the fingers slightly calloused. He glanced again at Hassan's hand, so much finer boned and lighter in colour than his sister's, lying limply on the divan. Then he solemnly felt Paka's pulse, prolonging the contact while her wrist jumped and quivered in his grasp. The warmth of her hand was not unpleasant, He remembered how, shortly after his arrival, she had come down to the guest's quarters one day with a can full of the small wood strawberries which grew in cover so thick that they were barely flushed with pink, yet they were ripe and warm to the touch. He had recoiled slightly from the idea that the fruit had been gathered by those somewhat grubby fingers, but all the same the strawberries had been delicious, and they were the only ones he had had in quantity, since Giorgio did not have the patience to pick them.

Both brother and sister were waiting for his verdict. Robert thought he had held the hand long enough. He cudgelled his brain for something to say.

'Your health is excellent,' he said at last. 'It should give you a long and happy life.' He hesitated for a second, and then went on, 'and many children.'

Paka tossed her head at this, but did not seem entirely displeased. It was Hassan who turned pettish.

'You do not care if I die,' he said, eyeing them both malevolently.

'You are not going to die. You could ride a hundred miles today.'

Hassan groaned again and lay back. Paka rushed to his side and held his head protectively. Robert felt there was nothing for it but to leave them.

It was Paka who ran after him, disregarding the loungers outside. He was halfway to his quarters when she caught him up and stood in front of him so that he was unable to pass.

'How many children shall I have?' she asked.

Robert thought for a minute. 'Ten,' he answered. 'All boys, all tall, as straight as that tree.' He pointed to a pine whose bare trunk towered to a vast height before it showed any sign of branch or leaf.

'What will their names be?'

'You will have to start choosing the names now, for so many.' Paka looked baffled. 'Shall I help you?' Robert dropped his voice to a more confidential tone.

Paka burst out laughing. 'Ten children! You have promised it.' Then in her usual exasperating way she ran off to herd goats, or tend poultry, leaving these promising beginnings unfulfilled.

Chapter 9

How LONG HASSAN's convalescence would have prolonged itself in the ordinary way was uncertain, but the news which brought him hurrying down to Robert's quarters a few days later, in restored health, alert and excited, concerned the Russian prisoners. They had escaped from the village where they were being held, and were presumed to be trying to make their way to the coast. Cast adrift without horses, without food, in an unknown and hostile country, with the frosts and rains of autumn imminent, their chances of success were reckoned slight, but what irked the Circassians most was the thought of losing these valuable hostages. It was deemed essential to recapture them before they lost themselves hopelessly and wandered and froze and starved to death. The whole village turned out on the man-hunt.

Robert enjoyed it, in spite of himself. It was quite aimless, as no one had the slightest idea what route or routes the escapees had taken, or where to look for them. The chase resolved itself into a series of exhilarating gallops up stony ravines and down through the towering forests, men and horses going hell for leather with the excitement of it all, but the noise, thought Robert, would have sent any fugitive instantly into a cover, of which there was plenty. From time to time the pursuers fanned out and began to quarter likely areas in a more systematic way, each man going at walking pace and making a solitary way for himself, circling in and out of the trees and the sudden outcrops of rock. In that enormous empty landscape one would have thought that any human movement could be instantly detected, but Robert riding with all his nerves stretched, inhaling the sharp, aromatic air with keen appreciation while his horse, which he left pretty much to itself, plodded indifferently over all the obstacles of the terrain, found that he was being constantly deceived into imagining movement where there was none. What seemed like something white waving high up on the hillside turned out to be the curve of falling water in the sunlight: the fuzz of dark green pines which clothed the mountain sides and strode along their crests took the shapes of men which he could actually see stepping forward on the skyline. At one time, when he was far from the rest of the party and only the noise of his own progress broke the utter hush of the afternoon, he became conscious of a strange whirring noise coming from somewhere in the dried stream bed where he had found a path of a sort. It might be an injured man groaning . . . He pressed forward, and came on a pool of brown, stagnant water. At his approach the noise ceased utterly, and something flopped into the pool, to be followed by further splashes. It must have been frogs, he concluded. He never knew before that frogs could make a whirring noise, but there was nothing else in sight to make it. The only birds were either tiny creatures no larger than a butterfly, which made infinitesimal movements in the cover of the bushes, or else crows which flapped heavily out of reach, and these carrion birds croaked, they did not whir. When the frogs had quieted, there was complete silence again, save for the crackling and buzzing of insects in the bushes, drunk with the heady smell which the afternoon sun had brought out, the smell of aromatic leaves and dried stems, the sweetness of the purple, yellow and white flowers which starred the bushes, mingled with an occasional putrid undertone.

The human chase at that moment seemed a hopeless one. Even the air which had begun to jump and dazzle on the bare rocks was deceiving. The beauty of the afternoon, Robert knew, would not last. He could see that heavy purplish clouds had come down on the hills to the east. It was just then that he really thought he saw the quarry. Something dun-coloured was moving cautiously round the side of a hill ahead of him, moving in and out of sight among the small oak trees which still held their leaves. Clearly it was a man trying to avoid observation. His heart thumping furiously, Robert pushed his weary horse forward: there was no need to avoid noise when he could easily run down a man on foot, and he comforted his scruples by telling himself that the Russians had no hope of survival unless they were recaptured. The thrashing of the oak wood ahead indicated that the man in front had seen him, and was endeavouring to get away, into a ravine where a horseman could not follow. Dodging the branches which slapped across his face, and tearing away a 'wolf's tooth' creeper which had attached itself to his shoulder, Robert followed at his best pace, catching fleeting glimpses of the brown object – surely a man's shoulder – moving ahead of him. Something tossed in the undergrowth like a hand thrown up, and gave him cause to pause. Could the Russian be armed? It seemed most unlikely, but from being the ardent pursuer, Robert became the prudent stalker. He pulled his horse to a standstill and for a moment sat in silence trying to see through the branches, but there seemed to be nothing but empty air where a minute before the brown object had been. Then the branches began to thrash again – the quarry was on the move – and Robert struck his feet into his horse's sides. The horse crashed through the undergrowth, stones shooting from under its feet, and Robert found himself looking at one of the dun Circassian cows, wild and scrawny beasts, which usually roamed at large on the lower slopes of the hills. The cow was standing halfway up a bank so precipitous that only a goat would normally have attempted to scale it, and was tearing at the leaves remaining on a tree which grew within its reach. The cow stared at Robert with great affrighted eyes, and then made off, with a prodigious spattering of dung, into another part of the ravine.

That was that! Robert looked round at the shimmering landscape before him. Above the oak forest grew the pines, clothing the hills to the very top. Where the pines ended, the cap of cloud was creeping down, covering the harshness of the rock. In the great misty bowl of land through which he had ridden the ridges tossed and tumbled like the waves of the sea, clothed also in a thick shoulder-height growth of sharp-scented bushes. The air from the pine woods blew down the hill into the sun-heated valley, and created sudden turbulences which swirled the leaves round in dusty spirals. There was a long low rumble of thunder away to the south-west, and a flash of lightning. The sky in that quarter was turning a dark purply-black.

It was time to return, or to find shelter. Since his earlier adventure when he had got lost and blundered into the Russian camp, Robert had been most careful to take note of his bearings,

146

and he was pretty sure of the homeward route. The way back, he thought, always seemed shorter than the way coming.

That might be so in other places, but in this tangled country the return was by no means as easy as he had expected, and his progress was wearisomely slow. A sudden clap of thunder overhead made him jump, and a shower of warm drops followed, just as if a giant rag had been wrung out over his head. Looking up, Robert was disconcerted to see how much darker the sky had become. He kept his eyes thereafter resolutely on the next landmark, which was an outcrop of rock dominated by a single pine tree with most of the bark stripped off, and he urged his horse towards it. But before he reached the rock he heard the rain sweeping up behind him.

He got to shelter only just in time. Under the side of the hill was not a cave but an overhanging depression sufficient to keep off the worst of the downpour. He crouched in it, holding on to the horse's reins with hands which steadily grew more cold and numb as the rain ran over them. At last it drew off, and he emerged from shelter and prepared to ride on among the shivering and dripping trees.

In which direction? Looking round, he realized that he had again been misled, or had misled himself. His shelter rock could not have been the rock he had marked, and he did not recognize the stretch of country ahead of him at all. However, leading down the valley was a definite track, and he decided to follow it. It led through places where wood had recently been cut, and in the distance he thought he heard the barking of dogs, a sure sign that there were people living somewhere near. Actually, there was only a little more of the narrow path to negotiate and he found himself in a village, as usual so well concealed among the trees that it was impossible to detect from any distance.

Actually the few houses hardly justified the name of village, and they were not even the fairly roomy timber-roofed structures Robert was used to seeing. Some of these dwellings were more like windowless caves, roofed with earth on which the grass was growing. At first Robert thought these were cattle byres, until he saw the children disappearing into the mouth of one of them, and veiled women standing nearby. In the centre of the village there was the usual open space of trampled earth littered with odds and ends of refuse and the ashes of old fires in front of the houses. A group of men was collected there, a ragged shock-headed crew, and they must have been engaged with some occupation which interested them extremely, for they paid no attention to Robert's arrival, even though announced by the chorus of dogs, until he was within a few paces of them. Then indeed they spun round, reaching for their weapons, and Robert was seized with qualms : he had not expected at this early hour to find a mass assembly of the inhabitants, and some of the men looked to him pretty villainous types. However, when they came forward and beat off the dogs so that Robert was able to dismount, he was relieved to see one familiar face. That of a man he had seen in Arslan's house, one of the old prince's feudatories, Azamat by name. Just now he seemed to be in high good spirits, and he and the rest of the men stood there grinning and jabbering. Looking past the group, Robert saw what had been the focus of all their eyes to the exclusion of himself.

It was two men, sitting on the ground beside some stones which had been piled up for a fireplace. They were seated, it first appeared to him, in the midst of a midden, but then he realized that the bones, the odds and ends of vegetable refuse, and the occasional brickbat, had been thrown at the men, and some of these missiles had reached their target. He saw that some of the children clustered nearby were still clutching an unsavoury object they had not yet had time to launch.

One of the two men presented a picture of utter exhaustion. He was slumped in an attitude of collapse, and he seemed also to have injured one leg, which was stretched out stiffly in front of him. He wore a long overcoat of European cut, splashed with mud and ragged round the hem, and his head was bare. The other man, who struggled to his feet at Robert's arrival, had a Circassian bourka draped round him, but underneath it a military tunic and trousers, also muddied and torn. On his head this figure wore a knitted woollen skull cap, a curious article of dress which did not belong to either east or west. He was not young : the hair that showed under his cap was grizzled, as were his moustaches. As he got on to his feet he swayed a little, but for all his dirt and exhaustion he retained a certain soldierly bearing.

'Russians!' said Azamat, grinning broadly, pointing to the pair.

The older man stared at Robert and Robert at him with growing recognition. The hollow cheeks, the white moustaches – it was the elderly lieutenant Robert had encountered in the Russian camp, the old officer who had taken his boots off. The old man recognized him.

'Ah, it's you, monsieur,' he said in his mangled French. 'Might I trouble you to ask these people to give us some food? We have not eaten anything for twenty-four hours. I am an old campaigner and I don't mind hardships, but my friend as you can see is injured, and he is about done. I have asked them myself,' he added, 'but they don't understand my Tartar.'

'Food – of course!' said Robert. He turned to Azamat. 'Well, they are Russians all right, but where is the third? There should be three of them.'

'There are only these two,' said Azamat.

'How did you catch them?'

The men grinned.

'They walked in by themselves, this morning,' said Azamat. We heard the dogs, and there they were. One of them has hurt his leg.'

'Well, you have caught them all right,' said Robert, 'and now you will have to give them food, if you want to keep them alive.'

There was general hilarity at this.

'Russians are like your Excellency, then, they have to eat every day,' said Azamat.

'Twice a day at least,' said Robert, 'for the large one.'

Azamat laughed and said something to one of the other men, who lazily walked off to one of the nearest cottages, to return a few minutes later with some hunks of bread under his arm, and a jug in his hand. He put these down on the ground within reach of the prisoners, and stood back.

'There you are, Ivan,' said Azamat. 'Now you can eat.'

The lieutenant nodded at Robert without saying anything, then he lowered himself painfully into a crouching position and reached for the bread which he proceeded to break into pieces. He took up the jug, looked into it and sniffed at it, then began to sop the pieces of bread in the liquid. The younger man still sat embracing his drawn-up knee, with his head down on his arms. The lieutenant touched his shoulder and when the young

149

man lifted his head, the lieutenant said something in a low voice in Russian and put a piece of bread into the other's hand. Robert meanwhile turned to Azamat.

'Have you sent a message to Arslan Bey to tell him that you have captured two of the Russians?'

Azamat shrugged his shoulders. 'There is no hurry. We will let Arslan Bey know presently.'

'Arslan Bey should know the news as soon as possible. A messenger will have to go to him.'

'All the horses are tired,' said Azamat, a patent untruth.

'Then take mine!' said Robert.

The animal had in fact been led away, he knew not where, while he was talking to Azamat.

'Ride your Excellency's horse?' said Azamat. 'Well, in that case . . . Ismail!' He called one of the young men over to him and a rapid interchange followed. Ismail went off in a leisurely way, and came back a few minutes later, mounted on Robert's horse. It did not look a particularly dashing steed with its unclipped coat, and stumpy legs, but under its present rider it caracoled effectively before setting off at a gallop in the direction of the coast.

'On your Excellency's horse, Ismail will fly like the wind,' said Azamat.

The two Russians had by this time finished the bread, both eating with steady ferocity. The younger man seemed to have revived somewhat. As Robert watched, the lieutenant picked up the jug and raising it to his lips, took a long pull. He lowered the jug, looked into it, and passed it to the young officer. The younger man drank avidly, then he put the jug down and passed his hand over his mouth, and pushed back the tousled hair which had fallen over his face. As Robert had suspected, he saw the face was that of the ensign Soutkine, now dirty and haggard, but still smiling and child-like. Soutkine caught Robert's eye and smiled at him, then indicated his foot with a deprecating gesture as if apologizing for his inability to rise.

Just at that moment an urchin standing among the onlookers hurled a ripe, a very over-ripe plum or some other dark red coloured fruit. It struck the bourka of the elderly lieutenant who was once more standing up, and burst into fragments, some of which dropped to the ground while a mess of juice and skin adhered to the hair of the bourka. The lieutenant who had barely started at the impact took no notice, but Azamat shouted at the child, who ducked behind the others.

The young man, who had put up his hand to shield his face from the flying fragments, looked up and laughed.

'You have had your food, Ivan, now you can sing for us,' said Azamat. Then he recollected his duties and turned to Robert:

'What about your Excellency? Does your Excellency wish for food?'

'Thank you, no,' said Robert. 'I am not hungry. I ate yesterday.'

This raised another laugh, but in truth Robert had forgotten the pangs of his own hunger in the face of the pitiable condition of the escaped prisoners: and knowing that in most Circassian homes the arrival of a guest of honour meant slaughtering some animal and quite a few hours of preparation, he did not think it politic to assert his own needs. What had been given to the Russians was very probably the only food immediately available.

A man came out of one of the cave-houses, stooping under the low doorway. In his hand he held a musical instrument of triangular shape with three strings. Robert wondered if this was the same thing as the balalaika he had heard the soldiers playing in the Russian camp, but what would a Russian balalaika be doing here in a Circassian village? The lieutenant accepted it from the man, and was looking at it doubtfully, when the young ensign reached up for it and laid it across his knee. He twanged the strings experimentally and twisted the pegs to which they were attached. Then he launched into a Russian song, accompanying himself by a few thrumming chords on the instrument. It was a simple plaintive ditty of several verses, each ending with a refrain which sounded something like
'dee dee dee dee dee dilly.'
The Russian syllables slid caressingly out of the young man's mouth, then
'dee dee dee dee dilly!'
The song came to an end. The Circassians could understand it no better than Robert, but they seemed pleased.

'What does it mean?' asked Robert.

The young man gazed into the watery sun. 'A boy is in love with a girl . . . on Monday he falls in love, on Tuesday he suffers, on Wednesday he is waiting for an answer, dee dee dee dee dilly – but by Sunday he has changed his mind, and so it goes on . . . dee dee dee dee dilly.'

He struck a minor chord and began to sing 'The black-eyed girl'. Robert could not tell if he really knew the Circassian words or whether he was just imitating them, but if so, the imitation was excellent, and so was his rendering of the shakes and quavers of native music. His last chord ended on a fine authentic wailing note.

This time there was no doubt the bystanders were delighted. The bundled-up women chattered under the veils and ventured to come a little nearer without incurring reproach from the men. Another child, a little girl this time, was pushed forward (but Robert noticed that none of the unveiled but nubile maidens was allowed to appear) with another plum, or apple it could be, in her hand. She approached to within ten feet of the prisoners before throwing the fruit. It went wide, but the ensign was able to put out his hand and catch it. Laying the musical instrument on a stone he waved his hand to the little girl and bit into the fruit. He took several large mouthfuls, then he offered the rest to the old lieutenant who waved it aside.

'Our own boys have picked up that song,' said the lieutenant, referring to 'The black-eyed girl'. 'It's quite a favourite with them. You hear that squalling noise going on all over the camp. It always sounds like cats to me. Still, they are not bad lads, the Tartars of these parts – not like those devils over on the east, I can tell you. When I was serving in the Army of the Right I got to know plenty about them.'

He sat down again on the stone and huddled the bourka round him. Robert was on tenterhooks. It puzzled him that the Russians had not been secured in any way, knowing, as he did so, the partiality of the Circassians for loading their prisoners with chains and fetters. Possibly the villagers thought the Russians were too exhausted to renew their attempt to escape and moreover the ensign was hampered by his injured foot. But Robert had no doubt that they were regretting their enforced surrender and had no intention of prolonging their submission. The lieutenant, with his bluff talk and old soldier's ways, was a cunning old fox. As for the young man, there was no way of telling the state of his injured foot, but it seemed to be no longer paining him. His head was thrown back, his eyes closed against the sunlight, and his dishevelled hair was falling across his forehead. But he opened his eyes to gaze round him with an active interest, and in spite of his state it was clear the young man had no intention of abandoning himself to despair.

The ring of half savage men who stood or lounged round them (for these villagers, except for Azamat, were far more primitive than any Circassians Robert had encountered so far) were for the moment in high good humour. But were the prisoners to make the slightest move to escape, Robert had no doubt that they would be cut down at once. He longed for the arrival of Arslan to take charge of a situation which he felt might at any time be beyond his power to control.

'Well, now you have had a song, where are you going to put them?' he asked Azamat.

'We shall keep them safe,' replied Azamat. 'Ghirei has a cellar under his house. We only need to dig the pit deeper, to hold the two of them. The boys are going to do it now.'

Some of the younger men began to rouse themselves at this, still in quite good humour, but without any great enthusiasm, and move off to one of the houses. There were still quite a number of spectators left, however, and Robert noticed in particular one old man wearing a particularly shaggy fur bonnet, who sat on the ground a little apart from the rest, with an arsenal of weapons slung round his person, and his carbine across his knees. He was not a genial looking old man, and he kept his unwinking gaze fixed on the captives. Robert hoped very much that Arslan would not tarry.

The two prisoners were talking quietly to each other in Russian, but on seeing that Robert's attention was once more with them they reverted to French. It appeared that the younger man had made some observation to the other about the circumstances of their capture.

'All the same, these tribesmen are not so bad,' persisted the other. 'What happened – well, I could have told Andrei Sergueievitch never to trust the word of a Tartar, but he wouldn't have listened. You young men, you are all the same.'

'You were never young yourself, Pavel Pavlovitch?'

'Ah, yes, a long time ago! I have been in the Caucasus for nearly thirty years. I served under Alexei Petrovitch' (he meant General Yermoloff, who formerly commanded in the Caucasus). 'It was after an assault we made that Alexei Petrovitch himself called me up to him and said he was going to recommend me for the cross. God knows what happened about that, they never gave it to me. Oh yes, I don't deny I might have made the same mistake, when I was young.'

'What is the old one talking about?' asked Azamat. He had not gone with the young men to dig the pit in the floor of Ghirei's house deeper, but remained in the sun with the loungers.

'He is talking about the battles he has fought in,' answered Robert.

'I can see he has fought in battles,' said Azamat. 'For a Russian, he is not such a bad one.'

Then a sudden call in a child's high voice gave the first warning that horsemen were approaching. The child must have been up in the trees above the village, for nothing could be seen from below.Then the women came pelting down, hugging their veils over their heads, by the twisting paths between the field patches and made for the boltholes which were the entrances to their homes. The loungers sprang to their feet and seized their arms, and the rest of the men emerged from their houses. First a single horseman appeared, riding full tilt between the wreathed wattle fences, to be followed by another and another, about a dozen in all. Robert recognized some of them as Arslan's men. They galloped into the open space and exchanged shouts with the men who awaited them there. All remained in the saddle except the leader, who dismounted in haste, and Robert, who had expected to see Arslan Bey himself, or at least Hassan, saw with dismay that the new force was led by Shekhir Effendi. As usual he wore a tcherkessa tunic and fur cap, but no one would have mistaken him for a Circassian. The Circassian brave swaggered for preference in a tunic full of tears and patches, making up for this calculated negligence by the set of his cap, the richness of his arms or the quality of his silk shirt. The escort also presented an unusual appearance of uniformity, clad alike in dark tunics with high white sheepskin caps. The villagers wore a motley assortment of headgear: Azamat and one or two others sported the flat fur cap with a cloth crown which Robert had gathered to be the latest fashion: others, including the silent old man, wore bonnets made of what appeared to be a wild cat's skin, pulled down to their eyes.

The effect created by the group of dark-clad riders was strangely sinister. Shekhir Effendi himself appeared to be in a high state of excitement, and his scarred face was bone-white as he threw the reins on the neck of his horse and strode forward.

'Where are they?' he demanded of Azamat, without pausing to greet Robert.

For answer Azamat jerked his head in the direction of the Russians. The lieutenant, who was already standing, stiffened at the sight of the Pole. The young man began painfully to climb to his feet. As he did so he jarred the balalaika, which emitted a short harsh note.

Shekhir was wearing a dagger, and he had one hand on the hilt. The lieutenant's hand went to his belt – there was nothing there – and dropped again. Drawing his head in like an old badger he confronted the Pole.

'It's you then, old friend, Lieutenant Kropff?' Shekhir said, in French.

'Why don't you speak Russian, Monsieur Zletzki?' said the lieutenant. 'You know how to.'

'Because I am not a Russian, thank God.' The Pole clenched and unclenched his hands on the hilt of the dagger. He seemed to be in an ungovernable fury. The lieutenant looked at him steadily. The young man said something in a low voice in Russian, and the lieutenant without turning his head replied. The ensign staggered slightly, and would have fallen but for the stick on which he was supporting himself. The Pole turned to him.

'I think I know who you are. I have heard about you, Ensign Soutkine.'

'I have heard of you too, Monsieur Zletzki,' replied the young man. 'You were stationed at the Nicholas fort, were you not, when you went over to the other side. The fort was attacked at night, not so long afterwards, and the tribesmen got inside and killed all the officers. The Colonel's batman fired the magazine when there were less than a dozen of our men left, and a good many of your friends went to glory with them – but not you, it appears. My congratulations.'

'You are pleased to be humorous, Ensign Soutkine,' said Shekhir, 'but I am not a Russian nor do I owe any allegiance to Russia. I am a Pole!'

'That is to say, a Russian. There is no Poland now,' said the old lieutenant under his breath.

'But you held a Russian commission,' said the young man.

'And what if I did? Does that bind me? Does your Emperor command me? I was in Warsaw in '30. I was a man *then*, when you were in your cradle. I tell you, there are rivers of blood between us.'

'I too have seen blood, Zletzki,' said the other.

'Nothing will wipe it out,' went on the Pole unheeding, 'the blood that Russia has spilled, until every single Russian soldier is dead.'

The young ensign made no answer and it was the old lieutenant who retorted.

'You to speak like that! You are a traitor, and that is all there is to it. A Pole you may have been born, but you engaged yourself in the army, you accepted promotion, you took our commission, then you went over to the enemy. A Tartar may act like that, but it's in his nature to lie and cheat, he knows no better, but you are a civilized man, and a worse traitor for that! I would rather not breathe in the place where you are. You poison the air!'

The Pole looked at him with hatred, then gave a wintry smile.

'That can be cured, Lieutenant Kropff. Your fate is in my hands, and I can oblige you by ridding you of the necessity to breathe in my company.' He turned and gave a sharp command to the riders. Two of them got down in a leisurely way from their horses. Robert saw that they carried coils of ropes on their saddles, and these the men proceeded to detach. Robert was relieved to see this, rather than otherwise. It seemed to him to be only a wise precaution to make the prisoners secure pending the further enlargement of Ghirei's cellar: work on this could not have been carried very far, for the men had come flocking back to the scene of events and were watching these developments. But instead of approaching the Russians, the two men, at a further word from Shekhir, walked off in the direction of a large beech tree which grew at one side of the clearing. At the bottom the trunk was quite bare: a large and solid branch grew out, however, about fifteen feet from the ground. One of the men threw his rope over this branch at the second cast. The other man was not so clever. With all eyes upon him, he made a clumsy throw and his rope not only fell short, but became entangled in projecting leafage from which he was unable to dislodge it. Amid general amusement, he accepted the necessity of climbing the tree and walked round to the other side from which the trunk must have been more accessible, for a crashing and falling of twigs and leaves announced that he was scaling it.

Robert was still bewildered. He had not understood any of the words of command : they were outside his vocabulary. He turned to Azamat who was watching the scene with his good-humoured smile somewhat clouded, for an explanation, when his eye caught that of the dour old tribesman still sitting cross-legged on the ground nursing his gun. Under the shaggy hat which partially obscured his eyes, that worthy gave Robert an unmistakable wink. His face contorted into a smile of pure malevolence and he ran a finger round his neck, at the same time letting his head fall sideways.

A thrill of horror ran over Robert, leaving his heart beating violently. He took a step forward, but the three principal protagonists in the drama were oblivious of him. The Pole was saying something, he could not catch what, and there was no doubt the prisoners had understood what was in store. The face of the old lieutenant was grimmer and greyer than before, but he answered Shekhir stoutly enough.

'I am too old to worry which way my end comes. At any rate I shall not have to rot in your friends' prison pits.'

'And you, Monsieur Soutkine,' said Shekhir to the younger man. 'Are you afraid to die ?'

The young man at first seemed hardly to have heard the question. He had detached himself from the scene. At the head of the valley the clouds had parted to show a patch of tender blue sky. Against it there stood like a white finger pointing heavenwards a distant snow peak. The young man's eyes were fixed upon it. For a minute he continued to contemplate the distant mountains, then he brought his attention back to the immediate scene, the soaking ground, the trampled and rubbish-strewn grass, the silent, savage onlookers. It was so quiet that the rushing of the streams could be heard from the nearby hillsides. He sighed, and answered slowly, choosing his words with care :

'I can think of nothing so bad I have done in my life that I should be afraid to die. Perhaps I have not done all the good that I should – all that I *could* have done. The world is so beautiful, we should all be happy in it. It is not enough, I see it now, to do good to one's fellow human creatures when we have the chance, we need ourselves to create the opportunities. Perhaps I have failed in that, and if so I regret it. Is that an answer to your question, Monsieur Zletzki ?'

The Pole said nothing. His face was working as if he was about to burst into speech, but he flung round to give some final instruction to his men. The man who had climbed into the beech tree was now sitting astride the big branch making the two ropes fast. Joking comments were called up to him from the ground.

The young man said something to his companion, who replied to him in words which sounded strange in his incorrect French (perhaps he had not realized that he was not speaking Russian).

'It's a bad business, Nicolai Petrovitch, but there's no help for it. If it's God's will we can't go against it . . . At least we know we have done our duty, we have nothing to regret.' Then raising his voice he shouted at the Pole.

'As for you, you should be ashamed to live. You are a traitor!'

It was at this point that Robert stepped forward. He forced himself to be calm, to speak slowly and distinctly, and he heard his own voice saying in an almost supercilious tone :

'Just let us wait one moment, Shekhir Effendi. I am tolerably certain that you have no authority to deal with the prisoners in this very high-handed way. They are being held as hostages' (he knew the Circassian word for hostage, and used it) 'against the time when exchanges can be arranged. They are certainly far too valuable to be thrown away like this to gratify what I can only suppose, from what I have heard just now, to be a private grudge. Moreover, I am quite certain that that would not be the will of the Council of Chiefs. Nor, I can assure you, would it redound to the credit of the Circassian cause in foreign countries.'

The Pole's eyes were blazing.

'In everything you say you are mistaken, Mr Wilton. I have ordered the execution of the prisoners, which is a justified measure in view of their attempt to escape, because I have complete authority over them which I exercise on behalf of the Council. The Council has delegated to me the power to deal with them as I think fit.'

'Precisely,' riposted Robert. 'The power to deal with them – not to make away with them. That is entirely outside your authority.'

He was surprised at his own calmness as he contemplated the furious anger of the Pole.

'I have power of life and death over the prisoners,' retorted Shekhir.

'Was anything specifically said about death?' asked Robert. 'Of what conceivable use would it be to hang the hostages, even if that were compatible with the civilized treatment of prisoners?'

He was tolerably certain by now that he could command support from the onlookers around, other than Shekhir's followers, and these, he calculated, were considerably outnumbered by the villagers. He sensed that Azamat and his friends were by no means anxious to see their interesting and valuable captives taken out of their hands and strung up in summary fashion and although they could not understand many words of the argument, it must have been clear to them what it was about, for they were muttering between themselves.

'Hostages! Valuable hostages!' said Shekhir. 'Do you know what these two are? Let me tell you Mr Wilton. This one –' he pointed to the lieutenant – 'is a lieutenant, after thirty years' service in the Caucasus. No doubt he has told you of the campaigns he has seen. He has served here all his life. But he is poor, he is of an obscure family, and he has no influential friends. That is why he remains a lieutenant. Do you think the Emperor would concern himself with his fate?'

The old lieutenant said nothing and remained unmoving, but the ensign's leg suddenly gave way beneath him and leaning heavily on his stick he sat down again.

'And this one,' went on the Pole, pointing to him. 'You would never guess who he is, so let me tell you. He is a writer, a Moscow dilettante, no less, a pet of the ladies. He used to serve in a smart regiment, on drawing-room duty most of the time.'

The young man gave an exclamation and attempted to rise, but the lieutenant's hand on his shoulder pushed him down again. 'Then what is he doing here? Well, after writing some very pretty little stories and articles and other pieces, all very acceptable to authority, one day he forgot himself and published something which was not so acceptable. I don't know what it was, as I have never been privileged to read it. Perhaps he was a little too advanced in his ideas. Perhaps he allowed himself to use expressions which might have been read as critical of authority. At any rate, the Emperor did not miss it: he never misses anything of that sort. His eye is everywhere. Our young friend was sent off to the Caucasus at twelve hours' notice – as expendable gun-fodder. Do you think he is going to be ransomed or exchanged?

'The only one of them who is worth anything at all to the Russians is the third one, Captain Lopokoff. Where is he?' he asked the lieutenant.

'How should I be able to tell you?' was the answer. 'We agreed at the outset to separate, and he made his own way.'

'If the Captain has not been recaptured, clearly the search must go on,' said Robert. 'It is vital we should get back and inform Arslan Bey of the position as soon as possible. The man will be getting near the coast by now, while we are wasting time here.'

The last sentence he managed in Turkish for the benefit of Azamat, and noticed that some of the other men also seemed to understand and approve what was said. Robert now felt more certain of his command of the situation. The man sitting up in the tree began of his own accord to detach his two ropes, and presently threw them down to the ground. The only dissentient voice raised was that of the old man, who when he realized that the hanging had been countermanded, began to protest. But Azamat shouted him down, and the other men began to laugh and joke about his evident disappointment. Shekhir also appeared to have accepted the situation. It was as if his blood-thirsty fit and its thwarting had exhausted him for the time being. He even deferred to Robert in asking,

'What about these two here?'

'Azamat and his people can surely look after them,' replied Robert.

160

'Where are you going to put them?' Shekhir asked Azamat.

Azamat began to explain about the pit in the floor of Ghirei's house and its advantages from the security aspect, when Shekhir cut him short.

'See to it, then, that you do keep them safe. Don't trust them to one man alone, this Ghirei or whatever his name is.'

'We will guard them safely, Excellency,' replied Azamat. 'On my head be it.'

'On your head then,' rejoined the Pole. To Robert he said: 'They have already dug their way out once.'

'Is that how they escaped?' asked Robert.

'Yes, the men put them in a cellar under one of the village houses which had a wooden lining. They made a tunnel behind the wood, and dug their way up outside the house.'

'Well, they won't get away with that twice,' said Robert.

Shekhir gave a bleak smile, then prepared to mount his horse. Someone without being told led forward a horse for Robert, which he mounted. It was better than his former one. From his elevation in the saddle Robert looked down at the scene. The early morning mist had condensed and was dripping from branch to branch, while on all sides the ceaseless running of water could again be heard. The gap in the clouds had closed, and the sky was a dull and uniform grey. The young Russian was once more sitting as he had been when Robert first saw him, with his head bowed on his arms, either sunk in dejection at the prospect of a further period of incarceration, or overcome with the pain of his injured foot, and the lieutenant was kneeling beside him with a hand on the young man's shoulder. Neither raised his head when Robert and the Pole, together with their followers, wheeled round and prepared to go. The horses broke almost at once into a gallop, Robert riding in the van with Shekhir. They took the steepest path up the hillside, disdaining the longer way round, and the women who had gone back to their work in the fields looked up from where they were crouching as the warriors passed, and watched under their veils until the men were out of sight.

Once the riders were out of the gloomy valley and round the shoulder of the hill, the mist lifted. All the way lay clear before them to the sea. A golden bird whizzed up out of the thicket on Robert's right hand and was out of range before anyone had a

161

hope of hitting it, but that did not deter one of the escort from trying a long shot.

'Don't waste powder and lead!' shouted Shekhir in a peremptory voice, but he smiled at Robert and shrugged his shoulders. Although on the open slopes the brush was as high as a man's waist, the ground below was firm and the horses cantered steadily on. The clouds had rolled back behind the mountains and the sun was shining overhead, though it was too cold for the trampling of the horses to release the heady aroma from the crushed herbage which Robert had smelt the day before. The last of summer, he realized, was over. But his spirits rose until he began to feel light-headed in spite of (or perhaps it was due to) the fact that he had not eaten for twenty-four hours.

It was almost another two hours though before they found themselves in the paths now familiar to Robert which led by devious ways through the woods to Arslan's village. As they prepared to descend the last slope, Robert caught sight of something moving on the opposite hillside – mounted men. The escort saw them at the same time. Shouting and whooping they urged their horses into a gallop in which Robert's mount joined. On such occasions Robert simply let his horse have its head and trusted to the animal's sagacity. There was no room for the whole troop of them on the track, such as it was, and the riders crashed through the bushes, avoiding by a miracle the standing and the fallen tree trunks, and the wolf's tooth tentacles. On their side of the valley the opposing band of horsemen galloped also, their answering shouts echoing back. Their slope was more open, which enabled them to get over the ground faster, and Robert's party spurred the horses on to make a final spurt which brought them into the space of beaten ground before the houses just at the moment when the opposing party debouched on to it from the opposite side. The mad impetus of the horses carried them on into each other's midst, the animals snorting and tossing their heads, their short legs going like pistons. Robert, concentrating all his attention on the avoidance of a head-on collision, felt a hand on his arm. His horse came to a standstill, blowing and sweating. There beside him Robert saw Hassan, his fur cap pushed back and tilted at a jaunty angle, his tunic of disgraceful rags and patches clipped in by his silver belt, his body swaying easily in the saddle as his horse jigged and fidgeted. The sunlight all at once seemed dazzling: the boy's smiling face became a blur, and Robert shut his eyes for a moment. His heart was thumping painfully, and a faintness oppressed him.

I need to eat, he thought.

He opened his eyes again to see Hassan laughing at him in the golden sunlight. How young and how happy he looked!

'What luck?' asked Robert.

For answer Hassan pointed to the two furry corpses fastened to his saddle. The fur was beautiful, soft and dappled, and when the wind stirred it, it looked alive. Only the faces of the wild cats were dead: one had the teeth still exposed in a snarl.

'The Russians?' Robert asked. 'Is there any news of the third man? Has he been recaptured?'

'Russians, no, but we have had good hunting,' replied Hassan. The other men too had dead beasts fastened to their saddles: four hooves secured together: streaks of dark blood on the horses' withers: golden wings hanging as if broken at the joint, showing the downy under plumage, as soft as the wild cats' fur. Smiles flashed in their dark faces as they displayed their booty.

Hassan leaned towards him. 'That one is for you,' he said, pointing to the golden spotted cat.

'I thank you, Hassan,' said Robert.

PART THREE

Chapter 10

THE WEATHER BECAME suddenly colder and sharper. Strings of migrating geese flew away overhead several times a day, and flocks of smaller birds suddenly appeared making noisy disputations in the coarse knee-high stubble, already trampled by the animals which had been turned in there to feed, which was left on the harvest fields. The moon had dwindled from a full blood-red sphere, to an ice-cold sickle which hung in the frosty night sky. The chill nights withered the flowers, but here and there the bushes flamed such a brilliant red on the hillside that it was difficult to believe they were not in full blossom. Game appeared in abundance, and Robert no longer had the feeling that the woods were empty of life. Near the village he saw quite a number of pheasants, but he did not recognize the little yellow berries, round and waxy, on which they were feeding so avidly that it was sometimes possible to get near enough to the birds to catch them in the hand. But the Circassians were amazed at the idea of anyone eating them. There were the tracks of other game as well, wild deer, roe deer, bear. The bears had moved in to the orchards as soon as the villagers left them unguarded, and gorged on the windfalls and the remaining fruit. They could be heard snuffling and scuffling between themselves at night, and from time to time there would be a crash as they broke the branches down. As well as these, other creatures who had so far kept themselves unseen made off through the bare branches with a flash of tawny fur, or a flapping of wings.

A villager trapped a lynx and everyone, Robert included, turned out to see it before it was finally despatched. Famished, but snarling and defiant, the animal padded round its prison pit and plunged its claws into the earth sides. A shaft of light penetrated into the pit, and in the centre of this the lynx crouched and turned up its pure and innocent face, banded with multi-coloured fur and embellished with tufted ears and bristling whiskers. Its yellow eyes met Robert's unblinkingly. The mouth opened and shut several times, but no sound was emitted beyond a faint hiss. It was as though the animal disdained to see or acknowledge its captors.

The sight of the lynx in its pit put Robert uncomfortably in mind of the two Russian prisoners in theirs, but he told himself they were better off there than dead. No further search was out for the third man, the man who Shekhir had said was the only one of the three likely to be exchanged. But there was a great chase of animals. It was the usual custom of the tribesmen at this season to organize a big hunting expedition down towards the south, thus combining two pleasures, the pursuit of game and the prospect of an encounter with their hereditary enemies, but this year however the old prince had forbidden this foray, and the men had to be content with such hunting as they could get in their own forests and foothills. Hassan was temporarily in charge of affairs. Shekhir Effendi had taken himself off, Robert knew not where, and Arslan Bey had not returned from the assembly of chiefs. Although Robert would have preferred to have known what was going on in that assembly, the war seemed very far away from this world of hunting and riding, wild beasts and men equally matched in their hardihood and gallantry, the bright coat of one vying with the shining weapons of the other, the tireless sinews and sharp claws of the quarry measured against the skill and endurance of the hunter. A young man was carried down into the village with his scalp half torn away by a stroke from a bear's paw: the boy had had no gun and had disturbed the bear at one of the wicker hives which the Circassians put up in the trees at points where they knew that the bees were likely to swarm. Robert patched the boy's head up as best he could, and the Circassian recovered.

A kind of hectic gaiety and liveliness pervaded the valley. It was as if everyone living there realized that the days of life were numbered before winter should set in, sending men and women to ground in the comfortless hovels which were their houses, to huddle there in semi-darkness, warmed only by the proximity of their livestock, until the spring. It was a season of feasting. The harvest was in, and the women, now that the hard drudgery of the fields was over, had more time for cooking. Food was abundant, meat in plenty, nuts and berries abounding on all sides. There were blackberries growing in the thickets along the stream, great bushes of them bearing masses of giant fruit, far more than could ever be picked. Giorgio showed no great enthusiasm for venturing among the thorns, so one day Robert set to work himself and found he had been joined by Hassan, who was plainly puzzled at his guest's choice of occupation, but Robert went on picking. Hassan made a snatch at one or two of the berries nearest to him: they were over-ripe and burst, reddening his fingers which he stuffed into his mouth. Liking the taste, he began to fill his hands and his mouth, and when the thorny bushes impeded him, he drew his sabre and slashed at them. Robert could not help laughing.

'You attack them as if they were Russians!' he said.

'Russians, Russians!' repeated Hassan, lunging right and left. The moustache which he had so carefully trained gave an artificial ferocity to his smile, but he could not disguise his natural gaiety. The hot midday sun poured through the leaves into the clearing. Hassan's face was smeared with juice: he passed the back of his hand over his mouth, but only succeeded in making matters worse. Then for some reason typically Circassian, instead of arming himself against the thorns, he decided to strip for action. He divested himself of his belt and its accoutrements, which he put on the ground at hand, then he pulled off his woollen tunic. Robert noticed that he no longer wore the gold bracelet on his arm, and could not resist teasing him.

'You are beginning to pay attention to what your sister says, you have given up wearing ornaments made by pagans!'

Hassan glanced round from where he was wrestling with the bushes in an attempt to reach the higher and most succulent berries. 'I have given it away. Although the thing was pagan, the gold was good, and gold is always a welcome gift. It was too small for me,' he added negligently, licking his fingers.

But it would fit a girl, thought Robert, laughing inwardly. However, he knew better than to mention such a topic.

Hassan suddenly tired of his occupation. 'I am going to ride, Jibrahil. Will you come with me?'

When Arslan Bey and his followers did not return, the feasting was redoubled, and the dancing. The dancing was less restrained than it had been when the old prince was there. Instead of the formal circles slowly gyrating, first the men and then the women danced in line to display themselves to each other, to the insistent rhythms of finger-drums. reinforced by a droning native fiddle. The men danced with all their arms clashing, their feet in morocco leather boots which had been shrunk on the limb to fit like gloves, stamping, twisting, making the tiny quick heel-toe movements faster than the eye could follow them.

Robert danced too, to roars of applause. He had always been a good dancer, and this was better than the Circassian Circle which had been the rage when he left London.

When the girls moved out in their turn, he sat with Hassan in the chief's place (Hassan was very much of a dandy these days. He had discarded his ragged old tcherkessa in favour of the smart white one with silver braid, and a new round-collared shirt of many-coloured silk showed in the open neck of the tunic. Almost as smart was his boon companion, Khassai, who also sported sabre and dagger with elaborately damascened hilts, and a silver belt.) First one girl, then another, stood in front of the line which postured and swayed behind her as she sidled up and down, until it was Paka's turn. Trailing her silk handkerchief before an invisible lover, every turn of her body beckoned, and every glance of her almond-lidded eyes concealed a smile – or so it seemed to Robert, who thought Paka and her friend Hafiza were undoubtedly the best of the women dancers.

Afterwards, she walked demurely behind her brother when he accompanied Robert back to his house, and sat, off the carpet, listening to the two young men talk. Once more Hassan interrogated Robert about foreign life. Everything enthralled him – Robert's account of a visit to the House of Lords, Robert's description of an English hunt, and of an English ball. This last pleased Hassan most of all, but Paka giggled so loudly at the account of the ladies' dresses that Hassan lost patience and broke up the party, Calling to her to follow, Hassan reminded Robert of a wolf-hunt on the morrow, and went out into the frosty starlit air.

In a night the weather turned its coat again. The wind howled round the houses, the rain poured down, and every morning fresh snowfalls crept lower down the hillsides. Men and women with rags over their shoulders hastily drove the cattle in. Outside Arslan Bey's house the ground was deep in mud, and the girls going over to the byres picked their way through it on clogs.

In the middle of a downpour Arslan Bey returned, the men of his escort and their horses soaked with rain and stained with mud. The prince's horse had nearly been carried away, fording the flooded river, and had strained a hind leg. The old man immured himself in his house where he remained invisible to his guest. On successive days Robert made attempts to see him, but he was turned away so often that he began to doubt if Arslan was there, and Hassan also was either elusive or preoccupied.

Finding inaction intolerable, and the rain no worse than a drizzle, Robert went out himself. He would have liked to ride, to work off his pent-up energies, but one of the minor irritations of the last few days had been that 'his' horse, the one which had been presented to him shortly after his arrival in Circassia, in exchange for the gifts of far greater value which he had made to Arslan Bey, was never available when he called for it. Whoever he told to bring it to him generally affected not to hear him, and when he sent Giorgio to the stables the result was the same. The obvious course was to protest to Arslan, but this was easier said than done, as he could not even discover whether the old chief was in his house or not. Thus, as his hosts were either absent, or preoccupied, it was with the certainty that he would not be furnished with an unwelcome escort that Robert went out to walk on the dripping hillsides.

It was easiest to follow a well-defined path, and the one on which he found himself turned out to be that which led to the grove inhabited by the Reverend Lewis Jones. Robert pursued the path until he came in sight of the clearing and the cabin.

Or rather, of the place where the cabin had stood, for to his amazement, it had gone. There was nothing there but fragments of timber strewn about in a circle, sodden with rain, round the remains of a beaten earth floor already beginning to disintegrate in the rain. Even the four corner posts of the hut had been torn down. Only the blackened hearth stone stood as it had. There was no sign of the Reverend Lewis Jones or of his belongings. Robert looked up to see if the crow's nest was still in the tree. It was, but there was nobody in occupation. The rope ladder dangled disconsolately. There was nothing at all at the foot of it, no platters of food, or pitchers of milk, or even signs of empty plates and pitchers to indicate that Mr Jones was in the vicinity. Only perched halfway up the tree, blinking angrily, was the small grey shape of an owl.

Robert called, but there was no answer. He debated climbing the rope ladder, and then realized that it had been cut off short and was now hanging far over his head, and out of reach. Alarmed, he called again, more loudly:

'Mr Jones! Where are you?'

His efforts were rewarded by a faint voice answering him, not from the top of the tree, but from somewhere in the undergrowth.

'Where are you, Mr Jones?'

'Here!' answered the voice, still indistinct, but languid with exhaustion rather than faint from distance.

'Are you all right?' exclaimed Robert, running in the direction from which the voice had proceeded.

Mr Jones emerged from a large hollow at the foot of a tree, dragging after him what at first sight appeared to be a bundle of dirty washing, but which was in fact the voluminous folds of his once-white robe. There was mud on his face and hands, and his long grey hair was plastered to his head. Robert noticed with surprise how grey it was: then he recalled that he had never seen the minister without some covering on his head. This had gone. Overcome with concern, Robert hastened to raise Mr Jones to his feet. The minister groaned, and with difficulty assumed an upright position.

'Mr Jones, are you hurt?' asked Robert, in alarm.

'No, Mr Wilton, I am physically unharmed, except for a slight touch of rheumatism natural after having spent a night out in one of the worst downpours that I have ever in my life experienced. But the Lord looked after his own to this extent, that he led my footsteps to shelter – of a kind!' Mr Jones looked with disfavour at the hole from which he had emerged.

'But how did this happen, Mr Jones?'

171

'You may ask me, but I cannot tell you the answer,' declared Mr Jones. 'I can only say that the wickedness of the inhabitants of this place is beyond belief. Indeed, I fear that they are in every way unfit to receive the light of truth.'

'Yes, but what happened?' persisted Robert.

'As you see, Mr Wilton –' and Mr Jones waved his hand towards the nearby scene of desolation – 'I have lost all the little I possessed. It may seem strange to you that that humble roof was the only shelter that I could boast, I, the accredited minister of the Zion chapel, duly elected by the majority of the men members of the congregation at a special meeting of the church, all according to the terms of the deed of trust, all faithfully observed. And now that has gone!'

'But who did this, Mr Jones?'

'It was a party of a dozen men at least who set about the work of destruction,' said Mr Jones. 'They may have been even more numerous. I was not well placed to make an exact account of their numbers, as you may imagine. As soon as I saw that trouble was afoot, I took myself to my post.' He pointed at the tree and the crow's nest. 'It was in my mind that they might follow me there, that they might even cut down the tree. But I called on the Lord with a loud voice and he hearkened to me. His fear must have entered then into these men, for they left me alone. But before they left they pillaged all that I had, though that was little enough.

'In the evening, I looked as usual to find sustenance, but there was none, and when I came to the end of my ladder, I found that it had been cut. I could not climb down and I could not climb up again, and in the end I had to let myself drop to the ground, to find what shelter I could for the night. It was by then nearly dark, and a violent rainstorm had come on, I could not hope to find my way to your hospitable fireside, Mr Wilton, so I had to do the best for myself. Indeed, you come now as a very friend in need. Again Heaven has shown me its mercy in guiding you to this spot.'

Giorgio was less than enthusiastic to learn that the Reverend Lewis Jones was to take up his quarters with them for an indefinite period.

'Arslan Bey has given this house to you, and not to the priest,' he protested. 'He will not like it when he learns that the priest is here. Nor will the mullah. Besides, he is mad,' he added.

'We cannot help it,' said Robert. 'It is raining, and he has nowhere else to go.'

Mr Jones sat in the guest's quarters reading his Bible, which Robert, aided by the unwilling Giorgio, had gone to a lot of trouble to retrieve from the crow's nest, together with the trust deed of Zion Chapel. The reverend gentleman's clothing was supplemented by various odds and ends of Robert's, and his robes were hanging up to dry by the fire, where they seriously impeded Giorgio's cooking. (He would have to be fed, too, thought Robert, with some concern in view of his now depleted supplies.) But it had to be admitted that Mr Jones gave very little trouble. His sojourn in the country had accustomed him to rough living and to scanty fare, which he accepted with resignation. Robert found it trying, however, to have to act as interpreter in the lengthy theological discussions which took place between Mr Jones and Giorgio – or perhaps it would be more accurate to call them discourses. Trust deed in hand (for this document, which never quitted his person, had survived the destruction of his former habitation), the minister expounded the doctrines it contained, article by article, while Giorgio listened and occasionally contributed a comment of his own.

'Why do you listen to the priest, when you tell me that he is mad?' Robert asked curiously, when Mr Jones was temporarily absent.

'I like to hear about English religion,' Giorgio replied. 'The English are very good people. I love all Englishmen. When I travelled with my English lord, he was also very fond of hearing religious talk. Wherever he went, if there was an English priest, he would invite the priest to come to dinner and to talk with him. Afterwards he would laugh and laugh. He enjoyed very much to hear priests' talk.' He hurried to the rescue of Mr Jones's robes, which were threatened with singeing.

When Mr Jones returned to the hut, he had come by some information. Robert had caught a glimpse of him in converse among the dripping bushes outside with a veiled figure which as it crept away momentarily lowered the drapery from its face to disclose the plump, sagging features of the Bezleni princess. The imprudence of the encounter struck Robert forcibly, but he was anxious to hear whatever news Mr Jones had been able to glean. This proved to be that the Russians had made a sudden and unexpected advance from the coast. A messenger, much delayed by the bad weather, had come into the village the day before with the message. Arslan had assembled what fighting men he could, and they had ridden off at daybreak. Hassan had also gone with the party. All this had happened, and Robert knew nothing of it!

The event was, in fact, just what he had foreseen. While warfare between the tribes came to a standstill when the paths became impassable, the Russians were not so hindered. The firm road which they had constructed and driven into the heart of the country was usable. To guard against ambush, they had cut back the surrounding forest for the distance of four hundred paces from the road – bullet range – but in any case, the leaves were now beginning to fall. A Russian column was on the march. There had been a fight. The princess knew nothing more.

'She may be able to find out more later,' said Mr Jones.

'I wonder if it is very sensible,' said Robert, 'to pursue this lady's acquaintance, after all that has happened. She seems to have made a good deal of trouble, one way or another.'

'The woman has also a soul to be saved,' said Mr Jones.

As usual, Mr Jones's argument was irrefutable, and Robert pursued the point no further.

Whan Arslan returned from battle, stern and sombre, at the head of his men, they carried with them the stiff, rain-drenched body of a young Circassian, roped to his horse. The dead man's eyes were open, and his lips drawn back to show the teeth. There were hacks and cuts all over the body, and a bullet wound in the chest, but the wounds had ceased to bleed. It was the body of Ali, the young cousin who lived in Arslan's household. The women who gathered round it set up a piercing wail at the sight.

The men were morose and cast down, and Robert did not find

it easy to gather the whole story, but at last it came out. The Circassians had made one of their surprise attacks on the Russian column, and this time it had failed, why nobody could tell. Either the Russians had been more on their guard than usual, or something – somebody – had given the alarm. The attack had failed to break the column, and after fierce hand-to-hand fighting Arslan's men had had to draw off, leaving the body of Ali behind them. Arslan Bey later sent intermediaries to the Russian commander to obtain its restitution. Two other men had been killed on the Circassian side, who had been buried on the spot, but che body of Ali, on account of his rank, had been brought back to the village so that the proper funeral ceremonies could be performed.

Robert saw Hassan standing on the outskirts of the group, his shoulders hunched, his arms folded across his chest, frowning and serious. He looked so lonely and so dejected that Robert went over to him, and saw the boy's face lighten for a minute.

'Hassan, you are back!'

Hassan did not reply. He stood looking at the body of Ali with a brooding air.

'Is your grief for Ali?'

Hassan looked up. 'I am not grieving for Ali, Jibrahil Bey. He fell like a warrior. My sorrow is for myself, that my father would not let us stay and continue the fight. Ali killed five Russians with his own hand. I would have made it ten!'

'Your father may have been wise,' said Robert, 'to break off the fight, if the odds were too great.'

'Odds! What odds!' exclaimed Hassan. 'The Russians are not men, they are ants, they are beetles. One stamp of the foot crushes fifty!' He ground his heel savagely into the earth, and began to look more cheerful.

'Why did you go off to fight without telling me, Hassan, my brother?' asked Robert.

Hassan looked embarrassed, and took his time in answering.

'These things are not for me to decide, Jibrahil Bey. It is for my father, and Shekhir Effendi.'

'Where is Shekhir?' asked Robert, sharply. 'Has he come back with you?'

Hassan looked surprised. 'I do not know where he is, Jibrahil. Somewhere away by the sea.'

175

And what is he doing there, thought Robert. Aloud he said :
'I do not know why Shekhir Effendi should decide for your
father's guest. He is not my *konak*.'

'My father did not want you to risk yourself,' said Hassan.
'I would have taken you with us.'

'For what have I come here ?' asked Robert. 'Does your father
think I want to encourage you with words, and then run away
when there are bullets? How can I tell them in England how
the war is going, when I do not see it?'

Hassan turned away his head, unwilling to speak, and at that
moment Paka, who also Robert had not seen for some days,
appeared behind her brother and began to try to catch his
attention. She was wrapped in a shawl, which she held partially
over her head.

'I hear your words,' Hassan said at last to Robert. 'I know
that you are a brave man, and that your heart is with us. But
it is not for me to decide these things.'

Paka pulled at his sleeve, and he turned and walked away
with her. Robert watched them standing at some little distance,
Paka with her shawl now pushed back from her head, waving
her hands, addressing her brother with vehemence, and Hassan,
half-embarrassed, half-bored, clearly anxious to escape. Robert
saw him finally shrug his shoulders with a helpless gesture and
turn away, breaking into a run when his sister threatened to
renew her importunities.

Robert returned to the hut where Giorgio was standing in
the doorway.

'The young man is killed – what a pity!' said Giorgio.

'Yes, a pity,' answered Robert.

'All this fighting – but these people are savages, they like to
fight.'

Robert, thinking he heard his name called, turned round and
did not reply.

'These people are certainly savages, and it rains all the time,'
continued Giorgio. 'This is a bad country. It would be better to
go back to Constantinople. That is a much better place for a
noble English gentleman.'

Giorgio was wrapped up against the cold in all the old
clothes he could find, and round his head he had folded as a
turban an old silk shawl which Robert had given him. In his

arms he held Fop, who was struggling to be put down in the mud for which the little dog always showed a strong propensity. In the glade the group of men still stood about and talked and gesticulated, their long guns in felt cases slung across their backs, the watery light glinting from their lances, but the wailing women had moved to the door of the chief's house, where they were clustered. As Robert watched, the men lifted the body of Ali on to an improvised bier and carried it slowly into the house.

When Robert finally succeeded in seeing the old chief the next day, Arslan seemed more stricken with grief at the death of Ali than Robert had ever expected to see him. One would indeed have thought that it was his own son who had died. He was also bitter.

'We rallied, as we had all of us sworn to do, under the same standard,' he said. 'Although it was not our land, I led out my men. But where were the others? You told us, Jibrahil Bey, that if we all fought together, the Russians could not withstand us. I listened to your words, but our allies were deaf, it seems.'

However he refused to discuss the matter which gave most concern to Robert, that the Russians had pushed inland, and established a fortified camp not so far away, and flatly declined any further initiative.

'That valley is not one of ours,' he said. 'Let the people there defend it!'

When Robert tried to raise the question of the party leaving without him, he drew blank again. Arslan only repeated what Hassan had said – 'We did not want you to risk yourself!' It was no use trying to get any more out of him.

Robert stepped out into the rain, and was rounding the corner of the house when a hand seized his arm, and he saw Hassan's face close to his own.

'I heard what you said to my father, Jibrahil Bey. You are right. We should not let the Russians go where they like in this country – it is a disgrace to all of us. I am going back to fight them, wherever they are.'

Robert saw that in addition to the sabre, dagger and pistols from which he was never parted, Hassan had his gun slung over his shoulder, and he was again wearing his old, patched tcherkessa. His eyes were glittering.

177

'Hassan, it may not be! What good could one man do? Besides, it is against your father's orders.'

'Jibrahil, you do not understand. My father cannot lead our men again into the fight. It is not our land. The men will not follow him. But I can go. It will be better to be one man alone in this work. Ali killed five Russians: you will see, I will make it a dozen!'

'It is better not to go against your father's will, Hassan, but if you will go, then I will come with you.'

Hassan laughed. 'It is not your kind of fighting, Jibrahil Bey. There is no sea to swim in, in the hills. When you are one against so many, you have to go like a hunter. I think you would make too much noise!' He stood irresolute.

'I do not care what my father says,' he said at last, 'but if you order me not to go, Jibrahil, I will obey you. I will stay here among the women.'

'Why among the women?' Robert asked, his heart lifting with relief. 'Do the men never sit and talk, when they are not hunting?'

At the word hunting a new light came into Hassan's eyes. 'The weather is getting colder. You will soon be needing a bearskin to cover you at night. If you would like it, we will go after one, in the mountains. The bears which live in the mountains are smaller than ours, and fiercer,' he continued, his eyes sparkling. 'Also their fur is better, they live all the year in the ice and snow. We can take Azamat with us, he is a great hunter. As soon as the day is fine, we will go and hunt bear!'

Hassan, at least was unchanged – he had no suspicions or reservations. As for Arslan, and the mystery of his altered behaviour towards his guest, there was someone behind it, and there was only one man who could be responsible. A reckoning with Zletzki could no longer be delayed. As soon as the bear hunt was over, he would go and seek out Shekhir, by the coast, in the mountains, or wherever else he was.

Chapter 11

To ROBERT'S DISAPPOINTMENT, although not entirely to his surprise, no steps were taken towards the bear hunt save a great deal of discussion. The Circassians never did anything in a hurry. *Yarin, yarin* – he was getting tired of the sound of the word Tomorrow. This time the men were even more dilatory than usual, and there was something disquieting in the absence of all activity in the village. Robert could not make out what was going on in the chief's house, and Arslan Bey, sitting brooding over the fire day in and day out, in the huge furred hat of the chieftain, was too morose to be approached. It was baffling, and Robert was beginning to lose patience.

Then he saw to his annoyance that Shekhir Effendi had once more joined the old prince's entourage. Robert did not know when he arrived, but the black-garbed figure of the Pole was certainly there, standing close behind Arslan, never smiling, hardly speaking, and when the Pole was there, Arslan seemed to be under a greater constraint than ever.

'That Polish deserter,' said Mr Jones to Robert, 'he is a trouble-maker, and I am sorry to see his face back here again. Indeed, he is no friend of yours, Mr Wilton.'

'That I have gathered,' said Robert. Nothing had ever been said openly regarding the Russian captives, but he felt that Shekhir's dislike of him had been much intensified from that time on.

'Did you know, Mr Wilton,' continued Mr Jones, 'that the Polish man is going round telling the people here that you are a spy – a Russian spy?'

'That is monstrous!' said Robert.

'Yes, it is so,' said Mr Jones, with gloomy satisfaction. 'But the people being what they are, ignorant and suspicious, are easily deceived. It is an ugly situation, Mr Wilton.'

Burning with indignation, with all his suspicions confirmed.

Robert went in search of the Pole, and came upon him almost immediately. Shekhir was standing near the chief's house looking at a horse which one of the Circassian retainers was putting through its paces. Robert at once recognized the horse as being his, and the sight greatly increased his anger, and spurred him to instant speech.

'I hear, sir, that you have been so good as to make statements to the effect that I am a spy,' he began.

The Pole was not visibly startled. He turned his curious green eyes on Robert, and inquired in measured tones, 'Who gave you that information, Mr Wilton?'

'It is of no importance who told me,' retorted Robert. 'It only matters that he is a reliable informant. It is clear to me, Monsieur Zletzki – I understand that is your name – that from the start you have gone out of your way to create difficulties between Arslan Bey and myself. I do not know why, since we are perfectly united on one point, that is, our desire to see the Circassian peoples continuing to lead a free and independent existence. I have come to this country at considerable expense and inconvenience to myself with no other object than to give the Circassians such assistance as lies in my power, and to carry back such reports as I am able to England, where I am convinced that support for the Circassian cause will continue to gather force. Why, then, should you wish to hinder me? And why have you put about the disgraceful slander which has now come to my ears? I demand an explanation!' Robert was beginning to work up a fine indignation.

The Pole smiled his slightly superior smile.

'Gently, gently, Mr Wilton,' he said. 'You go too fast, and a great deal too far. You have very much to learn about the Circassian people and their ways. They are deeply suspicious by nature of all that is outside their own experience. That is the result of the life they have led for centuries, absolutely isolated from the world. Everyone they do not know is suspected as a possible spy. It may well be that they suspect *you*. But I can assure you that it is no doing of mine.'

'These are all very fine words,' said Robert, too angry to be polite. 'But it can be no coincidence that these suspicions, if they exist, arose only with your own arrival in Arslan's house.'

The Pole shrugged his shoulders, still maddeningly calm.

'You yourself must be the judge of whether suspicions exist, Mr Wilton. But surely there are other grounds for these than the arrival of myself. You say you have come to help the Circassians. Forgive me, but I do not see how or in what manner you are proposing to help them. Moral support, yes! Promises of English support! But what are these promises worth? Your politicians talk, and what, after all, is done? Every year, Russia advances her frontiers in Asia – and what does England do? Nothing. The English government does not move.'

'It is because I and others like me hope to stir the Government into action that I have come here,' replied Robert. 'As to the help that I personally have contributed, and what it has cost me, perhaps you will allow me to point out that I have come here at my own expense, and no one else's.'

The innuendo in the last words, which was not intended, stung the Pole out of his self-command.

'What can you understand of this matter, Mr Wilton? You have never seen your country devastated by Russian hordes, your laws overthrown, your sacred rights and liberties trampled underfoot! You have never endured being dragged from your home and sent into exile, forbidden ever to return! All this has happened to me. I hate the Russians with every fibre of my being. The Circassians know that: they trust me as one of themselves. Moreover, I am an artilleryman, and I can teach them what they want to know. But what brings you here? Love of liberty, or curiosity? Can you be surprised if the Circassians do not understand your altruistic motives, if they treat you with suspicion? Particularly after you have been to the Russian camp,' continued Shekhir in a vindictive tone. 'How is it that you were allowed to leave, Mr Wilton, when there is an embargo on this coast, and a price on the head of anyone who supports the Circassians? Yet you were treated as an honoured guest and speeded on your way. Why?'

'That puzzled me also, Monsieur Zletzki, but I have since found an explanation. There is no law to prevent an Englishman from travelling in Circassia. No passport is required – Circassia is not part of the Russian dominions. The commandant would have no right whatever to detain me, or for that matter to expel me from the fort, although I entirely understand that he did not want me to see too much of it.'

'Yes, yes, the divine right of an Englishman to go where he pleases! You think the world belongs to you! I doubt however if the Russian commandant thinks so. In fact, he does not know what to think. There are so many agents and counter-agents in Circassia, who knows on what side a man may not turn out to be?'

Robert's fury threatened to boil over, and he took a step towards the Pole, but Shekhir stood his ground.

'*I* understand, of course, the feelings of an English gentleman – such a one would never condescend to play a double part. But we are in Circassia, Mr Wilton, where moral standards are different. When men are desperate, they think they are entitled to take desperate measures to save themselves. There is much more going on here than you understand. Take my advice, and go away. Go back whence you came. I warn you that you are in danger here.'

'How can I be in danger in the house of my *konak*?' asked Robert. 'Or do you mean, perhaps, that I am in danger from you? If that is so, let us speak frankly, as we are neither of us Circassians, although I can see that you are a man of two worlds. It would be interesting, for example, to know how you are so well informed on the subject of what goes on in the Russian camp.' Robert was pleased to find that he was now as cool as the Pole was heated.

Shekhir opened his mouth to reply, then shut it again. Robert followed up the advantage he had gained.

'If I have done you an injustice in imputing to you the responsibility for the unpleasant rumours I have heard, then, of course, I ask your pardon. It follows, of course, that you can have no possible interest in obstructing me, and I see now that the only person I should address myself to is our host, Arslan Bey. Allow me, sir, to bid you good day.'

He walked away before the Pole could answer, through the cluster of grinning Circassians standing by who became silent at his approach. But he did not take the way to Arslan's house. Some inner wisdom restrained him from approaching Arslan in the first heat of anger. He needed to think.

His suspicions about Shekhir were, he felt, pretty well confirmed. It all fitted in, there were so many events, inexplicable in themselves, which, added together, all pointed to one thing – the treachery of the Pole. There was the unexpected fire from the fort which had caught the reconnaissance party napping, there was the disastrous failure of Arslan's raid on the Russian column, which suggested that the raid had been expected. And there was Shekhir's obvious determination to get rid of himself, an embarrassing European observer, who might see too much. The Circassian who had led him nearly into the Russian camp – had the Pole's hand been behind that, too? Even the frantic spite Shekhir had exhibited against the Russian prisoners could be accounted for : in their extremity, they might well have given away something to his discredit, and in any case Shekhir's tirade about his devastated homeland rang true. The man was obviously a patriot of a fanatical order. But if the exile's only hope of regaining his homeland lay in showing himself to be a willing tool of the Russians, he had found a way to do it.

The situation now showed itself to Robert in stark outline. He *must* try to extract something more from Arslan beyond vague phrases and polite evasions. If he could not yet show Shekhir up as a traitor, he hoped he had enough to shake the old prince's confidence in this sinister adviser. He would tell Arslan that he must choose between the two of them. If the interview went badly, and it became clear that Arslan was no longer minded to extend his protection and his confidence to his guest, then there would be nothing for it but to depart.

At this point the difficulty of his position struck Robert forcibly. It was becoming unpleasantly clear to him that he had very little money, or the equivalent in goods which passed as currency in Circassia, left to him. He reflected that this sojourn in conditions of extreme discomfort, almost privation, had cost him rather more than it would have done had he passed the time in one of the best hotels in a capital city of Europe! It was ridiculous, but it was so. Since his arrival in Circassia he had been using instead of coin the goods which he had brought with him, partly as presents and partly to pay his way. These lengths of cloth, brass chains, compasses and pocket mirrors had disappeared at an alarming rate. In spite of Mr Jones's warnings Robert thought actual pilfering could be discounted, for the boxes were in the guest's quarters and under his eye, but many of the barefaced demands for presents which had been made to him were almost equivalent to thieving. His personal wearing apparel, equipment and arms he had managed to retain only by resisting very broad hints from would-be recipients. He was certainly in a most awkward situation. To be sure, there were funds available in the bank at Constantinople which could be drawn on in Trebizond, by arrangement with Mr Papandian, but that did not help him in Circassia, and how, without funds, was he to get back to Trebizond? And would the Circassians let him go?

Arslan Bey, when Robert finally judged the moment to be right to speak to him, gave no hint one way or the other on this last point. He was still sitting, hunched and brooding, in his house. He looked much older, and seemed to have shrunken physically since Robert had last seen him. The weight of his arms hung loosely upon him. He listened to Robert's protestations – for Robert was as impassioned as he knew how to be – with an impassive face. Robert could not tell if he was making any impression, since he could elicit no response from the old man. At last Robert produced his trump card. If everything was not put right between himself and his host – and he made another oblique reference to Shekhir – then he would have no alternative but to depart. Even this failed to move Arslan.

'You have been our honoured guest, Jibrahil Bey,' he said, looking not so much at Robert as through him. 'As to your going, be it as you desire.'

He began once more to run through his fingers the string of amber beads he was holding, and his gaze became opaque. Robert thought it best to leave the matter at that for the time being, and with a heavy heart got up to go. There were other subjects which would have to be broached later, such as horses for himself and for Giorgio (Mr Jones, he decided, could fairly be expected to look after himself), and a guide to take them to the coast. Once there, he thought, it might be possible to find a ship which was running the blockade to a Turkish port, and obtain a passage for himself and his servant on the basis that payment would be made on their safe arrival in Turkey. Other alternatives went through his head: of getting money or its equivalent through Mr Papandian's agency, then buying a safe-conduct from the local chiefs, and making his way east to the high mountains. Or, if bad weather prevented this, could he winter on the coast among a friendly tribe, or even in one of the deserted valleys where the houses were still standing, and make a further attempt in the spring to get himself to the seat of the war?

On his return to the cabin Giorgio met him, excited and full of news. 'The Armenian man' – and by this he meant Mr Papandian himself and not his agent – had come up from the coast and was at that moment in a village some miles away. Having heard rumours that all was not well in Arslan's territory, Mr Papandian had prudently decided to stay where he was until he found out how the land lay, and he had sent an emissary into the village, with whom Giorgio had talked.

'Has this messenger seen Arslan Bey?' asked Robert.

'No, he has not seen him. He has talked with some of the other men, and they have told him how Arslan Bey has become mad with his grief, and will not let any more strangers come into the valley, for trading or for anything else.'

'Where is he now, this messenger of Mr Papandian's?'

'He will surely have gone back to his master, to tell him what he has discovered. It will be no use for the Armenian to come here, when there is nothing to sell, and no money to buy. But he particularly wishes to see you. He askes you to let him know a time and place where he can meet you without these savages knowing.

'The messenger also brought letters for you – there they are.'

The packet was lying on the divan. Robert took it in his hand for a minute, while Giorgio watched him curiously. He felt the packet could only hold more bad news which, in his present predicament, was too much to contemplate with equanimity. It was the last straw, to have to carry the burden of moral responsibility for Henry Ginger's fate, when there was so little he could do about it. Even had he taken steps to return to England when he first received the news of Henry's arrest, he could not have got there before the trial. What he could do, which was to send funds for the defence, he had done. If his letter had reached London in time, Henry would have been properly defended, so far as any advocacy could help a poacher arraigned before a local jury.

Steeling himself, Robert opened the packet. Inside was a letter in a quite unknown handwriting.

185

'Carthage! The veritable Carthage itself,' was the heading which met his eyes. 'And indeed, *delenda est*!' He read on.

'Here I am, sitting on top of a hillock of brick and rubble which my guide assures me covered the remains of the cisterns which once supplied Rome's rival, and as soon as he has assembled his miscellaneous bits of rope, candle ends and so forth, we are to descend into the Pit itself, leaving our mounts, the smallest donkeys I have ever set eyes on, much less attempted to ride, to look after themselves. The works of Antiquity are liberally displayed on all sides here. On yonder hill smoked the furnaces into which mothers threw their babies before the altars of Moloch, and there are any number of pretty little Roman lamps, many of them quite genuine, to be had for a few pence from any urchin.

'Any aspiring Collector desiring to make a beginning here could do so at a very moderate cost. I acquired today two very handsome candle-holders in the form of hermaphrodite figures, each striding forward and holding in the right hand a torch which is the candle socket, all beautifully executed as to the (scanty) draperies and other details. These I bought for Ten Pounds the pair, after prodigies of bargaining, in the shop or rather den of a Maltese proprietor. The same dealer had some interesting sculptured heads dredged up from the Sea, and I bought one which particularly took my fancy as being the image of my Aunt's coachman, Hodge, a man with ten children. The Turkish work here is just what we saw in Constantinople, but not as well executed.'

Robert turned the page.

'. . . and on to Cairo in December, when the heat should have abated. You should come too – there is sure to be plenty of oppression going on for you to set right, when donkeys and Pyramids and Eastern charmers pall. I hear they have fine large white ones there (donkeys, I mean). Think about it, and the larks we had together under the dome of Sancta Sophia, and if you have got your Circassians liberated by then, why not join me in Cairo for Christmas?'

The letter was signed by the companion of Robert's sojourn in Constantinople, and even in his present condition, it made him laugh. The idea of setting off to Cairo was so ludicrous – as if timetables, steamers, letters of credit and tickets could be conjured out of thin air! But now to return to the business in hand.

'How is it possible to get in touch with this messenger again?' he asked, 'if we do not know where he is.'

'If you wish to see the Armenian, we are to climb to the top of that cliff –' Giorgio pointed to a spot on the opposite hillside – 'at noon tomorrow, and wait where we can be seen. Then the messenger will come, and he will arrange for the Armenian to come himself. I have told him that now we have no horses, we are prisoners here.'

'Very well. You will go to the top of the hill in the morning and wait for the messenger. When he comes, tell him that I will meet Mr Papandian –' he hesitated for a moment – 'at the Red Tower.' This seemed a reasonable choice of venue, far enough away from the village to be safe from prying eyes, yet accessible to Robert on foot.

'What time shall he come there to you, Excellency?' Giorgio did not sound delighted at the prospect of climbing the hill.

'As soon as possible. You will tell the messenger that I shall be at the tower at four o'clock.'

Giorgio hung around, clearly wanting to speak further but hesitating to do so. After a minute of this Robert asked him what he wanted.

'There is no more food, Excellency. That is, there is only a very little. Hardly enough for tonight. I suppose tomorrow we shall have to eat leaves and grass, like these people here.'

Robert made a decision.

'If there is enough for the priest and yourself, I myself will go and eat at Arslan's house tonight. Then I will mention the matter of tomorrow.'

Giorgio did not look much reassured, but there was nothing else for it. It was not a propitious time to send Giorgio to the kitchens of the old prince's house, and indeed, he wondered what sort of reception he himself would receive at Arslan's table. But for that very reason it might be wise to go, and not leave the field free for Shekhir to stir up more trouble behind his back.

Dusk had fallen, and the cooking fires were blazing outside Arslan's house as Robert crossed over to it. He entered the

187

main room where the company was already eating in a silence which nobody broke. Robert gave a wordless salutation which was acknowledged in a similar manner. A place was silently made for him, after a moment or two's hesitation, and he took it. Food was brought to him by a serving-man. There was no sign of the women.

Robert saw at once that Shekhir Effendi was absent: so was Hassan. The few people with the chief were mainly older men, except for a couple of young squires who were eating a little apart from the rest. The mullah from the village, he perceived, was also there, but he was eating nothing. His eyes were half closed, and he seemed to be in a trance. A small fire threw a flickering and variable light which made it difficult for Robert to see the food offered to him. In silence he masticated the strange pulses and grains which he found in his bowl. He had never got used to the absence of salt which rendered most of the dishes insipid and tasteless to him. A sweet and sickly-tasting brew was circulated to drink. Robert took as little as he could.

The silent meal proceeded to its close. One by one the other men made their salutations and departed. Robert hoped to see the mullah leave too, as he did not care for the influence of this hostile ecclesiastic, but the mullah was immovable, and in the end it was Robert who rose. Unless he could see Arslan alone, it was impossible to ask for what he wanted. Robert took his leave of the old prince, contented himself with the smallest hint of acknowledgment of the mullah's presence, and went out.

The fires outside the house were dying down, but as he passed the still-glowing embers, the odour of roasting meat pricked his nostrils, and he realized that he was still sharply hungry. It was always a puzzle to him how the Circassians could sustain their wiry bodies and warlike qualities on the very small quantity of food, unpalatable at that, which they ate. It ought to be possible to teach them to cook better, he reflected, but if the meal which he had just consumed had been a product of the old princess and her handmaidens, it was obvious that Giorgio's tuition had not produced much lasting effect. And there was still tomorrow to be provided for.

Standing there in the dark, Robert had a sudden inspiration. All round him were the woods. The half moon, just rising, showed through the branches where perched the low-roosting pheasants. It would not be difficult to knock down a sleeping bird! He would need a stick, though, and he slipped quietly into the hut to get one, without disturbing Giorgio who was occupied in building up the fire and did not notice him. There was no sign of Mr Jones.

Coming out of the hut again, Robert for the moment could see nothing, but his feet followed the familiar path in the darkness. By the stream the mist was hanging waist high, and the ground squelched under foot, but in a few minutes he was through the valley bottom and among the trees. The moonlight was just enough to see his way by. So far no dog had barked, and now he felt reasonably safe from their pursuit. But the moonlight, he found, was deceptive. Only the shadows were solid. The trunks of the trees glimmered faintly, like unsubstantial creatures which would vanish at a touch. It was like passing through a company of ghosts. More real obstacles were the countless spiny bushes and their tentacles which stretched across the path. The moonlight showed them as silvery cobwebs, whereas they were as strong as hawsers and barbed like dragons' teeth. Robert was gripped round the ankle by a tenacious creeper, and in his struggles to get free made a frightening noise. But nothing stirred: if anything the silence deepened, as if a hundred watchful eyes had opened to turn on him.

'Hsst!'

Robert peered into the darkness and saw, only feet away, the blur which was Hassan's face, separated by a screen of leaves. Hassan was laughing – or so it seemed.

'Whither are you going, Jibrahil Bey?' asked Hassan, with the faintest of mockery in his voice.

'I am going hunting, Hassan son of Arslan.'

'Hunting? Without a gun? What quarry then do you seek?'

'A quarry to fill the pot,' answered Robert, ignoring the first half of the question, although scruples about fine points of game law seemed hardly necessary in his present surroundings.

Hassan was evidently amused. 'Are you hungry, then?'

'I am not myself hungry,' replied Robert. 'I have eaten at your father's table. But the others with me have not.'

Hassan made no reply to this. It occurred to Robert that he

may have been embarrassed. They continued to stand still with the branches between them, their feet on two parallel paths.

'Jibrahil, they say in my father's house that you are going away.'

Robert did not answer at once, and Hassan continued, his voice low and agitated. 'You are leaving us!'

'Hassan, I have no choice but to go. Your father's heart has been changed towards me. Something – somebody – has crept into his mind and poisoned it with lies. Nothing has altered my love for your people, but I must go, none the less, for I cannot eat the bread of a host who listens to my enemy and denies me his ear.'

Hassan drew a deep breath, then he demanded passionately:

'What shall we do without you, Jibrahil Bey? What will become of us? Without support, we shall be lost. Where are your seven kings who promised to help us? When are they coming? Now even you are leaving us.' He seized Robert's arm.

'It has to be, Hassan. I cannot open your father's ears when they are closed, but I know, and I will prove, that someone very near your father's heart has a connection with the Russians, however much he may talk about his hate for them. You know who that person is!'

Hassan bent towards him. He grasped the branch which separated them as if he would tear it from the tree.

'You know that, Jibrahil Bey! You see very clearly, but you have not seen all the truth. Yes, I go to them, I talk with that Captain Lopakoff who thinks I am going to become a little Ivan, who has given me presents and pays well for everything I tell him. Only, what I tell him is no use. Sometimes there is a little truth, but only a little, in case he should suspect that he is giving his roubles for nothing at all, but I take care that he finds out nothing which would hurt our people. Like your book with writing – do you know how much he gave me for showing him that, and it was not even in English, you say, but in some tongue which nobody can speak now? He paid me nearly as much to see that book as for the golden bracelet which I sold him!'

'When was this?' asked Robert, as negligently as he could.

His ideas were racing through his head so that he could hardly keep pace with them. And it was hard to understand what a man was saying when you could not see his face clearly.

'I don't remember, maybe five days ago, maybe ten days. It took the Russian a long time to get back to their camp, walking!' He laughed with malice.

'You saw him, then, on the way?'

'I know which way he took. He is a good one, that captain, for a Russian. He must have walked all day and all night.'

'Almost as good as an Englishman.'

'Almost as good,' Hassan agreed. He began to sing softly to himself. Robert spoke urgently:

'Listen, Hassan, what you have told me makes me very unhappy. How do you know the Russians are not making a fool of you?'

'As if they could! Do not trouble yourself on that account, Jibrahil Bey.'

'If your people find out where you are going, will they not suspect you?' Hassan was silent. 'Is it worth it?' pursued Robert. 'What have the Russians to give?'

Hassan laughed. 'Their roubles. I need a pair of foreign pistols like yours. When I have enough money, and I have it nearly all, the Armenian will fetch them for me.'

'You can have my pistols, Hassan.'

'I know that, and I would have asked you for them, as we are friends, but there is also Khassai. He wants foreign pistols, also.'

Robert said nothing. There was nothing to say. Hassan went on:

'Jibrahil, do not leave us, I beg you. Do not go away.'

'I cannot stay, as long as this Polish man has your father's ear and tells him I am not a true friend to Circassia, when the Pole himself is a double traitor.'

'The Polish man?' Hassan was startled. 'I do not think he will betray us. If he does, I will kill him. If it will stop your going, I will kill him anyhow, Jibrahil. It would be quite easy.'

Robert could not help laughing, and Hassan laughed too. 'As for my father, he has not changed, I promise you. Nothing has changed. So you need not go.'

'If I can be of any use to Circassia, I will stay,' said Robert. 'But just now I am no use.'

191

At that moment he heard the dogs begin to bark frantically in the village below. Hassan heard them too, and led the way down the hill with Robert following close behind. Suddenly Robert became aware of something bulky advancing up the path towards them. He seized Hassan's shoulder and pulled him back into the midst of a spiny thicket just as a great dark shape parted the bushes in front of them. The thing passed them at a shuffling run, wheezing and panting. It was an enormous animal, as big as a house.

'Bear!' whispered Hassan.

They stayed where they were, as quiet as mice, until the coast was clear.

'It has gone,' said Hassan, still in a low voice. As if they knew that they were safe, the craven little jackals started to yap and scream on the other side of the valley.

Hassan and Robert got to their feet. Hassan began to laugh, quietly.

'We have come out to hunt a bear, without guns! Come now, Jibrahil, back to the house. Do not stay in the dark woods alone. There is no more hunting here. '

They began to make their way back, cutting through the tangled thickets which ran down to the stream. As they emerged into the meadow, Hassan checked. The guest cabin was in sight, with light showing dimly from the interior. As they watched, the figure of a man stepped into the open space, a man in long robes. The figure had all the appearance of stealth and secrecy. It flitted across to the door of the cabin, and as the door opened, the light showed up the face of the Reverend Lewis Jones.

'The old fox also has been out to look for food,' said Hassan, in a contemptuous tone. Before Robert could frame a suitable reply, Hassan went on, 'It would be better for that man to go away. There will be more trouble if he stays here. We do not need foreign priests.'

He went off quickly with his cat-like walk in the direction of the village houses, leaving Robert to go back to his own quarters alone.

Chapter 12

THE NEXT DAY dawned dull and sunless, and when Robert looked out (he woke late) he saw that the mist was down and filled the valley. It lay like a lake between the hut and the river. In spite of this, the air was not cold: it was a day of hot wind, the fever wind blowing from the east. Despite the lateness of the hour he could hear the cattle lowing in the byres. But otherwise the village was quiet.

Robert stepped out of the hut, and stood looking about. Immediately there was a flash, and something whizzed past his ear and thudded heavily against the doorpost. He spun round, to see a dagger, still quivering, driven fast into the wood. He studied it with interest, without withdrawing it. He did not recognize it. There was not much ornament on the hilt. The dagger might have belonged to any common man.

Robert stared into the mist out of which the dagger had come. Whoever had thrown it was somewhere out there, invisible, propably peering into the fog even as he was peering. He advanced a few paces into the squelching grasses and stood still, listening. There was a moment's silence, then a heavy body moved off through the soaking meadow, making no effort to be quiet, secure in the blanketing whiteness. Straight ahead lay the river, now too deep to be forded, on the one hand Arslan's house and the village huts. The only other way led up into the woods. Robert thought he could cut the man off, and ran, but his own noise betrayed him, and before he was out of the meadow he heard someone making off through the woods above him, by the same paths as he and Hassan had taken the night before.

Baulked of a capture, Robert walked back into the village. To his surprise there was nobody about. Even the dogs and the children had gone to ground. Arslan's house door was closed, and no sound came from inside.

Back at the guest's cabin, Giorgio had discovered the

193

phenomenon of the dagger impaling the doorpost, but for once even he was silent. There were too many possibilities, and none of them was pleasant, but the one which Giorgio later expounded was unexpected to Robert.

'There is the family of Aladji,' Giorgio observed, when he had finally succeeded in wrenching the dagger out of the wood, and was examining it in his turn.

'What about them?'

'They carry on the vendetta, these people here. Ibrahim, who killed Aladji, is dead, of course –'

'Then they should be satisfied,' said Robert.

'They are never satisfied, when it is a matter of money. They are saying that if you had not been here, they would have found a way of making Ibrahim tell them where he kept his gold. Since Kherim Agha took the horse away with him, they have nothing.'

The knowledge that, if Giorgio was right, Robert had an enemy in still another quarter seemed of little consequence to him. He was only just coming to terms with the momentous news which Hassan had let fall so lightly the previous night.

He could not believe Hassan was guilty of treachery, and indeed, what traitor would have disclosed intelligence which was so damning to himself. Hassan's escapades were no more than youth and irresponsibility, compounded with a dash of Circassian deviousness, and the powerful pleasures of taking a risk, as well as deceiving the Russians. Yet it was galling to know that Captain Lopakoff was a dispenser of unlimited roubles when his own pockets were empty, and that Hassan, who listened with such ardent attention to anecdotes of life in the west, had also been figuring, in imagination, in the ballrooms of St Petersburg!

Should he tell Arslan? No : it would do no good to make bad blood between father and son, nor would this go any way towards restoring the lost confidence between Arslan and himself. Should he stay? Or rather, was there any alternative to going? Robert paced the hut, but the realization was inescapable. He had no real alternative. Hassan, ardent, gifted and plausible, had little power. It was the old Lion alone who counted, the host who had closed his doors against him.

Robert was alone. Giorgio had started to his rendezvous with

Mr Papandian's messenger (he clearly preferred the rigours of the cold and dripping mountain side to remaining in the hut), and Mr Jones also had disappeared, ostensibly to meditate apart. If the situation had not been so desperate, Robert would have deplored this move, but he reflected that Mr Jones had his own ways of coming by information.

The sound of a light step outside made him snatch up a pistol. If it was Hassan, why did he not speak? Whoever it was seemed to be hesitating outside the door. It could only be Hassan.

'Enter!' called Robert, laying down the pistol on the divan. The door was pushed open, and he saw Paka standing on the threshold, her face set, and her great eyes fixed on his with fierce entreaty. She had a shawl thrown over her head and shoulders, concealing the lower part of her face, and heelless morocco slippers on her feet, as though she had run out on the spur of the moment. The slippers and her ankles were splashed with mud.

'You are going away!' It was a statement, not a question. 'Then take me with you!'

Robert was taken aback. He tried to temporize, piecing together the words in the mixture of Turkish and Circassian which they were forced to use.

'Why, Paka, you surely do not want to leave your home, your father and mother, your brother, your family? Where would you go?'

Paka advanced on him with her eyes blazing. She almost spat the words at him.

'My father wants to make me marry! With Kherim. I am to marry him next month.'

'I will send you a gift for your marriage,' Robert began, but Paka brushed his words aside. Her own came tumbling out.

'Marry Kherim, no! I will never marry him. I hate him.'

Her aspect became almost fierce as she tried to make him understand. She waved her hands and the shawl slid off her head and shoulders and fell unheeded to the ground. 'I do not want to stay here. Everything here is poor, everything is miserable. Look at my mother, how old she is! All the time working – what for? All the summer we make clothes for the winter, then in the winter we are cold. All the time, I am hungry!'

Her eye fell on the divan and on the red silk quilt which lay on it. She seized the quilt and draped the embroidered silk round her shoulders, stroking it lovingly.

'This is from Stamboul,' she went on, hugging the stuff to herself. 'Everything in Stamboul is very fine, very rich. The sun shines all day there, there are many rich pashas with great houses. Let me come with you to Stamboul, Jibrahil Bey.'

She planted herself in front of Robert with the red silk quilt bundled round her. At any moment, he thought, Giorgio or Mr Jones might return to find him in this ridiculous situation.

'Now, Paka, don't be a silly girl. You know this is all impossible talk. What would you do in Stamboul?'

'Live in a pasha's house,' she replied.

'This is just foolishness. You must go straight back to your mother.'

These words, far from having a soothing effect, seemed to inflame Paka more. She began to pant again and to glare, her eyes glittering dangerously. Robert moved towards the door with the idea of setting it open as a first step towards her expulsion, but Paka forestalled him. Whipping the silk coverlet off her shoulders and throwing it aside, she sprang back and planted herself between Robert and the door, her hands outstretched to ward him off. She looked like a young Amazon, in her shining breastplate and her little cap.

'I want to go to Stamboul!' she reiterated.

There was nothing for it but to put her out of the hut as gently as possible, but when Robert took her hands she twisted and struggled, contorting her body and throwing herself about. Robert shifted his grip and took hold of her shoulders.

Still she would not give way an inch. They stood there tussling fiercely in the dimly-lighted hut, Robert not liking to put out his full strength, Paka's eyes glaring into his. The breathing of both of them came short and fast. Neither said a word.

Then Paka changed her tactics. She ceased her resistance, and when Robert released her grip of her shoulders, she sprang on his neck and hung there, twisting her arms and legs round his body. Her head was buried against his shoulder, and his chin touched her oily, snaky hair. He staggered, for Paka was quite a weight, but managed to hold her up for a moment or two.

Then her body slipped slowly down through his arms till she stood on tip toe between his feet, her arms still wrapped round him. It was at that moment that Robert discovered his desire to put her out had gone, and as if she knew that she had gained her point, Paka raised her face to him, fierce no longer, but suffused with the vacant languor which he had observed on the faces of the serf-girls dallying with the men-at-arms in the fern-brakes and under the forest trees. Her eyes were half closed, and she smiled as she clung to him. Robert bent his head, and pressed his mouth firmly on hers. Paka immediately jerked her head away: her eyes opened wide with surprise. Then, greatly daring, she clasped her arms still more tightly round his neck, and gave him back his kiss.

Absurd recollections of their anatomy lesson floated through Robert's head as his hands fumbled with the silver belt which confined her waist so cruelly. It was easy enough to find the fastenings: he unhooked them and threw the belt aside. The tight-fitting pelisse which buttoned down the front was speedily got rid of, and the gauze shift below hardly counted as an obstacle, while Paka was already stepping out of her columinous trousers. But what was this? Robert's hands fell on something resembling a mermaid's skin which encased Paka's body above and below the waist and formed an impregnable barrier to his intentions. Then after a moment of bafflement, he understood. This was the famous deerskin corselette of which he had heard, which was put on to Circassian girls at the age of eight and not removed, except for ablution, until their wedding night. When that day arrived, it was the privilege and duty of the bridegroom to undo the innumerable knots which fastened the corset one by one, nor was he allowed to take the easy way out and cut them.

Where were the knots? Robert's hands searched frantically for some kind of fastening. Paka was no help to him. She was lost, so it seemed, in a dream of desire. Robert's fingers encountered something familiar, laces, ending in a knot. The question was, how many of these could there be. His cheeks were on fire, while his hands were cold and clumsy, and the musky smell of Paka's hair filled his nostrils as he struggled with the unyielding garment, as if grappling with some marine creature. Fortunately the principle of fastenings in Circassia

197

seemed to be much the same as in the case of similar garments in the West, there were two laces which held together the opposing rows of hooks, and the ends of the two laces were tied together. It was this knot which Robert could not undo, though he clawed at it with his nails till they broke.

'Help me,' he said angrily. 'Help me!'

This was the moment when, according to all he had read of Circassian girls, she should have drawn herself up and repulsed him. 'You are no man,' she would say, 'you cannot restrain yourself.' Then she would sweep out, with queenly carriage, reclasping her girdle round her waist. But Paka only laughed. She leaned down to where her belt lay shining at the foot of the divan, and came up with something in her hand. It was her little dagger, sharp as a razor, with its handle of rough turquoises and coral. She pushed the hilt towards Robert.

'Cut it!' was all she said.

The knot yielded to the sharp blade and the laces came free. The garment peeled off like a snake's discarded skin, and Robert heard Paka gasp as a swimmer does who comes up for air and fills his lungs before taking the next plunge. A vision flashed before Robert's eyes of himself and Henry bathing in the pool below the mill, of the boy's white shoulders and his arms, ending in clumsy work-hardened hands, cleaving the water. Henry's hands and arms were darkened by exposure to wind and weather, but his body where it was covered by his clothes was as white as Robert's. So was Paka's body white where the corselette had pressed. She threw her arms round Robert's neck and pulled him down, as Henry had done, but it was not into the depths of the cool mill-water that he sank, but into the depths of the red-embroidered quilt, dragged down in the embrace of this strange sea-creature, drowned in the depths of her snaky hair. He found himself locked with her in a mortal combat from which he could not free himself until he had mastered his opponent and achieved oblivion.

Whether the moment of oblivion lasted for five minutes, or for an hour, Robert could not tell. He thought it could not have been so very long, for while he lay torpid and exhausted, the patch of watery sunlight which filtered through an aperture in the roof on to Paka's foot had barely crept to her knee. When he came to his senses, the first thing Robert saw was the pistol lying between them – he moved it to the ground. He thought Paka was asleep, but then he saw – for she was lying on her side with her head turned towards him – that with the one eye visible she was watching him, and as he sat up, she did the same.

At that moment a footfall and a cough – Giorgio's – sounded somewhere outside.

'Remain outside till I call you,' shouted Robert. Paka seized the first garment to hand, which happened to be her shift, and covered her face with it. This gesture was sufficient to allay the demands of modesty, and it was Robert who had to pick up the rest of her scattered garments and urge her to put them on. He got her into her corset, but after that he was nonplussed. Not only were the strings to fasten it unlaced, but there seemed no possibility of the two sides of the garment meeting at all! It must be that she had swollen, or rather the top half of her had, before his eyes. What had been before the tightly compressed figure of a child now stood before him as a blooming woman, and Paka's young form refused to be confined in its former strait-jacket. Robert abandoned the problem: he tied the dangling strings loosely in front, hurried Paka into her trousers and her shift, and got her pelisse buttoned and her silver belt clasped, with a strong effort from himself, round her waist.

Paka leaned back against him.

'When shall we go to Stamboul?' she whispered.

Robert hesitated, but his will had been sapped: weakly he temporized. 'It will be difficult to arrange.'

Paka twisted round to face him. Her plaits of hair, which had not come undone, any more than the embroidered cap on her head had become disarranged, flew about as she nodded her head.

'No, not difficult! I have a horse. Then there is your horse. I can bring that to you.'

Suddenly she stopped and listened. A look of terror came over her face.

'It is Hassan,' she whispered. 'He is outside. He has heard us.' She held herself rigid, then she began to shudder. 'O Jibrahil, what are we going to do? My father will kill me now.'

Robert too listened, but he could hear nothing. Paka hid her face on his chest and shivered.

'There is nobody there, and nobody will kill you, you silly girl. I will take care of that.'

'You will take care of me?' Paka threw her arms round his body in a transport of gratitude. 'You will take me to Stamboul?'

The important point having been tacitly conceded, Robert became practical. Speaking still in an undertone, as Giorgio was presumably somewhere at hand, he asked:

'Where will you go now? What about your mother?' For he was afraid that Paka's present appearance would kindle suspicions in the least watchful of matrons.

'I need not see her till this evening,' answered Paka, 'when it will be dark, so she will not notice me. Then I shall tell her that I am going to sleep with Hafiza in the hayloft. We sometimes do that.'

Hafiza was Paka's favourite companion, a pert, forward girl. Robert wondered why they were in the habit of sleeping in the hayloft, a place which could be reached by an agile and determined person by other routes as well as through the women's quarters.

'Go then, now, go quickly, while the coast is clear. Keep out of your mother's way, and after dark I will send a message to you,' He urged her towards the door. Paka draped her shawl over her head and shoulders. It fell low enough to conceal her waistbelt and ornaments, and with her muddy feet (she was carrying her slippers) she might escape notice, and be taken for a serf-girl, it there was anyone hanging around to observe her. Robert held the door and she slipped out into the mist which luckily had gathered again. A few minutes later, having hastily straightened the disordered divan, Robert heard Giorgio whistling somewhere outside, and called to him to ask if the rendezvous with Mr Papandian had been arranged.

'You are intending, then, to bring away the young princess?' asked Mr Papandian. He sat on one block of carved stone within the shadow of the Red Tower, and Robert sat on another. The Armenian exhibited no surprise, or any other emotion.

'I have no alternative,' said Robert. 'The princess absolutely refuses to marry the man her father has chosen for her, and she has put herself under my protection. She is going in fear of her life.'

'Yes, if the girl has been promised in marriage, and she

refuses to obey, most certainly her father will kill her,' said Mr Papandian. 'A Circassian girl, whatever her rank, is not her own mistress in any way. She is the absolute property of her father, or if her father is dead, then of her tribe. The men can dispose of their women-folk as they please.'

He shrugged his shoulders.

'That is their fate. If a girl is not sought in marriage by another family of equal rank, then she will be sent for sale, in Constantinople. Most of them, of course, would far prefer that.'

'I cannot simply leave her to her fate here,' said Robert.

'No, indeed,' agreed Mr Papandian. 'If the princess has thrown herself on the mercy of your Excellency, it would be inhuman to abandon her. But it will complicate your departure.'

'What do you suggest?' asked Robert. 'I wish to leave as soon as possible, since my staying longer presents many problems. I have told the prince of my intention to depart, but I think it unlikely that he will provide either food, horses, or a guide.'

The afternoon was wearing on, and the clouds were hanging low. Inside the ruined interior of the Red Tower the gloom was intense, but it would not have been prudent to show themselves outside its walls, although Mr Papandian now wore the Circassian dress, with a small cap of grey curled wool on his head. He looked every inch a man of mountain stock – something Robert had not realized before – but his voice and his movements were decisive, and his merchant's faculty for making up his mind quickly was fully in evidence.

'These people,' said Mr Papandian, after some thought, 'do not rise early in the morning. It is not their custom to be abroad, particularly at this season of the year, until the day is well advanced. It would therefore be advisable to depart at the earliest possible hour tomorrow, and to omit any ceremonies of leave-taking, which can only lead to unprofitable delays. As for food, there is enough for the first day, and I can procure more. I have two guides. Horses will be a problem until we are out of Arslan Bey's territory and it becomes possible to buy them –'

'I hope to bring two horses,' Robert broke in. 'But if not, some of us will have to walk.'

Mr Papandian smiled politely.

'When you have arrived in Constantinople,' queried Mr

Papandian, 'what does your Excellency plan to do with the young princess?'

'I have no plans,' answered Robert. 'I suppose I shall have to make some when we arrive. The princess herself –' he smiled a little – 'wishes to enter the establishment of some rich pasha. Would it be possible, do you think, to find her a – a situation, with some suitable and respectable family?'

'Nothing would be more easy,' said Mr Papandian. 'There is a great demand for Circassians in Constantinople, now that the Russian blockade makes it so difficult to get cargoes through. Only last month, the Russians captured a boat bound for Trebizond with thirty girls on board. They sent them home! I take it that the young lady is personable?'

'Yes, she is certainly quite personable,' said Robert, colouring a little.

'The complexion is important. The fairer the better.'

'From what I have seen of her complexion, I should say that it is comparatively fair.'

'Can the princess sew and cook well?' pursued Mr Papandian.

'She can certainly sew,' said Robert, remembering the silver lace. 'Her cooking I am not sure I can recommend, but she can embroider very nicely.'

'Cooking is not so important, in a girl of rank, but embroidery is always a pretty accomplishment. No, I do not think you will have any difficulty in placing her suitably, Mr Wilton.'

'There is one important matter still to discuss,' said Robert, after a pause. 'I have no money –'

'That I understand. You would indeed have none here in Circassia.'

'– until I reach Constantinople, or at any rate, Trebizond,' achieved Robert. 'Once in Turkey, I have ample funds at my disposal, with which I can pay you the costs you will incur in making arrangements for myself, my servant, and the princess. But there may be some – difficulties, and if anything should go wrong, that is, should anything happen to me, you might find yourself out of pocket. I can only give you my undertaking that on my arriving safely in Turkey, I will reimburse you fully.'

'The word of an Englishman suffices me,' said Mr Papandian. 'If your Excellency engages to pay me on arrival in Constantinople, that is enough. As for the journey, we are all in the hand of God,' he observed, sombrely. Then reverting to the practical, he continued, 'We must be ready to move at first light tomorrow. There must be a place for meeting, not here, it is too far off the road, and the ground is too open.

'Where the path leads over the crest –' he pointed. 'Just beyond the crest is safest. I shall be there, at dawn tomorrow, Excellency.'

Shortly afterwards they parted, the Armenian slipping into the shadow of the forest which covered the ridge. Robert also took to the woods, to fetch a circuit back to the village, since the direct path to the Red Tower was too open for his liking. Looking down through the cover of the bushes, he saw a man hurrying up the path in the direction of the tower. The dark tunic and the black fur cap were familiar. It was Shekhir, alone and on foot.

On an impulse Robert pushed through the bushes and on to the open slope. He ran down, slithering in the wet grass, his course converging with the path. Shekhir, absorbed in his thoughts, did not see him until Robert was standing in front of him.

'Good afternoon, Monsieur Zletzki,' said Robert.

The Pole perforce had to stop. He was breathing hard from his exertions, and he looked harassed.

'Ah, the Englishman,' he said. 'Good afternoon, Monsieur l'Anglais. What are you doing in this lonely spot, may I ask?'

'I am going for a walk, Monsieur Zletzki. Is that permitted?'

'Walking! How like the English. But it is not very wise, monsieur, to go by yourself in the forest. There are bears there, and other dangers.'

The Pole made as if to pass, but when Robert did not give way, he asked abruptly:

'Where is Arslan Bey? And that son of his?'

'Why do you ask me, Monsieur Zletzki?'

'Why indeed do I ask you! What would you know, Englishman? Let me tell you, if you were to hear what Arslan Bey and your precious Hassan have been doing –'

Robert cut in, 'I do not think I want to hear it from you. It would interest me very much indeed, to have an account of what *you* have been doing for these past days, hour by hour –'

'Unfortunately, I have no time to spare for such an exercise, Mr Wilton, and certainly I have nothing to explain to you –'

Zletzki broke off, and Robert, following the direction of his eyes, swung round to see that a third man had appeared, and was standing under the walls of the Red Tower, almost invisible in his drab-coloured clothes.

'Kaplan!' called Shekhir.

The man detached himself and came towards them, a short stocky Circassian, with an ugly, impassive Tartar face, marked by a scar across the chin. He stood there, as if waiting for Shekhir's orders.

'Your man?' said Robert. 'The guide who led me on top of the Russians. Well! That explains much.'

Kaplan put his hand to his belt, but Robert was quicker. He whipped his pistol out, and covered Shekhir with it, saying:

'You had better put off your present errand, monsieur, and come back with me to find Arslan Bey. He shall hear your account of yourself, as you refuse to give it to me.'

Shekhir's eyes flamed, but he fell back, and began to expostulate.

'Your way lies behind you,' said Robert.

'Mr Wilton, you have misunderstood me,' said Shekhir, quickly. 'It is quite true that this man guided you wrongly, but it was not his fault. I can assure you that when you have heard the explanation –'

'Which we will hear in the house of Arslan Bey. Be pleased to proceed, monsieur –'

The blow from a pistol butt which descended from behind would have felled him, had it not been for his Circassian fur hat, which protected his head somewhat. As it was, Robert slumped on to his knees. His own pistol dropped to the ground. He was dimly conscious of Shekhir holding Kaplan back. The Circassian had his dagger in his hand now, and was clearly intent on finishing his work. Shekhir was saying something, urgently. Then there was the sound of the two men in flight towards the woods. After that, he was conscious of nothing but the ringing in his head, and a sensation of violent nausea which threatened to overcome him.

Painfully Robert raised himself from his hands and knees, after several long minutes had passed, and got on to his feet.

He looked for and found the pistol, and thrust it into his belt. It was nearly dark – the day was nearly over, and there was still much to be done, if he was to bring Paka, himself and Giorgio off safely the following morning. Staggering from time to time, and wavering somewhat in his course, he made his way back through the woods to the hut where Giorgio and Mr Jones, both of them in a state of some alarm, were waiting.

The preparations for departure had to be made before dark finally descended, for the candles were nearly at an end. There was not, however, very much to pack, although, confident that Mr Papandian's arrangements would be adequate, Robert decided not to abandon his books. He also decided not to take away with him any of the gifts which he had received from Arslan Bey, even though these had been given in exchange for presents of equal, or greater, value. He could not help the fact that leaving them behind might be regarded as a crowning insult. The boxes ranged against the wall had contained his store of presents, but their contents had nearly all been exhausted. What was left in them, the villagers were welcome to take. After some hesitation, he decided to keep the little leather purse which the old princess, Paka's mother, had embroidered for him with intricate patterns in beadwork. It would be ungentlemanly to reject a lady's souvenir, he thought, and besides, he had grown attached to the kind old lady.

Mr Jones's travel arrangements were simple, since he now possessed nothing but a blanket, the clothes he stood up in, most of which were Robert's, his Bible, and the trust deed of Zion Chapel. These last two things he packed neatly, ready for instant departure, for the minister had taken it for granted that he was to leave with the party, merely observing that although his mission in Circassia had not been as successful as he had hoped, still he trusted that some of the seed which he had sown would quicken, and Robert did not feel able to tell him that he must fend for himself.

The only crisis came when Robert looked for his own travelling clothes which he intended to assume immediately, instead of the Circassian tunic, trimmed with Paka's silver lace, which he had been wearing for the last weeks. This garment, like the other gifts, he intended to leave behind. The travelling suit was there, but it was totally devoid of buttons! Giorgio, called to account, protested vehemently, although in a stage whisper (they were rapidly coming to act like conspirators, thought Robert):

'All those buttons, you eat them! Every day I take one button, buy eggs, buy milk, buy bread. How else should we have been living? For many days now, no food has come from the house fit for an English lord to eat!'

There was nothing for it but to continue wearing the Circassian outfit, and to pack up the ravaged travelling suit.

Giorgio ventured on another topic. 'The young princess, she is to accompany your lordship to Stamboul?'

He had been quick to nose it out, thought Robert. Well, he would in any case have to be told.

'Yes,' he answered shortly.

'There is another girl in Arslan Bey's house who also wishes very much to go to Stamboul. She is a great friend of the young princess. Her name is Hafiza. I know her very well. She is a pretty girl, and clever. She will not be any burden to us.'

'It is out of the question to take any more girls,' said Robert. But Giorgio persisted. 'I think by now Hafiza will know all about our going. The young princess will have been talking to her. It might be best to take her with us, in case she should cause trouble.'

Robert reflected shortly. The presence of Hafiza could be of some positive advantage, for it provided the princess with a suitable female companion. Hafiza might be a doubtful influence in some ways, but she appeared to be a bright girl, brighter at any rate than Paka. This factor decided him.

'Very well, the girl can come with us. But both she and the young princess must be ready to leave at dawn. Can you get to speak with Hafiza?'

'Yes, lord, I go to her now. I know a way to reach her.'

'You had better be careful,' said Robert. 'It would not do for you to be caught.'

'No fear of that, lord,' said Giorgio. He was beaming. 'The loft door is barred, but I know where the window is. It is not too hard to climb up, not as difficult as climbing up the mountain. I have done it before!'

The devil you have! thought Robert. He was correct then in his surmise that Hafiza was no better than she should be. And what about Paka? A most unwilling suspicion crept into his mind that he might have been made a fool of, that there might be a more compelling reason than the one she gave, for her reluctance to go through with a marriage with Kherim. Still, it was too late to draw back, and he put the thought away.

'Very good. You go then to Hafiza, and give her this message. She and the young princess must get out of the house and meet us on the hill, above the Red Tower, at first light.' Robert described the place of rendezvous arranged with Mr Papandian, where the horses and attendants would be waiting. A sudden recollection of women and their habits made him add, 'Tell her that the girls are to bring as little baggage as possible – nothing that they cannot easily carry.' He hoped profoundly that Mr Papandian would be able to buy more horses, on the way to the coast. Mr Jones had grown used to fending for himself, during his sojourn in Circassia, and he could well walk, but he doubted the capacity of the two girls, should Paka fail to produce the promised horses.

When Giorgio returned about half an hour later and reported that he had successfully accomplished his mission, the last candle was about to gutter to extinction. It shortly afterwards expired, leaving them in total darkness. A sparse meal, procured by Mr Jones through some means into which Robert did not care to inquire, had been eaten, and there was nothing to do now but to wait for the morning. Robert lay down for the last time on the red silk quilt, fully clothed, with his pistols beside him, able at last to rest his aching and battered head. Giorgio and Mr Jones were soon asleep, and in spite of his many cares, and the recollections of the day which were spinning in his brain, Robert followed suit. He woke early though, before it was light, and in the chill of the icy dawn he roused the others. They shouldered their loads and crept out into the half-light.

Outside it was cold, with a crispness enough to stiffen the drenching grasses which reached above Robert's boots. The sharp air set Mr Jones off in a fit of coughing which he fortun-ately managed to overcome. Robert and Giorgio carried the portmanteaux between them, and in addition Robert shouldered his English saddle. Mr Jones carried little, since either as a protection against the morning chill or to give dignity to his withdrawal he had elected to wear his robes over his other garments, and he stalked imposingly through the meadow, impervious to the wetness round his legs, carrying the small bundle of his remaining possessions.

Robert led the way at the best pace he could muster, for the half-darkness was fast beginning to lighten. When they reached the shelter of the trees, where the path struck up through the woods, he hurried the party along, although Giorgio soon began to pant and flag and show signs of wanting to put down his load. The path grew more narrow, giving a bare foothold on the steep face of the hill. Round one more bend, and they would be at the meeting place.

From somewhere just ahead came a crashing noise and a threshing of branches. A rending, tearing sound followed, almost as if woodcutters were at work. Robert hesitated for a moment, then the sound stopped and he went on again. A turn in the path brought him within a few yards of a large cinnamon-coloured bear, which was standing on its hind legs on the edge of the path, tearing at the branches of a solitary chestnut tree which grew there. The bear, surprised and annoyed, looked round at the party approaching him, and Robert saw the animal's face with its boot-button eyes and sharp pointed muzzle peering out of the branches with a tuft of greenery adhering to the corner of its jaw. Instinctively Robert recoiled. Giorgio behind him uttered a gasp of horror, dropped the bags he was carrying, and began to flee back in the direction from which they had come. He was arrested, however, by the sound of horses' hooves approaching up the path from the direction of the clearing, and darted off the path into the midst of the under-growth, where he crouched as low as he could. Robert was tempted to follow him, but after a hasty review of the situation he abandoned the idea of flight as too ignominious, and in any case too late, for the bear, he felt certain, was capable of a greater turn of speed than he. His eyes lighted wildly on the trees immediately nearest to him, but apart from the chestnut which was engaging the attention of the bear, they were either beech or pine, smooth-boled to a height considerably above his head, and quite impossible to climb. He therefore stayed where he was, rigid with alarm. The only person who was unaffected by the panic was Mr Jones who had been walking at the rear of the party, seemingly sunk in his own thoughts and who now, drawing no conclusions from the sudden disappearance of Giorgio, continued his upward progress until he came abreast of Robert. Only then did he perceive the bear. The bear, struck by astonishment or perhaps by curiosity at this new apparition – for Mr Jones looked quite Biblical in his flowing garments – detached its attention from the chestnuts and reared up to its full height. With the advantage of higher ground as well, it towered over Mr Jones, who nevertheless remained confronting it over the leafy branch which was all that separated them. Mr Jones raised his right hand and said in a loud, though trembling, voice :

'*Gwell Duw na drwg ddarogan!*'

The bear looked puzzled.

'He can speak the tongues of beasts, then,' whispered Giorgio, who came crawling through the scrub to Robert's side. 'It is true, then, what they were saying in the village, that the priest is a sorcerer.'

The beast and Mr Jones continued to stare at each other, while Robert wondered how long the animal could remain poised on its hind legs. The bear began to emit a low rumbling sound. Mr Jones seemed rooted to the spot.

'Shoo!' exclaimed Robert, leaping to his feet, and brandishing a piece of stick in the animal's face. The bear coughed in an embarrassed manner, dropped on to all four feet, and shambled to the edge of the path. With an agility astonishing for so large and bulky a beast it disappeared into the bushes below. Mr Jones stepped over the fallen branch and continued up the path, followed by Robert and by Giorgio, who had to be induced by sharp persuasions to come out of hiding. They were nearly at the rendezvous, and one more turn in the path disclosed the rock, prominent on the hillside, which Robert had designated to mark the meeting place. In its shelter was a small group of men and horses, consisting of Mr Papandian mounted on a rough, sturdy local pony, two mounted Circassians with an *abrek* cast of countenance, armed to the teeth, and two more attendants leading baggage horses, one of which was already loaded.

'Where is the woman?' asked Mr Papandian.

At that moment a noise of hooves made itself heard again on

the path up which the party had climbed. Round the bend appeared a pair of shrouded figures, bending under the weight of bundles and tugging on the reins of the two horses which they led. One was Robert's 'own' horse, rough-coated and barrel-bodied, the other was the glossy Kabardan horse with its long tail dyed with henna which was the pride of Arslan Bey's stable.

Mr Papandian's eyes glowed at the sight of the horses, but Robert's first reaction was one of dismay. He did not know how much value Arslan attached to his daughter, but he had no doubt at all of the importance of the Kabardan horse. Still, it was a pleasure to have his saddle put on the beautiful beast, which pranced and sidled under the unfamiliar load. The two girls were assigned to one of the packhorses brought for the transportation of baggage, and Robert's portmanteaux were strapped on the other, which Giorgio bestrode. Mr Jones mounted the remaining horse, and the party moved off, with the Circassian guides in the lead, anxious to press the pace. Robert's mount could have forged away, and he had some difficulty at first in restraining it, but for endurance nothing could outdo the shaggy little ponies. Hour after hour they scrambled on, up and down the hills (but now there seemed to be more downs than ups), until late in the afternoon, when Mr Papandian called a halt and announced that they were out of Arslan's territory.

It was evident, too, that they had come down into a different climate. The tired horses stumbled through flowers which glimmered faintly in the dusk, and the air still held the heat of the day, not chilled by the breath blowing down from Mount Caucasus. Robert began to hope that they had got clear.

Chapter 13

THE PARTY SHELTERED for the night in a tumbledown rickle of stones which might have been a dilapidated Genoese watchtower, Turkish citadel, or even a shepherd's hut more substantial than most. Out of habit Robert went to assist the ladies to dismount, and lifted down the two swaddled bundles which dropped, groaning, into his arms, but he could not even tell which of them was Paka, and once on the ground the girls were allotted quarters behind a crumbling partition, in the innermost part of the hut. Giorgio and Mr Papandian – there was nothing Mr Papandian could not do – busied themselves with the preparation of a meal. Robert assisted to the best of his ability, while Mr Jones did nothing. The Circassian guides had meanwhile built a separate fire outside, and sat over it, talking. They apparently did not need or want to eat.

As soon as they had eaten the party one by one wrapped themselves in their blankets or bourkas and gave themselves up to sleep, all but the two Circassians, who kept up a desultory muttering round their fire. Robert alone found that tired though he was, sleep would not come to him. Neither his mind nor his body would leave him in peace, and he was conscious of the presence of Paka so close to him, on the other side of the partition. The shrouded figure she had become, silent and submissive, which would reveal its beauties only to the chosen one, enticed him infinitely more than the bold, unveiled girl who had herded lambs and goats behind her father's house, and gazed openly into men's faces. Under the robes and veils were the sweet rounded forms of womanhood which had blossomed under his hands : these dwelt in his mind rather than the young girl he had seen circling in the dance, rigidly corseted in her maiden attire. And he had possessed this hidden beauty! Paka was his, she called him her saviour. He had hardly seen her face since it had lain under his, flushed and gasping, on the red silk quilt. She had not been laughing at him, then!

Memories of Giorgio and the secret way into the loft came to Robert's mind. The building where they lodged was pretty insecure. Might it not be possible to effect an entry into the women's part of it by the back, and persuade the princess to come out? He began to extricate himself from the blanket. But the fire was still burning outside, and the two guides were sitting there, wakeful and watching. He would have to wait until they at last decided to go to sleep. But before that happened, Robert was asleep himself.

He woke up some time after midnight to find a violent storm in progress outside. The others were already awake, and Mr Jones was philosophically removing himself from the depression in the ground he had selected as a resting place. Promising comfort, it had ended as a quagmire. The rain was falling in torrents, and over the noise it made the crash of thunder could be heard. There was an outburst of exclamations and imprecations from the attendants who were wrestling with the frightened horses. Great gusts of wind and rain together battered against the stones. The rain penetrated freely inside the hut, there was no keeping it out, and in a few minutes everything was wet. Robert and the others huddled into the driest corners they could find, with their blankets and bedding seized up in their arms.

'Jibrahil!'

It was Paka's voice. Robert turned, and in the uncertain light of a torch he saw her head peeping over the top of the partition. She was unveiled and she was smiling at him.

'Paka!'

She stretched her hand as far as it would go across the wall which separated them, and Robert just managed to touch it with his own (he looked round quickly to see that neither Giorgio nor Mr Jones was an observer of this manoeuvre). Her fingers were warm, and jumped as if galvanized by the contact with his. Her face began to swim in a rosy flush before Robert's eyes, the features blurred and softened. She opened her smiling mouth, while the lids half closed over her eyes.

'I am coming round,' whispered Robert.

At that moment Mr Papandian, who had been to see to

matters outside, re-entered the shelter, beating the rain off himself. Paka instantly dropped down again out of sight.

'How much longer till morning?' asked Robert.

'Two hours, no more,' answered Mr Papandian. 'We must march at first light.'

'When we arrive at the coast, shall we be able to take ship right away?'

'Please God, yes,' said Mr Papandian. 'It would be most inexpedient to delay. I have sent a reliable man ahead to make all arrangements, and I trust he will have done so by the time we arrive.

'The Russian blockade has made things very difficult, just now. With their frigates patrolling, it is not easy to get a ship in or out of any harbour. And as if this were not enough, the Circassians are at each other's throats as well.'

'All this must be bad for your business,' said Robert, politely.

'It is very bad for business,' agreed Mr Papandian. 'There is no business. Trade with Circassia is coming to an end. What have they to sell? Their girls, mainly – formerly it was the boys as well, but that has mostly finished now – a few furs, perhaps, some chestnuts and honey. What do they want to buy? Cloth and salt and gunpowder, most of all gunpowder. All of these things have to go by sea, and they are heavy cargoes. It is not easy for a ship to run in during the blockade, as your *Vixen* found out to her cost, while the girls are not as simple to transport as skins. They have to be fed, and they become seasick. I can tell you, in an open boat, with twenty-five or more of them on board, all sick together, all wailing and screaming, it is not a funny thing.'

Robert asked whether Trebizond depended largely on its trade with the Black Sea ports.

'No,' said Mr Papandian. 'That is only a very small part of the business. There is a certain amount from the other Turkish ports, but the most part of it is the caravan trade with the interior. There are caravans which leave every day for Erzerum, Mosul, Baghdad, India.'

He was silent for a moment, contemplating the vast horizons which he had conjured up.

'Is Trebizond your native city?' inquired Robert.

'No, I was not born there. I come from a village in the

mountains, many miles away, near Erzerum. The people in my home village are very poor. They till the soil, they pay the pasha and the tax-gatherer, and somehow they manage to exist. When I was a young boy, and my father saw that I would be clever, he sent me to live with my uncle in Trebizond, to learn business. But it was not my wish. When I was a young man, I wanted to become a monk.'

His voice trailed off into silence. Robert leaned his head back against the wet stones and gazed out into the blackness of the night. The branches were still sighing and tossing, but the wind was subsiding. The air was chill and he huddled into his blanket and shifted his position on the portmanteau. He heard Mr Papandian's voice in his ear.

'Rest, Effendi, rest while you can. We start in an hour.'

The departure was a confused nightmare taking place in the half dark, horses getting their legs over the pickets and facing the wrong way round, wet ropes stretching, and men cursing. At last all was ready. The Circassian guides, having no possessions to speak of and thus the least to do, were in the saddle grimly waiting, and the two girls were summoned from their quarters. There also burst out with them, scrambling and panting at their feet, a small dirty white animal, doing his best to bark through the home-made muzzle which confined his jaws – Fop, who Robert fondly imagined he had left in safety many miles behind him, in the luxury of Arslan's kitchen quarters. But here he was, trying to fawn on Robert, attempting to scramble up his legs with dirty paws, and letting out strangled yelps of delight.

'Fobjee, Fobjee,' called one of the veiled figures.

The little dog hesitated for a second, then redoubled his attentions to Robert.

'Fobjee!'

Fop slipped down and ran back to Paka, who snatched him up and stowed him away somewhere in the folds of her voluminous coverings. His smothered protests could still be faintly heard, after the girls had taken their place at the rear of the cavalcade, while Robert and Mr Papandian followed immediately after the guides in the lead. The first night was over, and so far no pursuers had come out of the east.

214

Later in the day, however, when the sun grew hotter and hotter until the heat was like midsummer, and the cavalcade wound in and out of the scrubby oak and box thickets of the coastal hills, Robert was seized by a sensation of alarm and apprehension which increased, instead of lessening, with every mile they covered. He longed for a view to appear. The route they followed, winding between bushes and yet more bushes, never giving a glimpse of what lay ahead, was an endless frustration. Even though he was ignorant of the way, the fact that he could not see it increased his feeling of impotence. He did not doubt the guides : no useful purpose could be served by doubting the guides, for the party was completely in their hands, and he supposed that Mr Papandian chose competent ruffians. If they decided to cut the throats of the travellers and make off with the loot, it would be difficult to put up a successful resistance. As they selected the route, so they controlled the pace. He himself would have liked to push on as fast as possible, but in such tangled country it would have been foolish to let the rearguard drop too far behind, on the one hand, or to ride too far ahead of the party, on the other. He was constantly aware of some undefinable menace from behind. From where they were, the snow-flecked mountain peaks could no longer be seen, but nevertheless he sensed that they were there, the bastions of Arslan's territory. The fact that he could not decide what form the unseen menace took irked him the more.

The direction they were taking now led them into a marshy expanse of flags and reeds, where an undrained river filled the valley bottom. The path was broad, though, and well marked. This was clearly the way to the coast, and Robert for the first time that day felt his heart lift. Luck had been with them, so far.

Suddenly there was a whistle from the front. One of the guides came galloping back and exchanged a few hasty words with Mr Papandian. The grooms dragged the loaded horses into the shelter of a reed bed while the girls gave muffled cries of alarm. The guides peered in the direction of the opposite hillside. Robert peering also, could make out a movement behind the leaves which showed that a considerable party was passing that way, and he caught glimpses of their horses. The guides muttered to each other, and to Mr Papandian.

'Are they Arslan Bey's men?' Robert asked, at last.

'No, it is a messenger going to Arslan Bey's place,' answered Mr Papandian. 'The escort are bad characters. It is best to keep out of their way.'

'Who is the messenger?' asked Robert. His mind was on the possibility of the messenger carrying letters for himself.

'He calls himself Mikhail,' said Mr Papandian, 'but that is not his real name. He is a man of my race, but he is a Russian subject and working for the Russian commander-in-chief. He is the envoy the Russians are using to send to Arslan Bey.' He spread his hands.

'Had I known about this earlier, Mr Wilton, I should of course have taken steps to find you another *konak*, but the people of this country are like a boiling pot. With the lid on all is quiet, but once you take the lid off, you cannot see for the steam.'

'So Arslan Bey is treating with the Russians!' said Robert. 'Are you sure? How long has this been going on?'

'How long it has been going on I do not know, I cannot find out for certain, but I think only in these last few weeks. Arslan has not yet made up his mind, but as well as a treaty and Russian protection, they offer him gold. They are not mean with their roubles! The only thing is, they made a condition. He must give up to them the Pole who calls himself Shekhir, and that is not an easy condition to fulfil, for the Pole has his own bodyguard, and he is a brave and clever man.' Mr Papandian hesitated whether to go on, then continued: 'The thing which has troubled me most since I heard about this matter is this: if he could not give up the Pole, might not Arslan offer to give up *you*, instead? That is why I think you have done well in leaving, Mr Wilton.'

'Will Arslan pursue us, do you think?' asked Robert, calmly. After this further upheaval, his thoughts were settling down into the new pattern, and when the first crazy impulse to throw his hat on the ground and curse, or to laugh, or to cry, had passed, he felt more composed than he had all day. At least he now knew what he was up against.

Mr Papandian for the first time looked harassed.

'I do not know, but we ought to press on. We are not far now from the sea.'

He spoke to the guides, and the party moved off. They left

the valley bottom and turned into a tangle of scrub and oak woods. Wearily they plodded up another ridge, the counterpart of many others they had surmounted that day, and stopped at the crest to take breath.

'*Thalatta! Ecco di mare!*' said Giorgio, in surprise.

There it was, not sharp and clear and blue, but shrouded in a milky haze which blurred the junction of the sea and the sky. There was little wind on the land, but out on the water Robert could see white crests running southward. It was a deserted coast. There seemed to be no visible way down to the water, no beach, no way of approach. The woods ran straight into the sea, which beat uneasily somewhere down below. In the cover of some scrubby oak trees the party waited again, while one of the Circassians rode off alone. When he returned Mr Papandian dismounted, beckoning to Robert to do likewise and to follow him.

Mr Papandian led the way into the wood, taking the same direction as the guide had done, and they pushed their way through the bushes. No glimpse of the sea could be had, the prospect of taking ship seemed as remote as ever. Once more they were winding in and out of thickets and battling with thorns. The place was silent in the stifling midday heat.

'There is not much further to go,' said Mr Papandian.

The path took a downward direction and about fifty yards further on emerged from the wood. Robert found himself looking down into the marshy river valley which they had quitted some time back, at the point where the river waters, mingling with those of the sea, spread into a multitude of outlets, meandering over sandbanks and round rafts of purple and yellow water plants. The shore was fringed with the debris carried in by the waves, and glistening bubbles floated to and fro. Mr Papandian pointed.

'There is our boat,' he said.

There it was, an unpromising-looking vessel, perhaps, but certainly a boat, although it was considerably smaller than Robert had expected. One man was to be seen on board, and several others were squatting on their heels on the shore nearby.

'What next?' asked Robert.

Mr Papandian retreated until they were once more on the edge of the wood.

'I think this had best be our assembly point,' he said. 'I will have the luggage embarked first, and we will go on board when all is ready. It will be better to remain in cover until then. There is no need for you to trouble yourself, Excellency. I myself will go back and bring up the others.'

Left alone, Robert sat down among the buzzing and curious flies, which the gentle sea breeze was not enough to discourage. From this position he could not see the river estuary, or the boat. On a level with his head nodded flat plate-like heads of yarrow, which competed for the attention of the insects. The prospect to westwards was veiled and pearled with haze – a good thing, he realized, if there were any watchers out at sea. Rather to his amazement he saw that the time was still only noon. In some way he found this reassuring, and he was content to sit in the hot sun, watching the yellow butterflies – so late in the year! – which alighted on the yellow flower heads. He observed a bird hover hawklike overhead, but could not identify its species positively. In that heavy air all birds hovered rather than flew.

It was not long before he heard the jingle and subdued noises of the others coming up through the wood, and the riders dismounting, but he did not trouble to turn his head to see. With a groan Mr Jones subsided on to the ground beside him, and looked approvingly at the butterflies and the flowers.

'I wonder now, Mr Wilton, did you ever go into Wales?' he asked.

Robert admitted that he had never had that experience, adding that he regretted it.

'The north, now, that is a very wild country, almost as wild as it is yonder –' he jerked his head in the general direction of the vanished mountains – 'but the place where I was born is in the south. There are cliffs running down into the sea and the land behind is green. In the springtime it can be very beautiful. I am reminded of it now.'

Robert asked if Mr Jones intended to go back to his birthplace, to which Mr Jones returned a decided negative.

'Though the face of the land is beautiful, the people there are as wicked as can be found anywhere in the world,' he said, darkly. 'Did you know, Mr Wilton, that Pelagius himself was a Welshman? Morgan, that was his name. Sea-begotten is

218

what it means, and when he reached Rome he called himself
Pelagius – the same thing, you see. Some say he was an
Irishman, but the name Morgan is Cymric and he came from
Wales, more's the pity, to confuse men's minds with his
pernicious doctrines, until they were extirpated.'

Robert in a spirt of contrariness remarked that he himself
considered Pelagianism in some ways to be a healthy reaction
from the Augustinian doctrine which, if strictly applied, meant
that sinful man could blame all his lapses on his nature and not
on his failure of will, and this seemed to him little better than
the Mussulman's philosophy that everything was ordained by
God's will and that it was no good striving against it, be it to
rescue the drowning, or succour the orphan. If Pelagianism
were a heresy, it had in it more than a grain of common sense.

Mr Jones looked horrified.

'Indeed, how can you say such a thing, Mr Wilton? The
words of Scripture are plain.'

It was impossible to rival Mr Jones's faculty for proving his
case from the Bible, and Robert, although himself fairly
conversant with the Scriptures, did not attempt to challenge
him. Instead, he inquired again, in a polite manner, as to Mr
Jones's future plans, hoping that he would not be called upon
to further them.

Mr Jones appeared to be somewhat at a loss.

'My mission is to preach the Word, Mr Wilton,' he said,
'but I will not deny that I have been forced to regard these
Circassians as a hopeless case. They are a people without any
ideas of religion whatever! A pity it is, to leave them to the
bigoted tenets of Islam, but I do not think them even capable of
making good Mussulmans. Their land is indeed a habitation of
dragons, and a court for owls.

'But there are other places, not far from here, where I hear
that although the light of Christianity shines still, it shines but
darkly. The lamp needs plenishment. There are always devoted
men of my persuasion labouring to show the true way to these
poor people, who, Christians though they may term themselves,
are yet very near to idolaters in their observances, bowing
down to sticks and stones, revering mummified remains and
such-like heathen practices. I have it in mind to join a community of these devoted men I speak of.'

'And do you know where this community is to be found?' asked Robert.

'I know that it is somewhere in the land which was the ancient Armenia,' replied Mr Jones, 'but its exact location I am ignorant of. It will be necessary to make inquiries.'

'Perhaps Mr Papandian will know,' said Robert, rather thoughtlessly.

'Ah yes, it is very likely. You will be doing me a favour if you will be asking him for me, Mr Wilton.'

At that moment Mr Papandian approached, having occupied himself, while Robert and Mr Jones sat idle, in supervising the transfer to the shore of all the carpet bags and portmanteaux, in fact all the luggage, except for the two girls, who sat close together, covered with their cloaks, a little apart from the men, and whispered together.

Perhaps Robert did not put the question very tactfully, but Mr Papandian's countenance darkened, and he lost for once his air of obliging affability.

'I do not know which is the mission of which this gentleman speaks. There are many of them amongst my people, we have priests from Germany and other places, priests from America, even. Some of them are water-worshippers, some are throwers-down of holy pictures. I do not know why these foreign priests have come to our country when we have our own Church, the Church given us by the blessed Saint Gregory who expelled all the devils from Armenia and gave us the holy word of God. How can we have any need of foreign religions, who have been led to salvation by the Apostles themselves? We have the Scriptures already, and indeed, more of them than you have. We have the Testament of the Twelve Patriarchs, and the book of Asenath which you have not, and also the Epistle of the Corinthians to Saint Paul, and the Saint's reply to the Corinthians, of which equally your Church knows nothing, although they have been translated into the English tongue by your great Lord Byron.

'Some of the foreign priests who have arrived in my country are doing good, for they are bringing us our own scriptures in our own tongue, which are very scarce amongst us, as we cannot obtain them under the hand of the Mussulman. Also they have opened schools, and are teaching many useful things. All this

they are able to do because the Franks of the West are powerful, and our Lord the Sultan lets them have their way. But what can this man –' he indicated Mr Jones – 'do? He does not know the Armenian language. And if he were to learn it, he can only teach his religion, and we do not need his religion.'

'What does he say?' asked Mr Jones.

'He says,' replied Robert, 'that he does not know of any suitable mission such as you have spoken of.'

'Tell him,' pursued Mr Papandian, 'to go and preach his gospel to the Mussulmans. They are the people in whose midst we have to dwell, defenceless, forbidden to carry arms with which to protect our women and children. We have to make ourselves small and creep under stones not to be noticed. That is the only way we can keep our lives whole. Let your friend preach to these Mussulmans and alter their souls, if he can!'

Mr Jones, looking disgruntled, had risen, however, and wandered off.

'I agree that the conversion of the Mussulmans would be a worthy task,' said Robert, 'but it would surely be a hopeless one. It is not easy to persuade men to change when they are set in their faith.'

'Your Excellency is quite right,' said Mr Papandian. 'It is not easy, when the religion of the Mussulman offers him everything that he wants, freedom to sit idle and then seize the bread from the hands of those who have laboured for it, freedom to take what he wants in the name of his God, be it gold or silver, or lands, or women, freedom to cut off the lives of his fellow-men for a whim. All this – and paradise to come! Small wonder that he does not want to give up this religion, and it is not easy to persuade him.

'The other way round, it is not so difficult, perhaps.'

He glanced at Robert with a slightly quizzical air, and Robert recalled the somewhat incongruous picture of Egenye Bey, gay and dapper in his villa on the Bosphorus, with his pink and white cheeks, and his pink and green robes. He remembered, too, that only a minute number of Armenians, through centuries of oppression and degradation, had surrendered their own faith for Islam. But the flash of contempt in Mr Papandian's eyes was the matter of a moment only. The next second he bowed in his usual deferential manner.

221

'Everything should now be in readiness, and if you will permit me, I will go and see if the time has come for us to go on board.'

Our necessaries, at least, are embarked, thought Robert. It would have been sensible, no doubt, for him to have supervised the matter of their embarkation himself, but Giorgio at any rate had been there. Let him see to it. Robert was content to sit in the sun, bodily at ease, rubbing from time to time such insect bites as were accessible (for he had not acquired, and doubted if he would ever acquire, the necessary indifference to vermin which travel in this part of the world entailed) inhaling the odour of the turf and the flowers which was not so different from that of home, although the sea wind which murmured gently round his ears was a far remove from the blustery oceans of the north.

Chapter 14

A TIMID HAND touched Robert's shoulder from behind. He turned, to see Paka, with her veil wrapped round her so that only her eyes and forehead showed, She signed to him to follow her, and Robert crept after her into the shelter of the bushes. There was a patch of mossy ground there, with bracken waving over and round it. Robert put his hand up to the veil.

'Let me see you,' he murmured.

Paka made no demur to the removal of her veil, and she raised no objection when Robert took her in his arms. She was like a nut, warm, and brown, and sweet, or a ripe berry which only discloses itself when the leaves have been pushed aside. She returned shy caresses to his ardent ones, and she only giggled a little at his pronunciation when, with recollections of the French traveller's phrase-book:

'Oh, Paka, I love you very much,' he said.

They were not entirely alone in their private paradise. At a little distance off there was a sudden commotion among the bushes, and the strangled voice of Hafiza was heard, suddenly cut off:

'O Giorgio, amore mio!'

Giorgio's reply could not be heard, but a thrashing in the bushes and a convulsive panting indicated that Fop was foraging about on his own concerns. Paka giggled again. Robert paid no attention. He was watching Paka's face, seeing the smile on it fade, to be succeeded by astonishment (but why should she again have been astonished?) and then by a gaze of almost stern intensity, enough to stamp the picture of him forever on her eyeballs, which she bent on him until her long lashes came down on to her cheeks, and her arms dropped from his neck. The bracken fronds which had been lashing to and fro above their heads settled back into stillness, and the flies, which had risen in a glittering swarm, buzzing indignantly, returned to settle on their two motionless bodies.

Paka recovered herself first. She rearranged her disordered draperies, and sat up cross-legged, facing him.

'Jibrahil Bey,' she began. 'I am a Mussulman girl.'

Robert smile at her hazily, only half understanding what she was saying.

'Jibrahil, do you also become a Mussulman! Then we two can be happy together, in Stamboul, without sin.'

Robert was taken aback. He had not the words to explain to her how inappropriate was this idea. He sat up, in his turn.

'Paka, that cannot be,' he began.

'Cannot? Why not, Jibrahil?' Her mouth turned down, like a child's. 'If you love me, will you not do this for me?'

Just at this moment, Mr Jones could be heard calling, in increasing agitation, somewhere in the vicinity.

'I will come back,' he whispered to Paka, and brushing the leaves and bits of grass off his clothes, he emerged from the bushes.

Mr Jones was gazing distractedly around. The Circassian who had been sitting by his horse was still in the same place. The other man was nowhere to be seen, and Giorgio and Mr Papandian were out of sight.

'What is it?' asked Robert, seeing Mr Jones's agitation.

'I was thinking that I had returned to find you all gone, and myself left alone in the wilderness,' said Mr Jones.

'We are just about to go,' said Robert, 'but where have you been anyhow?'

'Oh, I have been only taking a walk round about,' replied Mr Jones. 'This is a fair country in many ways, Mr Wilton. It would gladden the heart to see such wealth as Nature has bestowed on it, were it in the hands of more worthy recipients. There is coal here, if I mistake not, and possibly other minerals besides.'

'What does he say?' inquired Mr Papandian, who came up at that moment.

'He says there is coal in this hill,' replied Robert.

'Coal! Does he know anything about coal?'

Robert translated the question.

'Has the man never heard of the Valleys?' queried Mr Jones, indignantly. 'Where does he think that most of the coal burned in Constantinople comes from, if not from Wales? And a wonderful and fearful sight it is to see valleys which before were deserts, with bare scant grass which would feed nothing but the sheep, resounding to the cheerful sounds of toil, and supporting men in their hundreds. Why, the few fields which are the endowment of our own chapel have increased more than fifty-fold in value since the coal was found under them.'

'He says he is familiar with coal,' translated Robert. 'He comes from South Wales, a remote part of England where large coal fields have recently been opened.'

'I know that,' said Mr Papandian. 'That coal is brought to Trebizond and further, Mr Wilton, while all the time there are large and accessible beds of coal on the Black Sea coast of Turkey which were worked in ancient times and never have been since.'

'I am surprised that someone – an enterprising man like yourself, for example – had not come forward to work them,' said Robert.

Mr Papandian spread his hands.

'Mr Wilton, I am a Christian subject of the Sultan – a *rayah* – the humblest creature that exists. What chance would I have of getting to the ear of a great man and obtaining a concession to work the coal, even if I dared admit that I had the money with which to buy it? But for an Englishman' (Robert doubted whether Mr Jones would like this description, but let it pass) 'it is a different matter. He has prestige. His Ambassador has the ear of the Porte. There are English consuls to protect him. Let your friend' (again Robert refrained from correction) 'be the prospective concessionnaire. Let him put off this priest's garb and put on proper Frankish clothes. Once he has found where the coal lies, I will put the money in his hand for the present he will have to give the pasha. We will be partners together in the enterprise.'

'What is he saying?' asked Mr Jones. Robert rendered the gist of it.

'That's not such a bad notion,' said Mr Jones. 'We must talk more about it. I like the man – he might almost be a Welshman. You tell him that from me, Mr Wilton.' He burst into laughter, and clapped Mr Papandian on the back. 'Here's my hand on it.'

Mr Papandian took the hand stretched out to him, but at this moment there was a wailing cry, a sound of summons, from the men waiting by the boat on the beach below.

Mr Papandian hastily looked down.

'It is time to go,' he said.

Robert also went to see what was happening. The travellers' bales and boxes had now been stowed away somewhere on board the boat, whose crew had assembled. Giorgio was now standing on the shore close by, engaged in disputation with one of the grooms who had presumably carried the loads down on their shoulders, as no horses were to be seen. Robert noticed that Giorgio had cast off his Circassian cloak, and shone forth once more in his customary gay clothes – short embroidered jacket and voluminous pantaloons, with a purple shawl round his waist. He must be happy to be getting away from Circassia!

'Where are the girls?' asked Mr Papandian. He called to them to come out. Hafiza was the first to answer the summons. She emerged from behind the bushes leading Fop on a string, and after a moment Paka followed.

'My parcel!' said Mr Jones, in sudden alarm, 'that I have carried all this way. Where can it be, I wonder?'

'Probably Giorgio has taken care of it,' said Robert. 'Why not ask him?'

Mr Jones hastened off down the path to the shore. Giorgio, seeing him coming, raised a hail. Robert could not understand what he said, but Mr Papandian did, and he too set off at a run.

Robert, left alone with the two girls, realized that this might be his last chance to speak to Paka about her future. He could only see her eyes, rather frightened now, as she held the veil across the lower part of her face.

'Paka –' he began. But he had no time to finish, for everything began to happen at once.

The crew were on board, Giorgio was still arguing with the porters on the shore, and the unhorsed Circassian was standing by. Mr Jones and Mr Papandian were three-quarters of the way and halfway respectively down the path. There was the sound of a shot from higher up the valley, and simultaneously a shout from the mounted Circassian who had been keeping watch from the edge of the woods. He now appeared galloping towards the sea. Into view at the head of the broad marshy valley flashed two horsemen. The black figures, at first so tiny, approached at an incredible speed. They were galloping on the lower path, making straight for the shore and the boat.

Mr Papandian also saw the riders coming. He and Mr Jones redoubled their pace. They seemed likely to reach the shore before the galloping horsemen, but what would become of the girls? They could not run, encumbered as they were with their wrappings. Where were the horses? They must be tethered somewhere within the wood, but Robert could only see his own. He ran to it and led it forward. Paka was watching the oncoming Circassians with horror-struck eyes. She began to wail and to beat her face with her fists.

'O Jibrahil Bey, it is Kherim! I am lost!' she moaned.

Hafiza now began to scream. '*Giorgio mio!*' Paka dropped on her knees on the ground.

Restraining a desire to shake them both, Robert seized Hafiza first and tossed her up into the saddle (his English saddle which Giorgio had forgotten to have taken off, but it was not the time to worry about the loss of it), then he took hold of Paka, who showed a disposition to go into hysterics at any moment, and got her up behind Hafiza. There was no need to give the girls the bridle, for he knew that if he could get the horse started in the right direction it would go better without one, and the sea would bring it to a stop. He led the horse, running by its side, part of the way down the path, and then released it with a smart clap on the flank. It set off with a plunge which almost unseated the girls, but they clung on somehow.

He himself stayed where he was. It was quite evident to him that he had no chance of reaching the boat before the advancing riders did. To his infinite relief, the Kabardan steed galloped down the hill in the right direction with the two girls managing to remain on its back, and a white object agitating frantically in Hafiza's arms. As the horse thundered up to the embarcation point, where Giorgio caught its bridle and brought it to a halt, Fop managed to wriggle loose. He landed on the ground with a thump which must have shaken the breath out of his body, but he gamely recovered himself and began to scamper up the hill again.

Scene then followed scene like the pages of a picture-book

being rapidly turned. Robert saw Giorgio and the crew hustle the girls on board. Mr Jones, his robes gathered up above his knees, was the next to board, then Mr Papandian. Giorgio and Mr Papandian made frantic signs to Robert to come at once. He made gestures back, and shouted, 'Get away! Get away quickly!' For he could see the riders galloping towards the shore while they, from their present position, could not. But there were now three riders in view, two galloping neck and neck in the valley bottom, the other, who was the mounted Circassian escort, was racing down from the hill to cut their course at an angle, but with what object Robert knew not.

That was the land picture. He turned to the sea again. On the shore the Kabardan horse was plunging and rearing, and the second Circassian was endeavouring, without success, to mount it. On board the boat confusion reigned, but with much splashing and shouting the crew had pushed out a certain distance from the shore, and were trying to hoist the sail.

The two riders reached the water's edge a good way ahead of the mounted Circassian. One was Hassan – Robert recognized him instantly – and a second man, who held a pistol in his hand as he galloped. This man was a short length ahead of Hassan. Without checking his pace he fired the pistol, and Robert saw it was Kherim. The Circassian let go of the Kabardan horse's bridle and fell first on to his knees, then forward on his face, with his hands outflung. Robert thought he could see the hands moving as though the man were trying to drag himself forward, but his body did not move.

As if it were a race, and the starter's signal had just been given, the Kabardan horse started off at a gallop for the open country, and Kherim turned his horse and raced after it. The mounted Circassian saw them coming, swerved, and joined in the pursuit. With incredible speed the thundering hooves of the three horses vanished out of the landscape.

Fop, panting and heaving, threw himself down among the grasses at Robert's feet, and looked up expectantly. Finding himself given no attention, he snapped at a fly, and sat up on his haunches.

Now there was only Hassan down by the shore, steadying himself as he leapt from his horse by the side of the dead man. He, too, had a pistol in his hand. Robert knew it, a native-made flintlock affair, with a round ivory butt and much inlay on the barrel, but very liable to misfire. Hassan did not attempt to use it, however. Instead, he reached for the long gun which was slung on his back. With this, Robert knew, he was an excellent shot. The boat was quite a long way out, the crew had got the sail up now, but even so, she was still within range.

'Hassan! Don't hurt your sister!' he shouted.

Hassan could not make out where the hail came from, and Robert could see the bewilderment on his face. 'Hassan! I am here!' he shouted again. Hassan looked in the right direction, and even at this distance there was no mistaking the fury which succeeded to the bewilderment. He mounted again and put his horse at the hill.

Robert ran like a hare, with Fop at his heels. Instinctively, he took to the thickest cover, reasoning that this would impede the horse more than him. On foot, he knew that he could out-distance Hassan. Instinctively, also, he made for the sea. The land had nothing more to offer him.

After five minutes of battling with the thick cover which tore his clothes and scratched his face, he came out on the top of the cliff. He found himself on a headland, from which he could scan the sea in three directions. Away to the south was the sailing boat, now going along at a fair pace. On the north the sea swept inland into a pretty horseshoe bay, no doubt with a beach which Robert could not see. In the mouth of the bay, lying at anchor, as fresh with paint and brasswork as though she were in a berth at Cowes, was a yacht. From this distance he could not read her name. So small she looked, and so incongruous, all alone against the immense backdrop of the sea and the shore, but it was unmistakably a European yacht, and a hope of sanctuary. Robert determined to reach it.

Getting down to the beach was even harder work than the struggle amongst the thorns and thickets on the cliff top. He hung from branches of small lichen-draped oaks, whose roots were precarious, he slithered down sharp slabs of rock. At one point where there was a vertical drop and no way round, it was necessary to lean over as far as possible, holding Fop at the furthest extent of his arm, and drop him on a ledge, before following suit himself. Streams oozed out of the rock face, and they both got very wet as well as dirty. Becoming finally tired and clumsy, Robert lost his footing and fell the last ten feet, but fortunately landed in a pool of water ringed with delicate harts' tongue ferns. This was the bottom of the cliff. He had reached the beach.

A carrion stench entered Robert's nostrils. It pervaded the air, already clamorous with insects. It was a stench compounded of decaying fish and putrefying flesh. Along the margin of the beach lay dotted here and there black carcases, some of them torn open. They were dolphins, driven ashore in last night's storm. As he advanced to the water's edge, two shapes which seemed to Robert's excited fancy to be as large as wolves started up from one of the carcases, and bolted up the beach. They were not wolves but wild pigs, attracted out of the woods by the smell of carrion.

Robert picked his way to the edge of the sea. No sign of life could be discerned on board the yacht. What if he was to hail her? But in what language should he do so? And dressed as he was, would anyone respond to the hail?

There was no time to lose. Robert took off his pistols. He had once hesitated about leaving them as a parting gift for Hassan. Now Hassan could have them – if he found them. He laid them on the sand. He also removed his boots, but nothing else. Minutes were precious, and anyhow he felt a curious aversion to meeting strangers without his clothes. He made his way to the edge of the water and walked into the sea, his feet sinking into the soft muddy bottom which oozed between his toes. Fop toiled after him, then suddenly finding himself waterborne, began to paddle.

The water came barely to Robert's knees, however, and the shore, as he remembered, was a gently shelving one. He picked Fop up and tucked him under one arm, the little dog striking out with all four legs at once, like a crab suspended in mid air. As soon as he was waist-deep Robert plunged forward, dropping Fop in a little ahead of him, and began to swim. The yacht, he now perceived, was not lying in the mouth of the bay as he had thought, but some distance out. He set a course steadily towards her, and Fop paddled doggedly at his side. Once through the fringe of floating jetsam at the margin of the bay, sea-wrack, branches, broken planks (where from? he wondered), with an occasional jellyfish, a bright blob, trapped in a patch of stagnant water, he encountered quite a strong current, but persevered against it. Thinking Fop was tiring, he tried to support him with one hand while swimming with the other, but Fop responded so energetically to this encouragement that he tore Robert's hand with his nails, and Robert had to let him go. Every now and again the little dog took a gulp of water which he seemed to relish, jellyfish and all. Robert concentrated on keeping his own head out of the water and seeing where he was going. The sun, now at its meridian, baked the top of his head (he had lost his Circassian hat in the last mad scramble down the cliff), the yacht never seemed to get any nearer, indeed he was afraid the current must be carrying him away from it. He forced his arms and legs to perform more strokes, and again more strokes. The weight of his water-logged clothes dragged at him – fortunate was Fop, who had only a string of blue beads to carry!

Water was beginning to come into Robert's mouth at every stroke. He spat it out, and shook the hair out of his eyes. The sea which had been so glassy smooth in the bay now started to run in all directions, with an uneasy motion which made his course still more difficult to hold.

Quite suddenly the yacht was there, rearing out of the water a little to one side of him. He let his feet sink and rested upright in the water, supporting himself with his arms. He read the name on her side – *Sea Sprite*, and hailed.

Still not a soul to be seen on board. Feebly, for by now he was nearly exhausted, he hailed her once more. No response. He tried again.

This time there was a flurry on deck. They must have all been looking out to sea on the opposite side, he supposed. He could discern something flapping. Heavens, it was a lady's skirt! A confused clatter of voices ensued, then he heard a man saying distinctly:

'Good heavens, I don't need a pistol, it is only one man. But you keep below.'

More confused expostulation, then the voice quite sharply:

'Please do as I say and get below.'

A man in a cap leaned over the rail. With the sun in his

eyes, Robert could not make out if he was young or old, short or tall. He called up:

'May I come on board, please? I am an Englishman.'

'English! Why yes, of course, come on board. Where's that ladder? McAdam!'

A ladder was lowered and wearily Robert clambered on board clasping Fop to his chest, to find himself confronting a man about the same age as himself, but already rather stout, who was attired in a tight yachting costume and eyeing him interrogatively.

'My name is Wilton, Robert Wilton,' he began. 'I have no card with me, unfortunately.'

'Sir William Enderby,' was the reply. 'Delighted to make your acquaintance, Mr Wilton. I am afraid we may not have heard you hail, at first. We were all watching that native craft away to the south over there, and wondering where she was making for, and also where she had sprung from, as this coast seems to have no inhabitants whatsoever.'

'She is making for Stamboul,' said Robert, 'and she is the boat I had intended to be on, but I missed her.'

'Missed the boat!' Sir William gave a loud and not un-friendly laugh. 'Well, we shall probably catch her up. We are making for Constantinople ourselves, although we may call in at Trebizond, if that's worth seeing, on the way. We shall be delighted to take you with us, Mr Wilton.'

'That is very kind of you indeed,' said Robert. 'It would be a great convenience to me. I am afraid I have no luggage at all. It was all embarked on the other boat.'

'No luggage?' Sir William seemed to take in for the first time that Robert was streaming water all over the spotless deck, also that the clothes he had on were not conventional in cut. Fop chose this moment to shake himself vigorously, and Sir William recoiled.

'I'll tell Blagg to find you something to wear now. Nothing of mine would fit you, but there are usually some spare clothes on board, and I suppose he can dry that – that travelling suit of yours. Blagg! Blagg! I want you here *at once*.'

'Yes, Sir William.' A bald-headed, elderly steward appeared and was given instructions.

'I will tell the valet, Sir William.'

'And now, if you will come below, Mr Wilton –'

Robert hung back. 'Well . . . I wonder. I have been living with the Circassians for some months, you know, and these clothes are, well, somewhat lively. The sea water will have killed a good many, I expect, but one can never be sure.'

Sir William stared at him for a moment, mouth agape, then recovered himself.

'Living with the Circassians? Very unusual that, but must have been interesting. I take it you are the English gentleman we were told about when we visited Count Williaminoff's camp. There were two Russian officers there who had been prisoners in Circassian hands until they were exchanged. They said that this Englishman had saved their lives. You must tell us all your adventures, Mr Wilton. We shall have an interesting trip to Constantinople.

'But now – the clothes. Why not throw those you have on overboard, my dear fellow. You can change up here.

'Blagg! Tell Baptiste to bring the clothes up on deck. And Mr Wilton will want a towel. That dog of yours – a bath, perhaps! Blagg, you attend to that.'

The Baptiste who brought the change of clothes on deck was a negro in smart European clothes, a man as solid and pompous as his master. He watched incuriously as Robert stripped off the Circassian tunic and breeches, and his own shirt, and dropped them over the side into the sea, then seized the towel and began to dry himself vigorously. Fop, cringing, with confidence momentarily deflated, was led away.

There was a sudden bang and a flash from the shore. Robert jumped as a bullet whizzed through the rigging just above his head. Baptiste dived head first down the companion way. Sir William, his hands in his pockets, walked to the rail with mild interest on his face.

'Firing at us, what impudence! There seems to be a man there on the shore, with hostile inclinations. And the general assured me that the country was perfectly safe! Is this character a friend of yours, Mr Wilton?'

'Not exactly a friend,' replied Robert. 'That is to say, there were misunderstandings.'

'Better move over to the other side,' said Sir William, and they both did.

'I can see him,' called an excited female voice from below. 'I am coming on deck.'

'No, you can't come on deck, Sybilla. Our guest hasn't any clothes on. You stay where you are, but let me have that telescope.'

The telescope was brought by Blagg, and Sir William adjusted it to his eye.

'Difficult to make him out among all those trees. Ah, now it is clear. Do you want to have a look at your old friend?'

Robert, who had got into a pair of trousers, took the telescope. He walked to the rail on the side nearest the shore, and it seemed to him that he would be able to see more clearly if he were to be raised up. He stepped on to a hatch cover, and raised the telescope to his eye.

The magnification was so high, the picture was so sharp and so clear, that he found himself as it were a few yards distant from Hassan. The boy was crouching on one knee. He had set up the forked rest on which the Circassians liked to support their long guns to take a shot, and his eyes met Robert's down the barrel of the gun.

Hassan's hat had also fallen off, his head was shaved except for the one long lock, he was frowning in concentration. With one hand he made a sign – could it have been the sign of the Cross, come down from the old days before Islam, designed to call down the blessing of heaven on his shot?

Yes, go on, go on, thought Robert, as their eyes continued to hold each other's. You could hardly miss a second time. The thought of taking cover never occurred to him.

Enderby was saying something which Robert did not hear, there was that girl's voice again, but still he and Hassan stared at each other, he holding the telescope steady as the yacht shifted and strained a little at her anchor.

It was Hassan who yielded first. He dashed his hand across his forehead to clear the sweat from his eyes, and rose to his feet. He put the gun back in its cover, then Robert saw him lead his horse out of the undergrowth. He swung himself into the saddle and rode away, not at a gallop as Robert was used to seeing him ride, but at a walk, for the cliff top was treacherous. He did not look back, and as Robert watched, horse and rider broke in among the bushes and disappeared.

Robert lowered the telescope. He felt all at once light-headed, betrayed and bereft – and also, desperately weary. He stepped down to the deck, to find Sir William Enderby scrutinizing him with interest.

'Wilton! Now I know who you are – been bothering me. You are a friend of Lawrence Fanshawe's, ain't you?'

'I used to know him quite well at one time,' said Robert. 'We were up at Oxford together.'

'At Oxford, yes. Well, they tell me he is a very brilliant man, and he is certainly wonderfully knowledgeable about all these foreign countries, and political problems and so on. He told me about some friend of his who had gone off to Circassia, when he heard I was to be cruising here, but I never expected I would come across you in quite this way! Jove, you must have had some extraordinary experiences. You are going to write something about it, I expect? You will find a good many people interested in you, when you get back to London.'

'Well, I may not go back straight to London,' said Robert. 'My future plans are still uncertain.'

'Good idea to winter in a decent climate,' said Sir William. 'We are thinking ourselves of spending Christmas in Cairo. I gather that there is one tolerable hotel there.'

The elderly steward appeared once more.

'Lunch will be served in ten minutes' time, Sir William, and Mr McAdam says there is a breeze coming up. Shall he be getting under way, he says?'

'Tell him to wait for half an hour. Let us have our lunch in peace, at any rate. Come along, Mr Wilton.'

The softly-stepping stewards down below continued with their preparations for the meal. The yacht suddenly heeled and swung a little, as two sailors began some operation connected with the anchor, just enough to transform her into a live thing, ready to plunge off southward in a storm of canvas.

As he was about to follow his host below, Robert noticed an English newspaper lying on a table nearby. With a murmured apology he glanced quickly down the columns. The first item that met his startled eyes was an account of the Queen's Proclamation.

'The Queen?' he said interrogatively.

'Yes, poor old King William's gone. It happened back in

June. We've got Victoria now. Good heavens, you have been out of touch!'

Sir William was showing signs of impatience, but Robert could not tear himself away from the several months' old newspaper. Nothing more of interest on the front page – but what was this? His eyes encountered a familiar name in a paragraph headed 'A Strange Affair near Norwich'. He read on :

'We are informed that considerable excitement prevails in the neighbourhood of Faxted, a village some ten miles from the City, as a result of a public declaration made by one Handyside, a gamekeeper in the employment of the Right Honourable Lord Shuttleworth. Handyside, who has recently become an adherent to the Methodist connection, has confessed that he gave false evidence in a trial held before the Spring Assizes of several criminals accused of poaching, which resulted in one of these men, Henry Ginger, being convicted of a crime under Lord Ellenborough's Act for which he was duly sentenced to transportation. Handyside has now stated that the man Ginger did not, contrary to what Handyside said in his sworn testimony to the jury, have a firearm in his possession at the time of the alleged offence. Further inquiries are being made.

In the meantime we are informed that an agitation has been started in the neighbourhood, which will no doubt be supported by those "liberal" persons who profess themselves opponents of the Game Laws, to have Ginger granted a free pardon. We hope the authorities will move with caution in this . . . over-riding necessity to ensure the protection of life and property . . . times of increasing lawlessness . . .'

Robert could read no more. He turned, smiling stupidly, to where Sir William stood, tapping his foot.

'Come and get ready for luncheon, Mr Wilton. Miss Enderby is waiting for us. You can read the newspaper later – in fact it will have to last you to Constantinople.'

As he made ready to follow his host below, Robert cast a last look behind him at the empty sea and the empty shore, quivering in the heat which veiled the stranded carcasses of the dolphins rotting on the beach. There was nobody on the shore, no living creature in sight, only trees marched down to the edge of the water.

Ridge after ridge rolled back as far as eye could see, the hills gaining height as they receded. It was hard now to make out whether the tiny specks on the horizon were clouds, or the distant tops of the snowy mountains which Robert knew were there.

Then as he looked, the mist began to roll down from the mountains like a curtain falling, covering first the sky, then the distant hills, then the nearer ridges, until all the sea-coast of Circassia was blotted out from view. Only on the water was the sun still shining with midsummer heat, the waves were as blue as a midsummer sea. The waves sparkled and splashed their white crests, the breeze blew gently but insistently. The current ran to the south, and to the south all the way was clear.

Chapter 15

Ten days later the *Sea Sprite* was lying at anchor off Seraglio Point, in the shadow of the domes and minarets of Constantinople. The voyage down the Circassian coast had been uneventful, and most of the time they sped along with a fair breeze behind. Sir William put in at Trebizond for a few days to take on water and to view the antiquities, during which time Robert pursued discreet inquiries of his own, without success. There was no news of the Circassian vessel, and Mr Papandian's shop in the bazaar was shuttered. The other party must have missed out Trebizond, Robert thought, and would put in at a smaller port along the coast to replenish their supplies, so there was a chance of overtaking them. But on the second day out from Trebizond a storm came up, one of the sudden Black Sea gales, and drove the *Sea Sprite* westwards in a cloud of rain and spray, in which they might at any time have passed the slower ship, ploughing along unseen. Robert, bracing himself on the pitching deck, exhilarated by the speed and the motion, could not but pity poor seasick Paka and Hafiza on board a much less well found craft.

Miss Enderby showed no signs of seasickness, and kept on her feet at the height of the gale, but his contacts with her were few, and mainly limited to mealtimes. Which was just as well, for he was lamentably out of practice in making small-talk with an English girl, and found himself rather nonplussed by this slight, pale young thing who listened gravely to her brother and himself, and kept her views to herself. The only occasion on which he had any real converse with her was at Sinope, where Sir William decreed they should be put in to remove all traces of the storm before arriving at Constantinople. Robert was deputed to escort Miss Enderby ashore and to the top of a hill which she desired to ascend in order to sketch the view.

The wide prospect of the Black Sea was indeed sublime, but Robert strained his eyes in the quarter where the peaks of Circassia lay. Too far, of course, he could not see them, but still they were there.

'What is Circassia like, Mr Wilton?' asked Miss Enderby suddenly, raising her eyes from her sketching block. 'Is it anything like this?'

Below them the slopes were clothed with green oak woods, and forested hills stretched into the interior as far as the eye could see.

'Yes, in some parts it *is* very like,' answered Robert. He did not enlarge on the statement. He was seeing in his mind's eye the dense greenery of the foothills, the icy streams and dew-soaked meadows of Arslan's domain, and above all, the harsh, forbidding mountains which had been before his eyes for so many weeks.

'How I would like to see it!' said Miss Enderby, abandoning her sketch. 'General Williaminoff said he would let us make a tour inland, with a Cossack escort, but we had to refuse as my brother did not want to spend so long away from the yacht. But I wanted to go, very much.'

'I do not think the general would have let you go far,' said Robert. 'The Russians have not conquered the country yet, you know.'

'Oh yes, I do know that the Circassians are putting up a tremendous fight for their independence, those brave people,' said Sybilla. 'Even Captain de Beaumont in the Russian camp was full of admiration for their courage – although he told us some very strange things about them,' she added. 'To think that you have actually lived with them – and fought for them!'

Her eyes were full of undisguised admiration, but before she could put the further questions which were on her lips Blagg, who had accompanied them to the foot of the hill, hurried up and announced that Sir William was making a signal from the yacht. It was time they were back on board.

Now the Enderbys, mustering their letters of introduction, took up residence in the hotel at Pera, and Robert returned to the boarding house which had previously accommodated him, where the first thing he saw was his portmanteau. He learned that Giorgio had deposited his belongings there a few days previously, and had been returning at intervals in the hope of obtaining news of his master. Going out to buy some soap and other necessaries, Robert ran into him. Giorgio rushed to kiss his hand, beaming.

'Praise be to God, you have returned in safety!'

He was at first too overcome with emotion to tell his story, but then it came pouring out, under the stimulus of Robert's questions. Their voyage also had been mercifully uneventful. As Robert surmised, they did not put in at Trebizond, but bought the food and other things they needed at small insignificant ports.

Where was Mr Papandian, Robert asked. And Mr Jones? And the two girls?

The girls! Giorgio grinned broadly. The girls were as happy as queens. Everything had fallen out for the best, and their futures were now splendidly arranged. Hafiza had been incorporated into the harem of one of the grandest pashas of the Porte, a situation which Giorgio, knowing an old Greek woman who had the entrée to the women's quarters, could vouch for as being one of the best, and –

'The princess!' interrupted Robert. 'Where is she?'

'The princess, ah –' Giorgio put on a mysterious expression. 'To have news of the princess, your Excellency should apply to Egenye Bey, the banker, he who has the yali by the Bosphorus.'

'Egenye Bey? What has he to do with the matter?'

'Why, it is he who has bought the princess, Excellency!'

For a moment Robert could not believe his ears. 'Egenye Bey has the princess?'

'Why, yes.' With his usual quickness, Giorgio perceived that something was wrong. 'It was the Armenian who arranged everything, no doubt as he thought your Excellency desired. Egenye Bey has a fine house, too,' he concluded, hesitantly.

'So the Armenian sold the princess, and Hafiza also?'

Giorgio nodded.

'In that case, where is their price?' asked Robert, with irony.

'It is all here.' Giorgio's hand went to his girdle. 'That is, it is written down what has happened to the price. The journey was very expensive, Excellency. There was the hire of all

those Circassian savages, there was the boat hire, the sailors'
pay, the food for all the men and the two girls –'

'Then what do I owe Mr Papandian?' asked Robert.

'Your Excellency owes the Armenian nothing. It is written
down in the paper which I am to give you. As to my wages, it is
all as your Excellency pleases – and in accordance with our
agreement.'

'Where is Mr Papandian now?'

'Gone!' said Giorgio. 'Gone to look for coal!' He recounted,
with frequent bursts of merriment, for his spirits could not
remain long under a cloud, that as soon as the future of the
princess and Hafiza had been "arranged", stopping only to
outfit the minister in suitable European clothes, Mr Papandian
and Mr Jones had sailed for the coal-bearing district a short
distance up the Black Sea coast, where Mr Jones intended to
initiate a survey immediately. Their ship, and the *Sea Sprite*
must have passed within hailing distance of each other, somewhere round about the Cyanean rocks.

'The Armenian excused himself a thousand times for not
being here to greet your Excellency, but he begged me to
present his humble respects and to give you this paper of
accounts which he has made out.'

Robert took it, but did not more than glance at it. His glance
showed him that Mr Papandian's two totals neatly cancelled
each other out.

'Will your Excellency give me a letter of recommendation
to other English gentlemen?'

'Yes,' said Robert, 'but not today. Come back tomorrow.' He
was restraining an impulse to rush off to the yali at Kadikoy,
and fortunately some inner wisdom came to his aid. It was too
early in the day for one thing, and there was another errand
which had to be discharged. This was a visit to the Embassy to
which he had, no doubt as a result of the Enderbys' duty call
there (for he had never made one himself) received a politely
worded summons. It was lucky the Embassy was back in
winter quarters at Pera, so it was a matter of minutes to reach
it, and to be admitted to the presence of a very youthful official,
who had already acquired such a mastery of diplomatic caution
that Robert never managed to gather his name. This young
man, while contriving to express a wordless disapproval of

Robert's recent adventures, nevertheless asked many discreet questions and made small careful notes of names and places. Finally he asked:

'And what do you plan to do next, Mr Wilton? Not write a book, by any chance?'

The question somewhat disconcerted Robert, who replied:

'Well, I have some business to attend to here, and I am also awaiting the arrival of a – a friend, who is coming out from England to join me. Then I shall probably make my way to Cairo –' he named at random the first place that came into his head – 'by land.'

'By land? You know the coast of Asia Minor is in a most unsettled state just now, and we hear the Arab tribes are fighting each other in the interior. You should have an interesting journey!'

The young man relaxed enough to smile, and Robert was emboldened to ask:

'What news of the *Vixen* affair? I have been rather out of touch, you know. Was anything done, in the end?'

Official caution was dropped, for a moment.

'What did you expect? There was more talk, and a packet of excuses was offered up in Parliament! Nobody wants to know the truth. Our politics nowadays are dictated by business men who never go a mile from the City. They know nothing of what is going on in the rest of the world, and they don't much want to know. The fact that we have a place to maintain, and that someone else will fill it if we don't, is something they prefer to ignore.

'Oh, you may be interested to hear,' the young man continued, 'that the Porte have at last been persuaded to act over your military confrère, Captain de Beaumont. He left yesterday on the Danube boat.'

'*Captain* de Beaumont?'

'He used to be in the army at one time, of course.'

'But I have never been in the army myself.'

The young man looked puzzled. 'Your name is R. G. Wilton, is it not?'

'Yes, but –' Robert was equally puzzled. 'I wonder if by any chance you are confusing me with my brother Reginald. He is with his regiment in India just now.'

'Still, I thought –' the young man stared, then recovered himself and shook hands civilly, with a formal expression of hope that Robert would enjoy his trip to Cairo. The interview was over, and Robert was free to pursue more pressing business.

This time he approached the yali of Egenye Bey by land. Taking a caique to the Asiatic shore, he landed at Scutari and rode north through the pretty villages which lay by the Bosphorus, where the villas at the water's edge were lapped in what seemed like summer's glow. One would have said it was late August in northern Europe. The current which raced furiously down the straits left quiet backwaters along the shore, where caiques were moored under the drooping willow-fringes. There were several tied up to Egenye Bey's landing stage, one of them draped with rich carpets which showed that it was for the use of harem ladies. Round the landward side of the yali ran a high wall, in the shadow of which two or three old men were sitting in the dust. Tossing the reins to a ragamuffin who appeared from somewhere to hold the horse, Robert found a door, and after some delay he was admitted to the presence of the master of the house.

Egenye Bey received him this time, not in the mirror-walled Turkish room, with its divan and its panelling of roses, but in an apartment which he evidently used for business, a room filled with elaborate French furniture and Lyon brocade. He had been writing at an escritoire laden with ormolu and marquetry. He had exchanged his robes for some kind of uniform, his turban for a fez, and the picture of a Frenchified Turk was complete. Mr Eugenius had come full circle.

Robert expressed the hope that he had not called at an inopportune moment, but Egenye Bey was cordiality itself, his manner at once joking and playful.

'Before you tell me your adventures, Mr Wilton, for I shall not let you go until you have done this, let me say at once that I have guessed the purpose of your visit.

'Yes,' he continued, 'I was sure that you would come at once to inquire about the welfare of your protégée.'

'I have no protégée that I know of,' replied Robert, 'for I am informed that the Circassian princess who accepted my escort to Constantinople has now passed, by a process of sale, into your hands.'

'From what I have been told, it sounds as if the young lady in question did not only accept your escort, but made full use of you to secure herself a passage to the destination of her choice, Mr Wilton, but perhaps that is an immaterial detail. On her arrival, as you were not here yourself, and she had, of course, to be provided for – and also her female companion – Papandian came to me and I arranged matters, for the best, as I thought. However, I fully acknowledge your interest in the girl – the princess, for so she is, I believe, in her native land – and I am entirely at your disposal to answer any question you wish to put to me on the subject.'

'Is it, then, the case that you have purchased the princess?'

'Yes, Mr Wilton, I purchased her, in the market – "open market", as you would say, although of course such transactions are done in private – and for the proper price. There was nothing underhand about it, I ask you to believe.'

'From whom did you buy her?'

'From your agent, Papandian, through a Moslem inter-mediary, of course. Papandian is a Christian, it would be against the law for him to own a Moslem slave, or you, for that matter.'

'I had not thought of the princess in the capacity of a chattel which could be bought and sold,' said Robert. 'If I may say it, it disgusts me that you, a man of Western origins, can do so.'

Mr Eugenius looked astonished.

'But, my dear sir, how else is it possible to settle the girl respectably? Do you think that we have here in Turkey employment agencies for young women from Circassia seeking situations? What employment, in any case, is open to this girl? She cannot speak French, or play the piano, so she is quite ineligible to find a place as a governess. You would not wish to see a princess working in the fields, or engaged in some degrading manual occupation. In her present state of life she will be educated, she will learn to read and write Arabic, even a little Persian, she will be given lessons in music and cooking, and also some religious instruction. In short, she will be able to acquire all the suitable female accomplishments. Even the piano is not excluded – I have one here! What more could you do for her? If you were minded to keep her for yourself, you could not do so here in Constantinople; there would be too many difficulties in your way. In what other manner could you assure her protection?' Seeing Robert was still unconvinced, Mr Eugenius led the way towards the door. 'Come, you shall see for yourself.'

Beckoning Robert to follow, he pushed back a heavy *portière*, and led the way along a passage which seemed to conduct from Europe back to Asia. Only screens of carved woodwork divided them from the Bosphorus, and Robert got the impression that water lay below the creaking boards they were treading. After running quite a distance the passage came to a dead end, but in the wall which faced them there was, high up, a small shuttered window. Standing on tiptoe (for he was not a tall man), Mr Eugenius opened this shutter and looked through the aperture, then he signed to Robert to take his place.

Robert found himself looking down through a wooden lattice-work into an enclosed space, a garden, or courtyard, within the walls of the yali. There were tall bushes of roses there, still flowering in profusion, and a fountain playing, while round the court were stone benches which had been spread with carpets and piles of cushions. Among the cushions an indolent, queenly creature was reclining. Robert could hardly believe his eyes when he recognized Paka.

She seemed softer, more voluptuous, and fuller in form than ever he remembered her. Her hair had been loosed from its plaits, and cut and combed so as to frame her head and shoulders. As well as the cloud of loose hair, there were two magnificent braids knotted loosely together at her back. A gauze chemise revealed most of her breasts, and a little waistcoat of patterned brocade did nothing to conceal what the transparent gauze disclosed. Paka's lower limbs were confined, as far as the knee, in flowing silk pantaloons, and she lay back on her piled cushions with one leg drawn up, in an attitude of complete abandon, apparently absorbed in contemplating the jewels which weighed down her arms and fingers, jewels which might have been chosen to show off the whiteness of her skin. A piece of embroidery work lay where it had been dropped beside her, and on a square of gauze lay skeins of many-coloured silks.

Sitting at her feet, also on a cushion, was another, younger girl, dressed in similar finery, but obviously an admiring satellite to Paka's full moon. She was talking with animation, and here and there Robert caught a word which was familiar to him. He realized that he had seen this girl also before – she was surely the untamed savage who had stamped and raged when she was shown off to him on his previous visit! And there, seated cross-legged in an embrasure, was the old negress, surveying her charges. Now that the whole of her face was revealed, she looked almost benevolent.

Robert was aware of Egenye Bey standing expectantly beside him, but he could not tear his eyes away, until a man's voice in the court, a high squeaky voice, made him jump. Did Egenye Bey's establishment, then, run to a eunuch? But the voice came from under the eaves, and Robert saw that there was a birdcage hanging there, the bars so elaborately jewelled and ornamented that the captive could not be seen. It was from the caged bird that the squeaky voice had proceeded. The girls laughed, and Paka looked up, in the direction of the lattice, as if she sensed that someone was behind it. The women must have been well aware of the existence of the peep-hole. Although she could not see him, she must have become conscious of a man's scrutiny, for she leaned back on the cushions, arching her neck and dilating her bust, as if to court it. The forbidden fruit was arrayed for his inspection. Negligently Paka bent a rose towards her, and buried her nose in it, giving by association the last refinement a voluptuary could demand, before she turned to her companion again.

The negress had a tambourine on her lap, and she suddenly struck it, setting all its bells jingling, before starting to chant in a harsh old voice. As if she had called the girls to attention, Paka picked up her embroidery frame and began to stitch at it, while the younger girl started to wind the skeins of silk.

Robert let himself down from the peep-hole, and followed his host back along the covered gallery.

'There she is, Mr Wilton, safe and happy,' said Mr Eugenius, as soon as they regained the study, 'and she will continue to be safe, I promise you, although I should tell you that it is not my intention to keep her here. As soon as she has had a preliminary polishing, she will be presented to a personage whose household

246

is far more magnificent than my own poor establishment. She will live in a palace, and who knows? a great fortune may be in store for her.'

'The picture is a dazzling one, I admit,' said Robert. 'I certainly could not offer anything like the same style of life. If ease and luxury is all the princess wants –' he broke off, in some confusion, for it was beginning to dawn upon him that the Paka he had known, and the indolent beauty who had just been displayed to him were creatures of a different flesh.

'Let us turn to another subject,' said Mr Eugenius, always a considerate host. 'Your adventures in Circassia have been most varied and interesting, I gather, and it is certainly good to see that you have returned in safety. I trust you have suffered no lasting discomfort from the blow on your head.'

He turned a smiling face on Robert.

Blow on the head? Robert threw his mind back to events which now seemed strangely remote. He was certain, however, that to no one had he mentioned that particular episode; not to Giorgio, not to Mr Jones, or to Mr Papandian. Nobody could know of the incident but the author of it. Observing Mr Eugenius as closely as Mr Eugenius had been watching him, Robert noticed certain resemblances which had before escaped him, but which were evident now that Mr Eugenius wore dark, semi-European clothes. Those odd pale green-coloured eyes, the pale greenish-blonde receding hair, the fluent French and near-perfect English. The face was more plastic, more mobile, and Mr Eugenius was capable of a greater variety of expressions, including affability, than Shekhir, but for all that the resemblance was there, a strong and striking resemblance.

'You are acquainted then, with the man who goes under the name of Shekhir Effendi, but whose real name I believe is Zletzki?' he asked.

Mr Eugenius's affable expression did not change.

'I have never met him, but of course I have heard of him, as any one must who has made the slightest study of events in Circassia. The whole of that coast is a whispering gallery. But you look as if the possibility of an acquaintance between us did not please you. Forgive me for saying it, Mr Wilton, but I hope you have not imbibed the national propensity for suspicion during your stay on those coasts.'

'It is very true that I did not form a very favourable impression of this person's conduct, and you will permit me to observe that there is a very strong resemblance between you.'

'Then a resemblance is all we have in common – that, and the circumstance that we are both of us exiles. I am not a Pole, Mr Wilton, but Poland is not the only country in Europe where freedom has disappeared. I come from one of the others. I can understand Zletzki, but there is this great difference between us. A Pole, try as he will, can never be assimilated into his country of adoption. His heart is always where he was born. I myself have no wish to return to my place of birth even if I could. I am in love with Turkey, Mr Wilton, that is, with the old Turkey. Oh, it is dying! Soon they will have steam engines and frock-coats here, there will be factories along the Golden Horn, and the ladies will wear Parisian toilettes in the harems. But it is dying slowly, and it will last my time. Beyond this I have no wish to look. I shall be, I hope, in Paradise, where the old ways will go on for ever.'

Robert was not listening. His thoughts were elsewhere. His mind was racing, juggling with and reassembling the puzzle he had almost given up hope of solving – where was the traitor?

Hassan – or Arslan? No, in spite of everything he could not bring himself to believe it. Who then were his other enemies? Aladji's cousin? Kherim? Unlikely that even Circassians could push a grudge so far, and besides, Kherim only wanted the horse!

Shekhir. Always he came back to this name. Now in his mind he crossed out Shekhir and substituted Eugenius. Indeed he could count himself fortunate that those boards he had crossed only minutes ago had not precipitated him into the watery cellars of the yali, where any amount of bodies could rot unseen. And this smooth spider in the centre of the web had taken Paka from him also!

But Mr Eugenius was still addressing him.

'Let us now decide the matter of your princess, your little Circassian beauty,' he was saying, smiling gently and touching his lips with a fine silk handkerchief, 'for the last thing I would wish is that there should be any ill-will between us. Rather, shall we let her decide? Surely, between gentlemen, that would be the better course. Nothing has been done that cannot be

undone : the paper of sale can be torn. I will have her brought
to us here, and the choice shall be with her – to stay with me,
or go with you.'

Slowly Robert shook his head.

'No. I have accepted your reasoning, sir. The princess also
is an old-fashioned girl.'

A memory came into his mind from many years before,
when in childhood he had cherished a scrawny farm kitten. His
mother disliking cats intensely, the kitten had existed on
sufferance in the kitchen, where Robert visited it sur-
reptitiously and lavished on it an erratic and guilty affection.
Finally it had been decreed that the kitten must go, and the
doctor's wife, a kind woman and a lover of cats, had offered it
a home. There it had flourished. The half-wild, skinny little
animal gained flesh and confidence, and developed into a large
and magnificent jet-black cat with long fur, the result, no
doubt, of some Persian strain in its ancestry. As the cat grew in
beauty, those who had known it before exclaimed in admiration,
all but Robert, whose former pet had become a stranger. The
day he remembered so poignantly, he had been standing on
tiptoe craning over the hedge which divided his father's land
from that of the doctor. In the doctor's drying ground, on the
grass, the daisy-sprinkled grass of spring, the cat was sitting,
reposing like a ball of black fluff. He knew that he should not
call her, but in spite of himself a tiny whistle escaped him.
Puss heard it : he could see the tips of her ears twitch when she
recognized his voice, and she looked in his direction. Round,
clear eyes looked blankly at him, lost in a moonface of black
fur. Puss licked her lips deliberately with a little shred of pink
tongue, yawned and looked away into the branches of an
apple tree where something engaged her attention. Robert
might never have existed. She had gone where the grass was
greener.

So it was with Paka. It was too late to whistle her back. The
only life he could offer her would be filled with trials and problems, even real hardships. What reason had he to think she
would accept the hardships – what right had he to ask that she
should ? In a Turkish harem she would be, as Mr Eugenius
promised, entirely safe. Nothing could not happen to her that
she had not invited.

Once again he took a ceremonious leave of an affable host. Once again Mr Eugenius escorted him to his gates, talking aimably about his return from Circassia, which Mr Eugenius obviously viewed in the light of a pleasure cruise.

'And a charming young English lady on board, as I have heard,' he concluded roguishly, but to this remark Robert made no answer.

When he emerged from the yali, the scene was unchanged. The same old men were sitting in a row under the same wall, and the boy was patiently squatting in the dust, holding the reins of the horse. Robert threw the child a coin, and mounted.

Slowly he rode back the way he had come, through the villages where veiled women were gathered round the wells, and graybeards basked in the last rays of the sun. Now that every link with Circassia had been cut, he felt not so much sad as empty. The peace of the road at evening soothed him : the horse ambled softly through the dust, and good aromatic smells of roasting peppers and baking bread came from the enclosed courtyards on either side. He heard the heavy thump of choppers as the evening meal was prepared, and a chatter of women's voices, and then quite suddenly, again from behind a wall, the wail of a fiddle and a man's voice singing a snatch of a familiar song – 'The Black-eyed Girl'.

Robert reined in sharply, to the surprise of the horse. He scanned the wall, and saw that it was high and blank, with no sign of a door or other opening. He listened, but at that moment the singer fell silent, as if he also was holding his breath and listening. Then the horse, heedful of its stable at the end of the road, moved on and carried its rider out of the village and on to the open shore. On the right hand the Bosphorus lay glittering in the golden evening light. To the left, the cypresses of the vast Scutari burying ground stood up, fingers pointing the way southward down the Cilician shore. A small, chill wind began to blow out of Asia, and Robert quickened his pace. The curtain was down over Circassia, and who could tell when it would ever go up again ? The stage was in front of him now, the golden world ahead.

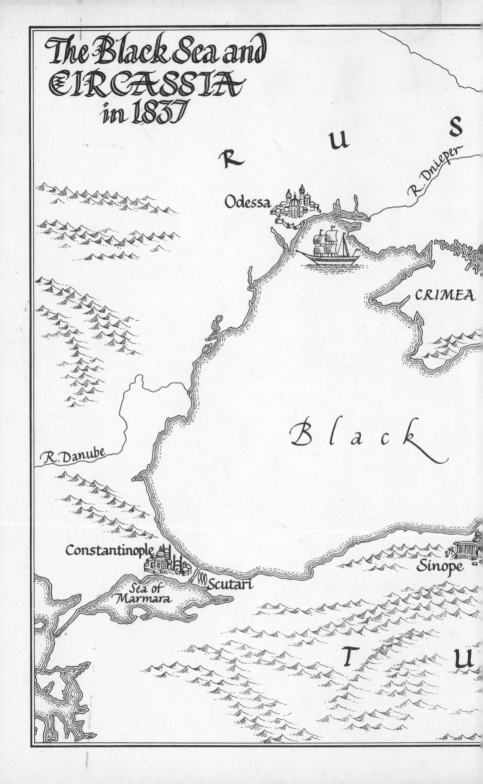